Politikill

Timothy Gene Sojka

Black Rose Writing | Texas

The author grants the final approval for this literary material.

First printing

This is a work of fiction. Names, characters, businesses, places, events, and incidents are either the products of the author's imagination or used in a fictitious manner. Any resemblance to actual persons, living or dead, or actual events is purely coincidental.

ISBN: 978-1-68433-904-4 (Paperback); 978-1-68433-983-9 (Hardcover)
PUBLISHED BY BLACK ROSE WRITING
www.blackrosewriting.com

Printed in the United States of America
Suggested Retail Price (SRP) $21.95 (Paperback); $26.95 (Hardcover)

Politikill is printed in Sabon

*As a planet-friendly publisher, Black Rose Writing does its best to eliminate unnecessary waste to reduce paper usage and energy costs, while never compromising the reading experience. As a result, the final word count vs. page count may not meet common expectations.

Praise for

Politikill

"Is *Politikill* a metaphor for present-day politics? It may be better thought of as a commentary on the eternal tendency for power to corrupt, and for at least one idealist to attempt to change the dishonest climate that may be the rule in some political circles."

–Carolyn Geduld, author of *Who Shall Live*

"Author Tim Sojka masterfully tackles controversial issues of the day in a way that is both entertaining and thought-provoking."

–John Hazen, author of *Beyond Revelation* and *The Correction*

"*Politikill* is another winning, highly-recommended thriller by a master of the genre."

–A.J. McCarthy, award-winning mystery suspense author

"*Politikill's* dizzying details and deception make for a satisfying conclusion to this crime thriller with fascinating characters. Sojka has created a thought-provoking, historical yet timely tale of political intrigue."

–Lisa Petrocelli, Author of *The Gloves Come Off*

"A tangled web of characters, backstories, and motivations in the vein of a Stephen King epic. And much like that, you won't be able to stop turning the pages."

–Luke Swanson, author of *Epicenter* and *The Other Hamlet Brother*

Political misconduct meets its match when vigilantes decide to hold their leaders accountable with deadly consequences. From the smart and sexy FBI agents, scheming politicians, watchdog reporters, and the enigmatic socialite with a mysterious past, the characters weave together through the tangled web of murder and corruption that leaves the reader quickly turning pages to find the next unexpected twist.

–Nola Nash, author of *The Crescent City Series*, and *Traveler*

"Thought provoking, quirky, and at times painfully realistic, Politikill will have you ducking for cover and turning pages all night long."

–Laya V Smith, author of the 2021 Maxy Awards Best Thriller *The Lumbermill*

To Margaret Sojka.
The first to believe, even though I gave you epic reasons to doubt.

*"Ninety percent of the politicians
give the other ten percent a bad reputation."*
Henry Kissinger

Politikill

Important author's note:
No actual politicians were killed in the making of this book. Do not
murder corrupt politicians...or anyone for that matter.

Warm Up the Crowd

September 1991
Some movie stars become so big, so famous, so wealthy, fans wonder, "can they burn any brighter?" Then the movie star lands their career-defining role, and despite all odds the star goes supernova—bigger, more famous, and yes, wealthier. Interestingly, star turns occur outside the human realm. Sometimes, places enjoy star turns too.

For obvious reasons, this place, the Watergate Hotel burst into America's collective conscience before today. The Watergate scandal rocked the early 1970s. President Richard Nixon infamously resigned his office, and for a moment, the Watergate became the most famous hotel in the world.

Most observers doubted the Watergate Hotel's ability to author another twistedly historic footnote. At least, most people doubted *before* September 1991.

• • •

"I need to be in that room with you," Anna Hamp demanded. Those were the last words to her boss, Senator Alan Greene, before he exited the lobby. Far from a stay-in-the-lobby type of assistant, the political veteran considered herself a right hand, a coordinator, and a protector. She ran Senator Greene's day, schedule; hell, she ran his life. Frustration reverberated from her every pore.

Emoting at her disinterested lobby-mate seemed an equitable distraction. "Do you really have to call him Eagle, seriously?" asked Anna.

"Yes, we call him that," said Tammany York, Senator Eagle Thompson's beleaguered assistant.

"I can't believe your guy and my guy will occupy the same room…alone," said Anna, prodding for a response.

"Yes, strange, huh?"

Anna's guy, California Senator Alan Greene, the youngest and most liberal senator in America, brought Anna along every stop of his political career. Greene recently spent his inheritance to defeat a five-term incumbent dinosaur. Greene led with his heart, fought for the environment, championed underdogs, and loved his constituency. Anna stared across a coffee table at Eagle Thompson's assistant, seated in a cushy chair, reading *Town & Country* in the Watergate Hotel lobby. Tammany appeared unconcerned with their situation. Conversely, Anna felt discarded.

Greene alerted Anna of this meeting yesterday. So, she prepared her senator. Anna studied Texas Senator Elroy "Eagle" Thompson. He retired from the military in the 50s. Eagle was not the most original name for a WWII era pilot, still, Elroy Thompson earned the approbation. The former pilot recorded fourteen confirmed kills, escorted dozens of bombers over Germany, and spent twenty-two years in service. Eagle held his senate seat since '68. Party leadership considered the veteran a Vice-Presidential option in '76. Eagle drove hard, pushed his staff harder, and bullied rivals.

According to early newspaper articles, Eagle arrived in Washington with a solid agenda and a reputation for integrity, a hero in every way. Her research suggested the system corrupted Eagle. A quick analysis showed significant gains in the older senator's financial position, especially in the last dozen years, without support for the fiscal windfalls. Records labeled Thompson a multimillionaire.

Conversely, she knew Alan Greene's precarious financial situation. More diverse senators shared a room in the 200+ year history of the United States. Still, Anna, new to DC was unsure of how often.

"Why are we down here if they're meeting alone?" asked Anna.

"I don't think they're meeting alone," answered Eagle's indifferent assistant.

• • •

Senator Alan Greene rapped on the door. He understood the need for firmness. He knew the temptations when he took the meeting. His host's words masked root issues while dripping implication. Greene never met today's host, but he knew three facts:

1) First, due to the hotly contested election, Greene's coffers rivaled the emptiness of his rival's campaign promises;

2) Second, to carry out long-term change, he needed the financial support of strong political action committees and committed donors;

3) Finally, when an envelope containing $50,000 cash arrives on your desk with a note requesting a meeting, you say yes.

Greene planned to return the money. Keeping the cash, no matter the senator's precarious financial footing, reeked impropriety. Still, a DC player capable of placing $50,000 in an envelope for a meeting may possess more appropriate means of financing Greene's re-election.

An unusual, but pleasant voice called. "Please enter, Senator Greene."

When Greene walked into the room, Senator Thompson sat brandishing a highball. Thompson rattled his glass, stood elegantly, and greeted Greene. "Hello, Alan." Thompson extended his hand delivering a bone-crushing handshake.

Greene, surprised by the familiarity, paused, then responded. "Hello, Eagle." Thompson smiled, acknowledging his moniker. Thompson stood 5'8"of knotty, old-oak muscle. Greene observed the older senator's firm features. Greene towered over Thompson; even so, Eagle, reeking of coiled aggression, owned the room.

Greene noted their host focused solely on the two politicians, signaling disinterest for anything else in the room. The host motioned for everyone to sit. "Welcome, Senators, thanks for taking time to meet. We have much to discuss. My name is Hiram Long, and I represent a conglomerate in need of men with your diverse political views."

Greene noted his speaker did not look or sound like someone named Hiram Long. The host efforted to mask an accent. Greene made note but remembered his own battle to cover the California surfer lexicon of his youth.

Their host continued, "I need your word that this discussion is private. The $50,000 you received is for your commitment to privacy and nothing else. Your recent…financial upgrade…does not bind you to my request. Do I have your commitments of privacy?"

Greene watched Thompson assent. Turmoil coursed through Greene; internal debate raged. "I'll listen, and I commit to privacy, but I cannot keep your $50,000." Greene gulped removing the stuffed envelope from his coat, dropping the cash and the political horsepower the money represented on the table. His host made no move to recover the money.

"Senator Greene, it's your money. You're welcome to do as you please. I can donate to the charity of your choice."

"Thank you," said Greene, relieved.

"At the end of our time, tell me your chosen charity, and they will receive an anonymous $50,000 donation. Will this donation ensure your silence?"

"Yes," said Greene, grateful to have the awkwardness behind him.

Thompson scrutinized Greene. The older man made no motion to return his $50,000. Eagle turned his attention to their host. "I would like an additional $50,000 donation to a charity of my choosing, to secure my commitment."

The host considered the older senator knowingly, nodding his agreement. Eagle glanced at Greene, looked longingly at the $50,000 table ornament, and shook his head.

"The money is inconsequential; can we move on?" The delay perturbed their host.

Both senators nodded.

"A bill recently navigated the House, setting aside an additional 350,000 acres for Native American tribes across five states. The bill barely passed for a multitude of reasons. I won't elaborate, you both understand the roadblocks."

Senator Greene recently read Anna's analysis of the bill. The powder keg issues included: the closing, or downsizing of an Air Force base, and removing thousands of jobs from an aching community. Additionally, expansive farms, both corporate and family endeavors, dotted the land.

"I need this bill to pass the Senate. I need you two to make it happen."

Internally, Greene questioned his invitation to today's meeting. He planned to support the legislation; he already voiced his position. Greene understood Thompson's presence. Thompson announced plans to battle the bill with every ounce of his considerable political pull. Thompson and his backers' doctrine demanded protection of military jobs.

"I can't support that bill. I'd get slaughtered," Thompson asserted.

"Yes. But I didn't say I needed you to support the bill publicly. I just need you to ensure it passes. Swing the vote of Hitchens, Hood, or Collier. Each senator owes you a favor."

Thompson seemed unconvinced.

Hiram Long continued. "We'll work with...other friends to attach a rider to the bill supporting three new casinos."

Now Greene understood his role. He diametrically opposed casinos on Native American grounds. Casinos offer a financial upside. However, the money's disbursement presented problems. Select members of the tribe prospered, while others received no positive impact from the casino. Legalized gambling presented pros and cons. The arrival of casinos invariably cannibalized other business. More importantly, the junior senator understood casinos invite corruption, addiction, prostitution, and a myriad of vices.

Greene championed a plan to bring non-gambling related industry onto tribal land. The young senator spouted up. "I can't support the casinos."

"Yes, you can, for the greater good. The 350,000 acres added to Native American tribes represents the greater good. One hundred twenty thousand of those acres rest in your home state. A boon for your supporters. You support the bill like you planned, and I need you to bring one senator riding the fence with you."

"And...?" Senator Thompson asked.

Their host smiled broadly, broadcasting his lack of surprise. "Senator Thompson, my sources confirm your impending retirement."

"Yes, how did...?"

Long ignored Thompson's incomplete question. "Upon retirement you agreed to join Barney, Jones, and Dupree, Houston's largest law firms. They offered you a comfortable salary. They expect little work from you, they covet your influence and desire an ex-senator's name on their letterhead."

Thompson nodded.

"We arranged for your annual salary to double. When you leave today, confirm with Larry Barney, the senior partner. I funded a $500,000 golden parachute, if you part ways with the firm."

The older senator sat stunned. Countless corruptors purchased his vote with a menagerie of incentives. Still, today's act bordered grandiosity.

"Young Senator Greene. You're busted. You possess grand dreams about changing Washington. Still, you can't change DC if you don't get re-elected. You just won your seat, but six years is a millisecond in Washington. Trust me, your competition's compiling a war chest. Taking down a one-term senator is simpler than defeating a two-term incumbent. Your rivals can't afford for you to get re-elected. I have...influence over a large political action committee sharing your beliefs. They may support your next election, but they fund multiple lawmakers. I'll ensure their favor shines upon you. I won't discuss the amount in front of Senator Thompson, but I've written a number here."

Long slid a piece of paper across the table. Greene nervously unfolded the paper and gasped. Senator Thompson snickered, his countenance broadcasting one word: *rookie*.

Greene rechecked the figure. The number dwarfed his last campaign budget.

"I've included the phone number for the PAC's director. Call upon your departure. Remember, Senator Greene, this is for the greater good. With the finances funneled your way, you win re-election and have an additional six years to fight future tribal casinos. Our interest rests with the aforementioned casinos...only. So, gentleman, you on board?"

Greene remained stunned. Thompson spoke first.

"I'll validate your offer."

"Of course. Once you validate the offer, are you on board?"

Senator Thompson took a deep breath. Greene understood Eagle's struggle. Thompson nodded to the host and Greene. "Yes."

"Senator Greene, this bill benefits your constituency?"

Greene pondered, a mirror of Rodin's famous work. Most senators are beholden to various benefactors. Many served as power brokers' neutered pets. Greene aspired to be unblemished, unchained, and...unneutered. Still, this contribution's game-changing girth promised financial independence. Worry about the next election ended. The money meant less time chasing donors and more time fighting for significant legislation.

"I'm in, I guess," mumbled Greene.

"I don't need your guess, are you *in*...or not?"

"Okay, I'm in."

A door behind Hiram Long sprung open. Greene worried, *did the FBI or CIA just bust me in a corruption sting*? Greene's worry promoted to horror when he spotted the gun. Before Eagle rose from his chair, two muffled Glock discharges obliterated his skull. Greene tasted terror's appetizer. He rose as Eagle's assassin turned to serve the main course.

Act 1: Introduction or Exposition

Introduction of major characters, scenes, and setting

Silsbee, Texas
Gertrude Arrington sat across from her daughter, Allie, in the small-town diner. The retired teacher's posture was rigidly straight, a lingering reminder of a long-ago youth spent in corsets. She sipped her tea and studied the TV. Gertrude's posture and grace reflected almost identically on the other side of the table. Her daughter's lack of interest in the television was the most obvious difference.

Someone killed—maybe executed—two senators at the Watergate Hotel. An assistant discovered the politicos' bodies, after the senators failed to return from a meeting. No one knew what happened. Currently, the network only reported the murder of two powerful members of the DC politocracy.

Gertrude directed her attention to the porcelain cup. "Bob, your tea, excellent, much like your father's. Your scones, far superior. You have perfected your craft," said Gertrude, a slight British lilt endured despite decades in Texas.

"Thanks, Ms. Gertie," Bob said and beamed. "Will you be back tomorrow?"

"No, grand plans await us tomorrow." She did not elaborate.

Smiling, Bob nodded before returning to the kitchen.

A few days a week, at 4 p.m., Gertrude and Allie visited this diner for a proper afternoon tea. Bob's father, the diner's founder, did not serve tea before Gertrude arrived in town almost a half-century earlier. Still, he started carrying Taylors of Harrogate Tea for his favorite customer. Bob's dad added homemade scones and clotted cream a few years later. People, especially men, tended to overachieve for Gertrude.

In the past, Gertrude met at the diner for parent-teacher conferences or after-school meetings with the many clubs she oversaw while teaching high school. Because Gertrude drank tea at the diner for years, several former students or students' parents developed the habit. So, strangely, despite the heat, the small Texas town of Silsbee became a hot tea drinker's haven.

Passing the table, most male diners' eyes surveyed one or both women. Accustomed to stares, neither woman made note. The cursory glances found the women almost identical in height, build, and beauty. Gertrude's light gray hair and carefully managed wrinkles stood as the most noticeable genuflection to Father Time.

Ashen blond hair defined Allie, her features similar to her mother's but sharper, more regal. A youthful innocence offset by deeply intelligent eyes intrigued and confused potential suitors. Her bearing ended the confusion, crushing men's confidence before they dared imminent rejection.

Gertrude riveted by the TV, failed to see a woman waddle her way to their table, wave, then wedge between Gertrude and the newscast.

"Ms. Gertie?" asked the woman.

"Is that a question or a statement?" asked the former teacher.

"Why, a statement…you are Ms. Gertie, right?"

"Yes, I am."

"My son Greg had the biggest crush on you when he was in your political science class. He studied British history to impress you."

"How sweet. Was it Greg Garvey? I recall he enjoyed discussing Great Britain."

"Yes, it was. He'll be pleased you remembered."

"I was 45 or 50 years old when Greg graduated. You must be mistaken about the crush; I assure you a younger teacher enamored him."

"I'm quite certain it was you," replied Mrs. Garvey.

Gertrude desired to return to the news report, still, decorum demanded her attention divert to Greg's mother. "Well, that warms my heart." Gertrude smiled, hoping to terminate the superfluous conversation.

Her daughter added gas to the situation. "When you were in your 40s, Bo and Wyeth came home beaten to a pulp after football practice." She paused; then continued, "Bo and Wyeth defended your honor. The rest of the football team voted you the teacher they most wanted to…"

"Allie," interrupted Gertrude, "I doubt Mrs. Garvey's interest in your vulgarity."

Mrs. Garvey appeared keenly interested.

"Mrs. Garvey, this is my daughter Allie."

Allie nodded in Mrs. Garvey's direction.

"You're beautiful, like your mother," said Mrs. Garvey.

"So, you're saying I look like the teacher the football team most wanted to..."

"Allie," interrupted Gertrude again. Allie smirked.

"I am sorry, Mrs. Garvey, her brothers spoiled Allie. Not much I can correct now; she is almost 40."

"I'm sorry about the twins," said Mrs. Garvey. "Sorry for your loss."

"Well, it's been years now since we lost Bo and Wyeth, we carry on."

"Everyone called them twins because they were in the same grade," said Allie. "But they weren't twins, Bo was a year older."

"Oh, I'm sorry," said Mrs. Garvey.

Allie continued, "They were very different."

"Like I said, her brothers spoiled Allie; the three of them were inseparable," explained Gertrude.

"You must be proud of Bo and Wyeth's friend, Congressman Book; he's doing so well."

Allie rolled her eyes. Gertrude beamed. "Yes, he is."

"Ms. Gertie, can I ask you one last question?"

Gertrude agreed, hoping to end the conversation. "My son and his friends called you Lady Arrington, because of the accent...were you royalty, back in England, I mean? Were you a princess or something?"

"Of course, I was not a princess," answered Gertrude. She smiled at Mrs. Garvey and returned her attention to the television and a reporter in front of the Watergate Hotel.

• • •

FBI Special Agent in Charge Natalie Liu's insufferable day continued. She flew, middle seat, on a crammed commuter flight with two stops. Her boss left her no time to arrange military transport. Earlier she met the deputy director. He sent her to Houston, Eagle Thompson's hometown. Her job: investigate Eagle's death. Another SAC traveled to Palo Alto to study Alan Greene's demise. The leadership team stayed in DC led by Liu's boss, Deputy Assistant Director Henry Moss.

She viewed the video earlier, terrifying. Only a matter of time before the grainy film leaked to the ravenous press. The ramifications of the video were immeasurable.

Introductions to her Houston team and a local briefing awaited when she hit the ground. She nodded off into troubled sleep. She dreamed of gunmen, executions, slowly expanding blood puddles, last breaths. Watching a final breath, even on video, reeked of inappropriateness, rawness, peeking behind the curtain while death performed its most notorious task. Unbeknownst to her, Natalie moaned in terror.

Liu's aisle mate nudged her awake. The man smiled politely, rose, and left. The starkness of the plane's brightly lit cabin offered a diversion, allowing the dream to drain from her, much like the blood drained from Senator Greene.

Liu ran each morning at 5 a.m. Exercise and long hours usually ensured solid sleep; so, she seldom slept on planes. Standing slowly, she stretched and let the passengers behind her go ahead. Last off the plane, not a problem; her team knew to wait. She grabbed her quickly packed carry-on and started down the aisle.

Liu exited the jetway, spotting another agent. Identifying one of her own was a simple task. Natalie walked in his direction and heard him utter one word. "Wow."

"Excuse me?" asked Natalie.

"I said wow," replied the man with tightly cropped curly hair. His square jaw set in a way that looked crooked as he smiled.

"And by that, you mean?"

"Does it need explanation," said the other agent extending his hand.

Natalie shook his hand begrudgingly. She walked away from her subordinate, then realized she did not know their destination. He caught up and tried to take her bag. She glared, conveying she did not need his help.

"Look…" She waited for him to fill in the blank.

"Special Agent Tanner Tucker."

"Agent Tucker, I'm one of the few female Special Agents in Charge in the country. I'm currently the only minority woman in the position."

"And?"

"I don't need you harassing me. Am I clear?"

"Ma'am, I just said wow because…"

"This is Texas, you boys are used to being in charge. Flirting is your state sport, and I know you think it's okay but…"

Tucker reached out wiping her cheek and chin. "Wow, you had a large line of drool running down your face, wow."

Tucker turned and marched off. Liu followed him. She did not speak until she arrived at his car. He opened the trunk; she deposited her bag.

"So, where do we meet the rest of the team?"

Tucker looked confused.

"*You* are the rest of the team?"

He nodded.

"Has the media gotten a copy of the tape yet?"

"Not yet. Won't be long now."

"Have you seen it?"

"Yes."

Liu wondered if he watched it all, or only the edited version. "And your thoughts?"

"The shooter and his compadre never looked at the camera. Not once. They are smooth. Deadly. I didn't hear the audio, though."

Liu realized Tucker viewed the edited version, so he had not seen the ending. "Have you seen the version with audio?" he asked.

Liu nodded.

"And?"

"This world's about to go mad."

"Wow." He made eye contact and smiled.

She returned his smile, despite herself.

"So, you have a plan for tomorrow?"

"Yes, I do. We'll interview Thompson's widow, and then we'll visit an old friend."

"That's your plan?"

"So far, that's all I got," replied Tucker.

"Your friend better be worth it."

"Trust me, he is."

• • •

September 26, 1991

Foxx Kauffman endured a sleepless night. The reporter assumed few Washingtonians slept well, as yesterday's news rumbled into city news outlets, political meeting rooms, and dining table conversation. Foxx, no longer a beat reporter, cashed every hard-earned favor to uncover the details of the seismic news. Videotape of yesterday's murders existed. Insiders called the tape "the video."

Sources stated that leaking "the video" ended careers, maybe worse. Each confirmed a tape existed. Getting a copy topped each news outlet's wish list.

Foxx's humor carried him far in life. He wrote a column for *The Times*, freelanced segments for network newscasts, and guest-hosted radio programs. Friends joked Foxx was omnipresent. The columnist replied he preferred actual presents.

Foxx walked into his editor's office and plopped down. "What do you know, Tye?"

"I know there's a video, that's it. Foxx, you're a columnist now, a personality. Not a real reporter anymore, not for years. Why don't you let the reporters handle this?"

"One, I have more connections; two, the execution of senators at the Watergate Hotel is the biggest story in ten years; three, everyone wants this story, even an African American Jew like me."

"There are no African American Jews like you. Hell, Foxx, there's no one like you."

"Thanks."

"Not a compliment. If you're on this, keep me informed. We pay your salary. Yes, you make a pittance from TV and radio appearances, but we're your cash cow. Anything you get, we get first fruits. Clear?"

"Yea, I'm clear. I am on this like a fat kid on a chocolate buffet."

"Be careful, Foxx, I was a fat kid."

"Like a frat boy on free beer."

"I was a frat boy too. Please stop."

"Like a stoner on a bag of Nacho Cheese Doritos."

"Get out!"

"Just wanted you to know I'm on it."

• • •

Houston, Texas
Natalie Liu's internal thermometer bumped past annoyance, redlining to pissed off. Eagle Thompson's young widow refused to stop staring at Agent Tucker, below his belt. Liu wondered if Mrs. Thompson possessed the willpower or sobriety to look away. When

Liu glared at Tucker, he shrugged. Her partner's refusal to feign embarrassment, even for her sake, vexed Liu. While internally admitting she stole glances at her partner's physique this morning, Liu's frustration for the widow threatened to bubble over.

Because of a proliferation of average FBI movies, people assume FBI agents wore suits. In truth, FBI work to blend into their environment, and jeans carry the day in Texas. Liu, with Tucker's guidance, wore the only pair of jeans she packed. Liu thought she busted Tucker earlier, sneaking glances at her backside.

Liu checked her watch—10 a.m.—and Eagle's widow, Eliza Thompson, bordered the states of toasted and plastered. She offered the FBI agents a Screwdriver upon arrival. Of course, the two refused.

"Mrs. Thompson…" Natalie paused and waited for the widow's eye contact. *Look away from Agent Tucker's bulge, Mrs. Thompson.* Natalie imagined herself telepathically sending the thought to the widow. Blocked by the booze, Liu surrendered her attempt. Natalie smiled at Tucker and shook her head. The Special Agent in Charge already assessed her new team member's mental fast twitch, so she signaled with raised eyebrows. Tucker stood a foot behind Liu and five feet to her right. Tucker winked to confirm he read her mind and slowly moved behind his new boss. The senator's widow's eyes predictably followed, finally settling on Liu. The SAC offered Tucker a glossy smile as thank you, then turned her attention to their hostess.

"Let's tackle the big question. Do you know anyone who would want to kill your husband?"

"Hell yes," she slurred.

Eliza Thompson's liquor-assisted answer signaled the tenor for the day. "Can you clarify the 'hell yes'?"

"Well, there're the husbands of the women Eagle screwed."

"Can you give us a list of those women?" asked Liu calmly.

"Sure, he shared all the women he screwed with me." Eliza cackled. "I don't have a list. I just know."

"And how do you know?"

"He screwed me before he divorced his last wife. You know men like Eagle. At least I do. I understood when I married him. Still, who wouldn't marry a senator?"

"Who can identify the women Eagle…?"

"Screwed," Eliza added. "One of his assistants might."

"Is there anyone else who would benefit from his death?" asked Liu.

"I'm not an FBI agent like you two." She paused, winking at Tucker. "With my philandering husband dead, buncha' people'll move up the totem pole. I'd gander their way. Course, I'd consider all the broken promises."

The widow remained in stasis for two uncomfortable minutes. Deep in thought, or absence of thought, Liu started to prod when words cascaded from Eliza's mouth. "Eagle made plenty'a promises to plenty'a people. I don't know a senator who can keep 'em. The promises. Do you?" She paused again. After the lack of forthcoming answers, she continued, "They start thinking they'll keep all their promises, then settle for some of 'em, then a few of 'em. Then the promises become an afterthought.

"There was a time he kept his political promises, if not his marital ones. Still, in the end, he punted in both areas, all of 'em do. Despite everything, I loved the old son of a bitch."

Without a view of Tucker's tight jeans to keep her awake, the widow nodded off. Natalie snapped her fingers. Eliza's eyes lazily reopened.

"Who were the people he made promises to and couldn't keep?" Liu pushed.

"Wooo!" Eliza laughed. "If the line started here…it maybe ends near the Canadian border, and that's a soft maybe."

The questioning continued for thirty minutes. Mrs. Thompson tried to serve herself another Screwdriver, but Tucker dissuaded her. Later, when wrapping up, Liu offered, "I'm sorry for your loss, Mrs. Thompson."

"Ya, ya, ya," said the widow while wonkily wobbling to her bar.

"Have you made the funeral arrangements?"

"Not in my court, honey, there's three kids about my age. They'll take it and run with it. My bet is you know more than me."

Liu said nothing. Moments later Liu and Tucker showed themselves out as Eliza mixed her fourth or fifth, depending on who's counting, Screwdriver.

As they walked from Thompson's River Oaks home to their car, Liu said, "I don't understand why we're interviewing a Rice University history teacher."

"He's more than that. After you meet him, you'll pitch to your boss to use him as a resource."

"You're confident."

"Very," offered Tucker.

Tucker tried to open Liu's car door. She shot him a *go to hell* look, and he relented. He walked around the front of the car and Liu caught herself checking him out. *I am no better than Eliza Thompson*, she chastised herself.

Earlier, Liu showed Tucker the unedited tape. Tucker sat listening to the audio, mouth agape. At the end of the tape, after the big conclusion, he sat speechless for minutes, then asked, "Is this real?"

"Yes."

"Can't be, can't be real…because if it is…"

•　　•　　•

Erasmus Luther, or Professor Raz, as his students christened him, brimmed with energy as the new semester stumbled into September. August classes sucked Luther's life force. Houston's August heat hung heavily over campus. Students grumpily trudged to class coated in perspiration. Additionally, the student body, no matter how bright, arrived unprepared for Erasmus' pace. Once the calendar surrendered to September, the weather cooled slightly, and students fell into a rhythm. Luther noted young minds rose as leaves fell.

Luther beamed at his class. He taught three classes most semesters at Rice, but this class remained his favorite—"A History of Political Assassinations."

"Many historians dissected the famous US political assassinations, Lincoln or Kennedy. I've been honest from the beginning. Kennedy's assassination shaped me, brought me to this lectern."

Luther raised an eyebrow as his former student, Tanner Tucker, and an alluring Asian female entered the room. He nodded, returning his attention to the class.

"I lived in DC. I saw Kennedy speak; whew. I was the perfect age to feel afraid, heartbroken, haunted, and intrigued by Kennedy's death. I teach this class because I'm fascinated by assassination. Still, we don't know exactly why assassins targeted Kennedy…which makes his assassination less interesting in a way.

"If we understand the why, we experience the rage the assassin carried. We taste the revenge. We indulge the urge to traipse through the assassin's psyche. Humanity rightly detests the act of murder but desires—needs—to understand the why.

"The why often appears insignificant to observers but looms large to the assassin. Charles J. Guiteau killed James Garfield. Guiteau did not receive a political appointment after Garfield became President. Basically, Guiteau threw a pity party when passed over for a job and killed...a *President*. A President that many historians propose possessed Rushmoresque potential.

"Let's stay with Guiteau for a moment. Because I mentioned him for a reason. If you analyze American assassinations, the number one motive is loss of a job or influence. Several defeated political candidates murdered victorious rivals. George L. Rockwell, the Commander of the American Nazi Party..."

Luther paused for boos. "Yes, yes, agreed. Anyhow, John Patler executed Mr. Rockwell after Rockwell dismissed Patler from the party. In Patler's mind he lost influence, power."

Luther registered the time, nodding toward his guests. Probably smart to wrap class early if two FBI agents awaited.

"So, back to *why*. The why fascinates me, and hopefully fascinates you. I appreciate your patience. I know what you're dying to ask. Will we study the deaths of two senators in a DC hotel? The truth, I'm not sure. We're unsure if yesterday's murders qualify as assassinations. I'm betting they do, so I'm betting we'll scratch our curious itch. Just allow me time to process and research. Then we'll go off agenda. For now, a former student stopped by to see me. Since he has a badge, I'll make time."

Students filed from the room, examining Tucker and Liu upon departure. Luther moved to his desk and selected a leather-bound notebook. He smiled at his former student, while considering Tanner's friend, obviously an agent too. What the hell do FBI agents want with a 40-year-old history teacher?

• • •

Liu watched Luther wrap class. She recognized the professor, of course. She waffled between feeling perturbed with Tucker for not telling her who they were meeting, to measuring the veracity of Luther's words. The professor's question troubled Liu. Why kill

Greene and Thompson? Yes, she saw the end of the video, still it didn't calculate. Why did someone drop $50,000 envelopes off with zero promise of a meeting? Why did someone do the research necessitated by the charade? Liu jotted questions to ponder later. The *why* loomed large.

Luther appeared 10 years older than her but dashing in a professorial way; fit and in decent shape, but not covered in lean, solid muscle like Tucker. She stole a glance, as Tucker rose, firmly shaking Luther's hand. She stood to greet the professor.

Agent Tucker spoke first. "Agent Liu, this is Erasmus Luther, my former teacher, and one of America's foremost experts on assassination. Erasmus, this is Special Agent in Charge Natalie Liu; she's my boss, at least for the next few weeks."

"Tucker didn't tell me who we were visiting, Dr. Luther. He wanted to surprise me." Liu offered Tucker a cutting glance. "I'm excited to meet you. I've read all your books."

"Thank you. I'm glad you did; I have a mortgage to pay," Luther said.

He motioned for them to sit. He occupied the aisle next to Tucker.

Liu started. "Before we get official, I've always wondered about your name. It's unusual. Your last name is Luther, no one chose that for you. Your first name is Erasmus, though. I'm dusting off my religious history, but weren't Erasmus and Luther rivals during the Protestant Reformation? Luther left the Church and started the Protestant movement. Erasmus believed in reform but stayed and defended the Catholic Church. They disagreed over free will, I think."

"Nicely done, Special Agent in Charge Natalie Liu. Long title, by the way."

"Please, call me Natalie or Agent Liu."

"My father wanted me to consider both sides of an issue; he wanted me to understand the motivations and needs of adversaries. Hence the name. He taught history too, but specialized in the history machinery played in war…"

"Wait a minute, your father's Roland Luther. He worked for Secretary of War Stimson during World War II and participated in the planning of the Normandy Beach attack. He's credited with the creation of two war machines used that day."

Luther nodded toward Tucker and smiled. "Roland was my father. Between his specialty and mine, safe to assume the dark side draws Luther men. Where'd the FBI find you?"

"I grew up in a traditional Chinese family, a family of tailors, but my parents pushed their kids hard. Dad hoped I'd become a doctor like my brothers, or a professor. I was working toward my master's in history, when a friend invited me to an FBI recruiting event. I went on a lark, and something fit. Ironically, my friend never joined."

"Where'd you complete your degree?"

"Princeton."

"Well, I'd relish another student like you. Brilliant. What an overeducated pair."

"What do you mean?" Liu asked.

"A master's in history from Princeton and a doctorate of philosophy with a political science emphasis from Rice." Luther turned to Tucker.

Liu's looked to Agent Tucker. "You have a doctorate in political science?"

"Sure," Tucker said, avoiding explanation. A raised eyebrow from Liu encouraged continuation. "Politics is a family business. I'm not ready to join the family business," answered Tucker.

Liu chastised herself for not knowing Tucker's background. The SAC usually researched team members to understand how they ticked. *Cut yourself a break, Moss hadn't assigned the team yet when you boarded the plane*, she resigned.

Luther pressed. "Okay, we know the players occupying the poker table. Now, explain the variation we're playing. I prefer Texas Hold'em, if you have no preference."

Liu ignored Luther's analogy. "I'm working with Agent Tucker to find out about Eagle Thompson and who killed him. Tucker believes you'll make a valuable consultant. I'm not sure yet. Still, if I'm sure, I'll need to push for approval from..."

"You won't."

"Excuse me?"

"No need to push for approval, I already consult for the FBI and CIA. I'm preapproved, as it were."

"Did you know?" Liu questioned Tucker. He shook his head.

"Few do; I only consult on specific cases," Luther added.

"What have you heard about Thompson's and Greene's deaths?"

"Nothing, no one's brought me into the loop. Still, I'm willing and want a seat at the table." Luther looked at her with expectation.

Tucker nodded.

Liu pondered before starting, "I'm sure you're approved. But I need to check with my direct report. Can we meet tonight? I have something to show you, you'll catch up fast, trust me."

"I'd love to, but I can't tonight. Tonight's my favorite night of the year. Got plans. I'm happy to reconvene in the morning. I don't have a class tomorrow. How about 8 a.m. in my office? Tanner remembers the spot. The crime won't get solved tonight."

Liu battled exasperation, but honestly needed an early evening. The thought of reporting back to her boss in DC, getting Luther's approval, and falling into bed before 10 p.m. intrigued her. The three shared farewells.

Liu grumbled to Tucker as the agents navigated campus. "Thursday night in September. What the hell makes this his favorite night of the year?"

Tucker shrugged.

• • •

Luther adjusted his tuxedo for the fourth time. Their arrival imminent, his excitement peaked. The Arrington AIDS Art Gala endured as the biggest annual fundraiser for Rice. Texas is not the most progressive state, nor is Houston the most progressive city. Still, by 1991, many people lost loved ones or friends to AIDS. Therefore, the event became a local touchstone. The Rice administration hosted the event in and around Lovett Hall on a Thursday evening in September each year.

Luther enjoyed art but infrequently attended galas, usually only upon his dean's direct request. Tonight, he arrived of his own free will. He attended the gala's inaugural event in 1986, out of faculty obligation, but one glance of her guaranteed the professor's future attendance.

Each year, Rice engaged a limousine service to chauffeur Gertrude Arrington and her daughter Allie from some backwoods Texas town to Houston. Each year, Gertrude spoke, greeting attendees, and each year her daughter said nothing. In 1986, Luther rallied the courage to ask the daughter to dance. She turned away countless suitors, so when she obliged his invitation, the professor panicked. Dumbstruck, he failed to utter a syllable. He smiled, hoping to appear cultured. When the dance ended, Luther remembered stuttering "thank you."

Since "86, Allie spent the evening chatting up one man. They laughed like old friends, no one else existed in their world. Because of the man's presence, Luther never vied for another dance. Luther did not know the guy, but he hated him. Luther prepared and practiced multiple icebreakers, hoping for another opportunity.

Luther lived steps from campus in a tidy home he shared with two art history professors. His last book, *Garfield & McKinley: The Other American Tragedies*, sold enough to make a down payment, and his tenured salary covered the note. The other professors' rent payment provided additional income.

Luther stepped out the front door and walked under the cover of mature oaks onto campus. The heat and humidity made Houston unbearable for pedestrians most of the year. Still, fall arrived earlier, and the event began late enough to make the short stroll pleasant.

Luther walked to the main entrance, to enjoy the full effect of the night, greeted by an arbor of light-drenched oaks. Ribbons announced the theme of tonight's event. Luther took a deep breath, sturdied himself, and embraced his favorite night of the year.

•　　•　　•

"Allie, when I was a young woman, men thought I was gorgeous," reminisced Gertrude.

"I know, Mother," answered Allie. She looked out the window as the limousine lilted onto Main Street, almost there.

"Still, I do not think I ever looked more lovely than you do tonight."

"Thank you, Mother," replied Allie, surprised by the rare compliment. Her mother reserved accolades for Allie's deceased brothers, Gertrude's former students, or the horses. "You look lovely," Allie acknowledged sincerely.

"We have to represent the boys." Gertrude said, fighting off tears.

"Yes, we do, Mother, yes, we do," Allie said, losing her battle. A passion for horses and protecting Bo and Wyeth's legacy brought the mother and daughter together, their only shared interest.

"Pete will be there; he is giving the opening address."

"Yes, Mother, I know," said Allie. The mention of Representative Pete Book always cooled camaraderie between them. Allie pulled out a silk kerchief, dabbed her tear, and located her compact to check her makeup.

"I know you and Pete don't exactly get along, but you get to see Kyle."

"Yes." Allie returned to staring out the window.

The limousine pulled into the main entrance of Rice University. The gorgeous lit oaks and the grandeur of Lovett Hall greeted them. Out her window, Allie spotted the handsome, awkward man who asked her to dance years earlier. Allie seldom remembered gala attendees who requested a dance, but she remembered Mr. Awkward, or at minimum the situation. He said nothing as they danced; not an awkward joke, an inappropriate innuendo, a compliment, nothing. She consistently caught him glancing in her direction and she recognized him, but never placed him. Her curiosity coaxed her to ask others his identity; however, she had yet to surrender to the temptation. She wondered if he might approach her tonight, doubting the chance.

•   •   •

An hour later, Rice's president moved to the podium. The president surveyed guests and smiled at the array of Houston business executives, athletes, politicians, and artists as he stepped to the microphone. "Thank you all for coming tonight, for one of Rice University's most prestigious events, the Arrington AIDS Art Gala. I have one job tonight, to introduce one of our own, a 1971 Rice graduate and US Congressman. He made a name for himself, for his zeal for the Constitution and considering current laws before enacting others. He's a member of the powerful House Ways and Means Committee and sponsored the Book-Purdy Senior Citizens Act. Ladies and gentlemen, may I introduce Congressional Representative Pete Book."

Gertrude winked at Pete as he peacocked to the podium and smoothly adjusted the microphone. "I'll start tonight with a moment of silence, so each attendee can pray, if they choose, for the families of Senator Thompson and Senator Greene." Book bowed his head. Pete said nothing about either politician, not praising or denouncing them. Gertrude assumed selecting a position signaled recklessness. A prayer for the senators' families presented a safer political move.

Gertrude watched her most successful former student control the atmosphere. As prayers ended, Pete smiled and began. "I'm here to introduce Gertrude Arrington, a woman I've known most of my life. I grew up playing with her boys, learned to ride a horse at her home, but most importantly, I was blessed to have her as my political science teacher. Ms. Gertie, or Lady Arrington as we called her, may have been born in Great Britain but she possesses passion for our system of government. She appreciates America and the opportunity this country granted her and her children. Few people love America more. She gave me that love for our country as a gift. She taught me to induce change the right way—by the book, using the laws our forefathers put in place. Like many teachers, Ms. Gertie inspired. I'm a product of God's blessing and outstanding teachers. Please pause to thank her and our teachers for making America great."

Pete paused, surveying the assembly.

"Also, a reminder, the Arrington family requests no cameras or photos this evening. They prefer tonight to be about Rice University and finding a cure for AIDS. It's an unusual request for a gala, but please respect the family's wishes. For your convenience there are photo booths. Volunteers can point you there. With that, my teacher, mentor, role model, Ms. Gertrude Arrington."

Pete hugged Gertrude as she stepped toward the podium. Gertrude noted Pete smiling at Allie. Her daughter returned a frigid stare before continuing a lively conversation with Pete's Congressional Chief of Staff, Kyle Kenner, Allie's best friend since elementary school. Gertrude watched as the congressman coolly returned his attention to the crowd, waving good-bye to make room for his former teacher.

"Hello everyone and thank you for your attendance. My three children graduated from this fine university. So, I am blessed. All three arrived on full or partial scholarships, and I have spent years trying to repay Rice University for the generosity. I watched my oldest son Bo play football here. My youngest son Wyeth started his art career here, and my daughter Allie attended Rice on full academic scholarship.

"Wyeth achieved some fame..." Gertrude paused for applause. "He achieved some fame as the most innovative and sought-after young painter in the United States. His patron, Cassandra Hinds, sponsored dozens of painters, but told me recently, no one mastered the human form like our Wyeth. Wyeth was all of ours..."

She smiled and paused again. "Wyeth's most famous painting, *Arrington's Aphrodite*, sold at auction for the highest amount of any living painter in 1979. That painting helped Wyeth become a household name. I am his mother, so if it sounds like I am bragging...I am." The audience chuckled.

"Unfortunately, Wyeth died in 1983. My son became one of the first celebrities to die from AIDS. Wyeth was our heart, our artist. Allie and I want to share him with the world." She looked to Allie. Allie smiled, waving back to her mother to draw the attention away from herself.

"Bo...our blessing. The hardest worker I knew. He founded a start-up oil company at 27 and was a multimillionaire before 30. Unfortunately, he died the year after Wyeth. Bo...he died from..." Gertrude paused, not for applause but to disguise raw emotion. "He died from...depression.

"Bo's financial legacy blessed Allie and I beyond our needs. So, we chose to contribute to causes the boys believed in. This event started simply. Allie—my ally—and I used some of Bo's money to throw a gala. We donated one of Wyeth's paintings for an auction. To honor Bo, half of the proceeds go to Rice University. To honor Wyeth, the other half will go to help those battling AIDS." She paused for a lengthy applause. "The first painting sold for substantially more than we planned..." she paused, again interrupted by applause. "The University requested the one-time gala become an annual event, so here we are.

"The event transformed over the years. Tonight, we have one of Wyeth's paintings to auction. I believe Representative Book will act as our auctioneer. We have much more, though. After year one, other artists generously donated their works. Tonight, we have works from three world-renowned artists. Plus, the Hinds Trust generously donated a private collection painting for the auction. The Astros, Rockets, and Oilers donated auction items, and several sports celebrities mingle among us tonight. The beautiful artists from the Houston Ballet will entertain us later. Oh yes, the Houston Symphony sent over a quartet to keep the night lively. Enjoy your night, do not forget to bid generously on the art, and thank you for coming."

•   •   •

Luther watched her all night. Allie Arrington, stunning beyond measure, remained out of reach. He wanted a second chance with her, more than he wanted to know who killed Kennedy, and his specialty was political assassinations, for God's sake.

The same annoying man dominated her time, not leaving her side. Other suitors hovered like moths to a Texas porch light; some asked to dance. Allie, pleasant but short with each, barely looked away from her handsome counterpart. Once, Luther thought he caught her glancing in his direction. He chuckled; she probably remained unaware he existed.

To distract himself, Luther danced with female colleagues. He chatted with politicians and professors. Still, his eyes traced her, despite trying to ignore her. Luther watched disinterested as Pete Book auctioned Wyeth's painting. Finally, he spotted an opportunity.

Pete Book waved to Allie's companion. The annoying man hugged Allie, then followed the congressman from the room. Luther's excitement bubbled. The professor walked to her, reciting in his head all his pre-prepared questions. Before Luther pounced, the University President approached Allie and extended his hand. Luther's dream girl smiled and complied. Luther watched dignitary after dignitary (men you don't turn down when you are trying to raise money) escort her to the floor.

Luther sulked, leaning against one of Lovett Hall's arches, resigned to failure. After an hour-long pity party, he walked to where chauffeurs circled to collect Houston's luminaries.

He dropped onto a bench, loosened his tie, and embraced the night's beauty. While sitting, Luther smelled a mix of jasmine and vanilla before Gertrude Arrington approached.

"Hello, young man." The evening's host sat beside him. Luther estimated she was twenty plus years his senior. Still, her accent and grace induced enchantment. Luther, not immune to the moment, embraced the surreal texture of the encounter.

"Hello, ma'am, I'm…"

"You're the young man who asked my daughter to dance and forgot how to speak. Now, you stare each year but do not say hello."

"That obvious?"

"Oh yes. There is always next year."

"Yes, ma'am, maybe next year."

Gertrude smiled, patting him on the knee and walked to her awaiting chauffeur. Moments later Allie Arrington walked past Luther toward the limo. Just before opening the door, she glanced his way and smiled.

To Erasmus Luther, the night ranked as a stupendous success.

• • •

September 27, 1991, DC

Foxx Kauffman understood his role today. He was being used. Congressman Pete "By the" Book rode a red-eye commuter flight from Houston back to DC. Book's Chief of Staff, Kyle Kenner, summoned Foxx to note the fact. Foxx's mother once said, "An eight-year-old can do nothing unwatched." The columnist's version seemed more appropriate: "A lawmaker can do nothing honest, socially correct, thrifty, or heroic…without alerting the press."

Many congressmen finagled private jets or first-class upgrades on the taxpayer, but not Book. Kenner and the congressional representative's staff aggressively broadcast Book's reputation for honesty and thriftiness. Savvy and smart, Book's DC stature rose each election cycle.

Despite Foxx's misgivings about today's charade, he would mention the congressional representative's commuter flight, saving taxpayer dollars. In reality, the congressman also invited Foxx to ask one question. Kauffman waited in an airport meeting room which Book's team arranged. Two cups of coffee into the morning, Foxx stood when the congressman and Kyle entered. Foxx noticed Book's limp.

"What's wrong, Pete?" asked Foxx.

"There's no leg room on those damn commuter flights," stated Book.

Well, that took two seconds, reflected Foxx. "Pretty rough?"

"My 42-year-old knees are killing me; man, I wish I had my 18-year-old knees back."

Foxx retorted, "If I wished for something from when I was 18, I'd pick something a little higher."

The congressman and Kyle fought smiles while feigning offense, an unusual combination. Foxx sensed their amusement, despite the shattered decorum.

"I mean my dick," Foxx clarified. "I'd want my 18-year-old dick back."

"We got it, Foxx," said Kyle firmly, assuming the subject closed.

Known for taking points too far, Foxx bulldozed forward. "I'd go again, again, and again."

The congressman sat. Foxx, mentally noting Book's attempt to manage the circumstances, reluctantly joined Book. Kyle stood to the side. Foxx seldom spotted Pete without his chief of staff in tow. Kyle was the perfect staffer. He controlled Pete's schedule, staff, budget, and election procedures but seemed allergic to taking credit. Not needing credit—a mighty nice trick to master when working politicians.

Foxx started. "Why'd you call, Pete?"

"I thought you'd want to inquire about Eagle. I prayed for his family at an event last night."

"Hmm, interesting. A more interesting question strikes me—'who'll the Texas governor pick for Eagle's spot?'"

"I'm not sure, Foxx, there's several great candidates to take over for Eagle."

"You interested, Pete?" asked Foxx, knowing the answer.

"I'm in a prominent position on Ways and Means, I'm not sure I can walk away. The party needs me. Members of the Ways and Means Committee raise massive contributions for themselves and their party."

"Thanks for the lesson," the columnist replied sarcastically. "Still, why am I here, Pete?"

"I told you earlier, I'm here to answer any questions you have."

"Hmm." Foxx decided he had poked Pete enough, extracted payment for the forced pomposity of today's proceedings. Everyone knew the question Book's team summoned Foxx to ask.

"If your governor and party leaders felt you could better serve the country by taking the senator's post, you would…?"

"I'd do it. But only if it were for the betterment of the great State of Texas and our nation."

Foxx chuckled; his caramel-coated baritone as apparent in his laugh as his words. "Is it okay if I print that?" he asked, knowing the answer.

Pete Book nodded.

• • •

Houston, Texas

A firm rap rocked Erasmus Luther's door. "Come in," he said.

Liu and Tucker entered. Luther motioned for the agents to sit. Tucker, dressed in pressed jeans, boots, and a button-down Ralph Lauren shirt, shook Luther's hand. Liu wore the same jeans as yesterday, but a more flattering top. The Special Agent in Charge appeared rested, unlike yesterday, and honestly gorgeous. No need to dress beautifully, prepare a speech, or summon the calvary; Luther coveted this opportunity.

"Good morning, Dr. Luther," Tucker said, a broad grin adorning his face. "Did you enjoy your favorite evening of the year?"

"Spectacular," he said, smiling. "Unless I'm being investigated, let's stick with that."

Tucker nodded. Liu let the boys lead, remaining silent. Seeing opportunity, Luther asked his question.

"Yesterday, before we started, Agent Liu, you had questions for me. I'm hoping to ask one today?"

"Sure," Liu replied.

"I found nothing mentioned about Thompson's and Greene's protection or security detail."

Liu answered, "John Wilkes Booth assassinated Lincoln while the President's lone security guard drank at a bar. We've come a long way since Lincoln. Now, a comprehensive security detail protects the President. Smaller details protect the Vice President, Speaker of the House, the Whips, etcetera. Still, most congressional representatives and senators have little or no security detail. Neither Thompson nor Greene hired protection."

"Wow."

• • •

Liu attempted to mask surprise. She assumed a professor studying assassination knew more; still, Luther studied the past and not the present. "With your permission, Dr. Luther, we're here to bring you up to speed. I spoke to my direct report, and he called the director. You're on board, assuming you want this."

"I do."

"You understand, everything is confidential."

"Agreed, Agent Liu."

Liu paused, signaling Tucker. "We want to show you something. Do you have a VCR?"

"Yes," Luther said, intrigued. "There's a VCR and television behind you."

Liu handed Tucker the tape. Her partner turned to the audio/visual cart. Tucker, the antithesis of an A/V nerd, still smoothly navigated the equipment and inserted the tape. Tucker adjusted the volume.

• • •

The final moments of Greene's and Thompson's lives transfixed Luther. He noticed the clarity of the audio and the graininess of the video. Luther's nerves rattled like a wooden roller coaster. The professor rooted for Senator Greene when he returned the $50,000 and attempted to hide shock by how easily the host bought Thompson. Most disturbing was Thompson's comfort with the proceedings.

The historian's heart broke as Senator Greene accepted the bribe. Witnessing two powerful men transform to lapdogs, someone's bitches, disturbed Luther. The assassin's appearance and execution of Thompson riveted the room. Two head shots. The assassin turned slightly and delivered a bullet to Greene's torso.

When Greene crumpled, the assassin unloaded two shots to his skull. Without glancing toward the camera, the assassin emptied his pistol into Thompson. Tucker rewound the tape three times upon Luther's request.

Luther dissected the Kennedy-Zapruder film and videos of various executions hundreds of times. Still, he had seen nothing this close, staged, or visceral. Tucker stopped the tape each time the assassin unloaded his suppressed pistol. Luther saw enough.

Agent Liu asked, "So what d'you notice, Doc?"

"The audio's incredible. I hear every syllable. Seemed strange, considering the poor video quality."

Liu nodded. "Our technical team assumes the assassins placed microphones in and around the senators' seats. High tech. Well planned. Pretty obvious the audio's importance to the perp. Someone wanted us to understand they bought and sold two senators."

"Why is the video grainy?"

"Not sure. We received the video later that day. A 16-year-old kid on a bike delivered an envelope to our onsite agents."

"A kid on a bike?"

"Yes, but that's a dead end. A masked guy on a motorcycle gave the kid $1,000 in unmarked twenties. The guy never removed his helmet. The motorcyclist instructed the kid to deliver the envelope to guys in suits snooping around the hotel. The kid endured lots of questions. He's probably wondering if the $1,000 was worth the interrogation. We took the $1,000 to examine the bills. We're processing them now."

"Will the kid get the money back?" asked Luther.

"Least of my concerns," she said and shrugged. "Still, to be honest, I hope he does. But to answer your question, I don't know why the video is grainy. What else did you get from the video?"

"The killer and the host never glanced at the camera."

Tucker responded, "Not once...takes discipline. They could've edited it out."

Liu nodded and kept pushing. "What else, Doctor?"

"Did anyone recognize the guy's voice?"

"No," answered Liu. "Don't think these guys hit the FBI radar before. They follow a specific template; we'll know if they strike again. Seems the host attempted to hide an accent."

"What type of accent?"

"Unsure...so far," answered Liu.

"There're more copies, correct, this isn't the original tape?"

"No. Each agency has at least a dozen copies."

"Then this will get out?"

"Yes," Liu said flatly. "Want to see the rest of the tape?"

"There's more?"

"Indeed."

"Why didn't you show me the entire tape?" asked Luther.

"If we showed you the end, you wouldn't be able to think of anything else," responded Liu.

"Sounds ominous," replied Luther. Tucker and Liu said nothing. Tucker hit the play button. In the video, Thompson is dead in his seat. Greene is bleeding out on the floor. The gunman walked out of the camera's scope to the left. The man who had acted as emissary exits camera right. Then from the left, a poster board, like any high school student used for history projects, appeared in front of the camera. On the board, using cutout lettering from newspapers, is a message.

•　•　•

HELLO WASHingtoN

TaKE A bribE

Meet Your Maker

Shame on You

I'm Watching

"

—

The professor's jaw dropped. Tucker nods to confirm what Luther witnessed was real. Washington, DC, was about to explode.

• • •

Washington, DC

After the conversation with Pete Book, Foxx Kauffman needed assurance his 40-year-old member performed to his standards. He traveled to his favorite DC bar. Foxx remained handsome, even at 40, maybe *especially* at 40. He aged well, and at 6'3" towered over rivals in the dating jungle. His dark skin and green eyes proved irresistible to many. Foxx, a bit of a local celebrity, took full advantage. He refused to complicate his approach. When this evening's goddess asked what brought him to the bar; Foxx stated, "I'm looking for an intoxicatingly beautiful woman who yearns to make a terrible decision." The line, a nonstarter for most men, worked for Foxx.

Foxx now relaxed in bed, his naked goddess adorably snoring beside him. The reporter considering awakening her for a fourth… interview…when a knock fractured the silence. Foxx waited for the banging to stop. He had no intentions of leaving bed, or the company beside him. Then Foxx heard a voice tapped to childhood memories—of adventure and friendship, the...

"Kauffman, open the stupid door; I flew from Houston to make you a legend." The dulcet tones of Erasmus Luther. The only man sporting a more bizarre name than his own, the only friend Foxx would willingly leave his current goddess to see.

•   •   •

Foxx's beautiful bedmate departed, shooed by Luther. Coffee brewed as two old friends stared across the living room. Foxx made the first move and stepped to Luther for a hug. Foxx relished the embrace, smiled, then motioned for Luther to sit.

"What brings you to DC, old friend?" asked Foxx.

"I'll stand by my word; I'm here to make you a legend."

"I'm already a legend," Foxx declared.

"With the beautiful woman I pushed out the door, I'm forced to agree. Still, you only thought you were a legend before today. I brought you a gift."

"A gift? You ruined my plans; better be a stupendous gift."

"I have a video, the..."

"You have a copy of *the video*?"

"Well, I haven't heard it called *the video*, but yes, I think so."

"And how do you have a copy?" asked Foxx.

Luther shrugged. "I watched it. My...let's call them *friends*...told me a few dozen copies of the video existed. We agreed it would get out soon. I convinced them it would be best if they controlled how. I told them I trusted you. Also..."

"The Feds used me to release stuff before because I keep my mouth shut."

"Exactly. I talked my friends into letting me deliver the tape. On the condition you found it on your doorstep in the dead of night."

"You, sir, are a god," said Foxx.

Luther popped the tape into Foxx's VCR. The reporter, mouth agape, sat as stupefied as Luther hours earlier. Foxx repeatedly mustered an, *is this real?* look. Luther nodded. Foxx rewound the tape a half-dozen times in spots. Once he deconstructed the information, he took a deep breath and stared at Luther.

"Holy mother of…" he stopped short of taking the Lord's name in vain. Foxx joked nonstop, slept with any woman who did not kick him off, but never blasphemed God.

"Yes," interrupted Luther. "What do you do next?"

Kauffman smiled.

• • •

1937, New York City

"Philippa Harrington?" the uniformed inspector barked, eyeing her papers.

"Yes," Philippa answered, summoning a heart-melting smile.

"You're clear," he pronounced, returning her papers. Philippa thanked him, making her way from the entry port to the street. She marveled. Philippa traversed London and Paris, both beautiful, romantic, and grand. Still, New York, shiny and fresh, possessed palpable energy, even in the depressed economy.

Philippa battled fear, but simulated confidence as she walked New York City streets. She selected New York for simple reasons. First, the name reminded her of home. Second, a ship bound for New York departed in her time of crisis.

Philippa hoarded birthday, Christmas, and chore money before blossoming into a young woman. Most of her savings were spent on first-class passage from Yorkshire, a final extravagance, before the harsh realities of life without wealth's umbrella. Her purse possessed enough financial firepower for a month of food and lodging. Philippa, gorgeous like her mother, but taller and leaner thanks to her father, continued her walk. Her tailored dress accented tantalizing curves. The 18-year-old's presence swiveled the heads of even the politest gentlemen. Female pedestrians stared, equally intrigued by her couture as their male counterparts by her form. Philippa's arresting appearance was counterpoint to grimy surroundings.

Exhausted from her travels, she walked slowly, taking in everything. Traveling alone and on the run presented challenges. She planned for today most of her life. The teenager pushed back regrets, embracing forward momentum.

She walked hours before stumbling upon O'Connor's Irish Pub. Stares from downtrodden patrons nursing pints greeted Philippa upon her entry. The servers sported outfits tight around the waist and hip and loose in areas men appreciated near the top. She asked a beautiful redhead, with *Claire* stitched on her dress, where to locate the proprietor. Claire carted pints in her hands, so the beauty motioned her head toward a bearded man working in a darkened booth.

Philippa beelined to him and stood in view of the proprietor, waiting for his address. When he looked up, he grumbled, "You're blocking my light, girl."

"Oh, sorry," she said and stepped aside.

"Can I help you?"

"I am inquiring about a waitress position," she said in a beautiful Yorkshire accent.

"Lots of people looking for jobs, girl. Rough out there."

"Well, sir, I have few options, so I will work especially hard for you."

He stared at her, slowly, up, and down, like it was his right to explore every inch of her form. Philippa stood horrified. Men admired her often, but this was different. The proprietor examined her. Using her upbringing, Philippa rose above the inappropriateness. She endured; her head held high.

She assumed he was imagining her body in the establishment's tawdry waitress uniform. He stood, spending additional time focused on her decolletage. She doubted eye contact in the near future. After a few seconds, he surprised her.

"I'm O'Connor. Have you waited tables before?"

"I am very familiar with serving," Philippa answered deceptively.

"Where you from?"

"Here and there," she answered.

"Keep the accent. The boys'll approve, it'll lead to extra tips. When can you start, girl?"

"Now, if I can be of assistance," she answered.

"No time like the present. Girl quit earlier; guy grabbed her caboose. Happens." O'Connor waited to see if his words frightened his new recruit. Confirming the contrary, he continued, "You'll have'ta wear her uniform 'til we can get one of your own."

The man rose, motioning Philippa to follow. He took her to the supply room and foraged for the uniform. "Here, try this on," he said, making no attempt to leave. Philippa raised her eyebrows and O'Connor exited in a huff. She pushed the door shut and changed.

Philippa folded her clothing before wiggling into the snug-fitting outfit. She examined herself in the cracked mirror crookedly fastened to the door. The uniform fit, but Philippa was unfamiliar with being so ...exposed. Still, her needs overcame her modesty.

She exited the supply room. O'Connor thoroughly inspected her, spending extra time examining her mostly exposed breasts, then he smiled approvingly and nodded. "Oh, that'll do, girl." Philippa noticed O'Connor shifted his weight, she assumed to hide growing indiscretion. "Wear the uniform until I can get you another. We get the girl's name stitched on their uniform." He pointed to her chest, letting his finger linger longer than her liking.

Philippa looked down, noticing the name stitched on the uniform—*Gertrude*.

"Well, today is our lucky day. You need not order a new uniform. This one appears new, and by coincidence my name is Gertrude."

"Funny, you don't look like a Gertrude."

"Yes, funny indeed," Philippa/Gertrude answered.

• • •

Early Summer 1943, New York City
"Let's compare tips, I bet I beat you last night," challenged Claire.

"I feel improper discussing money," taunted Gertrude. The waitresses occupied two of the four bunk beds jammed into the cramped flat they shared with Mary and Elizabeth.

"You're afraid I'll win," bragged Claire, always the competitor. "If I spoke in a beautiful English accent, I'd make more every night."

"I have never told you how much I make," replied Gertrude. The two sat dressed in their uniforms.

"Maybe I should try a French accent...or Spanish."

"You are drop-dead gorgeous, have flaming red hair, and work in an Irish pub. Possibly an Irish accent?"

"You're a genius," said Claire. They laughed irrepressibly. "I love the new Chinese box you place your tips in."

"The box is not new or Chinese; it is Japanese."

"I haven't seen it before."

"No, I hid it for some time, but I finally have four roommates I trust, so I displayed the piece."

"The box is too beautiful to hide. Where did you...?" Claire stopped cold as her roommate shared the look. Gertrude and Claire trusted each other implicitly. Time together taught boundaries even their friendship dared not cross.

Upon arrival in New York in 1937, Gertrude boarded in a horrid hotel before locating this flat. Claire moved in with Gertrude days later. A procession of workmates cycled through. Some moved out when they married or returned home. Others just moved on. Since World War II began, the current foursome remained intact. Mary and Elizabeth started working at O'Connor's in February 1942 after the Army deployed their husbands. Both women moved into the apartment a month later.

With the rent Gertrude charged, the apartment transformed into a profit center for her. The other girls did not mind. Gertrude paid the bills, arranged groceries runs, and handled the landlord. Mary, Elizabeth, and Claire considered the extra rent they paid a convenience fee. The girls took turns cooking when necessary. Gertrude did not cook when she arrived stateside, but with Claire's help became a passable culinarian. O'Connor provided the girls meals most nights. Their boss wanted his fabulous foursome in the pub as much as possible.

The ladies mostly ignored decor. Mary's husband's picture rested on a table in the living room. A picture of Elizabeth's family at her wedding stayed by her bed. Claire and Gertrude never displayed photos of any kind. The most prominent picture showed the beauties in pub regalia, arms around each other, smiling at the camera, each heartbreaking in their own way.

Mary and Elizabeth emerged from the bathroom, dressed for work. Several months ago, O'Connor started scheduling them on the night shift. The four worked together like gin and vermouth. Recently, O'Connor paid the girls extra if they dressed at their apartment and walked to work together because soldiers and businessmen followed.

The four started down the stairs. Claire and Gertrude tall, lean, and well proportioned, the younger of the foursome. Mary, 5'4" of pure curves, perfected a distracting walk that extracted tips even from the emptiest wallets. The elf-like, waifish Elizabeth reminded O'Connor's customers of a perfect, petite porcelain doll.

"How are your studies, Gertrude?" asked Mary as the foursome descended the stairs.

"Fine, almost done now," answered Gertrude.

"You really want to teach…children?" asked Mary as they stepped outside.

"I cannot wander through life while inebriated sailors peep down my blouse," said Gertrude.

"Why not?" questioned the bald hulk standing at the bottom of the steps. "Sounds like my idea of heaven, inspecting under your hoods."

"Well, you may find it charming now, but not when I am 80," responded Gertrude.

"Girls, I'll love you when your hair is gray, and your tops are fighting their way to your bottoms," spouted the man through an unruly orange beard.

The girls laughed as Claire, the foursome's flirtiest said, "Hello, Tolbert." She kissed him on the cheek like she did each night. Tolbert blushed like this kiss was his first.

Tolbert did not work at O'Connor's, not exactly. He only walked the girls to and from their apartment. In return O'Connor comped his old friend's pints and meals. Tolbert needed no payment. The Irishman considered himself the luckiest bloke in the world while in the foursome's company. The girls' protector found himself the envy of each male passerby. Claire and Elizabeth walked ahead, and Mary and Gertrude assumed positions on Tolbert's tree-trunk arms.

Gertrude found herself overjoyed in the company of her girls. Mary grew up in Manhattan, and Elizabeth spent her youth in Brooklyn and Queens. The native New Yorkers loved to indoctrinate their roommates to the five boroughs' charms. Claire the youngest, remained a mystery. Gertrude surmised Claire arrived from the Midwest, though she knew little of her friend's past. Claire was a flirt but also uncommonly streetwise. Gertrude wrestled sadness when imagining why the beautiful redhead needed those survival traits. Gertrude wanted her past unexamined, she granted Claire the same indulgence.

Gertrude breathed deeply, enjoying every moment in her new city. Manhattan morphed since her arrival. She understood her luck landing a job in late 1930s New York, the city mired in depression. Dozens of Gertrude's new friends and favorite patrons lost their lives in the war. Weekly, gloom fell over the bar when attendees of another Irish wake stumbled in to drown regret.

While New Yorkers struggled to find meaning in the deaths of loved ones, New York thrived financially. Few cities benefitted more from the World War II driven economy. O'Connor's became a profitable recipient of the city's resurgence.

As they started walking, Tolbert looked to Gertrude. She detected his attention, so she looked into his eyes.

"Taking a gander down my top, Tolbert?"

He chuckled. "Sounds lovely, but no." Tolbert did not speak for several steps, then said "Gertrude, may I ask a question?"

She nodded.

"You have a British accent, but you never say British words, like bloody or cheeky, or fish and chips."

"I am an American now, I try to speak like an American. I cannot rid myself of the accent, though I have tried. I can concentrate on the words I use, and for an unknown reason, I find word selection easier to master."

He pondered her words, then continued, "Claire seems to think you were some kinda lady in England."

"Does she now?" said Gertrude, not answering the question. Gertrude shifted her weight on Tolbert's arm, letting her breast brush over his triceps. Expectedly, Tolbert lost track of his question, and his tongue. Gertrude, awash in relief, walked quietly.

Tolbert and the girls strolled to the bar amidst unrelenting catcalls. The five, familiar with the routine, continued forward unaffected. As expected, a small line formed behind them and continued growing during their stroll to the pub. The girls entered their second home moving directly to their positions.

In time, each kissed O'Connor on the cheek. O'Connor, a lecherous and lascivious man, too ancient now to be a threat, still hunted ogling opportunities. He watched after them all but seemed most enamored with Elizabeth. Their boss protected his fabulous four like family. Over time Gertrude became a little sister to him, and she loved him as her big brother, despite his flaws. He handed her an opportunity when she needed one the most.

Hours later, patrons packed the bar. Fogs of smoke, rumblings of drunken conversation, and smells of beer and fried food permeated the atmosphere. The packed bar bristled with activity; a thin layer of perspiration coated each customer, the cooks, O'Connor, and even the girls. Gertrude noticed a fresh crop of soldiers admiring Mary's departure from their table. Gertrude spotted Claire tip-flirting with a mass of sailors while dropping off pints. Elizabeth manned the bar with O'Connor. Happiness engulfed Gertrude, as the once familiar emotion dotted her early childhood. Then she heard the voice.

"Philippa, is that you?"

Philippa/Gertrude turned toward the voice she knew her entire life—the cook's son from the estate, the voice of a playmate.

"Hello, Ronald," she said. The waitress had not seen him since her hurried departure. "You look quite handsome …in your uniform." The two played together for a decade, sneaking away from parents, and escaping the terrors of Philippa's brother.

"Thank you," he said and blushed. She wondered why a British soldier stood in her New York bar. He probably failed to comprehend how she landed among the proletariat. "Your father searched the ends of the earth for you; we thought you were dead."

"Then it is best if it stays that way," said Philippa/Gertrude.

"Philippa, we were heartbroken when you disappeared. I am duty bound to tell your father I have found you."

"Ronald, I have little money, still I have saved. I will give you every penny if you just…promise to tell no one you saw me."

"Do not insult my honor, Philippa," he said.

She surveyed her beloved bar. No one noticed her crumbling world amidst the backslapping, laughing, and drunken distraction. She breathed, inhaled, staring into her former playmate's eyes.

"Ronald, I think you loved me once."

"Yes, Philippa, how could I not?"

"Many times, in our youth, I felt much the same."

"That is the greatest honor I have ever received," announced the proud soldier, with a broad toothy smile.

"Ronald, I work in an interesting place…" She paused, soaking the bar into every pore. "Despite the flirting sailors, begging businessmen, and charming drunkards, I have never been kissed. In a moment, I will step forward giving you my first kiss."

Ronald shifted his footing, signaling nervous energy.

"As you will experience my first kiss, my efforts may be awkward, still, I will strive to do my best. When I give you this kiss, I hope you find my first effort enough to…muddle your memory. I do not expect you to promise me not to tell my father. I only ask that you kiss me this once. Do you regard this as a fair proposition?"

Ronald nodded.

Philippa stepped into him, close enough for the soldier to experience all of her. She sweetly guided his arms around her waist. She stepped closer, kissing him, much longer than he hoped, even in his oft-visited fantasies. Kissing Ronald, she also experienced all of him.

The bar erupted into applause, whoops, and huzzahs. Ronald heard none of it, his brain muddled beyond hope.

"Good-bye, Ronald," she said. The waitress nuzzled him away, leaving a heartbroken soldier in her wake. Ronald, who traveled to New York with a group of select soldiers to train for covert missions, died months later. Each day of those months, he considered himself a fortunate man, and each day he forgot again to send word of their meeting to Philippa's father.

The only girl Ronald ever loved pushed through the rambunctious crowd to O'Connor. When she reached the bar Gertrude hugged O'Connor, kissing his bald head. Surprised, O'Connor said, "Hello, British beauty," before Tolbert pulled the proprietor back into a Bronx Bombers debate with two frothing Yankees fans.

Gertrude searched for Claire, spotting the redhead working tables in the back. Gertrude dodged drunks and overflowing pitchers before wrangling her best friend. She hugged Claire. The first person she met at O'Connor's, her first American friend, and the one person Gertrude knew harbored as many secrets as her, looked knowingly into her eyes. They shared a look that only women who escaped horrors understood. They hugged again, holding the embrace. The twosome said nothing, but tears traced their cheeks. Claire mouthed, "I love you," as Gertrude turned to leave.

Gertrude/Philippa navigated to the pub's exit. She enjoyed one last moment, taking in the rank, but now beloved aroma of stale beer and sweat and the exhilaration of chaos. The waitress and future teacher endured the pain of leaving her hiding place, her buffer from the past, her haven. Then, as she did on her terror-drenched eighteenth birthday, Philippa/Gertrude disappeared into the night and a vastly different future.

• • •

Fall 1991, Washington, DC

"A New WHIRLED"
Foxx Kauffman / Columnist / *The Times*
Washington, DC

No, I did not misspell "World." I pinned and understood my headline simultaneously. Like many Washington pundits, my life differs today. I am in a blender, the world of Watergate II, the senator slaying, the "Politikill." Whatever we label last week's murders, make no mistake, we are being whirled.

I write saddened by lives lost, no matter how disappointingly the lives ended. Still, as a columnist, expressing opinions remains my responsibility. Last week you read the transcript from Senators Greene's and Thompson's assassinations, each indicting themselves with their words. Our readers were the first to experience these transcripts. *The Times* released the tape, now known as *the video*, to national media. Because I secured this tape, I feel driven to offer opinions.

The United States of America is a great country. Industry, capitalism, innovation, and religious freedom the most commonly credited doctrines of our success. Each doctrine contributes, however, our government nurtured them, protected them, and allowed them to flourish.

Our government remains imperfect, broken even. Still, make no mistake, despite flaws, our government incubated the best qualities of this great nation.

These assassins, executioners, "politikillers," opened a dirty, stinking, puss-filled box of secrets. Every citizen knew about the box. Still, we turned away, holding our noses as we passed. Each of us knew the rich and powerful influenced, even directed, the political automatons. We prayed influencers that shared our beliefs paid off our representatives.

Based on last week's events, now seems the perfect time to address the difference between a bribe and the actions of political action committees:

Bribe: verb; persuade a person to act in your favor, illegally or dishonestly, by a gift of money or other inducement; Synonym—influence.

Political Action Committee: noun; an organization that raises capital privately to influence elections or legislation, most commonly at the federal level.

As a lifelong DC resident, I understand the difference between a bribe and a political action committee. Bribe is a verb. Political Action Committee is a noun.

Okay, I understand a bribe is illegal. I also understand the government's attempt—or to be honest, *failed* attempt—to regulate the movements of political action committees. Still, the line is blurry and often crossed.

Lines are hard to see when you spend your life straddling them, like career politicians often do. Each definition shares a key word: *influence.*

Once, wealthy farmers or successful executives spent a few years away from their professions to fulfill their duty to this country by becoming short-term politicians or lawmakers. Over time, the unplanned and unwanted creation—the *career politician*—replaced successful farmers or business owners. Career politicians systemically embrace self-serving agendas.

Historically, the wealthy and powerful influenced politicians and governments. Neither Santa Claus, Glinda the Good Witch, nor these philosophically fascinating assassins possess the magic to correct this chasmic fault in our country.

Still, I wonder if, in the short-term, Republicans and Democrats quake. Most likely authorities capture Senators Greene and Thompson's assassin. Odds say they never strike again. What if authorities cannot apprehend the assassins? What if they do strike again?

Just for giggles, for morbid curiosity, let's imagine the scenario. What if accepting bribes terrified lawmakers? What if PACs acted within the law's parameters for fear of retribution? What if lawmakers decided key issues based on their conscience or constituency? What if the government ran as our Founding Fathers intended?

Let's get crazy. What if courageous legislators put term limits in place, so politicians returned to the regular world and lived with laws they passed? What if we disbanded PACs? Imagine if politicians answered to...their voters. What if policies placed caps on politicians' media spending? What if listening to voters returned as the political endgame?

Crazy, right?

I cannot solve government corruption in one news column. I am not obtuse. I understand there is a better chance of a documented alien landing than our government correcting the political inbreeding.

Am I a horrible human to admit I am intrigued to see what happens next? Or I prefer my politicians a little afraid—okay, *terrified*—of taking bribes? Can I express sadness for Greene's and Thompson's deaths and admit my voyeuristic desire to watch politicians clumsily navigate our new WHIRLED?

• • •

Winter 1991

Le Donphant remained legendary in DC circles. Locals understood the name played on the prevailing political parties' mascots. Uninformed visitors incorrectly assumed the restaurant's French origin. Just blocks from the Capitol, and serving signature food, the bar navigated the test of time. Senators, congressional representatives, judges, and presidents visited the bar for summits, budget debates, bullshit, or to eat the locally famous fried chicken. Le Donphant featured private dining rooms, remote corners, and conference rooms perfect for the business of politics.

The restaurant's most sought-after corner, famous in its own right, was aptly named Nixon's Nook. The corner booth featured a dedicated server. Nixon's Nook remained *the place* to be seen without prying ears, powerful in the political spectrum. Le Donphant servers vied for years to service Nixon's Nook, only few received the honor. A Nook server's best qualities were the ability to hear nothing, remember nothing, and repeat nothing. One slip, just one, and servers are jettisoned from the Capitol's service industry forever.

Today, Chad Cash, the fast-rising Colorado Congressman, occupied the Nook. Chad mastered the art of leading, and to a degree, controlling the Swing Wing. The Swing Wing was a group of 10 to 15 congressional representatives who showed a propensity to vote with their heart, brains, or constituency, instead of along party lines. The Swing Wing grew and retracted based on elections. Still, Chad sought members who demonstrated philosophical fits. The Swing Wing rode high after just shooting down the Conger-Watson Bill. Insiders shortlisted Cash for a potential presidential push in 1996 or more likely 2000.

Cash rose to greet his tablemate, longtime acquaintance and local real estate legend, John "The Heater" Hall. John earned his moniker. He reheated floundering legislation that benefitted real estate holders. Cash led the Swing Wing, but Hall's donations via assorted PACs made the mogul the prominent benefactor. Governmental agencies and reporters investigated Hall's alleged improprieties. To date, nothing stuck. His closest brush with indictment happened seven years earlier, more than a full election cycle, and a DC eternity.

"Hello, Heater," said Cash, motioning for Hall to sit. A server dropped a whiskey neat in front of The Heater.

Hall popped his knuckles, releasing the day's stress. "Good to see you, Cash. I hope you don't mind; I'm rushed. My assistant called ahead and ordered for us."

"I don't mind," Cash said. "Nice to have someone thinking ahead." Cash finished his sentence, as the Nook's waiter delivered plates of fried chicken. Cash, used to living in this world, knew Hall preferred to skip pleasantries. "To what do I owe the honor of our meeting?" he asked as The Heater attacked the golden fried feast.

"Where are we on the Decker Urban Housing Act?" The Heater asked while chewing.

"Heater, the bill's clogged up in Committee. About one in seven bills make it out of Committee. I doubt Decker will."

Chad observed his tablemate's plate. The Heater burned through half his meal. The congressman's first bite rested on his fork.

"Cash, you're the ranking member of the Financial Services Committee. I think it'd benefit our country if Decker made it out of Committee. Then, it'll be even better for our country when it passes."

"Heater, I'm happy to work with you, but Decker is stuck. Not much I can do," said Cash.

"I delivered tons of support your way. You and Rivers are on the Financial Services Committee. Hell, she heads the Housing Subcommittee. She's part of your Swing Wing. I need Decker out of Committee this term. Period. If you can't, I will find someone who can."

"Are you saying if I don't get Decker out of Committee, I can't count on your support?"

"I'm saying it's good for the country if this bill passes," said Heater, handpicking his words to avoid crossing a line.

"Okay," continued Cash. "Then I'll say better legislation will come along. Decker's stuffed full of pork-barreled trade-offs. It's bad legislation."

"Pass the damn bill or else."

"I worked with you because I believed in the legislation you backed; the new laws benefitted you…and my constituents. Heater, I got elected before you came along, and I held my seat before we met. So, even if you're threatening me, I'll pass."

Veins popped in The Heater's neck. "Look, you Colorado hippie, I groomed you. I helped build your fucking Swing Wing. So yes, I'm threatening you." Spittle sprayed as he continued. "You don't get Decker out of Committee, I'll drop every penny I spend on you. Then I'll spend it on whoever runs against you next election. Pass it or I'll treat you like a bloated baby treats a fresh diaper."

The congressman dealt with PAC pressures before, but never a direct threat. Heater polished off his meal in between threats and glares. Cash's hunger diminished as his anger built. The congressman questioned, *what the hell do I do now?* He watched colleagues trounced in re-election bids much the way Heater described. When finances swing, campaign ads swing, voters swing, victims to the advertising spending of the prevailing powers.

Cash fumed silently. Not dealing with this crap seemed worth losing his seat. Even though Cash's food sat uneaten, the server dropped two banana puddings and another Whiskey neat.

Cash stared to tell his tablemate to screw himself when Heater's eyes flashed terror. Cash heard Heater's last words, "What the hell…" The congressman turned and spotted two men wearing papier-mâché elf heads, dressed in green spandex leggings, red felt tops, and black patent-leather belts and shoes. One toted a sign. Holy shit, the other elf carried a…pistol.

· · ·

Houston, Texas

Gertrude Arrington smiled from the stage. An elegant bonnet covered her hair and obstructed the view of her face. She witnessed Kyle Kenner directing chaos backstage, as Interim Senator Pete Book funneled through the throng, shaking hands on his path to the podium. Earlier staffers decked the Grand Ballroom at the George R. Brown Convention Center in red, white, and blue bunting and Pete "By the" Book election posters.

Pete and Kyle were not her sons, nor could they replace Bo or Wyeth. Still, Pete and Kyle blossomed as her students. Both spent extended time at her home and little time with their families.

Gertrude prided herself on being active in students' lives. She participated in Pete's political rallies and fundraisers. A smart woman, she understood Pete used her as a rallying call for his election. She believed in Pete's political efficacy; he remained the second brightest student during her teaching career. They shared an awkward moment after Pete's high school graduation, but she forgave him and many of her male students' similar missteps.

Pete neared the stage as Gertrude searched for his parents. Pete's mom and dad seldom attended events. Ninety minutes separated today's events from their hometown. Gertrude understood Pete's pain, still she lacked surprise. Pete's parents' small-town wealth assisted the Congressman's rise, but he operated without their emotional support or familial guidance.

Pete walked toward her, pulled her up, and hugged her. The crowd cheered as Pete raised her hand. He waved and walked toward the podium as she gracefully returned to her chair.

"My fellow Texans, months ago the Governor of our great state, Ben Swindell, asked me if I'd vacate my comfortable position in the House of Representatives and risk it all to become Interim Senator of this great state. Now, I stand for you, for him, for Texas, in the upcoming special election to decide who represents the Lone Star State.

"Ben Swindell proved he is this state's greatest champion, bringing the economy to new levels." Pete paused, allowing applause. "So maybe you should take his recommendation." He paused again for chuckles. "Maybe the endorsement of Houston's mayor, who is attending today, sways you." The mayor stood and waved to the cheering crowd.

"Or just choose a family champion. A vote for me is a vote for parents, children, and teachers. I championed legislation that cut budgets while adding funding for seniors. Hard to do, but we've done it. I worked to increase programing for children right here in Texas." He held up his hands, encouraging applause.

"Then, of course, I spent time on my passion, supporting the outstanding teachers of the United States of America. Teachers like my political science teacher, Gertrude Arrington." Pete paused until the crowd coaxed Gertrude to wave.

"Teachers who change lives, who inspire. If you vote for me to represent this great state as a senator, I will find innovative ways to reward our country's best teachers. We'll share best practices and make learning accessible to even the most challenged. Helping children by empowering teachers is my charge.

"I'd be remiss if I didn't mention the emphasis on government corruption since the Watergate assassinations earlier this year. But God bless Texas, we're in great hands. Because we do things…" Pete stopped, allowing the crowd to finish… "*By the Book!*"

●　　●　　●

Liu stood at the back of the ballroom with Tanner, shaking her head. Her time in Texas prolonged past initial estimations. Her boss, Henry Moss, planted her in Houston with Tanner and Luther to root out more about Eagle Thompson. The investigation, started with incredible momentum, but stalled as the FBI failed to identify the Watergate assassins. Liu, following the words of Eagle Thompson's widow, investigated politicians who gained from the senator's death. Hence, her attendance at a political rally. Liu nudged Tanner, and they walked to the private room Book's team arranged.

The agents waited for the interim senator. A half hour later, the senator strolled into the room. "I'm sorry, I helped Ms. Gertie to her car, and I had to thank some dignitaries. I appreciate your patience."

Pete shook Tanner's hand before moving to Liu. He smiled maintaining extended eye contact. Liu held her grip and stare, refusing to back down. He released his grip, sat, then pushed the conversation. "How can I help the Federal Bureau of Investigation?"

"We've intended to meet for some time but waited. We wanted as much intel about your past as possible before meeting," said Liu.

"Sounds ominous," said Book, holding a perfect smile. Liu pictured Book practicing in a mirror to perfect his grin. He looked to his right as Kyle Kenner entered the room.

"Not really," replied Liu. "We know you're from Silsbee, Texas. You were elected to the House in a special election. You rose in rank quickly, making it to the Ways and Means Committee in your second term. We know you run a clean campaign, have a spotless record and reputation."

"Thanks. But cut the perfunctory courtesy. Why are we visiting?"

"One reason; no one gained more from Thompson's death than you."

"True," answered Pete, glancing to Kyle. The chief of staff remained silent. Pete continued, "I'll admit it's a good reason to meet. I'll ask again, how I can help the FBI?"

Tanner nodded and Liu continued, "For starters, besides you, who'd have a motive to kill Thompson?"

"My first thought, the husbands Eagle cuckolded. His philandering was Capitol Hill's worst kept secret. You can toss that, though, when you consider Greene. Why kill Greene, unless to throw you guys off track? I barely knew the guy, but everyone loved him."

They paused as a junior agent, now assigned to Liu's team, busted into the room. The agent passed Tucker a note before departing. Liu paused as Tucker read the communiqué. He signaled for her to continue, but his somber expression indicated crisis.

"Any other theories?" questioned Liu as she turned back to Book.

"Lately, I assumed the assassins killed Greene and Thompson over the bribe. Consider the senators they picked. Greene new to DC, inexperienced in the temptations we face—a babe in the woods. Thompson, bought and sold, been in DC longer than the Lincoln Monument. The dichotomy convinced me. Now, no other motives make sense."

"Have you heard of other bribery attempts?" asked Liu.

He laughed. "Of course. But politicians don't sit around campfires comparing bribes. And with my slogan, I'm not the confidant other lawmakers would choose."

"No," she agreed.

He continued. "After the murders, I bet politicians tighten their inner circle. I doubt even the most corrupt politicians plan to play Russian roulette with their lives...or careers."

"Thank you, Senator," she said, standing to signal the meeting's conclusion.

Book stood, smiling smugly.

Everyone exchanged polite good-byes, then the senator and Kyle departed. As Book exited the room Liu overheard him remark under his breath, "FBI must mean Fine, Bitchy, and Intelligent."

Liu started out of the room to confront Book, when Agent Tucker corralled her, with a hand on her shoulder. "Hold on, Cowgirl. We got bigger fish to fry."

•   •   •

Liu and Tucker trekked under Lovett Hall's arches onto Rice University's campus. They turned toward Luther's office, now their designated brainstorming location. While walking, both processed the day's information. Elves, or more correctly assassins dressed as elves, executed John "The Heater" Hall in front of dozens of people at a DC restaurant.

Even as disturbing questions filled her head, Liu laughed as coeds checked out Tucker. The Special Agent in Charge shook her head.

"Are you oblivious to the fact that these smart, beautiful young women are trying to command your attention?"

"What?" Tucker questioned, emerging from a daydream, or the newest death's details.

Liu, proud of her question, repeated it.

Tucker nodded to a male student, catching the younger man assessing Liu's form. "I'm not alone in being admired, Special Agent in Charge Natalie Liu."

Tucker called her by her full title anytime she referenced his appearance. An obvious jab. She admitted the fairness of his stance, after the agents' first meeting. She committed each morning to not flirt with him and counted most of their days together as a success, others less so, and a few utter failures. Tucker proved difficult to dislike, impossible not to...well. Liu allowed no time to process that prickle.

They transitioned to friends over the last months. To his credit, Tucker labored to ensure her comfort. Still, the palpable sexual tension became an additional, and unwanted, or to be fair, occasionally wanted, member of their team.

They reached Luther's office and stepped inside without knocking. Months of scattered research material stretched across two small tables. He barely addressed them as they entered.

Tucker and Liu walked to the TV. "What do you have so..."

"Shhh," the only sound Luther offered before turning back to the TV. They picked up a reporter mid-sentence.

"...*Congressman Chad Cash remained unharmed but made no comment. Witnesses said the gunman targeting John Hall, pushed Cash into the booth, then removed something from under the table. The accomplice held up a sign for everyone to read.*"

The anchor asked the onsite reporter, "*Have witnesses shared the sign's message?*"

"*Multiple witnesses gave similar testimony. Luckily, a party for a retiring judge occupied a nearby table. Guests brought Polaroid cameras; one took snapshots.*"

The reporter held the picture up to the camera.

taKE A bribE

meET yoUR MAKeR

STiLL WATCHing

"

"Shit, same guys," said Liu.

"Yes," replied Luther. "Are you thinking what I'm thinking?"

"If you think the gunman pushed Cash back to grab audio equipment, then yes," said Liu.

Tucker added, "If you assume the audio will be released soon, then yes."

Liu continued, "If you believe they took their equipment because it's one less way to track them, also yes."

The group traversed briefly into their own thoughts. Liu contemplated a return to DC. The FBI agent in her wanted to return to Washington. Her intuition screamed she needed to remain here; she just did not comprehend why.

• • •

Washington, DC

John Hall's sparsely attended funeral ensured Foxx's front-row seat. One of The Heater's ex-wives occupied the front row. Four of Heater's six children filled out the front pews. Another reporter, caring nothing about the family's grief, detailed Hall's missing offspring's return to rehabilitation facilities. Members of Hall's staff dotted the cathedral's rear. Story-starved reporters stood out as the only other spectators of the once powerful man's nearly vacant service.

Despite Hall's former political potency, none of the politicians who dined for free in Hall's restaurants, used his private jet, or visited his Caribbean resorts attended today. Each politician's absence served as an additional indictment of character. The DC residents who battled for seats at Hall's luxurious events deserted their former benefactor, scurrying from his memory like cockroaches from floodlights.

Someone mailed the audiotape of the Hall/Cash interaction to multiple media outlets. The assassins bypassed the FBI and other government agencies. Foxx pondered the shift in delivery method. Maybe the killers wanted this tape released sooner. Conceivably, the killers taunted FBI agents by sending the first tape to them. Foxx assembled a dozen theories. None arose as a favorite.

Chad Cash rose from the manure surrounding Hall, smelling like freshly cut grass. The congressman's political star reached heavenly heights. Some proponents discussed a governor or senator's role as a stepping-stone to a presidential run.

Foxx processed the facts. The killers were technologically advanced. Most importantly, they adapted, morphed. If the assassins emerged again from their cocoon, the reporter wondered how different their methods may appear. Foxx considered the assassins—terrifyingly driven and strangely beautiful in the execution of their agenda.

Still, the assassins used recording equipment twice, giving away much. The assassins showed a pattern. Patterns = weakness. If Foxx headed the investigation, canvassing DC haunts for recording equipment climbed the priority list. If the FBI found audio equipment tracking their quarry became an easier task.

Upon departure, the columnist offered condolences to family members. Guilt overtook Foxx when he asked himself, *Do I really want the killers captured?*

•   •   •

Late May 1951, Silsbee, Texas
Gertrude swaddled Allison Antonia Arrington. The proud mother stared into her newborn daughter's eyes. "Well, Allie; us against the boys, I guess." Gertrude planned to bear children until she conceived a girl. She loved her boys more than words. However, looking into her daughter's eyes comforted her soul. Gertrude loved her life as a little girl until…well…

Gertrude turned her attention from her daughter to Milly Rae Hillmore, Gertrude's friend, and neighbor since 1943. Milly served as babysitter to each of Gertrude's children. Today, Milly brought her niece Candy Lynn. Candy, a new teacher at Silsbee High School, badgered her aunt for an invitation to Gertrude's home. Candy, an area native, did not hide her fascination with the glamorous Gertrude Arrington. The three sipped tea from a bone china set Gertrude rescued from a yard sale.

"You started teaching at the school when…?" asked Candy.

"When I arrived in Silsbee, in the heart of the war, 1943. I had a fresh teaching certificate and love of literature. They hired me right away. Ironically, they asked me to teach American government and political science. Though, being fair, the school was short-staffed."

"Everyone there kinda loves you," said Candy.

Gertrude smiled, unsure of how to respond.

"I think it's the accent," said Candy.

Gertrude nodded, allowing Candy's continuation of her polite, Southern-fried interrogation.

"The kids call you Lady Arrington in the halls, but Ms. Gertie in class. Does that bother you?" Candy continued "It makes you sound…old.".

"No," replied Gertrude. She understood her novelty in Silsbee or any rural town.

"I didn't mean to imply you're old. You're gorgeous, I mean *gorgeous*. You're 30 something, but you look 22. Heck, my boyfriend has a crush on you. I don't mean it like that, it's just…" She stopped frustrated, not getting it right.

"Candy, if you want another invitation to tea, let Gertrude breathe?" Milly Rae scolded.

Milly Rae, 20 years Gertrude's senior, understood Gertrude, at least more than most. The grandmother watched over the young Brit since her arrival. Milly Rae babysat the boys during the school year and planned to take on Allie next year.

Gertrude loved Milly Rae. Still, the older woman's nosy nature rivaled her niece. The past Yorkshire resident/former waitress/current teacher comprehended the power of carefully selected words. The words Gertrude chose protected her children and safeguarded anyone *in the way* if the past paid a visit.

Candy grimaced as the boys screamed, toddling after a mongrel dog. Milly Rae and Gertrude failed to notice the commotion.

Wyeth turned two, days before, and Bo turns three next week. The dog Gertrude labeled the "Interloper" became "Loper" to the boys, making himself at home.

Milly Rae wrinkled her nose. "You're keeping that mutt?"

"I am British, trained to be a gracious hostess. I bathed him, fed him, hoped for his departure. He chose this as his home, despite the boys' persistent torture. I must keep him."

Gertrude sensed the question brewing again. Milly Rae's question simmered since the announcement of Allie's predicted birth month. The question nagged Milly Rae, like a small burr under a saddle nagged a stallion. Gertrude sighed, watching Milly Rae's face, sensing her friend's losing battle with curiosity.

Milly Rae blurted, "Your children are all May babies, their birthdays are all within weeks of the others; a strange occurrence, don't you think?"

"Not so strange. I only see my husband once a year," answered Gertrude, prepared for the question.

"When will I meet your husband? I've known you for years, and I've never seen hide nor hair of him," pushed Milly Rae.

"I have mentioned my husband served in the war and is now on special assignment for the US and British governments. He remains secretive. He does not feel safe meeting anyone close to me. We live on forty acres, so when my husband visits, he can maintain a low profile."

Candy could not restrain herself; words stumbled from her mouth. "Your children don't look a lick like each other."

"Yes, peculiar," said Gertrude, offering no explanation. Sidetracking nosy women proved more difficult for Gertrude than distracting men.

Gertrude read her houseguests. Both itched to continue the questioning. The new mother remained quiet and waited for the women's enthusiasm to dim. After awkward moments and no further explanation, the women surrendered.

Frustrated, Milly Rae turned the conversation. "What'll ya do when this heat gets worse?"

The oppressive Southeast Texas heat seemed poised to test thermometers' top levels. "For now, we will sleep on the screened porch. Soon, I will trade tutoring for another used fan."

"My husband rounded up volunteers to do some general maintenance next weekend."

"Yes, sweet," Gertrude replied.

Gertrude's home rested on poorly placed cinder blocks, featured an oft-patched leaky roof and peeling paint. The home lilted precariously southwest. The home improved from unlivable, to passable, to decent in Gertrude's occupancy.

"How long have you lived here?" questioned Candy.

"I bought the home soon after my arrival," replied Gertrude.

When Gertrude bought the home, a small hole surrounded by a rotting and ever-expanding damp spot highlighted the bathroom. A midnight trip to the loo led to interaction with rats, a cat living under the home, or on one occasion an opossum. The bathroom, kitchen, and bedrooms were repaired as Gertrude traded tutoring for contract labor. Despite neighbors' initial concerns, the home endured, well-worn, musty, but charming.

The house neighbors called "the dump" continued a slow march to a respectable homestead. The dump sat on forty ugly acres of underbrush and trash trees that Milly Rae's husband, Gus, sold to Gertrude for a song. Gertrude assumed no other fool wanted the property. She saved her tips from years at O'Connor's. She paid Gus her hard-fought savings and he owner financed the balance. Per their deal, Gus and his adult sons cleared part of the acreage. Gus begrudgingly agreed to leave the old house on the property. He told her to tear it down. Gertrude's attraction to the acreage overrode her distaste for the home. More so, slight savings and a teacher's salary limited her options.

Surprisingly, the home had not crumbled yet, and Gertrude understood it would not. The cleared acreage now featured a small barn her students' fathers erected three summers ago. Her barn boarded five horses and Gertrude planned for more. Gertrude's barn also housed Victoria and Edward, her own mounts. Gertrude got lucky; another neighbor tired of the chores associated with owning horses.

She slowly paid off the home. Several sweet PTA mothers gifted Gertrude hand-me-down furniture soon after she arrived. Gertrude replaced the worst of them, keeping favorites. So now the income from boarding horses, riding lessons, tutoring, and her salary allowed her to renovate. Gus' sons repaired Gertrude's home in exchange for riding lessons for their kids.

Despite her beauty, the young teacher did not threaten other women, because of her married status. She must be married. Three May babies provided proof.

Gertrude beamed at the newest joy in her life. She imagined this moment as her happiest—a dainty girl to enjoy tea with, to dress in lace, to gossip with when the boys moved away, as boys invariably do.

Just when Gertrude thought Milly Rae and Candy completed the interrogation, she heard a "Ha, hmm," from Candy. "Gertrude?"

"Yes, Candy?"

"The picture on your coffee table, who are the three beautiful girls with you?"

Gertrude struggled to not let her previous life flood back too vibrantly. She missed those girls; she missed that bar. "Those were my coworkers when I waitressed...back East. The girl to my right is Claire, the best friend I ever had, will ever have."

"She is stunning," said Milly Rae.

"Yes, she was, still is, I assume."

"The outfits were quite...revealing," said Candy.

"Yes," replied Gertrude.

"Do you talk to them anymore?"

"No."

The conversation paused for several seconds. "You're hard to get to know, Gertrude Arrington," said Candy.

Gertrude smiled, a subtle acknowledgment to the correctness of Candy's words.

"I've been trying to crack ya for years," said Milly Rae to Gertrude. "Still, I will one day. I like puzzles, and I love you, and I want to know you better, so you'll spill everything one day."

Gertrude looked around her modest home, mulling over how dangerous her cracking would be—for Milly Rae, for Candy, for Bo, for Wyeth, now Allison. How dangerous indeed.

•   •   •

Silsbee, Texas, 1951 to 1965
Having settled into her teacher role and with Allie's birth behind her, Gertrude Arrington turned her energy to her home and her childhood love—horses.

Even in 1962, Gertrude's home featured no phone, television, or frivolous distractions. Her children learned the lesson her father taught her long ago: Education started at school, real learning and ability arose from books read and work completed after school. Gertrude discussed anything the children learned and put lessons into action when possible.

Gertrude started Allie in school a year early, so Milly Rae, no longer the children's babysitter, now enjoyed her role as adopted aunt. She, Gus, and their boys became the closest Gertrude's children had to aunts, uncles, and cousins. Gertrude held Bo back a year; she wanted Wyeth and Bo in the same grade. The two operated symbiotically, deriving joy, strength, and yes, a talent for mischief, from the other. Allie started school early because of extreme precariousness and an attachment to her brothers. Only one grade separated the threesome.

Most locals called the boys twins, even though they shared few traits. Gertrude thought of the threesome as triplets. The three proved, in all ways, dedicated to the others. Instead of the boys torturing each other, they worshipped each other. Bo transformed into a force of will—big, strong, dominant. Wyeth's traits seemed tailor-made to compliment his brother's—fast, coordinated, and cool. The "twins" shared a love of horses, the worship of their mother, and a desire to spoil Allie.

The boys read to Allie before bedtime, prayed with her, played with her. She lit the twins' world. So much so, Gertrude found few opportunities to spoil her daughter. The tea parties Gertrude imagined were replaced by cowboys and Indians or knights and dragons with the boys. Allie admirably performed the role of maiden or princess. The boys battled over chances to save her. She often demanded scenarios of rescuing them from tragedy as well. Since Gertrude received few opportunities to spoil Allie and did not wish to spoil her boys, she gifted her children time and the lessons of work.

The summer Bo turned eight, he towered over 12-year-olds. He and his mother started clearing the property's remaining acreage. Wyeth, still small for the task, watched and spoiled Allie. The following summer, Wyeth and Loper joined Bo and Gertrude. Gertrude charged young Allie with chores and meal preparation. The offerings, simple sandwiches, or stew at first, bordered on extravagance years later. By the time Allie was nine, she completed chores by 11:00, delivered lunch by 11:30, worked with her brothers a few hours, then returned home to prepare dinner. Even during the school year, when the children completed their studies, the family shaped the property.

To Silsbee residents, the Arringtons appeared in perpetual motion. Gertrude's equestrian businesses dominated the time not spent working the property or devoted to schoolwork. In 1959, the homestead met Gertrude's exacting standards. With Gertrude's encouragement, her children spread their wings.

Twelve-year-old Bo, Wyeth, and their woodshop teacher renovated the Arrington's main house in 1960. In return, Bo and Wyeth worked on the teacher's contracting crew after school for a year. With their new skills, the boys turned the barn's loft area into what they renamed the Romp.

The Romp featured a functional bathroom, two bedrooms occupied by the twins, and an enormous room for sleepovers and parties. Bo and Wyeth's crew, which rounded into an army of teenage boys and girls, spent a good portion of their weekends occupying the Romp. After the Romp's completion, Bo commandeered any boys who slept over. The group built flower beds, cleaned stables, or trimmed trees. Then, with a burst of inspiration and his mother's support, Bo put together a crew of teenage boys and their fathers to build stables.

A selfish endeavor for Bo and Wyeth, the stable build proceeded swiftly. The brothers wanted the barn for themselves and tired of waking to the smell of fresh horse excrement. Expansion of the property's living quarters allowed Gertrude and Allie to enjoy private bedrooms in the main home. The additional stables benefitted the Arringtons, multiplying boarding income from the horses and increasing space for riding lessons.

While Bo led the stable project, Wyeth organized his mother, Allie, and friends to repaint and redecorate the home and barn.

Gertrude's dump off FM 418 transitioned to the most desired home in Silsbee. Gertrude still taught school because she loved her students, though she now made more money instructing inexperienced riders and boarding horses. Her children rivaled her skill on horseback, and each served as part-time instructors to make extra money.

Cod Haney, a dirt-poor farmer, but the best hunter and angler in Hardin County, wanted riding lessons for his daughter. Unfortunately, lessons exceeded his budget. Wyeth, as usual, explored all angles. He considered Cod's daughter Savanah a magnificent creature. Wyeth taught Savanah in exchange for one used Marlin 336 rifle and four hunting and fishing trips with Cod. He planned for Bo to accompany him, but Allie finagled an invitation. Under Cod's tutelage, the threesome developed hunting, fishing, and foraging skills.

The Romp became the teenage mecca, and over the years Gertrude witnessed hundreds of kids wandering about the property. Kids from school, riding lessons, and dozens of unfamiliars passed through the property's gate. She loved them all and aimed to teach each life lessons. Still, Allie proved Gertrude's greatest challenge.

Gertrude prayed for a daughter like herself. God laughingly granted her prayer. Smart, stubborn, defiant, and quick to decision, Allie decimated contemporaries in debate, when she engaged, which was seldom.

Gertrude knew why everyone told her that dads spoil girls and moms spoil boys. In Allie, Gertrude saw herself mirrored. Like most mothers, she wanted more for her daughter. So, Gertrude pushed Allie hardest. Traits she tolerated in her boys, she corrected in Allie.

Gertrude understood this about herself. She loved Allie as much as her boys, probably more. However, displaying her affection proved arduous. Gertrude, whose relationship with her father molded her, bemoaned the absence of a father for Allie.

Beyond precocious, Allie became the best student in her grade and the best in the school district. Worse, or better, Allie carved out a place as the youngest member of Bo and Wyeth's crew. Gertrude loved Allie's ability to assimilate.

But right now, Gertrude questioned her parenting choices.

Fourteen-year-old Bo, Wyeth, his girlfriend Savanah Haney, Allie, Pete Book, and Kyle Kenner disappeared days ago. Dozens of members of the boys' crew and their parents prayed in the Romp.

• • •

September 24, 1992
Liu and Tucker occupied the back of Erasmus Luther's classroom, embracing a break from the investigation. Liu observed a few days last spring, and with FBI approval now audited Luther's class. Erasmus, in rare form, transfixed each student.

"One of the most interesting and least known assassinations in America is New Mexico Governor Charles Bent. Bent lived an interesting life. For instance, he counted legendary frontiersman Kit

Carson among his friends. Bent became Governor of the New Mexico Territory in 1847.

"The appointment angered the Native American population. Taos Puebloan Tomas Romero and a group he organized broke down the door of Bent's home and attacked with bows and arrows!" The class, including Liu, gasped.

Luther mimicked a bow, releasing arrows. "There's more." The class waited in rapt attention. "Imagine, arrows impaled his body, but Bent lived. So, Romero and his crew lifted Bent to a sitting position." Luther again acted it out. "One of the Native Americans held up Bent's head and scalped him." Luther pantomimed the knife pulled across Bent's forehead. Then the professor mimicked holding up the scalp. Liu, like others, gasped again. "In front of his family." He waited, building suspense.

"It doesn't end there. Bent, a tough man, hard to kill, was alive." Murmurs passed through the class and a few "Ewws." Luther held everyone in the palm of his hand. "I'm not sure what happened next, but I read that the would-be assassins locked Bent, his family, and friends, including Kit Carson's wife, in a room. The group dug through the adobe wall into the next room before Romero's crew discovered them, finally finishing Governor Bent. The insurgents, freedom fighters, assassins (depending on your point of view), left the women and children unharmed but killed several government officials.

"Why was the governor killed?" he asked the class.

Answers varied from, *"New Mexico citizens did not want to be part of the US,"* to *"The Native Americans felt excluded from the process just like our forefathers at the Boston Tea Party,"* to *"Revenge for abuses they suffered."* Luther entertained each answer.

Still the room's brightest student, the one who needed FBI approval to attend, the one who hit more dead ends in the last few months than she could stomach, was not thinking about why Romero murdered Bent. Liu considered how amateurishly the assassins carried out their plot. The assassins proved incompetent, unpracticed.

A thought bounced through her brain, like a super ball gaining momentum, bouncing faster, harder with more spring. Thompson, Greene, and The Heater's assassins bordered on perfection. How did those assassins improve their craft? Did they ever stink? Was there a trail of poorly planned assassinations? Did she miss them?

• • •

Per their tradition, Tucker and Liu stayed after class to brainstorm with Luther. Liu remained quiet on the walk to Luther's office giving her ideas time to percolate. Tucker peppered Luther with questions about Kit Carson.

When they arrived at the office, the men sat. Liu paced. Tucker and Luther understood how she processed information. She stopped mid-stride and turned to them.

"We've spent a year on this. We've interviewed everyone that benefitted politically from Thompson's death. Actually, a few times. Nothing. We've interviewed his exes and family. Basically, the people who gained financially from his death—nothing. We've cleared everyone over the last year. I've read everything collected on Greene; Tucker, you've read everything on John Hall, nothing. Luther, you tried to find a political link between Cash, Greene, and Thompson, a bill or piece of legislation, nothing."

Luther added, "Greene just got started, no chance for them to cross paths politically."

Liu continued, "The FBI's brightest tell us these assassins' trail materialized at Watergate. Not on anyone's radar before Thompson and Greene. The two arrived perfectly formed killers."

Luther and Tucker let Liu run. "The most interesting thing about Bent's assassination is Romero's poor execution. Why weren't the Watergate killers ever bad? Doesn't it seem like they'd operate poorly at some point?"

"So, your point is…?" asked Tucker, pushing her.

"The DC team, they're searching for good assassins. Maybe we investigate bad ones, assassins-in-training."

"Hmm," echoed Luther and Tucker.

Tucker offered, "Nothing new since last year, no high-ranking assassination, hell, no low-ranking ones. People are aiming too high. What if our guys started small, like a mayor or city councilman even?"

Liu shook her hands, signaling for him to continue.

Tucker asked, "Luther, any small-fry assassination in the last 10 years?"

Luther considered, then spoke, "Sure, but it is definitely not something I've studied—small local killings. I stick with the big stuff. I'd bet most of the small ones are passion based."

Liu raised her hands as if screaming, *Yes!* "That's how we find them—their passion, that's how it started."

• • •

Excitement about her plan overwhelmed Liu's thoughts. After their discussions, she handed out responsibilities. She tasked Tucker and a team of Luther's brightest students to analyze New Mexico to the West Coast, including the Southwest, California, the Northwest, Hawaii, and Alaska. Liu asked Luther to assemble a team to search for patterns on the East Coast and Midwest. She assigned Luther the most populated portion of the US, the biggest project. The Special Agent in Charge and her team focused on Alabama, Mississippi, Louisiana, and Texas. Liu wanted each team member to tackle areas unfamiliar to them.

Still, as she stood in her recently rented condo, pouring herself into her lavender evening gown, she admitted her excitement about her plans for Dr. Luther. For weeks Luther battled distraction, looking forward to the last Thursday in September, the Arrington AIDS Art Gala. Last month Luther finally admitted why the last Thursday in September highlighted his social calendar. So, tonight, Dr. Erasmus Luther had allies, wingmen, a tag team with one mission, *get Luther another dance with Allie Arrington.*

Liu admitted to herself, and only to herself, her desire to see Tanner Tucker in a tuxedo. She was more excited about him seeing her. Her best friend went to Liu's DC apartment to retrieve and Express Mail this dress. Girlfriends dubbed this dress "the jawbreaker" because when Natalie wore this dress, jaws hit the floor.

Still, Natalie only wanted to impress one man tonight. One man whose crooked jaw she wanted to hit the floor. That man picked her up in ten minutes.

• • •

Erasmus Luther stood in front of his mirror and thought he looked surprisingly good. For months, each morning, he ran with Tucker,

Liu, or both. Working out with younger, faster, professionally trained agents fine-tuned his body to near perfection.

The Balani custom-tailored tuxedo Liu chose for him fit perfectly, though tighter than his usual attire. Liu's family owned a dry-cleaning and tailoring business. She worked with the Balani tailor to personally fit his tux. Luther indulged himself, remembering the tuxedo fitting. Having an armed and beautiful FBI agent measure his inseam challenged the professor's gentlemanly thoughts.

Weeks earlier, when she offered to help select a new tuxedo, he accepted, to make Tucker jealous. The professor understood Liu offered her help for the same reason. Luther scored a perfect-fitting tux and Liu made Tucker jealous—a win for everyone.

The professor knew, hell, everyone knew Tucker battled to hide his schoolboy crush on Liu. Luther understood why. The female agent dripped with intelligence and confidence. Liu's competitive fire burned nonstop. On morning runs, Liu set the pace, not Tucker. A simpler explanation arose for Tucker's, and most men's, infatuation with Liu. Despite her modest day-to-day wardrobe, and best efforts, the agent failed to disguise her electric eyes and near-goddess-like figure.

Still, while Natalie Liu's beauty intrigued most men, the professor's heart belonged to a woman who remained a mystery. Tonight, Erasmus Luther intended to change that fact, because tonight the professor had backup.

• • •

May 20, 1962

Because of past perils, Gertrude Arrington seldom experienced raw fear. Today she battled that emotion with every internal fiber. She watched from her porch as Milly Rae drove to Gertrude's gate. Milly Rae waved violently, and Gertrude, paced by Loper, raced to the gate. Several of her children's friends and parents started toward the gate as Milly Rae motioned for Gertrude.

Cod Haney and local police officers found the Arringtons' beat-up farm truck three days before, a mile up FM 418 near Village Creek. Fourteen-year-old Bo drove since he was 12. With his mother's permission, he traded two years of riding lessons for the old truck. Since Gertrude lacked the desire to drive, Bo or Wyeth drove the family to and from school. In rural towns, authorities often ignored family's underaged drivers.

Some neighbors assumed the kids drowned in a freak accident. Gertrude struggled to wrap her head around that scenario. Her kids grew up swimming in the creek. Also, she assured herself, even if they died in the attempt, there was zero chance the twins allow Allie to drown. Since Allie failed to come home screaming about her brothers' deaths, Gertrude knew her children were not floating at Village Creek's murky bottom.

No one voiced a reason Bo, Wyeth, Allie, Savanah, Kyle, or Pete disappeared. Select friends spoke of a secret project, but none knew the origins or reasons for secrecy.

Gertrude's full sprint brought her to Milly Rae. A crowd gathered around the two women.

Gertrude fell to the ground weeping uncontrollably when she overheard someone mumble, "They're alive, they are all alive."

As she lay crying, Loper licking tears to comfort her, one boy said, "'Course they're alive, Bo and Wyeth are with 'em."

She could not be prouder until overhearing a girl whisper, "Someone told me Allie planned it, and if Allie planned something, it'll work." Gertrude found herself in a familiar position with Allie, proud and furious.

Gertrude rose to her feet, with help from a few boys, then completed her trip to Milly Rae. The mother demanded, "Where are they?"

"In Galveston. Pete Book called his dad, who's driving to pick up Pete and Kyle. Gus lent his truck so I could drive ya down. Savanah's mom wants to ride with us, she'll be here in minutes."

"Galveston is 100 miles away. How did they get there?"

"It's 125 miles. You want answers, climb in the truck and ask your kids."

While they waited for Savanah's mom, Gertrude thanked each parent who prayed for her children and brought her meals. She locked the house and asked Bo and Wyeth's crew to feed Loper and the horses. A long drive awaited. Gertrude never visited Galveston, nor had the kids, at least not until today.

Milly and the mothers drove through Winnie, Texas, to Bolivar, and boarded the ferry to Galveston. Once the ferry launched, the women departed the car to enjoy gulf views. Gertrude watched as children threw white bread for the seagulls. Each throw ignited a gull war, as birds battled for torn pieces of Mrs Baird's bread. The cawing gulls swooped, snatching bread without fail.

Gertrude wondered if her children rode this ferry on their misadventure. She took a deep breath and smiled despite herself. She recalled a three-month-old conversation foretelling today's events, forgotten before this moment:

Allie excitedly entered Gertrude's bedroom, a room the two shared before the boys moved to the barn. "Mom, I want to do something special for the boys' birthdays."

"Something special sounds spectacular, Allie. What do you have in mind?"

"I miss the boys living in the house, I don't see them as much since they moved to the Romp. I've saved my money for a long time. I want to take you and the boys to Galveston. There's the beach and an old candy store and..."

"Allie, the old truck will not..."

"I understand, Mom, but..."

"Allie, the answer is no."

The ferry's horn signaled passengers return to their vehicles. Gertrude shook her head, knowing she needed to be firm, while only wanting to hug her children. Like the truck's other occupants, Gertrude found herself overcome with curiosity. How did Allie pull it off?

• • •

Milly Rae, Gertrude, and Savanah's mother Sally lounged in Hotel Galvez's lobby. The women arrived the night before, exhausted from their trip and onslaught of worry. After greeting the children, they voted to stay overnight in Galveston. Milly Rae booked a room for the mothers, whose emotional fuel tanks ranged from anger, relief, and happiness to a confusing concoction of pride. Gertrude, too exhausted to question the kids that night, used silence and demeanor to forecast the pending punishment her troublesome threesome faced.

The kids stayed at the hotel the night before but had run out of money. Milly Rae paid for their room as well. Gertrude promised Milly Rae that Bo, Wyeth, and Allie would repay every cent. Milly Rae laughed, admitting she considered the drive, room cost, and inconvenience repaid in full; if Gertrude allowed Milly Rae to hear the kids explain their misadventure.

According to Bo, Mr. Book dragged Pete, with Kyle in tow, out of the hotel. Now, this morning, Allie, Bo, Wyeth, and Savanah sat in front of their southern Star Chamber, with Gertrude ready to begin the inquisition. Gertrude struggled not to smile, summoning the turmoil she suffered the last few days to broadcast a tough facade.

Sally, happy to see Savanah alive, did not participate in the questioning. Milly Rae considered herself an interested party, so she stayed quiet.

"Allie, I am guessing this was your idea."

"Yes," she said, head high. Gertrude understood Allie proceeded, fully considering the consequences.

Of course, Bo stepped in to protect her. "Mom, it was Allie's idea, but we decided together."

"Tell me what happened, starting with how our truck got to Village Creek."

"Well, it started before that," said Bo. "Allie ordered Wyeth and I a six-man inflatable raft for our birthday."

"That was your gift, an inflatable raft?" Gertrude asked.

"That was part of the gift," answered Allie, offering no more.

"So where is this raft?"

"Somewhere near Sabine Lake," Wyeth said and laughed.

"Wyeth, don't laugh, you are all in trouble."

Wyeth smirked and lowered his head.

"Tell me how this started," demanded Gertrude.

Bo began, "Allie got us the raft. She handpicked our crew too. Me and Wyeth, because it was our birthday. Pete had money. Kyle is Allie's best friend. Savanah because she's Wyeth's girlfriend, and she had two bikini tops."

"What?" interjected Savanah's mother.

Wyeth starred at his bare feet. Savanah blushed. "We'll get to that," said Bo.

"In early March, Allie's science teacher mentioned Village Creek and the Neches River have been running high and fast. Allie ordered the raft right away. She shipped the box to Kyle's house, 'cuz the Kenners are never home. Pete wanted to come. Allie made him bring fifty bucks. Wyeth and I pooled our savings. Kyle brought over the raft and borrowed his dad's cooler and a pistol. We packed the cooler with jerky and summer sausage from the deer Wyeth killed. Allie made a list of everything needed for a campout, so we dropped the raft in Village Creek and off we went."

Bo paused, awaiting questions, before continuing. "We felt pretty confident. We took turns rowing. Everything went smoothly. Then, Village Creek hit the Neches River. The Neches was choppy, we hit some sandbars, but handled it. Allie's map made navigating easy."

"We pulled up for the night before we hit Sabine Lake. We camped out and prided ourselves on the first leg of the journey. Then our luck ran out. Sabine Lake was tough. The current pulled us one way or the other, but we reached Sabine Pass, then the Gulf."

"You took an inflatable raft into the Gulf of Mexico?" asked Milly Rae, horrified.

"Not for long," said Wyeth.

"Wyeth, your smarmy remarks add no value, sit there and be quiet," ordered Gertrude.

Bo continued, "According to Allie's research, there's a real fishing contingent always near the mouth of the Gulf. So…"

"So?" asked Gertrude. She noticed Savanah's blush returned; Allie stared defiantly.

"So, Allie, from a distance looks…older, very mature for her age…" He paused again.

"And?" Gertrude demanded.

"And Savanah, well, Savanah…" Bo stopped talking.

"And?"

"Allie coordinated the plan. If we couldn't navigate as well as we wanted…"

"Yes?" pushed Gertrude.

"Savanah and Allie stripped off their shirts and waved for help," said Wyeth, relieving his brother.

Allie hit him.

"What?" He looked at Allie. "They wore bikini tops. Fishermen arrived lickety-split. When they got close, they saw we were kids. Savanah and Allie smiled their best smiles, Pete paid the captain twenty bucks, and we had a ride. Allie told the captain it was our birthday. He dropped us near Bolivar."

With the sensitive stuff handled by Wyeth, Bo began again. "From there we took the ferry, with Pete's money, and we got to Galveston yesterday. Allie reserved a room at the Galvez. We shared a room of course." He looked at Savanah's mom. "The girls took the bed. The boys slept on the floor; I promise."

Sally looked upset but stayed silent. "We spent time visiting the places Allie researched, La King's Confectionery, which is awesome. We pooled our money to eat at Gaido's and visited Bishop's Palace. When we ran out of money, we combed the beach. Then Pete called his dad."

"It was exceptional," added Savanah.

"The best days of my life," said Bo. "Pete and Kyle thought so, and they're in tons of trouble."

Wyeth took his sister's hand. "Outstanding, Allie. Outstanding."

Then Gertrude witnessed something she had not seen since her daughter's fourth birthday. A single tear traveled Allie's cheek.

•   •   •

September 24, 1992
Natalie Liu opened her door and smiled at Tanner Tucker. The jawbreaker delivered. Tucker's handsome, crooked jaw dropped.

After a beat, Natalie said, "Better shut your mouth before you collect mosquitos." Natalie Liu always dressed professionally on assignment. She also dressed conservatively when she and Tucker dined as coworkers. Tonight, seemed the appropriate time to impress. The lavender dress hugged her lean midsection. A slit ran to her hip, exposing toned running legs, but Tanner's usually polite eyes had yet to clear their maiden voyage of her cleavage.

"Wow," he said. She motioned for him to step into her room. He obliged. She turned to collect her purse. Liu intentionally left her clutch on the bed. She needed to bend to pick it up. She turned, catching Tucker's eyes riveted to her backside. He looked dashing, but her usually cool partner stood shell-shocked.

"You look handsome, Tanner," she said using his first name, communicating they were off duty.

"You look...wow." Tucker glanced at her petite purse. Liu translated the one thought taunting her partner's brain, and...other areas. "Where are you carrying your gun?"

Liu hoped to answer the question at some point. She elevated one of her four-inch heels onto the bed. The slit in her lavender dress peeled back, showing most of her leg and part of her inner thigh.

Tanner stared at her softly muscled legs and followed them from heel to thigh where he helplessly ogled her strapped weapon. Liu held her leg in place a second longer.

She returned her heel to the ground, smiling innocently. Natalie hoped she delivered to Tanner, the man that wanted her for twelve months, the most tantalizing interlude of his life. Her success was confirmed by a quick glance below his belt.

"Whoa, I don't have to ask where you're keeping *your* gun," she ribbed.

Tanner looked down, horrified, and blushed. "I am so, so sorry." Tanner aspired to be a gentleman in her presence. She battled a tinge of guilt; toying with him felt unfair. Speaking of toys, Tucker looked like a little boy staring at a Christmas present, knowing his parents got him what he most desired. One thing she comprehended: Tucker hungered to unwrap this present. She turned and smiled but made no movement to leave.

She risked another discreet glance at Tucker's indiscretion. "Don't worry, I'll consider your…condition…a compliment," she said, while thinking, *an enormous compliment.*

Tanner Tucker took a deep breath, attempting recovery, then held out his arm. "We should get going, we have a professor to rescue."

"But, will our plan work?" asked Liu as she embraced his arm.

"Natalie," he said, addressing her for the first time by that name. "I have zero doubt after seeing you in that dress."

• • •

Erasmus Luther, following Liu's instruction, arrived thirty minutes later than usual. He did not understand her reasoning. The delay allowed thirty fewer minutes to pursue Allie Arrington. The auction started before he arrived. Liu told him about a plan but shared no detail. Liu worked with Luther, helping him prepare, running through questions.

Luther watched Gertrude Arrington chat with the Rice University President. Senator Pete Book again acted as the auctioneer. Luther tried not to stare at Allie Arrington and succeeded to some degree. Still, the dress she wore demanded his attention. Once again, she talked to the same annoying guy. They laughed, enthralled in conversation.

He felt confident. A beautiful Houston Symphony violinist, 10 years his junior, asked him to dance. While dancing he peeked at Allie. She smiled curiously, seemingly in his direction. Now he stood near the bar, hands in his pockets, wondering where the hell Tucker and Liu were. A familiar voice startled him. "Ready?"

Tucker stood beside Luther. "Where'd you come from?"

"I'm an FBI agent. If I can't sneak up on history professors…"

"You're pretty good. Where's Liu?"

"She's waiting for me to get in position."

"So, this plan of hers…"

Tucker sighed. "Her plan is going to fucking work. Trust me, you're the luckiest SOB here. Every male will comprehend that *fact* momentarily."

"Okay," said Luther, confused.

"So that's Allie," Tucker said, motioning with a turn of his head.

"How did you know?"

"How could I not? Hottest woman here, or she was. This'll be simpler than I expected. I know the guy talking to her. That's Senator Book's right-hand man, Kyle Kenner." Tucker bumped Luther, grinned, then left. The FBI agent marched toward his prey.

Luther remained unsure of his role, so he stood in place. Tucker stopped 10 feet short of Allie.

Moments later, Luther witnessed a deity crossing the room. He predicted her arrival before she passed into his line of sight. Murmur marked her entrance. Professional athletes, politicians, and the cream of the Houston elite littered the room. Yet, each privileged head turned to drink in the lavender-clad goddess. More incredibly, the head-turner in lavender stepped toward him with purpose.

Then he recognized Special Agent in Charge Natalie Liu, and like most men in the room, his jaw hung agape. If Luther could register, which he could not, he would notice women elbowing their dates to regain misplaced attention. Each step Liu took showed an intoxicating amount of thigh. Each time her stilettos stuck the ground, her breasts seemed predestined to escape her gown. As Liu continued toward Luther, she smiled and waved seductively. He admitted he loved her plan. She walked toward him, taking his arm. Luther now grasped Tucker's extreme understatement. Erasmus

Luther embraced his role: not the luckiest man at the gala, the luckiest man in the universe.

•   •   •

Liu whispered, "Ask me to dance."

Luther did so. "Agent Liu, I don't know your plan, but I really like it."

Liu smiled. "Act like you're enjoying yourself."

"That will not be hard."

Liu looked across the dance floor and winked at Tucker. He nodded in response.

•   •   •

Allie watched as the awkward, handsome man, who made staring at her an annual event, danced with a stunning woman in lavender. Annoying pangs of jealousy taunted her for a second time tonight. Allie returned her attention to Kyle; he recounted his recent trip to Ann Arbor. Lost in thought, she half listened.

A moment later, a rugged man walked up and addressed Kyle. Kyle recognized him. Allie overheard the conversation.

"I just talked to Pete," the rugged man stated. "Book needs you stage side ASAP."

Kyle thanked the man before departing. Unlike most male guests present, Allie noticed this man fit precisely into his tux, lean and handsome. Without pause, he walked to her. "I need you to dance with me."

The words resembled a polite, intriguing order. He wrapped his right hand around her waist, and they were dancing. "I don't recall saying yes."

The man's arched eyebrows, signaling he did not understand.

She continued, "When you asked me to dance."

The handsome man smiled. "I didn't ask. I'm Tanner."

"No, you didn't, I guess. I'm Allie. Did Pete really ask for Kyle?"

"No."

"You know Kyle and Pete?" asked Allie.

"Yes and no," he said, smiling crookedly. "And you?"

"Kyle and I are best friends. I've known him since birth almost."

"You're friends with Pete, too?"

"No," said Allie, offering nothing else. She hoped her partner did not feel her body go rigid, if only for a second. However, when she looked into her dance partner's eyes, she registered comprehension. He paused, saying nothing, she guessed absorbing everything. Allie adroitly changed subjects. "So, you wanted to dance with me?"

Her dance partner's face mirrored a simple expression...*duh*. "You're breathtaking. There's not a male attendee with a pulse who'd decline a chance to hold you this close." Allie appreciated the compliment. The man appeared five years her junior, maybe more.

He turned her, his lead firm and fluid.

He continued, "But no, I said I needed you to dance with me."

"Need?"

"I work with the lady in lavender." He tilted his head toward the beautiful Asian woman dancing with Allie's annual admirer. "She's my best friend and..."

"You have a bit of a crush on her?"

"Yes."

"She enrolled in Dr. Erasmus Luther's class. I think she's infatuated with him." Allie pondered the name, Erasmus Luther, eerily familiar. She grasped for the reason, which alluded her.

"How does that involve me?" asked Allie.

"Dr. Luther and I are friends. Before Natalie arrived, I noticed him staring at you."

"He's been staring at me for years," Allie said before catching herself.

"Perfect. As one of the most beautiful women I've seen, I need two things from you."

Allie hated to admit her level of intrigue. "And they are?"

"I need you to dance close enough to make the girl in lavender jealous."

He pulled her to him, his hand lowered interestingly close to her backside. Allie experienced his muscled body glissade over hers during the next perfectly executed turn. *Not torture*, declared Allie's internal monologue. Her partner's leads precise, firm; suggesting more than ordering the next dance step.

"You're an excellent dancer," Allie said.

"Yes," he offered.

"You said two things. What is the second?"

"You'll find out as we go along."

A sharp tap on Allie's shoulder signaled the second act of her dance partner's plan. She turned to see the stunning woman in lavender behind her. "I'm cutting in," the woman said. Allie noted the woman stated, not requested the intention.

Allie winked at Tucker before stepping aside. Then the handsome, awkward professor stood in front of Allie. He stepped forward with confidence, and again, without being asked, she discovered herself in a man's arms.

Allie noted something different about him. He radiated confidence, yes, but he also carried more muscle. "Hi. I'm…"

"Dr. Luther," she said. "Your friend told me."

"Oh."

"And what are you a doctor of?"

"History; but I specialize in assassinations."

"Hmm," Allie sounded, now understanding why his name rang familiar. "We danced together once before?"

"Yes."

"You are…more talkative this time."

"I'm trying, yes." She witnessed her dance partner battle a variety of pained expressions, considering, selecting words, as if from a thesaurus. "You are…mmm, I got tongue-tied, more so my brain failed to function. You stupefied me."

"Professor Luther, what a sweet and charmingly awkward collection of words."

Luther shrugged.

"Your friend who danced with me and your beautiful student in lavender?"

"Yes?"

"They must be fantastic friends, to execute such an elaborate plan, to get you this dance."

• • •

The Next Morning

Tanner Tucker displayed rare form. Erasmus Luther failed to show for the morning run. Usually, Liu set the pace for their jaunts. However, this morning her partner offered no quarter. Liu stayed with him but battled to keep pace.

Intoxication almost overtook her last night. Not alcohol, but the intoxicating thought of inviting Tucker to her room. Natalie wanted him for months, maybe as badly as he wanted her. Natalie Liu, enamored by her handsome partner, battled her desires. Still, Special Agent in Charge Liu understood the decision's ramifications.

Tucker handled himself professionally the last year. However, before last night he possessed a boyish nervousness. Still, when he danced, Tucker took charge. Each step smooth and manly, a rare combination. She found herself intrigued, tempted, even infatuated.

He presented himself politely the entire night, but he stared at her...hungering.

During the car ride home, indecision ripped through her. Unsurprisingly, the Special Agent in Charge won. When they arrived, she thanked him for an enjoyable night, confirmed the morning run, then exited the car before he petitioned to come up.

Walking to her room, she felt guilty about toying with Tucker. Was she fair to him?

This morning, as their run continued through Hermann Park, Tucker was polite but not talkative. She did not know if the increased pace quieted him. She considered his silence a possible ramification of the way she played last night. Sweat coated them both. As they turned to approach her condo, he slowed, letting her coast into the lead. They chatted and everything seemed normal.

A few steps before her door, she turned to thank him, but could not. She found herself speechless. Tucker removed his shirt. A jagged lightning shaped line divided his abdominals. Lean ropes of muscles striated his chest. She found herself mesmerized. Tucker's actions played in slow motion. He wiped his forehead as she stood and watched. Tanner Tucker never removed his shirt in her presence, never after a run, never.

He winked at her before walking away. Natalie's mouth formed a perfect O. Tucker said nothing. His action communicated two words, "Game on."

•　•　•

Washington, DC

Anna fidgeted, but tried, like every nervous person, to appear unfazed. Another candidate waited in the lobby. Anna knew her. Like Anna, the other candidate was extremely qualified. Working for Pete Book pulled against a majority of Anna's political beliefs. Still, in Washington, few politicians offered more opportunity.

Anna watched from afar as Book's staffers moved from his team to other incredible opportunities. Book's Chief of Staff Kyle Kenner seemed universally respected in Washington. Honestly, Anna wanted to work with Kenner more than for Pete Book.

Kyle stepped into the lobby and smiled. "Ms. Hamp, this way." She followed him to a perfectly decorated office. He motioned for her to sit. "Would you like coffee, water, anything?"

"Something to tamper my nerves," Anna answered, hoping to break the ice.

"Tequila shot?"

"Maybe after I get the job."

"No need to be nervous; we would love to have you. But you worked for Alan Greene. Our political agenda doesn't mirror your former boss's."

"No."

"So why are you here?"

"I need a job."

"Anna...may I call you Anna?"

"Yes."

"Anna, I want you on our team. Still, let's save time. How married were you to Greene's political agenda?"

"I helped Greene build the agenda, so I'm married and pregnant."

"Hmmm...our agenda, not a deal killer for you?"

"No."

"After Alan's death and the release of the Watergate tapes, you got offers to sell him out. One talk show offered you $20,000."

"Yes."

"You didn't take it?"

"No."

"So, the ability to keep your mouth shut comes with the Anna Hamp package."

"Yes." She shifted in her chair, not sure where her answer may lead.

"Do I have your word...on that?"

Anna paused, looking for clues in Kenner's eyes. He gave none. "Of course."

"Perfect. Then I'll ask again why you are here? The *I need a job* answer doesn't fly. Clement and Row recruited you, so did Thames."

"Wow, you're informed."

"It's my job."

"Then let's slice through the pleasantries. I watched member after member of your staff move to peach positions in DC. Your reputation, Mr. Kenner..."

"Call me Kyle."

"Your reputation, Kyle, you get people promoted."

"Yes."

"I have zero intentions to stay here long. Still, you know I'll improve your team. My ambitions go well beyond working for Pete Book."

"Hmm. Thanks for your frankness."

Anna felt a box checked inside Kyle's head.

Kyle continued, "I need you ambitious."

"I am."

"So, Thursday?"

"I'm sorry?"

"You start Thursday."

"Wow, okay, I'll be here."

"Perfect." Anna translated something that resembled melancholy pass over Kyle's face before he stood to usher her out.

On the walk home, Anna struggled with the feeling she passed some secret test, a test for which only Kyle Kenner knew the answers. She never forgot Kyle's last words to her that day, as he walked her to the stairs outside Book's office. The implied warning that she only grasped with the passage of time. "Bring your ambition; you'll need it to survive."

●　　●　　●

November 22, 1992

Gertrude Arrington sat in the small Silsbee diner. Thankfully, Allie agreed to escort her for tea. Tears traversed Gertrude's cheek as she remembered the horrors that inflicted the world twenty-nine years earlier.

November 22, 1963, she stood in her classroom, her students released for lunch. Of course, Bo found her, told her, held her—her oldest son, the rock, the only person capable of calming her. Sweet, reliable Bo. Her oldest son helped her process raw emotions.

Because of Gertrude's past, she remained wary of men in authority. John F. Kennedy, two years Gertrude's senior, evoked faith and confidence. She sobbed as Bo held her. His calming voice echoed in the recesses of her memory. Bo became the man of the family on November 22, 1963.

Wyeth was nowhere to be found.

• • •

Allie, like her mother, sat in the diner watching vintage newsreel coverage from 1963. Like her mother, Allie's memories overwhelmed her. To this date, 1963 remained one of the worst years of her life. Her brothers and mother were at the high school campus. Eighth-grade Allie found herself stranded in junior high. She and her brothers, for years inseparable, now occupied campuses miles apart. The three operated as a unit, each understood their roles, the other's personalities and needs. The school day severed Allie from her pack. She hated the isolation.

She convinced herself the year could not get worse; it did, plummeting to an unexpected nadir.

Over the intercom. Principal Keller announced that President Kennedy had died. Allie remembered sitting, stunned for fifteen minutes. She struggled to remember her words to her teacher, to be excused. Allie never forgot stepping into the hall. Wyeth sat on the floor outside her classroom, waiting. Bo and Wyeth heard the news together, earlier. Bo stayed to comfort their mother, but the brothers wanted someone to console Allie. Wyeth wanted the job. He hurried from the high school campus to be with her.

She remembered every syllable he spoke. Yet, what she recalled clearly was her funny, sarcastic brother holding her and telling her one day everything would be okay. Now, 29 years later, she hoped, one day, he would be right.

• • •

Washington, DC
Foxx Kauffman watched the Kennedy coverage. Like many, he remembered the day his world changed. Foxx and Erasmus Luther,

his best friend ruled the eighth grade. They worked to perfect "the game." Foxx postulated to Erasmus that when girls thought you were nice, polite, even chivalrous, they told other girls. If several girls shared the same story, the story must be true.

Foxx's invention—the game—proved a masterstroke. The game featured specific rules.

Rule 1: Both boys concentrated on making one girl, just one, feel special for a week.

Rule 2: They never stopped being nice to that girl after the week; they now counted the girl among their friends.

Rule 3: They never spoke of the game.

Rule 4: Neither boy asked a girl out within two weeks of her inclusion in the game.

Their goal remained simple: make someone feel special. Were ulterior motives involved? Absolutely, they were 12-year-old boys, not saints. They...appreciated the young girls blooming around them. Hormones ruled Erasmus' and Foxx's decision-making processes.

The game included every female from teachers to lunch ladies to girls they crushed on and girls they did not. Foxx's logic proved sound. Someone felt good. The game worked; the boys benefitted. The game usually benefitted Foxx more. Despite time under Foxx's tutelage, Erasmus failed to move one girl from friend to girlfriend.

This day, the game focused on the beguiling Tisha Johnson. Foxx liked her a lot. He remembered suffering as Erasmus chose that day to excel at the game. Astonishingly, Erasmus charmed Tisha. Foxx's dream girl giggled at every Erasmus move. The green-eyed monster flamed in Foxx, exacerbated with each Tisha eyelash flutter.

Then Foxx's world changed. He overheard two teachers talking. "Kennedy's shot...just a few minutes ago, yeah, it's going to be terrible to tell them. We're supposed to wait until they're in class, so they find out together. So, they can hear it from someone..."

Foxx wished to turn back time. He selfishly longed to enjoy a few more moments of innocence. Foxx regarded his best friend, flirting and laughing with Tisha Johnson. He relished those sweet smiles and laughs. Foxx, no longer jealous of Erasmus' spot next to Tisha, but jealous of his extra moments of innocence. He wanted to protect his friend's last minutes of childhood. Because Foxx understood that minutes from now, his closest friend would never be the same.

•   •   •

Houston, Texas

Erasmus Luther, the man named for conflict, enjoyed this day. Most November 22nds found him in class teaching. Not this year. This year the anniversary of Kennedy's death fell on Sunday. Luther, not wanting to mope at home, hosted Tucker and Liu at *Taste of Texas*, a legendary Houston steakhouse. On Luther's recommendation, they arrived in taxis.

After trips to the salad bar and perfect steaks, a filet for Liu, T-bones for Tucker and Luther, the three remained to empty another wine bottle. All three of them blitzed, not tipsy, not light-headed, drunk.

The two FBI agents took turns interrogating him about Allie Arrington, but Luther reported no news. Luther stuck to the story he repeated the last two months. "I hit it off, I thought. She danced with me. We talked the rest of the night. I asked for her phone number. She declined but took mine." He paused for effect. "There is something new, though."

Tucker and Liu leaned in.

"Friday, I got a copy of my book in the mail, *Garfield & McKinley: The Other American Tragedies*, with a request for an autograph and a self-addressed, stamped envelope from Allison Arrington."

"At least you have her address," stated Tucker.

"PO Box."

"That bitch," said Liu. They all laughed.

"Thanks for being here." The agents signaled "you're welcome" by tapping glasses with Luther. "This is a rough day for me. When I have class, like I do most years, I tell the students about my experience."

Tucker motioned for Luther to continue.

"I was hitting on a girl to make my best friend jealous. For once, I enjoyed a miniscule amount of success. I glanced at Foxx, and I knew something cataclysmic happened. I gave up my coveted spot next to Tisha Johnson. I went to him. He shook uncontrollably, but repeated, "Everything's okay." In class our teacher, Ms. Westbrook, told us. The news wrecked her too. Foxx knew, he said later, he wanted me to enjoy my innocence a few moments more. I appreciated him for that. Those minutes meant a lot. I loved Kennedy. I wanted to be him. Who didn't?" He paused. "Where were you when Kennedy was assassinated?" the professor asked.

"I was three, I don't remember. My parents tried to protect me," said Tucker.

"I wasn't even a year old, so zero memory for me," followed Liu.

"You guys are no fun. Even drunk."

"That hurts," said Liu.

"We all changed that day. Kennedy's assassination trampled my innocence, wrecked my faith in the world, taught me the meaning of fear, and became my obsession. I can't imagine how November 22 warped people, how it changed their world view forever."

●　　●　　●

December 10, 1992
"Everyone ready?" asked Liu.

"I can tell you are," said Erasmus grinning. "Give me a moment," he said, pulling piles of paper into an organized presentation. Luther's, Liu's, and Tucker's teams worked separately to avoid influencing the other's efforts.

Tucker leaned back, smirking. Two legs of his chair dangled in the air. Liu glared, shaking her head. "You're not in college; sit like an adult." Tucker shrugged. He recruited additional coeds to complete his project. The young women organized, cataloged, and created reference manuals for Tucker's team's research.

"I'll go first," said Liu.

"No, you're the Special Agent in Charge. You go last," ribbed Tucker.

Liu dropped into her seat dejectedly.

"Raz, you go first," added Tucker.

Luther stood behind his desk. "Okay, six East Coast and Midwest deaths appear politically related. Sounds like a ton, but it's one every few years. Miniscule compared to the population. Three deaths appear to be standard bullshit. One candidate loses an election, he kills the winner. So, no legs there. One incumbent caught his wife in bed with his rival. The incumbent unloaded his revolver into the pair. Interesting but doesn't help us."

"Someone killed Steph Joseph, the former mayor of Levittown, Pennsylvania. He'd been out of office six years. Still, he stepped down during an ethics investigation. I almost didn't include it. He died in a hunting accident, still unsolved."

"Hmm," said Tucker, leafing through his notes.

"Like I said, we almost didn't pull it, but I'm glad we did. You'll see why."

"This last one, there's something here. A judge from Pennington, in Jersey, named Urey Little, was indicted for accepting bribes in 1988. Yet, the locals never prosecuted him. Probably called in favors, got off clean. No charges."

"I don't remember that," said Liu.

"Didn't get much national attention. Anyway, police found him dead from an overdose weeks later. He left a typed note admitting to the bribe."

"Why kill yourself after wrangling to get charges dropped?" asked Tucker.

"Because he had no intention of killing himself. This might be one of our guys' first targets. Not tons of news coverage, but some. The guys who killed Thompson and Greene showed a propensity for finding the rotten fish. Potentially the story drew the killers to Judge Little. That's my guess."

"He admitted he took bribes in his typed note. He hand-signed the note, his signature. Since it looked like a suicide, it got processed as a suicide. Still, a few facts scream it's not."

"Continue," prodded Liu.

"Levittown, Pennsylvania, and Pennington, New Jersey, are thirty minutes apart. A local reporter wrote an article about Judge Little. The Associated Press picked up the piece. So, it ran nationally. The article chronicled examples of political wrongdoing. Guess who else got mentioned?"

"Your Pennsylvania mayor."

"Bingo. One newspaper article mentioned two corrupt politicians. The two died within months of each other."

"What year was that?" asked Tucker.

"Eighty-eight."

"And no one put that together yet?"

"Unless you're looking through our lens, with tons of hindsight, why would you? One hunting accident and one suicide. No one spotted the association," answered Luther.

"There's something else."

"What?"

"The shot that killed the mayor, Steph Joseph."

"Yes?"

"Head shot. Most hunting accidents, body shots, more mass, simple logic. Not in Joseph's case. Head shot, or if not an accident, kill shot."

"Do Moss and the DC team know this?" Tucker asked Liu.

"I don't think so. I get weekly updates. But a lot of politics are involved in this case. Who knows?"

"Anything else, Erasmus?" asked Liu.

"I'll get more on our crooked judge and mayor, but that's all."

Liu addressed her partner, still frustratingly leaning back in his chair. "Okay, Tucker, you're up."

"Well, I thought I had nothing. But Luther showed me I might."

"What do you mean?" followed Liu.

"Well, technically no political assassinations. We went back 10 years. Three politicians were murdered. Two were domestic disputes, the other an old-fashioned mugging. Authorities closed those cases. Because I didn't want to appear lazy, my team researched other causes of death.

"There were a few suicides, I'll poke those harder now. I ran across a California congressional representative, Wally Lane, died in an Alaskan hunting accident. Seemed random, but maybe not. Gunshot. A little strange, more hunters die from avalanches or exposure in Alaska than gunshot wounds. The reason I logged it was because it was unsolved and..."

"And he was under investigation for something else," stated Liu.

"Misappropriation of campaign funds and illegal fundraising. Headed for trial in the next year."

"Was there news coverage?" asked Erasmus.

"Some, but it was a state congressman, not the DC variety."

"Maybe the news report drew the assassins," added Luther.

"Sure," replied Tucker. "Our suspects seem advanced now. But when they started, maybe they followed news stories. Might have stopped because they felt predictable; no one put it together yet."

"Tucker, you have homework. Find out," started Liu.

"Did our California Congressman die from a head shot? Also, did the same gun..."

"Exactly," said Liu, cutting him off.

"Already in my notes," Tucker said. "Once we have ballistics, let's pull hunting deaths and see if we find a connection."

"Good idea," said Liu.

Erasmus asked, "What year did the California Congressman die?"

"1986," answered Tucker.

"Hmm," Liu and Luther said in unison.

"Anything else, Tucker?" asked Liu.

"I enjoyed making you wait." Tucker smiled, appearing pleased with himself.

Liu groaned, "I've felt for some time, I needed to be in Texas. Our project confirms my intuition. Here's what I got. Police found two female school board members in Beaumont, Texas, dead from an overdose in '89. The case remains unresolved. Police guessed a home invasion led to the deaths. Until they found $10,000 stacked on a table with a note."

"Holy crap," said Tucker.

"Agreed," said Liu. "The note said, 'Track the money'. Upon investigation, police found a building contractor paid the women ten grand to secure votes on a $750,000 school remodeling bid. There were no newspaper articles before someone executed the women. No one knew about the scandal before police found the women dead. News outlets covered the story after the deaths but nothing before. The women's names, let's see, Candace Cole and Amy Freel. This time, the assassins selected someone not already in the news for fraud, corruption, or bribery. Maybe by '89 they advanced. Something to note—this is the first-time the assassins targeted females."

"Anything else?" asked Tucker.

"Like you guys, I ran into a few others. Deaths in Alabama, Florida, Louisiana, and Texas. Police solved all but one."

"And?" asked Luther.

"It's not connected. A US Congressman died in 1986. According to a witness, Ollie Whiteman, a well-connected good old boy sat at a bar in Port Arthur, Texas. The bartender remembered a woman entered and sat beside Whiteman. The two left 10 minutes later. Cops found Ollie dead the next morning, multiple stab wounds. Cops never found a murder weapon. Investigators believed the assailant used an ice pick. Locals wrote it off as a deadly mugging. The woman stole Whiteman's wallet and car. Cops never found the car either. No one used Whiteman's credit cards. I don't think this case fits our profile. A woman's the culprit. Looks like a mugging or good old-fashioned passion crime."

"Stats on the perp?" requested Tucker.

"The bartender's the primary witness. He said the killer wore sunglasses and was tall, beautiful, brunette. About Whiteman's age. The bartender struggled to pin down an age."

"We keep it in the queue," said Erasmus. "I think we kick this info to Moss and the DC team."

"I think the 1989 school board murders are related. Not sure about Whiteman in '86. Still, I'll hunt for more," said Liu. "Great work, everyone."

"Don't mark '86 off, 20 miles separate Beaumont and Port Arthur. Liu, guess who took Whiteman's spot in Congress?" asked Tucker.

"Who?" said Liu.

"I know because my family pushed my brother to run for that seat. You met the guy," teased Tucker.

"Pete Book," answered Liu, mad at herself for not knowing.

"Pete Book," confirmed Tucker.

• • •

November 1966

Despite November's arrival, the heat in the Arringtons' barn remained stifling. Most of the Silsbee High School football team, their girlfriends, some cheer squad, and band members hung out in the Romp. Friday night awaited, their final high school game, the last time Bo, Wyeth, Pete, and Kyle played football together. Most of the crew lounged in the barn talking, but Wyeth, Allie, and Bo sat shoulder to shoulder, just outside by themselves.

To Allie's right, Bo rocked back and forth, drunk. Allie was jammed between her brothers, her favorite place, trapped in an Allie sandwich. Wyeth's rhythm and condition mirrored his brother's to Allie's left. The youngest sibling overjoyed being her drunk brothers' keeper tonight.

"Have you wondered what he's like?" asked Bo.

"Who?" asked Allie.

"Dad," answered Wyeth.

"You still believe that crap? Our dad's off protecting the world," she prodded.

"What do you mean?" asked Bo.

"You two are both going to Rice, don't tell me you're that stupid."

Wyeth stared at her.

"Hasn't it occurred to you; we look nothing alike? I mean, we resemble Mom, but that's it. We share zero qualities. Bo, you're huge, muscular, determined, thick in the neck. You reek intensity. You don't tan, you turn different shades of red. Wyeth's coolness matches your intensity. He's lithe, coordinated, fast, and infuriatingly relaxed. Even his hair looks relaxed. He tans in the shade. And I..."

Wyeth continued, "You're tall, impossibly thin, light, and utterly breathtaking."

"Thank you, Wyeth," said Allie. Flustered, she stalled to regain composure. "Here's my theory: We have the same mother, but different fathers."

"What the hell are you saying?" slurred Bo.

"Look, Bo, we love each other. We just have different dads. I'm not saying Mom slept around. Men flirt with Mom daily; she shuts them down. She puts us first."

Wyeth looked on, interested. Bo battled curiosity and anger.

"Think. Mom wanted children." Allie held up a finger. "She didn't want to marry. I don't know her reasons. The fact is the most sought-after woman in town, our mom, remained single." Allie raised a second finger. "Then created a fictitious husband."

"And..." Wyeth led.

"We were all born in May." The boys stared quizzically. "Can't be a coincidence. Count backward. What does Mom attend nine months before our birthdays each year?"

The boys calculate. "The high school reunion," they answered in unison, staring at each other.

"Wait, Mom slept with high school kids?" asked Wyeth.

"No, no. Bo, you were born nine months after the five-year high school reunion of Mom's first class. She was about 29. Boys who graduated from her first class would have been 23. I bet she seduced your dad, Tony Creighton."

"Tony Creighton, he attended USC on a football scholarship?"

"That's him," answered Allie. Bo sat dazed. "He attended five or six of your football games. Mom introduced him as a former student and old friend. You standing next to Tony, talking after a game, exact same height, similar mannerisms, launched my theory."

Allie continued, her brothers sobering rapidly. "She picked Tony. I looked him up. He graduated valedictorian. Classmates voted him most likely to succeed; he captained the football team. Hell, he played the same position you do. Mom needed a first son to make her feel safe. She couldn't pick a more perfect first son out of the Sears catalog."

"What if Mom had a girl instead?" asked Bo.

"Would have been a big girl," answered Allie.

Wyeth's head bounced from Bo to Allie, back to Bo. "I see it, man. Hate to admit it, but I see it. Okay, Allie, do me."

"Wyeth, you already know, don't make me tell you." Allie waited.

"Our Fourth of July party. Lyle Vallone comes every year. He goes out of his way to hang out with me."

"And..." Allie pushed.

"He gave me my first paint set, my first camera, my first set of charcoal. He implied it wasn't a big deal. Here's my old paint set, I found this camera at a garage sale. He's my dad?"

Bo chimes in, "You stand like he does; you walk like he does."

Allie continued, "He wasn't class valedictorian, but the girls voted him most handsome and Homecoming King. He attended Rhode Island School of Design, the best art school in the country, I looked it up. Now he owns an advertising agency."

"Is that why I love art?"

"He bought gifts showing you he loved art. He nudged you in that direction."

This time Wyeth sat stunned. Moments later he considered Allie. "Who is your father?"

"Hell, even I can guess," said Bo, now less drunk, engaged. "Coby Crowell brought your mare, Cherish, for your tenth birthday. He played it off. Just happened to be in town with an extra horse. He gave Mom a car to thank her for being his favorite teacher. Mom doesn't drive, so you drive it. Coincidence?"

"He owns a car dealership," added in Wyeth. "Okay, Allie, tell us more."

"Mom's favorite student of all time. Known for gargantuan pranks. Coby hot-wired a school bus and took 40 classmates to Crystal Beach before finals. They went missing days before anyone found them. On his senior trip to New Orleans, chaperones found a voodoo queen in Coby's hotel room conducting a seance for the kids. Weeks later, Coby's parents bailed him out of a Matamoros jail. He attended UT, got kicked out, transferred to LSU, got kicked out, then graduated from Texas Tech. Coby's the guy you want on your side; he always had an angle. Parties seem to follow him. Unfortunately, the parties sometimes devolve into entertaining train wrecks. He's my dad."

No one spoke. Bo broke the silence. "How'd she keep them quiet?"

"Well, Mom was between 29 and 32 and beautiful. She waited 'til the five-year reunions. Remember, we raise horses, so I'll use horse logic. Mom picked guys she considered good…this will sound harsh…breeding stock. She watched them, analyzed them for four years. Mom chose guys who possessed traits she liked. And guys who could and would keep secrets."

"So, Mom seduced her students?" asked Bo.

"Again, not exactly. Mom seduced men in their 20s who were smart, strong, creative, fast, bright. I'd bet she tried for children other years and failed. There's a gap between you two and me. Mom will never tell us, but I can't imagine what tragedy shaped her. What'd she go through to make such strange decisions? I can't fathom why she selected her method to bring us into this world. Still, she did. I'm strangely grateful."

Allie turned because she noticed something move out of the corner of her eye. She watched Pete Book bolt around the barn. Kyle Kenner stood there stunned.

"How much did you guys hear?" demanded Allie.

"The last few minutes," answered Kyle.

Allie ordered her brothers to search for Pete and keep him quiet, but no one found him for hours.

• • •

"Kyle, walk me down to the creek," Allie asked her best friend. Kyle Kenner nodded. Pete Book remained missing. Bo still hunted him. Wyeth quit the search long ago and relaxed nearby.

"I'll take you," said Wyeth. An anticipatory grin adorned his face.

"I didn't ask you."

Allie walked to the creek path hundreds of times. She needed no escort, she needed a watchman, and the opportunity to ensure Kyle's allegiance.

Humidity engulfed them as they started down the path. The trail of foot-worn, hardened dirt divided knee-high grass. Allie waited until they approached the creek's pine tree border to engage Kyle. Before her first word, Kyle blurted, "I'll keep my mouth shut." They walked in silence. She considered addressing the real problem before he read her mind, "I'll keep Pete quiet too, don't worry."

Allie took a deep breath, relieved. "Thanks, Kyle. I'm going to miss you and Bo and Wyeth when you go off to college."

"Will you miss Pete?"

"No," she said without elaboration. "Kyle, you've been my date to Homecoming, Prom, everything as far back as I can remember. You were my first crush."

"I know," he said and blushed.

"You're my best friend, Kyle," Allie said while navigating the pines to her favorite spot.

"You're my best friend too, Allie. You always will be. We keep each other's secrets."

Allie and Kyle pushed through limbs and underbrush to the creek.

"You're also the only one I trust for this little rendezvous," she said. "You know the drill, stay alert."

Kyle does, he turned around, guarding the path. Allie removed her top reveling in the heat. Her head turned as if on a swivel, her ears prickled searching for the sounds of trespassers before unzipping her shorts. Allie dove in, loving the embrace of the cool water on her naked frame. She spotted Kyle, who took his role as sentinel seriously.

A few minutes in the creek's cool water removed the day's stress and completed her cooldown. Allie enjoyed the creek longer than needed. She stepped out, using her shirt to dry off before slipping it back on. She wiggled into her jeans shorts before kissing Kyle on the cheek. "Thank you, Kyle. Watch out for my brothers next year the way you watch out for me."

"I will, Allie, I promise."

Allie and Kyle's heads whipped at the crisp crackle of snapping limbs. The pierced silence confirming they were not alone. "Which of you perverts is up there?" Allie screamed while sprint-climbing the path to confront the Peeping Tom. "I'll find you and I'll skin you alive."

• • •

"Allie, you've seemed distant the last few weeks," said Gertrude as Allie drove them home from school.

"Yes," Allie mustered. Gertrude resisted learning to drive. When she could not ride a horse for an errand, her children, another teacher, or neighbors drove her. Today, the task of Gertrude's chauffeur fell to Allie.

"You haven't been hanging out with the boys and their friends."

"No," said Allie.

"Any reason?"

"Just need time to myself."

"You've always been right there, by Bo and Wyeth's sides."

"Mmm," Allie muttered.

Gertrude checked the rearview mirror. The same car followed her home again. Allie paid attention to everything in front of her. Her daughter failed to register the trailing vehicle. Gertrude spotted the car yesterday right away. When you look over your shoulder your entire life, it does not surprise you when you finally find your fears following. The tailing car stood out like a naked sumo wrestler in a church baptismal pool. Gertrude, not a car expert, still understood, olive BMW convertibles did not litter Silsbee's countryside. Her pursuers chose not to disguise their presence.

She remembered the relief she felt last year. Gertrude sat in the school library and read about her father's death in the *Houston Chronicle*. Not surprisingly, shockwaves of his death reached the US. Gertrude allowed herself a prideful moment but prayed the search for her died with her father. She felt guilt his passing supplied some relief, or hope.

Now, looking in the rearview mirror, she was haunted by the fact it had not. Scarier still, what if her father knew where she was; what if he protected her from afar? What if his death emboldened her pursuer? What if…

Yesterday, the BMW passed when Allie turned into their driveway. Today, the green convertible repeated the pattern. An icy chill dripped down Gertrude's spine.

Gertrude understood this challenge fell to her. The children cannot know, no one must. The burden remained too heavy for anyone to carry, still she alone, like always, would carry it.

Act 2: Plot Arch or Rising Action.

Rising action is an element of the story arc. Usually, rising action comes after exposition or the basic story introduction.

Silsbee, Texas

Gertrude peered out her window, spotting two figures creeping toward the barn. Sleep eluded her the last few nights. Despite her heightened awareness, she would not know of the men on her own. The stirring horses alerted her to intruders afoot.

She checked the wall clock: 2:24 a.m. Time to face her past and what may unfortunately be her end. She scrutinized as two men inched toward her home. Gertrude jumped as a hand rested on her shoulder. She turned to see Allie. Her daughter, a horsewoman too, peered over Gertrude's shoulder.

"Someone's outside," whispered Allie.

"Yes, two of them," said Gertrude without turning. "Where's our gun?"

"In the barn, with the boys. What do we do?"

"The boys have the first move. Give them a minute, stay calm."

"Are you sure they're awake?"

"You are awake because I raised you around horses; they grew up in the same home."

The two men slithered closer. One figure, a behemoth of a man, brought his hands up from his midsection to his chest, indicating he carried a pistol. Gertrude squeaked before she fortified herself, trying not to pass the terror to her daughter. Allie pulled closer to her mother.

Before stepping into the light, the larger intruder considered the surroundings, measuredly, as if repeating a tactic, drummed into him through military training. Finally, the massive man stepped into the yellow glow of the porch light. Then the second man, the one-eyed man, followed into the light.

Gertrude hissed one word, "Jonas."

A tightened grip on Gertrude's shoulder confirmed her daughter recognized both men carried guns. The crisp crack of a rifle rang from the barn. The behemoth crumpled to the ground. Before Gertrude reacted, Bo leapt from the dark, tackling the second man. Loper's unrestrained barking echoed from the barn.

Gertrude gripped the door handle and rushed outside. Bo's crushing momentum knocked the gun free from the one-eyed man. Gertrude reached for the gun as her son fought a life and death battle with her past. She watched in terror as Jonas pulled a six-inch Japanese hairpin from his coat and raised the silver antique to stab her son.

Before the one-eyed man struck, Allie engulfed his arm, stalling the attack. The intruder wrangled, leveraged against Bo to free his other arm, and in one motion slugged Allie. She crashed backward and tumbled to the ground. Just then, the barn door flew open and Loper, despite his advanced years, sprinted, leaving Wyeth in his wake.

Loper ripped into the intruder's arm, drawing blood immediately, snarling jaws tearing and pulling. The intruder screamed before jamming the sharp silver pin into the dog's neck. Blood covered his gray and yellow coat. Not until the seventh insertion did Loper yelp, passing from consciousness, jaw death-locked on the intruder's arm. Bo took advantage of Allie and Loper's sacrifices, wrapping his thick arms around the intruder's throat. The intruder stabbed into Bo's thigh, but Gertrude's son never released his grip. Gertrude experienced the sickening sound of a neck snapping and the final gurgles, hisses, and moans of death. Bo collapsed backward, exhausted, bleeding, spent, the task complete.

Wyeth finished his trek from the barn holding the family rifle. His head, a slow-moving swivel, surveyed the homestead. He stood sentry as the others recovered.

Gertrude raced to Bo. "Are you okay, are you okay?"

"Yeah," he said, removing his shirt. "Horses woke me. Wyeth spotted the guns. We had to do something." Bo wrapped the shirt around his thigh.

"I know, son." Gertrude crawled to Allie, but her daughter stood, wobbling, then stumbled toward Loper. She dropped to the family's only four-legged member. Loper's jaws remained clamped to his family's attacker. Allie searched for signs of life. She looked to her mother, Bo, and Wyeth, shaking her head. The four cried for Loper, ancient, loved, and now gone.

Gertrude considered the familiar six-inch Japanese hairpin, the long-ago gift, locked in the disgusting dead man's hand. Gertrude understood Jonas intended to plunge the pin into her chest or temple. The vile man waited decades for revenge.

Wyeth knelt beside the man he shot. He nodded, communicating the man joined Jonas in hell. Gertrude understood she must navigate her family through this terrible night. She looked to Bo first, as always.

"Bo, I need you to help me bury these bodies…somewhere."

"Okay, but I'm burying Loper first."

"Wyeth, somewhere around here you will find a green convertible," she said.

"Cool."

"Not really, I need you to make it disappear."

He appeared disappointed, picturing himself behind the wheel she assumed, but like his brother Wyeth nodded. "Allie, I need you to go with him. You always have your wits about you. Follow him in our car and bring him back."

"This must happen before sunrise. If Milly Rae or the neighbors ask questions about the shots…"

"Bo and I were shooting racoons and possums," said Wyeth.

"Loper died of old age," added Bo. "Hell, no one will miss him but us."

Gertrude nodded approval.

"Mother, what's this about?"

"I am sorry, Allie. This seems an inopportune time to explore my past. Please dear, just do what I ask."

Like her brothers before, Allie nodded.

• • • •

The Houston Chronicle, November 17, 1966
Bryce Hardin

German business executive Jonas Hysler went missing on Monday, November, 14. Conference attendees spotted Hysler and bodyguard Ernst Müller leaving the Houston International Trade Conference. They departed their hotel in a dark green BMW. Police report no leads. Multiple sources claim they spotted a dark green BMW in Kountze, Lumberton, and Silsbee, Texas. Police question those sightings. None of Hysler Industries' sub-companies headquarter or manufacture in those locations.

Hysler took over Hysler Industries in the late 1940s after his father, Nazi supporter and war criminal, Dieter Hysler's conviction for war atrocities. Dieter Hysler, called the Furor's Financier, died in prison.

Jonas, considered a shrewd business mind, grew Germany's Hysler Industries after the war by healing relations with most European countries, including Belgium, France, Norway, Greece, and Denmark. Hysler Industries, once a dominant force in Great Britain, never regained prominence in the UK. Long-standing House of Lords fixture, Earl Augustus Harrington, successfully battled to bar Hysler Industries from Great Britain. Augustus and Dieter Hysler, former business partners, fell out in the late 1930s. Neither man addressed this split. Since the late '30s, the discord between Harrington Partnerships and Hysler Industries grew to legendary proportions.

Jonas, known for his distinctive eye patch, lost an eye as a young man while hunting, according to family sources. The family has offered a $100,000 reward for information regarding Jonas Hysler's or Ernst Müller's location.

• • •

March 5, 1993
Texas Governor Swindell requested Senator Book act as a VIP host for the Southern Governors' Conference. Since Swindell endorsed the new senator a year earlier, the request resembled an order. Book and Kyle Kenner's limousine approached the Texas Governor's Mansion.

"Kyle, please tell me I am done with FBI interviews."

"I believe so."

"How many times do I have to tell them? I wasn't running for Congress before someone shish-ka-bobbed that old shithead Whiteman. Swindell asked me to run for Senator; I didn't ask for it."

"Well, not directly," said Kyle. "I understand their point of view. Looks pretty incriminating."

Pete Book rubbed his temples. "No one runs a cleaner campaign than me. You're my chief of staff; you know I'm not on the take."

"Yes, I do, Pete. We share too many memories. You're a shitty friend and an asshole for a boss. But you're the most honest politician in DC. That's what I told the FBI. Because it's the truth."

"Will they finally leave me alone?" asked Pete. The driver slowed, pulling behind the line of limousines, just short of their destination.

"Yes, you're due for some air. Unless another assassination makes you President, then you'll never leave an interrogation room again."

•　•　•　•

Natalie Liu sipped her cold beer and smiled. She and Tucker decided to enjoy a night off before returning to protection detail. Scholz Garten, Texas's oldest Biergarten, brimmed with activity. A deep belly laugh rolled through Erasmus, despite himself. Foxx Kauffman recounted, and Liu guessed, embellished, the embarrassing story of Luther's first kiss. Foxx met Natalie a half hour earlier. He obviously considered embarrassing his oldest friend a suitable tactic to ingratiate himself to her.

"So, I have you two to thank for me getting a copy of the Greene and Thompson video in '91?" asked Foxx, knowing the answer.

"Video?" questioned Tanner. Natalie shrugged.

Foxx began another foray. "Special Agent in Charge Liu, it's a warm Friday night. We're in Austin, moments from the University of Texas campus. Beautiful coeds pass us, in various stages of undress, and I haven't seen one woman more breathtaking than you."

"A drink's in front of me, we're off duty, call me Natalie." She smiled. "Thank you for the compliment; Luther mentioned you're a shameless flirt," said Natalie.

"That, lovely lady, is true, but it does not change the veracity of my statement. Ask your partner, he can't keep his eyes off you," retorted Foxx.

A blush rose to Liu's cheeks. Foxx failed to fluster Tanner Tucker, an FBI agent raised to be a politician. "She'll do in a pinch, I guess," said Tanner, deflecting the situation.

Liu jammed her elbow into her partner's ribs. Tucker ceded no indication of damage done.

"How do you like Texas so far?" Tucker asked, changing the subject.

"I find the women enrapturing." Foxx winked at Liu. "But the air here sits on you, it's heavy. I picture myself wading through oceans of humidity. Also, I just saw a mosquito raping a turkey, those bloodsuckers are huge."

They laughed before Foxx adeptly mixed humor with his lust for information.

"So, you guys drove to Austin for the Governor's Conference?" Foxx asked.

"Yes," Liu answered.

"Not giving a reporter much. Can't blame you," said Foxx with a smile. "I was hoping..."

"Why are you in Austin, old friend?" distracted Luther.

"I decided if I came to Austin, my oldest friend would visit me. I'm in Texas to see you."

"Bullshit," replied Luther.

"Okay, truth. I'm a columnist. I need material. True, I travel sparingly. What's driving me crazy—our political assassins disappeared a year and a half ago. The story seems to have fizzled for now."

"Just the story?" asked Tucker.

"There's no news. The assassins remain on the loose. The FBI released nothing to imply impending capture. A source told me they're interviewing Pete Book again. But nothing new came from that. Everything's played out."

"What do you mean?" asked Liu.

"Well, I thought things may change. Public outcry called political action committees to task. Politicians ran scared. I don't mean to imply Washington ran honestly, but politicians tried to walk a straight line...out of fear mostly. Unfortunately, politicians settled back into old habits recently. Nothing changed, the momentum died almost as fast as Thompson and Greene."

"Boo," said Erasmus.

"Too soon?" said Foxx.

Erasmus led his old friend. "Did the story about the California state congressman and the mayor from Levittown affect anyone? Both shot by the same caliber bullet, probably the same weapon."

"Got some play in Washington. But it was old news, I don't think it scared the DC gang like the Greene, Eagle, and Heater assassinations. After Heater died, DC blossomed into full shitstorm."

Liu and Tucker talked this case to death. Still, she enjoyed a fresh perspective. So, she pushed for more. "Foxx, in your opinion, is this all connected?"

The reporter surveyed Luther and Tucker, then focused on Liu. Foxx enjoyed a long drink before answering. "I've rolled this around my head. I don't know everything you do, but I understand motivations. Something's brewing."

"What's that?" asked Tucker.

"Based on the hunting deaths, and rumblings, my gut tells me these guys aren't new to the party. They've morphed, though."

"What do you mean?" pressed Tucker.

"Well, at first they tried to fix it. With zero fanfare, the assassins killed corrupt lawmakers. The assassins decided they couldn't fix the problem by killing a few corrupt politicians. Corrupt politicians are as plentiful as maggots on a cow carcass. Killing a few larvae does not repel the horde. So, the killers changed philosophically. The assassins announced their presence, sent a message if you prefer, with Thompson and Greene. They killed Heater to drive the point home. The assassins hoped, in vain, the reverberations from their message served as a rallying cry to correct corruption. Their plan worked, a little, briefly, but caused no long-term change. Maybe that's why our assassins stopped...or paused."

"Paused?" Tucker asked, intrigued.

Foxx continued. "They may've gone dark for lots'a reasons. Gathering the data needed to select a mark takes time and copious research. Or our assassins shifted philosophically. Probably, they're more careful, averse to risk. You guys know their systems now. For instance, the FBI now routinely sweeps political gathering spots for audio equipment. Of course, something else drives our assassins."

"What's that?" asked Luther.

"The messages tell me one thing. Our assassins are idealists. Idealists are driven by something they feel is greater than themselves. Throughout history, idealists proved they'll die for what they believe in; that's what makes them scary."

• • •

Erasmus Luther smiled to himself as the valet pulled up his 1975 International Harvester Scout. He arrived in Austin last night to see Foxx. Luther splurged and stayed at Austin's historic landmark, the Driskill.

FBI agents are not the only ones who harbor secrets. At noon, Erasmus' much-awaited rendezvous commenced. As he told Liu and Tucker months earlier, Allie Arrington mailed the professor a copy of his latest book for him to sign. He failed to mention he returned the book with a letter and an invitation.

> *Ms. Arrington:*
> *Please find the autographed book per your request. I'm honored by your interest. I could be coy, but with your intelligence, I'm sure you would see through guise or misdirection.*
> *Straight to the point, as you've ascertained, you fascinate me. I've attended the Arrington Gala for years in hopes of mere moments of your time.*
> *I request the opportunity to take you to dinner and look forward to learning more about the men you honor each year—your brothers. Truthfully, I'm more excited to spend time with the bright, beautiful woman I danced with weeks ago.*
> *Regards,*
> *Erasmus Luther, Admirer*

When his letter went unanswered for months, he abandoned hope. After checking his mailbox each day, he let the task pass to his roommates. Then a handwritten card arrived. The communiqué, brief on romance, full of specifics, said:

> *Dr. Luther:*
> *Your letter intrigued me, as did the ruse your friends executed to arrange our meeting. Also, you complimented my intelligence before my beauty.*
> *Smart. Honestly, quite singular.*

Meet me at my family homestead, the first Saturday in March, around noon. Map included and directions. I hope you like horses.
Regards,
Allie

Erasmus turned onto US 290; a plotted map occupied his driver's seat. He possessed no inkling of how today may unfold. The day presented itself as a blind undertaking. Erasmus acknowledged a pull, similar to stepping alone into a dark room with no light source, riddled with anticipation.

• • •

"Special Agent in Charge Liu," said Deputy Assistant Director Henry Moss. "You're the one who asked for heavy FBI coverage for the Southern Governors' Conference. What've you got for us?"

Liu studied the 10 agents present. "There's already security here, lots of it. Governor Swindell arranged unprecedented protection for the conference. I hand-selected this crew, many of you worked the Assassination Task Force from its genesis. You're not here to provide security, you're here to spot the unusual. Tap into your heightened senses. We've swept for listening devices. Nothing. The assassins are smart; I doubt they'll use the same tactic again.

"Here's what's in your report. Assassinations started in '86. Based on the Houston team's research, our killers simulated hunting accidents, staged suicides and possibly muggings to target victims. Put nothing past these guys; think, process, act. Our assassins proved they're smart, high-tech, and organized. An added bonus, they probably possess sniper skills. Our strength…most attendees don't recognize you. Blend in. Unlikely the assassins strike today but be ready for anything. Tucker and I will roam the conference floor. The rest of you review your assignments."

• • •

Hours later, Tucker tapped Liu's shoulder and handed her a sad-looking sandwich. Liu nodded. After taking two bites, she said, "Thanks."

"No problem."

"Anything?"

"No, so many reporters here, there's barely room for politicians," replied Tucker.

"I meant to ask. You're from a political family. Do you know Governor Swindell?"

"Most of my life, yes."

"Is he a good man?" asked Liu after taking her third bite.

Tucker considered before answering. "He's a politician. I never viewed him out of politician mode, so I don't know. He's done wonderful things for the state. But Texas is tough, big oil's the bull, the star of the rodeo, and the governor just tries to survive for eight seconds."

"I'm sorry, I'm not from here. I don't get the reference," said Liu.

"At rodeos, in the bull ride, the cowboy must stay in the saddle for eight seconds. Without getting bucked off. That basically sums it up."

"You didn't answer my question. Is the governor a good man?"

Tucker shrugged. "He may be. I've met honorable politicians. Most people don't believe me, but it's true. To answer your question, I just don't know about Swindell."

"How about Pete Book?"

"Now's not the most opportune time to answer." He nodded as Kyle Kenner, Pete Book, and a show-stopping blond walked toward the FBI agents.

The woman's appearance unsettled Liu. The FBI agent struggled to pinpoint why. Liu assumed the blond, dressed exactly like a politician's wife, was Pete Book's bride.

"Officer Liu, Officer Tucker, you remember Senator Pete Book. This is his wife Samantha," said Kyle Kenner.

"Yes, of course," said Tucker.

"I'm happy to see two FBI agents not interested in interviewing me," said Pete. "I'm sure you've heard I've been under increased scrutiny lately."

"Yes," Liu confirmed. She looked from Pete to Kyle to Samantha. Tucker's raised eyebrow was his only response.

"It's a pleasure to meet you both," Samantha said extending her hand. "The governor asked Pete to help host for the conference. I volunteered to coordinate the entertainment for spouses in attendance. Thank you for your service today, the more protection the better. I am grateful to you both."

"You're welcome," said Tucker.

Liu found herself entranced, examining Samantha Book. Liu felt Tucker bump her, coaxing her back into the present.

"Yes, you're welcome," Liu muttered.

Kyle pointed to his Rolex, then directed, "We have to get moving. There're more reporters here than we're used to, and if we stay in the halls, we'll get suckered into unscheduled interviews."

The Books shook the agents' hands then departed.

Liu started, "Did you notice anything?"

"The senator didn't flirt with you with his wife around," said Tucker.

"No, I mean..."

"Did I notice Samantha Book looks exactly like the woman Luther drools over at the charity event, what's her name?"

"Allie Arrington. Samantha Book is almost a twin of Allie Arrington," answered Liu as she watched the senator's wife walk away.

● ● ●

Erasmus' truck stopped in front of a wrought-iron gate. He investigated; no speaker, no buzzer. As his search continued, he noticed a hedge-obscured camera. When nothing happened, he stretched, releasing a belting yawn. The professor opened the Scout's door and stepped onto the soft, uneven St. Augustine grass.

His trek from Austin to Silsbee proved uneventful, allowing him to listen to his homemade Texas mix tapes. Not a Texas native himself, over time, Willie Nelson, Waylon Jennings, Charlie Pride, Lefty Frizzell, Doug Sahm, Billy Joe Shaver, and the Georges, Jones and Strait, worked their way into Luther's heart. Weekend road trips to eat at the Gristmill and dance at the legendary Gruene Hall introduced him to Robert Earl Keen, Jerry Jeff Walker, Townes Van Zandt, Nanci Griffith, Jimmie Dale Gilmore, Lucinda Williams, Joe Ely, and Lyle Lovett.

Luther's Texaphile roommates shaped his taste. They indoctrinated him into the cult of blues god, Stevie Ray Vaughan. Today, Luther felt especially blessed for their gift. The pure want and desire Vaughan expressed with each chord mirrored Luther's longing for Allie.

With the drive behind him Luther decided to decompress. He turned off *"Pride and Joy"* and removed his loafers, allowing his bare feet to enjoy contact with terra firma. Luther closed his eyes, stretched again, before hearing the clinking of an opening gate. He opened his eyes, spotting no one. He hesitated, grabbed his shoes, then hopped back in the International Scout. He drove toward the small but elegant cottage home.

He got out and surveyed the picturesque property. Horses: grays, chestnuts, one black, and a pinto grazed the property. Luther noticed solidly built stables capable of supporting a dozen more horses. A cream-painted barn rested a short walk from the cottage. Erasmus pivoted from home to barn multiple times. The barn appeared more fastidiously maintained than the manicured grounds.

After a moment, he started toward the home. He stepped up on the sturdy, southern porch, an obvious addition, added many years after the old home's completion. Luther took four steps on the deck before an elegantly dressed Gertrude Arrington opened the door.

The matriarch remained radiant but appeared frailer than during her last gala appearance. "My Bo built this deck for me, as a teenager; his first project. Fine work, preserved well, squeaky, though. The squeaks serve as an alarm of sorts."

"Apologies, I failed to introduce myself when we met a few years ago; I'm Erasmus Luther."

"I taught political science, but occasionally dabbled in world history. Your name reeks of contradiction, Mr. Luther. Oh, listen to me go on, step in, my name is Gertrude, most of my students called me Ms. Gertie."

"Which do you prefer?" he asked.

"How sweet of you to ask, people seldom do. I prefer Gertrude." She stepped back to let Luther walk into the bright farm-style home.

Luther looked around, spotting pictures of Allie and her brothers. Many pictures featured Gertrude's children on horseback. Stylized horse photos dominated the decor. Luther examined the room, trying to learn everything possible about Allie. He stopped to note a picture of an old dog. He paused, recognizing the place of honor the cur's photo occupied.

"The family's only canine member, the Interloper. The kids just called him Loper. A pitiful mongrel who chose this family years ago. His decision blessed us."

Luther continued his intel; Gertrude watched. He spotted photos of the boys he heard so much about. Then Erasmus helplessly locked in on a picture of Allie between her brothers. The boys sported swimming trunks, Allie a flattering, microscopic bikini. Luther summoned willpower and moved to the next picture. The picture featured four fetching females in tight, revealing waitress outfits. Luther picked out a young, gorgeous Gertrude. He found himself equally reluctant to look away.

"I've noticed, men spend a disproportional amount of time admiring those two photos," she said wryly. "I put the two together, as a service to ease their efforts."

Luther re-examined his surroundings. There were dozens of pictures of the children, multiple horse photos, but only one picture of his hostess. Luther continued viewing photos and discovered three Marines in dress blues. Erasmus recognized Senator Pete Book and the annoying man who dominated Allie's time at the Arrington Galas. "That's my boy Bo, with his best friend Pete Book. Pete's a senator now. The other man is Kyle Kenner. He's Pete's chief of staff. Kyle and my boys were friends, but Kyle was Allie's best friend. Kyle escorted Allie to Homecomings and Proms."

Jealousy pinged Luther, despising Kyle Kenner more than before.

Gertrude continued, "I assumed Kyle and Allie would marry; I was mistaken." Gertrude smiled, before redirecting the conversation. "I prided myself that the boys served our country. I felt blessed they returned home. Many boys did not."

"So, they enlisted together?"

"Yes, Bo led their pack, so when he joined the Marines, Pete and Kyle followed. Luckily for me, they failed to see action. My other son chose not to enlist. Wyeth loved Bo but declined to follow his brother's every move. Wyeth did not think the US Military needed painters. He went straight to New York after graduation and started painting."

As Erasmus continued around the room, he stopped at a stunning Japanese lacquered box. The box displayed an equally breathtaking six-inch silver woman's hairpin. "Crap."

"Excuse me," replied Gertrude.

"I can't claim to know much about the pin, but when I worked on my doctorate, I studied in Japan for a summer. I fell in love with the art of Japanese lacquered boxes. Your box rivals the finest I've ever seen. Do you know the value of this piece?" Erasmus rambled. This piece, casually displayed in Gertrude Arrington's country home, belonged in The Met or the Houston Fine Arts Museum. "A master created this box, probably commissioned by an emperor, this piece predates the Edo Period."

"Well, how nice," Gertrude said, downplaying the compliment. "Where did you find this?"

"Not much of a story. Before my mother married, a young man gifted her the box and hairpin. She passed the two to me for my 18th birthday. I lost the pin several years ago; however, the pin returned to me in the strangest way."

Luther remained quiet, awaiting details. After some time, Luther realized none were forthcoming.

Gertrude motioned for Luther to sit, "Please sit, Mr. Luther, would you care for tea?"

"No, thank you. I'd love some water." Gertrude moved gracefully but carefully toward the kitchen. Luther remembered how spry she appeared months before. Then he spotted the clue— an IV pole pushed to the corner. A crochet blanket hung over the contraption, a poor disguise for the unmistakable shape.

Gertrude peeked back in the room. "Do you prefer ice?"

"No ice, thank you."

Gertrude looked from the pole to Luther. "Well, you are an observant young man."

Gertrude disappeared back to the kitchen and returned with two glasses of water. She placed Luther's glass on a coaster to his right. His host smiled, then moved to an upholstered wingback chair. "Cheers, Dr. Luther," she said before sitting.

"Are you sick?" he asked.

"Sick, such a broad term. Cancer," she said, reducing the villain to one word. "Allie, such a jewel, treated me like a queen. She nursed me these last months. One reason for her delayed response to your letter."

"One of the reasons?" Luther led.

"I lack experience in today's dating rituals. Perchance, she desired your anticipation to build."

"So, today is a date?"

"I assume so," answered Gertrude. "Although my opinion bears no weight."

"What type of cancer do you have?"

"Thank you for your concern, but I do not have cancer. I am clear, as they say. Still, the doctors said that before. As for the type of cancer, I am British, my family rarely discussed maladies."

Luther's thoughts returned to Allie. "If this is a date, when will it start?"

"Well, the date started, of course. I am traditional. Now is the meet-the-parent portion of the date. I know what you're thinking. Allie's age exempts her from a mother's intervention. Still, our family follows protocols."

"Okay."

"Allie mentioned you wanted to know more about the boys. Allie chooses not to talk about Bo and Wyeth, and I love to talk about them, so I am here."

"I want to learn about Bo and Wyeth, but I'm more excited to learn about Allie."

"How fortunate. You cannot learn about Allie without learning about the boys."

For an hour Gertrude told Erasmus stories of the Arringtons' childhood. Despite his longing to see Allie, Gertrude's storytelling engaged him. Gertrude shared stories of the property's origins and the boys' misadventures. Erasmus marveled at the story of the long-ago birthday boat ride to Galveston.

However, when Gertrude transitioned to her children's adulthood, things got interesting.

"You attended the gala for several years. You know each of my children attended Rice on scholarship. As I mentioned, Pete Book grew up in my home. His father played football in 1937, the year Rice won the Cotton Bowl. Just ask Pete's dad; the man will recount each detail. Anyway, Pete's father became a major donor to the university. The old man probably wielded some influence over Bo and Wyeth's good fortune. Not Allie, though. Allie gained admission and earned her scholarship with no assistance.

"She valued time with her brothers and Kyle. But, after her junior year of high school, she abandoned Bo and Wyeth's crew. She outgrew them, I assume.

"Anyway, once the boys graduated Rice, they each went their own ways. After his time in Vietnam, Bo moved to Odessa to learn the oil trade, and you know about Wyeth. When Allie graduated, she worked in finance, babysitting the assets of the wealthiest Houstonians. One day Allie received a call from Wyeth. His career took off, and Wyeth never mastered details. So, Allie dropped everything and flew to her brother's rescue."

"I recall Wyeth painted a lot of nudes," offered Luther.

"Yes. He loved the human form. Anyway, Wyeth possessed interesting idiosyncrasies. For example, he completed four slightly different paintings of each model. He always gifted the model one of the four portraits. Allie hated this practice. She stressed, based on the value of Wyeth's work, he would come out ahead paying models a standard sitting fee. Wyeth disagreed, telling her he planned to become famous. By giving a painting away, in the short term he lost money. He stressed that when the word spread, and the paintings gained value..."

"His choice for models became unlimited," finished Luther.

"Dozens of the world's elite actors, models, and athletes posed for him. In time, his fame surpassed many of his subjects. He also kept one painting for himself, an expensive indulgence. Because he painted four similar paintings, Allie created an opportunity for a steady income. Rare for a painter."

"How?"

"Wyeth made money selling his paintings. However, his income remained erratic. Allie understood Wyeth needed a patron. Cassandra Hinds, the premier gallery owner and collector in New York, showed interest in Wyeth. His first two shows had been at rival galleries. Allie approached Ms. Hinds, explaining Wyeth's process. My daughter told Ms. Hinds she could receive two paintings of each of Wyeth's subjects, one to sell and one to keep. Allie proposed that by selling only one, and keeping the others off the market..."

"Painting prices escalate."

"Correct, Cassandra drove up the price of each sold painting, while keeping one painting of each model for her private collection."

"Driving up the value of her private collection."

"Yes, Dr. Luther. Cassandra received the first right of refusal for Wyeth's gallery shows. Allie's strategy allowed Wyeth to keep one of the four paintings, give one to the model, and make money from the one sold at the Hinds Gallery. Ms. Hinds kept the fourth painting for her collection. She has yet to part with one. In return,

Ms. Hinds paid Wyeth an unprecedented monthly allowance. The paintings Wyeth kept for himself are the paintings auctioned at the charity event each year."

"I don't understand. Why replicate the same painting of each model?"

"Each painting differed slightly, increasing the intrigue."

"Several famous people posed for him. Still, his most famous painting, *Arrington's Aphrodite*, featured an anonymous model."

"Yes."

"Wait, you inherited Wyeth's painting when he passed. Are you saying you own another rendition of *Arrington's Aphrodite*?"

"Sadly, no."

"The model's copy never turned up?"

"The model as yet remains unknown to the public."

"So, the model owns a painting worth millions."

"Yes."

"At the gala, you mentioned the copy that sold at the Hinds Gallery auction set a record for a living painter."

"Correct."

"Ms. Hinds held on to her copy?"

"Yes, many investors tried to pry the painting from her personal collection; all have failed."

"Have you seen it?"

"Yes, spectacular."

"I love *Arrington's Aphrodite*. I'm not an art critic, but it's the most beautiful painting I've seen. I live with two art history professors. That's why I attended the first gala, at their invitation. One night over Chianti, they discussed the reason for *Aphrodite's* value. First, when Wyeth painted nudes, he more often painted males."

"Yes, true."

"My roommates claim the Aphrodite rising from the water remained Wyeth's most stylized nude. Different. Mostly, he painted posed models. The Aphrodite appeared painted from a dream or foggy memory and possessed an element of action. Also, Wyeth's studio models face the artist. The Aphrodite does not. If she turned, just an inch, she'd be recognizable. The painting's value is in the mystery, the almost completed turn, the admirer's ache to discover Aphrodite's identity."

"Since you can't ask Wyeth, I guess you'll never know," answered a voice behind him. Allie entered the room. She wore snug fawn riding pants and a tailored white shirt. Erasmus found his excitement level climbing.

"How long have you stood there?"

"A woman has a right to her secrets," Allie answered.

• • •

New York City, 1976-1980

Allie Arrington's cool demeanor deserted her. She peered out the plane window at New York City's skyline. Before today, she never crossed Texas' State Line. Allie breathed deeply, before checking the survival guide she created for her first flight. While her plane prepared for landing, she buoyed herself for the onslaught of new experiences. She corralled her excitement. Surely the woman next to her felt the energy radiating from Allie.

The excitement of her first plane flight, Broadway shows, dinner at the Russian Tea Room paled compared to the reason she glowed. In less than an hour, she would hug Wyeth for the first time since his college graduation. Yes, she wrote often. They telephoned, but she had not held Wyeth in years. He seemed different now, distant. Still, Allie's ability to contain herself evaporated hours ago. She looked out the window at her new home, New York City. Awaiting her, a new adventure

Wyeth bought Allie a first-class ticket, so she departed the plane first. She expected to find him waiting; he was not. A hurried counter agent pointed Allie to baggage claim. After finding her bag, Allie again looked for her brother. Still no Wyeth. She anticipated this moment for weeks. A chance to hold him, to talk, to reconnect. His unexplained absence troubled her.

She pulled her notes and searched for Wyeth's address. Allie had never navigated an airport. She stood confused, calculating her next action. A handsome uniformed man, probably a pilot, walked up to Allie and said, "May I help you, young lady? You look lost."

Allie smiled in relief. "I assumed my brother planned to pick me up, but I guess he's not."

"Do you know his address?" the handsome man asked.

"Yes," she said, showing him proof.

"That's close to my place, you can share a cab with me."

The handsome pilot appeared nice. Still, Allie did not feel safe riding in a car with someone she just met. Growing up in Gertrude Arrington's home made her careful. She thanked the pilot, then watched him depart toward the taxi stand. Allie noted the stand's location before continuing the search for Wyeth.

After 20 minutes of futility, Allie walked into the cool evening air and made her way to a cab stand. She arrived in front of her brother's Brooklyn residence an hour later. She confirmed the address, then lugged her bag inside the building. A handwritten out-of-order sign adorned the elevator. She checked her notes, confirming her brother's fifth floor location. Allie sighed, lifted her luggage, and found the stairs.

When she reached the third floor, she heard the thumping of heavy base above her. She knew instantly where the music originated. Only a Texas-raised prodigal would blast ZZ Top's "La Grange" in New York City. She climbed the stairs as her anger bubbled. Upon reaching the fifth floor, the amplified rhythmic pound of Gibbons, Hill, and Beard flooded the hall. Of course, her brother's door opened to the hall. Impaired partygoers streamed in and out. Smoke and the smell of stale beer assaulted her nose. She stepped inside the room, dropped her bag, then searched for her brother. He was nowhere.

A grimy curly-haired man handed her a lit hand-rolled cigarette and asked if she wanted a hit. She returned the skunky-smelling cigarette and continued to scan the room. Dozens of revelers littered the room, some stood upright, most occupied the floor in various states of consciousness. Still no Wyeth.

Wyeth's apartment resembled industrial space more than living quarters. Near the back, Allie spotted two metal doors. She reached the first and found people waiting outside. She assumed the door led to the apartment's bathroom. Allie walked to the second door. Twisting the knob, she found it locked.

Allie knocked.

"Go away, go away, go away." The voice relieved and infuriated her. She banged on the door this time. "Didn't you hear me? Go away."

"Open the door, you idiot!" Allie yelled.

"Allie, is that you?"

"Who do you think it is, asshole?"

"Give me a minute…okay…just give me a minute."

Allie overheard the interplay of multiple voices through the door. Moments later, the door squeaked open. Breathtaking twins exited, shooting Allie sideward glances. Then Allie saw him—Wyeth—or a stylized version of the brother she remembered. Shirtless, thin, painfully so, stoned, her brother rocked slowly. Allie looked down. "Wyeth, your dick's hanging out of your pants."

He smiled the "Wyeth smile," his "get away with anything" smile. He maintained eye contact, corrected himself, and zipped his pants. Not the meeting Allie envisioned.

"Look, Allie, I'm sorry..."

"Shut up and hug me. I've missed you, you horse's ass."

• • •

Allie spent the next months learning what a sheltered life she led under her mother's wing. The leeches surrounding Wyeth did and said unimaginable things. Allie spent the following months protecting Wyeth from...well, Wyeth. Allie negotiated Wyeth's early lease termination. The landlord, overjoyed to see him leave, severed the lease-waiving penalties. Allie found Wyeth a Classic Five Manhattan apartment. She and her brother had their own bedrooms. Allie transformed the formal dining room into Wyeth's studio. The siblings' use of the floor plan did not lend itself to parties, per Allie's plan.

Allie failed to share the new address with party friends and hangers-on. Wyeth's New York party crew called Allie "The Bitch from Back Home." Allie considered protecting Wyeth, not pleasing sycophants, her priority. Wyeth flourished under Allie's steadying influence. His income increased but remained erratic.

Allie dealt with galleries, worked as Wyeth's saleswoman for direct sales and commissions, and in a masterstroke found his patron, Cassandra Hinds. Cassandra basically adopted them both. Allie worked for her brother until Cassandra assessed the younger woman's competency. Cassandra hired Allie as the gallery's special events coordinator.

Allie learned Cassandra's breadth of talents. More than an art patron, Cassandra oversaw profitable businesses while influencing a network of Manhattan elite. With Cassandra's blessing, Allie assimilated into Manhattan's core and soaked in everything.

Cassandra, like many women of means in New York, fell for Wyeth. Although they engaged in a dalliance, the art dealer mostly enjoyed the youthful, impish energy the reckless artist added to everything. The threesome spent the next year creating, crafting, and growing a celebrity around Wyeth.

At his peak, Wyeth did not seek models, actors, athletes, or Broadway stars to paint. They sought him. Allie became desensitized to finding world-famous soccer forward, prima ballerinas, or the hottest star posing in her dining room.

Her time in New York opened once-in-a-millennium opportunities. She witnessed the Yankees win the World series in '77 and '78, the city electric with excitement. The small-town Texan enjoyed a Broadway renaissance. She occupied Cassandra's premium seats to A Chorus Line, Annie, Ain't Misbehavin, and The Best Little Whorehouse in Texas.

Terror surrounded the city too. After her arrival, The Son of Sam murders engulfed New York in fear. They watched the news every night together. After David Berkowitz's capture, the city roared back to life. Allie's toughest test revolved around her brother. She often arrived home to find Wyeth passed out drunk or worse with a needle dangling from his arm. Allie fought for Wyeth. When home, she kept Wyeth in check. Still, no one possessed the ability to corral him 24 hours a day.

The fighting started. Wyeth resented Allie acting like his mother. Allie hated having to monitor him like a child. Allie enjoyed no social life because she could not leave Wyeth alone. Bo flew to New York to tug Wyeth from the brink. Bo dragged his brother to rehab, which worked briefly, but once Bo returned home, Wyeth faltered.

Gertrude visited too. Allie sensed her mother's discomfort. After her arrival, Gertrude seldom left the apartment. When she did, Allie caught her mother glancing over her shoulder. Their mother stayed for a month, giving Allie a break, nursing Wyeth, and getting to know Ms. Hinds.

Once Gertrude returned home, Allie persevered but Wyeth's energy for destruction proved overwhelming. In 1980, Allie's time in New York ended.

Allie arrived home finding Wyeth painting. Four canvases spread around the room, as was his practice. Two works neared completion, two canvases blank. Wyeth, bottle in hand, wielded a paintbrush in the other.

Allie stared at the paintings, horrified. "Wyeth, what the hell is this?"

"It's my fucking masterpiece," he slurred.

"Wyeth, your fucking smile won't get you out of this. What the hell are you doing?"

"I'm painting. It's what I do."

"Not this, Wyeth, not this. You don't do this."

Allie marched to her room and packed. Moments later, a door slammed. When she emerged from her room, she found herself alone; two wet canvases left behind. Allie dried the paint with her hair dryer, wrapped the canvases, as she had many times, and set them aside. She wrapped other paintings Wyeth gifted her over the years. Then she called the bellman and a taxi.

Allie never saw Wyeth Arrington alive again.

•   •   •

March 6, 1993

Liu's head rotated, scanning the food court of the Austin Convention Center. Foxx Kauffman found Liu earlier and flirted a few minutes before other DC reporters pulled him away. Reporters packed the place.

She spotted Tucker. He stayed close, examining the face of each passerby. He predictably worked his line of vision back to her. The

Special Agent in Charge admitted she enjoyed Tucker's proximity. In her past, Liu proved she did not need protection. Still, as female reporters' passing glances in Tucker's direction confirmed, Liu's situation could be worse.

Tucker winked, smiling his crooked smile. Something he mentioned ricocheted through her head: "...*so many reporters here, there's barely room for politicians.*"

Liu fought to pinpoint why, but his words bothered her. The assassins morphed a few times in their progression. From hunting crooked politicians via newspaper articles to detailed traps like the Watergate Hotel to using smartly planted audio equipment to target the Heater.

What if the assassins morphed again? Liu stared at the reporters carrying microphones.

Tucker read her face and pushed to her.

"The recording equipment, it's here already," she said to Tucker.

"Can't be, we scanned the place..."

"The conference staff set microphones in every damn room for the press conferences and political roundtables before we got here. The killers bugged the existing microphones. That's what I'd do. I'd put something in the stationary microphones, it's simple. Why didn't I see it?"

"Liu, that's a good guess, but it's just a guess."

"I'll get Moss. Stay here."

Tucker's look confirmed he did not want to let her out of his sight, but he followed orders. Liu raced to the command center and found Moss eating lunch.

Liu pushed through a contingent of agents and blurted, "The equipment, their recording equipment, I think I know where it is."

"You think?" Moss asked, glancing up from his sub sandwich.

"Yes."

"Any proof?"

"No."

"Just a hunch?"

"Yes."

"Liu, this is my first break today."

"The assassins bugged the conference center microphones. The conference staff positioned the mics in advance. Plenty of time for the perps to tamper with them. We cased this entire site for independent recording microphones, under tables, in the walls. Putting a bug inside of existing microphones—that's genius. Who searches for recording equipment inside a microphone? How do we isolate bugs from the microphone's inner workings?"

"Great question. Got a great answer?"

"We don't understand the equipment, but the cameramen might."

Moss wiped his mouth and nodded. "Okay."

"Okay, what, sir?"

"Get Tucker, grab a few guys, figure it out."

• • •

Liu and Tucker wrangled a hulking cameraman returning from lunch. "What's your name?" asked Liu.

"Ben."

"Ben, what do you do?"

"I'm a cameraman for…"

"If someone tampered with a microphone, could you tell?"

"If I cracked it open, yeah."

"Or any piece of recording equipment?" interjected Tucker.

"Yes."

"Follow me. You're unofficially working for the FBI."

• • •

Ben scored immediately. He located the first bug inside a dais microphone, in the conference hall. An hour later, Liu stood in front of Moss. Three identical, miniature, high-tech recording devices splayed in front of him.

"So, our assassins, they're here?"

"Probably, at least they were," answered Liu.

"Why'd you pull them, the bugs, why not leave them in place? To trap the assassins?"

"We found others; there's likely more. We pulled three to test. Probably useless. They may know we found them, not sure. Our action may have scared them off, maybe not."

"Why'd they bug the conference room tables and dais? The politicians see the mics."

"Sometimes you forget a mic is live when it's just sitting there. Remember in '84 , Reagan almost started a war when he joked during a mic check. Politicians live around microphones. So, they forget any mic can be a hot mic."

"Solid point. Check the streets for sound trucks or anything resembling sound trucks."

"That's why Tucker isn't here. He and a few agents hit the streets. Nothing yet."

"Okay, everyone's on high alert," Moss snapped to his left. "Kemp inform the boys in blue. This ain't a pissing match. We don't care who wins. Protect the men and women here. Make it happen." As Kemp headed off, Moss barked, "Sytkowski, the locals have every door covered. Get our guys on as many doors as possible. Look for anything strange, anything." Sytkowski gave a thumbs-up, departing as quickly as Kemp. "Lackland, collect a few dorks like yourself." Moss paused to let the insult to his oldest friend marinate. "Get one team to the conference center security hub. Analyze the videotapes. Also, analyze the bugs Liu found."

"Liu, your team located the bugs, find out if anyone spotted unauthorized personnel tampering with equipment. *Anyone.* Everyone clear?"

"Do we alert the governors?" asked Lackland smugly, pleased to point out something Moss missed.

"Hell, I guess, but start with their security detail if they have one. Smaller states don't. Try to get protection on everyone. Cade, that's your job. We didn't bring enough agents. So, use the resources here. I'll get more asses on the way and notify the boys in Washington."

Liu, like the other agents, fell out, but Moss grabbed her shoulder. "Liu, you've been at the forefront of this. What are you thinking, did we stop them?" asked Moss.

"They've been recording for 36 to 48 hours. I'm not sure what they have."

"And...?"

"And I sure as hell don't know what they'll do next. I have a funny feeling we'll find out. If we don't do our jobs, someone's going to die."

• • •

Silsbee, Texas

Perfection. Erasmus struggled for another word to describe the day. He failed. The professor and Allie rode horses around the Arrington property line, with her serving as tour guide. "Bo and Wyeth turned the barn into living quarters. When I moved back to Silsbee, I updated the barn and moved in. Mom lives in the house. Honestly, we enjoy the arrangement. If we need each other, we knock. Once, after a heated battle of wills, we didn't see each other for eight days."

Allie proudly pointed out the south pasture. She, Bo, Wyeth, and their mother cleared the property over a decade. Erasmus cursed his eyes, drawn too often to Allie's backside as it bumped up and down in the saddle.

After an hour of trotting around the property, they stopped near a path cut between pines. "Let the horses graze here. You and I can walk to the creek. Want me to lead, so you can stare at my ass some more?"

He laughed. "That would be fantastic. Does anything get by you?"

"Not much."

They started down the path, and Erasmus enjoyed the view.

He noticed a few tattered scarecrows and the strangest thing: a noose hanging from an oak.

Before he asked, Allie volunteered, "Mom hosts a haunted trail ride for her students. We never bothered to take down the scarecrows. They're scarier weathered."

"And the noose?"

"Eerie, huh? We hang a mannequin to look like a dead body from the noose, scared the crap out of the kids."

Luther spent a moment considering the noose, then happily returned his gaze to Allie's backside. She turned, catching him, and shook her head.

After she returned her attention to the trail, he asked, "How are you not married?"

She turned back, a betwixt expression adorned her face. Luther prided himself. He caught Allie off guard. "Why are *you* not married?"

"I asked first," said Luther, staying on point.

Allie stopped walking. "My mother's theory: Bo and Wyeth spoiled me. No man could measure up."

"What would you say?"

"Mother's an observant and insightful woman. My brothers dominated my world. Bo, Mom's firstborn, served as her protector. Wyeth chose the role of my guardian. Both spoiled me in different ways. For instance, freshman year of high school, usually tough on kids. Not mine. Everyone knew Bo, respected him. No one dared mess with me. Because of Wyeth, everyone assumed I was cool. My brothers pre-punched my popularity ticket."

"You may have been popular on your own? You're smart and well…"

"I looked coltish as a freshman. Maybe, I could've made it by myself. Still, I'll never know. The three of us did everything together."

Allie turned and continued down the path. Erasmus' senses reveled in the beauty surrounding him, dense trees, sunlight cutting through their arbor in ribbons. The unmistakable smell of pine filled his nostrils. The haunting whistles of mockingbirds danced through his ears. In the distance, the soft bubbling of the creek played a distinctive melody. Instantly, the temperature cooled, conditioned by the air's interplay with the water. Goose bumps rippled along Erasmus' arms, celebrating the sudden humidity drop.

As they approached, Erasmus spotted a wicker basket atop a handmade quilt. "Is this where you bring all your beaus for a first date?"

"Well, so far," said Allie. "I made sourdough bread earlier. Mom contributed pimento cheese, Aunt Milly Rae's recipe. You game?"

"Absolutely."

Allie spread the blanket. The two relaxed and enjoyed a late lunch of chilled pimento cheese, homemade bread, and lemonade. Allie asked about Erasmus' classes and his books. To Erasmus' surprise, she read each one.

The professor embraced the beautiful setting, which seemed strangely familiar. Had he previously visited this place in a dream or memory? Déjà vu overtook him, until he pushed the sentiment aside.

He asked her about the horses. She detailed the shared family's passion. Conversation flowed. Then everything halted with one question.

"Was it tough for you that your brother was gay?"

"What?" said Allie.

"Was it tough that Wyeth was gay?"

Allie examined Erasmus, then almost seductively answered, "Wyeth was not gay."

Erasmus paused processing before he spoke. "He died of AIDS, he painted a lot of male nudes. I...assumed."

"No, Wyeth wasn't gay. He struggled with addictions. He probably got AIDS from an infected needle or a woman. Still, I'll never know. He painted a lot of male nudes, lots of female ones too; he loved the human form."

"You're positive he wasn't gay?"

"Yes, two reasons. When I lived in New York, I saw him sleep with dozens of women. He never showed an interest in males."

"You said two reasons."

"Yes." Allie did not elaborate.

"Oh, come on."

"I could tell you, but your ability to hold a cognizant conversation will evaporate. I've enjoyed talking to you, and I would prefer to keep it that way."

"Allie, it's just going to bug me."

"I know Wyeth was not gay, because this is the spot I've skinny-dipped since I was in high school. I often brought someone to serve as lookout because Wyeth constantly tried to spy and..." Allie stopped.

Erasmus wanted to prove her wrong, but he misplaced his ability to speak. He looked at Allie, then the water. Then pivoted to Allie again. He repositioned his paper plate to hide his growing indiscretion.

"Before you say something stupid, no, we will not go skinny-dipping. Yes, I understand, despite your gentlemanly efforts, you're picturing me naked at this moment. Which explains why I chose not to elaborate. Take a minute to pull yourself together. I'll sit and eat in peace." She calmly ate pimento cheese, waiting.

•   •   •

Erasmus understood his next word's importance. So, he remained silent. A few times in his life, he comprehended that words would forever define a relationship. The magnitude of this moment crippled the professor. He considered his options. He deemed a flirtatious remark shallow and inappropriate. A joke seemed a tasteless alternative, even if he mustered one applicable to the situation. Unadulterated honesty tempted him, but honesty meant explaining the picnic plate covering his lap.

He remembered she welcomed frankness before.

When he broke his silence, he selected each word carefully. "I beg for mercy. I possess no talent to handle this situation. I'm not cool, I don't know what to say. I'll admit that the thought of you…"

Allie smiled, raising her hand like a crossing guard protecting children from traffic. "You were doing great, maybe stop there."

"Okay."

"I warned you."

"You did. Let's talk about anything else, anything."

"What do you have in mind?"

"We've covered my books and classes; we've talked about horses. Your mom said you don't like to talk about your brothers."

"I don't."

Erasmus perked up. "How about your mother, tell me about your mother?"

Allie waited a long moment. "I've had an incredible time, Dr. Luther, and all incredible times must end."

She started collecting the items from their picnic.

Erasmus felt a wall materialize between him and Allie. He stood, vacillating. He did not want their date to end. He embraced silence as his ally. He aided Allie in packing their lunch supplies. Then he led their climb to the horses, so she could not accuse him of staring at her backside.

Moments later, Allie expertly mounted her horse, quilt in hand. He awkwardly climbed on his horse while balancing the basket. Allie rode over, held out her hand, and took the basket. She said nothing.

With each stride the horses took, Erasmus felt Allie pull further away.

They rode back to the stable. After dismounting, Allie took Erasmus' reins and unsaddled the horses. She led both horses into the stable and returned.

Then, Allie led Erasmus to his vehicle.

He opened the door of his vehicle and stood, stunned. Erasmus battled the temptation to say something superfluous about having a pleasant time. Instead, he decided the last time seeing her must end as the first time, punctuated by his stupefied silence. Erasmus noted the symmetry. After appreciating the beauty of his personal enchantress, he added today to his cluttered collection of blown chances.

To his surprise, Allie spoke. "That's it. You're giving up that easy?"

Erasmus stayed with what worked so far and said nothing.

"Sometimes a woman…everyone…needs time to think."

He nodded.

"And sometimes a professor needs to find his words before he loses his chance."

"Can I take you to dinner soon?"

"Yes."

"I'll need your phone number to set something up."

"No need, there are things I need to attend to. I'll meet you six weeks from Thursday at your office. After your last class. When making dinner reservations, consider I'll dress to dazzle."

Luther took a minute to catch his breath, pondering. How could she dress more dazzling than at the galas, or today? "Let me give you my schedule. My office is in…"

He looked to Allie, who shook her head. She already knew. She researched him. You do not examine someone unless they interest you. Allie was interested in him. For Erasmus Luther, the globe tilted on its axle.

• • •

Austin, Texas

"I won't nod off; I won't nod off," Foxx Kauffman repeated. The conference leaders allowed press members to attend select meetings. For obvious political or national security reasons, other meetings remained closed to the press. Foxx attended two snooze-fest political roundtables earlier and now resided in the food court. Then the reporter spotted Tanner Tucker and two similarly fit agents jog past with purpose. Tucker took no notice of Foxx.

Foxx reassessed his surroundings, noting a different mood, an uncomfortable vibe. Officers, relaxed earlier, appeared on edge. Foxx sensed bedlam afoot. He searched the posted schedule, asking himself, *Where's the action?* The Governor's Panel on Tourism started soon, open to the press.

Moments later, Foxx sat in a crowded room with reporters, governors, and politicians. Senator Pete Book acknowledged the crowd. "Our governor granted me the honor of introducing our all-star panel. First, from the great State of Florida, Reilly Steel. The man credited as architect of Florida's booming tourism economy." Pete paused as Reilly walked into the room and took his seat.

"Next, he's not a southerner, or governor, still he's here by Ben Swindell's special invitation—US Congressman and Colorado Gubernatorial Candidate Chad Cash." Foxx noticed Book, who probably considered Cash a rival, failed to introduce the congressman with the same vigor as Steel. Pete did not pause for Cash's entrance.

"The great State of South Carolina's governor is here, Sonny Howe. In Sonny's tenure he oversaw the expansion of tourism in South Carolina, whose collection of beaches, golf courses, and hotels offer something for every tourist. Like Florida, South Carolina possesses one of America's top tourist-driven economies. Give a grand Texas welcome to all three guests of the governor."

Pete Book waited for the applause to die down. Few played crowds better.

"Finally, I'm honored to introduce the man who leads Texas. Our governor oversaw the relocation of 17 manufacturing facilities and 11 corporate offices to Texas in the last four years. Due to his work, Texas moved into the top 10 in tourism dollars. He's the governor of the 28th state, but he's number one to me, my friend, Governor Ben Swindell."

Applause enraptured the room, as Ben Swindell, the politician pundits considered a front-runner for his party's 1996 presidential nomination, entered the room. Swindell shook hands as he sauntered to the table and joined the panelists.

Foxx now noted additional security everywhere. He waved as Natalie Liu took a position by the back door. She did not acknowledge his greeting. Despite the added security, the tourism roundtable proved nothing more than standard political fare. Each man bragged about their state, tourist-friendly economies, and construction projects to boost tourism.

Foxx rose to excuse himself when he heard the click.

Foxx's head jerked around the room, searching for the click's source. His first thought—a shotgun, chambering a round. The thought dissipated as he realized the sound originated from everywhere. The auditorium sound system clicked again, this time louder. Next, audio feedback pummeled the room. Foxx covered his ears guarding against the unforgiving sound onslaught. Then as quickly as it started, it stopped.

Foxx recognized the familiar voice of Ben Swindell. "Do I have your attention?"

A heavily edited basic rap ensued, "*Do I, do I, do I have your attention? Do I, do I?*"

Ben Swindell and the other speakers rose. Liu, bracketed by officers, rushed the stage to protect the politicians.

"*Do I, do I, do I have your attention,*" played again. Then silence. Foxx watched as the conference center staff searched the room for the source of the audio anomaly.

Then another click. "Do I have your attention, Sonny, Reilly?" Clearly Ben Swindell addressed his two fellow governors. "Argon Oil is pulling in their horns internationally. They're tired of the graft in Africa and South America. They need to expand their US presence."

Foxx looked to the stage. Agents and law enforcement surrounded the panelists. The reporter watched Governor Swindell's head dart around the room. "*Stop this!*" he screamed. Reilly and Sonny's panic matched the Texas Governor's. Chad Cash looked intrigued. Pete Book listened, confused.

"What does that mean to us? They need more offshore rigs now. Yesterday."

"Ben, I'm topped out, I can't bring more offshore rigs near our coast," said the voice of Governor Steel.

"My political base will crap if I allow more drilling offshore," added Governor Howe.

"Look, Sonny, Reilly, if it were easy, Argon wouldn't need us. The Feds control almost everything, but we control our states' drilling rights. Argon could not make progress with the feds for deep offshore drilling, so they're coming to us. Each of our states control drilling rights three to seven miles offshore. Argon needs another platform from you, Sonny; they need two from you and me, Reilly."

"Fuck," the audience heard a voice mumble.

"*Turn it off*!" screamed Governor Swindell again.

Foxx watched hotel staff scurry about the room looking for the source. Liu took control, holding up her badge. "Special Agent in Charge Natalie Liu, do not turn a damn thing off, let it play."

"Argon contributed a lot of money to your past campaigns. They need this, they need us. We'll each have two million sitting in our accounts if this happens. It's all three or no deal."

"Okay," said a voice.

"Okay what, Sonny?"

"I'm in."

"Sonny's gotta push through one offshore rig, I have to push through two. I want three million."

The audio stopped, only the slow clicking of a tape remained. The room stood aghast.

Foxx watched Agent Liu oversee law enforcement agents take Governors Swindell, Steel, and Howe into custody. Chad Cash and Pete Book stood stunned on stage.

Foxx Kauffman barrel-laughed. His rich roar enveloped the room. He grinned, holding his hands in the air. Foxx panned the room, booming at Liu, "God bless Texas, everything is bigger here. I gotta big old *news woody*." He smiled, beseeching his contemporaries, "Don't pretend there's not a collection of news erections in this room."

● • ●

Liu's boss, Henry Moss, witnessed everything. But he let her run the show, watching the circumstances test her limits. Natalie and her team surrounded the podium.

"Governors Swindell, Steel, and Howe, I'm placing you under arrest on federal bribery charges," Liu stated. Her team handcuffed the formerly powerful men, their fiefdoms laid to waste seconds earlier. Liu knew each man considered pulling rank or threatening her. However, the three failed to regain cocky assuredness. FBI agents escorted the governors for processing.

"This the same group that murdered Greene and Thompson?" asked an approaching Moss.

"Yes," answered Liu.

"They didn't kill these guys for taking the bribe."

"They did worse. Whoever created the recording took everything from the governors and made them watch. These governors face jail time, lawsuits, public humiliation. If the three died, their families received sympathy, life insurance, an ending. This way their families receive disdain. The governors' wives receive front-row seats to trials and news interviews. Swindell, Steel, and Howe's kids get to visit their dads in prison. Based on the research, our assassins change their M.O. Maybe they realized what they did today is scarier to politicians, scarier than knocking them off. Still, I'd assign Swindell, Steel, and Howe serious protection."

Moss nodded before Lackland pulled him away, leaving Natalie Liu standing alone. The thought occurred to her that today may be her biggest arrest, and she felt disheartened by the empty space beside her. Damn, she missed him.

Tucker failed to report since he departed to check for sound trucks. Then, she knew.

She radioed, "Has anyone heard from Tucker?"

"Negative."

"Negative."

"Not at command."

"Bates here, he left with Harmon and I, but we split up to cover more ground."

"Harmon here, haven't seen him since."

"Tucker…Tucker…"

Liu sprinted out of the Austin Convention Center and studied her surroundings. Nothing. After a second of indecision, she assessed her partner's tendencies. A line of delivery vans parked to the left. She followed her instinct and started toward the vehicles.

Two shots caused her head to whip toward the river, then silence. The distinctive sound of a revving boat engine greeted her next. Four erratic shots fired, then six shots in succession. The boat engine continued to rev, but the sound differed somehow. "I got gunshots, toward the river," she announced into her radio, then raced toward the Colorado River. Looking over her shoulder, she spotted Bates and further behind, Harmon.

Liu led the sprint toward the Colorado River, with one thought dominating her psyche: *Tanner Tucker, you better not be dead, not before I can tell you...*

Liu burst from the wooded trail onto the makeshift beach and boat dock. Her first action was to process the surreal surroundings. Kayakers swarmed to their kayaks. A small boat, engine roaring, circled senselessly on the river. The erstwhile captain slumped over the boat's wheel.

A bevy of bathing suit beauties gathered around a fallen man. *Tucker. Of course*, Liu thought to herself. As she started to Tucker, she shouted, "Harmon, Bates, commandeer a boat or kayak, I don't care, and get to that boat before the locals. Bring that boat in. No one gets onboard but you. Secure it. Be careful."

She parted the young women surrounding her partner. Tucker appeared as if he awoke from hibernation. Liu found herself relieved and pissed to see his crooked smile. "I wondered when you'd show up," he said. A beautiful, tanned blond pressed a blood-soaked knit bathing suit cover against his left arm, above the elbow. A bullet hole punctured his shirt dead middle but failed to do damage, thanks to Tucker's bulletproof vest. He grasped his service pistol in his right hand.

"Ladies, I need some space. But stay close, agents will arrive in minutes, and need to interview you."

The blond, before departing, smiled at Tanner. "Look, you need to keep pressure on the arm. And if you need anything, come visit me at Austin Care Clinic. I work later...in case you want to stop by." The blond's smile dissipated as she turned from Tucker to Liu. The flirty blond disappeared, and a young but worried ER nurse occupied the same body. "Keep him talking, be on the lookout for shock. He lost lots of blood."

"Thanks for your cover-up, sorry I ruined it," Tucker called as the girls stepped back. Tucker watched his nubile savior depart, as agents and officers swarmed the scene.

"You're getting hit on by a beautiful woman in a bikini after a shootout. Only you, Special Agent Tucker. Only you."

Tucker's crooked smile flashed. "Jealous?"

Liu considered a snide remark, then remembered missing him earlier. "A little...but if you tell anyone, I'll shoot you."

"Get in line." Tanner Tucker grinned broadly, a smile she had never witnessed. Liu realized the smile was a new creation, just for her. Liu lamented that no matter what her life held, this smile would be a highlight.

"You okay?"

"Just a chip shot to the meat of my arm. Got knocked down by the chest shot. Not sure if I hit my head, but I blanked out."

"What happened?" asked Liu. "Why didn't you answer your radio?"

Before he answered, a paramedic kneeled beside Tanner. Like the bikini-clad nurse, the paramedic was gorgeous. A miffed Liu's internal monologue shrieked; *can a girl get a break*?

A second paramedic, a burly man in his 50s, arrived soon after. "Ma'am, give us some room."

"I'm an FBI agent, I need to talk to this man."

"Sure, you will, but not now," barked the paramedic. "Our job is to keep this man alive; he can't answer your questions dead."

Liu begrudgingly gave in. She took Tucker's gun. "We'll need this." The paramedics worked her partner onto their stretcher, then hurried him to the awaiting ambulance.

Liu understood her job was here. She would debrief her partner when doctors allowed. No one talked to him before her. Liu wondered, if in the FBI's history, two agents had more interesting stories to share.

• • •

March 9, 1993
Tanner Tucker dreamed or assumed he must be dreaming. Because he long ago memorized her smell—lavender and coconut, soft, subtle. Still, he never recalled the naked proximity, seemingly a half breath away. Since their dance, he daydreamed about her soft and arrestingly curvaceous form brushing against him. Here, now, in this nirvana, he experienced her in intricate detail. Tucker fluttered in and out of consciousness, unaware of day or time. Tucker's only surety, the only known fact, he lay damaged in the aseptic world of a hospital room.

This experience, this juxtaposition of her body to his, must be fantasy. In a moment of cognition, Tanner force-fused his eyes shut, recognizing that opening his eyes ended the fantasy's tantalizing opportunities.

His rational mind understood the impossibility of her warm breath so close. So close he almost tasted her kiss; suddenly, he did taste it, the warmth of her mouth on his, the softness of her lips, her delicate nose nuzzling his. He grasped his mortality, understanding he passed to the next world, accepting death, happily departing the sterile hospital room, and stepping through Heaven's gate. If this interlude previewed Heaven's wonders, Tanner Tucker faced death joyfully. Then he heard a whisper.

"Don't you fucking die on me, Tanner Tucker."

Was cursing allowed in Heaven? If angels allowed cursing, he suspected the f-bomb would be off the menu. Possibly an occasional "damn."

"I'm surprised my sins did not damn me to Hell," for instance. Slowly, his senses alerted him of the improbability of his Heavenly residence. A throbbing arm and grating chest pain greeted him as he unwillingly departed the half-sleep. Stringent smells of cleaning products intermingled with scents of illness assaulted his nose. The *beep, beep, beep* of the assorted equipment connected to him served as an annoying reminder of his present location. Carts rattling up and down the hall jerked him to reality. Stark light, found only in hospital rooms, overwhelmed his opening eyes.

He blinked to reality, balancing the harshness of this environment with his dream. He surveyed the room. Liu sat beside him, perusing an ancient copy of *Sports Illustrated*.

Tucker focused on her, taking in her beauty. A luxury he rarely allowed himself, partly as a professional courtesy to her, but honestly to protect his heart, which she owned from the moment she groggily stepped off the plane the night they met. He analyzed by nature, so he allowed himself time to put pieces together before speaking. "Did you just kiss me?"

"No," answered Liu. She continued to read *Sports Illustrated*.

"You sure? Because I could swear you kissed me."

"I did not."

"Pretty sure you did."

"You're an FBI agent…prove it," said Liu, obviously intrigued by his questioning.

"Well, I've never seen you read a magazine. Seems you're hiding something."

"That's circumstantial."

"I smelled your perfume, close to me, very close."

"You recognize my perfume?" Liu said. She seemed strangely complimented.

"With every ounce of my soul," he said, staring into her.

"Circumstantial. I leaned over and checked on you. That's what partners do."

"I taste your lipstick…on my lips. Explain that."

"Maybe a nurse kissed you when I stepped out; they fawn over you because you're handsome…" Liu stopped.

"Did you just say I'm handsome?"

"The nurses think you're handsome. I don't, you're not my type."

"So, a nurse kissed me."

"Must have."

Tucker licked his lips. "Well, this lipstick—*your* lipstick—has a specific feel. Kiss me again and we'll compare?"

"Not going to happen. We'll ask your nurse to step in and kiss you. Or kiss them all, to conduct more conclusive research."

"What if I said I possess proof you kissed me?"

"Impossible, because I did not kiss you, still I'm willing to listen," Liu answered.

"You never mention sports; you yawn if Luther or I broach the subject. Now you're pretending to read *Sports Illustrated*."

"It's the only magazine here, your dad left it when he stopped in."

"You met Dad?"

"I met your entire family. Loved your mom. They took me to El Arroyo. The tacos were awesome. Oh, and your brother has a crush on me."

Jealously gouged Tucker, irritation ran rampant inside his broken body. Then, his old friend logic took over. "Wait, they had time to…how long have I been out?"

• • • •

Liu watched as Tucker downshifted from jealousy to confusion. She considered Tucker's question, trying to grasp how lost he must feel.

The toughest man she ever met looked vulnerable, not physically as much as spiritually. Bringing him up to speed gradually seemed important.

"Four days," answered Liu, admitting to herself she enjoyed seeing Tucker jealous seconds earlier. Still, seldom in her career had she so embraced a topic change.

"Four days, what happened? I was just shot in the arm."

"Well, a lot happened. Do you mean medically?"

She remained quiet as Tucker gauged the depth of her response, the many directions their conversation could travel.

"Okay, yes, medically first."

"You've lost a lot of blood. The bullet that struck you hit an artery. The...beautiful young nurse slowed the bleeding. She saved your life. Examiners found your blood pooled in three separate locations. I thought the chest shot knocked you out, but you passed out from blood loss. You went into shock. It was touch and go for hours. Then the doctors dealt with blood clots. I'm not a doctor, but they repeatedly said you're lucky to be alive."

"The two men from the shootout?" Tucker asked. Liu extrapolated he dreaded the answer.

"Leon Loyola and Arturo Tigre. Dead."

"Ohh..."

Liu respected his need to grieve. She waited for him to ask.

"Were they...were they the ones...?" Tucker let the words hang.

"All the evidence points that direction, yes."

"Good." He sat in stasis for several minutes. Then he looked at her. Liu watched as Tucker inspected her, spending extra time investigating her lips. She knew his thoughts revisited his waking moment. Liu flushed and quickly changed subjects.

"We collected witness accounts, but I need to know...from you, what happened on that beach, when you're up for it."

"I'm up for it," Tucker said, his tone professional but his words dripping innuendo.

Like the kiss Tucker sought to prove, Liu could never confirm his words were unprofessional. "Well, Moss is staying at a hotel a few blocks away. If we're taking your testimony, I want him here. I'll have one of the guys track him down. Give me a second."

Liu tried to hide the excitement of not only having her partner back but getting to tell him everything. Much happened since they last talked. Before she exited, she smiled and vocalized words that fell short of the enormity of their situation. "We have a lot to tell each other."

• • •

Airborne
A fawn-like flight attendant glided through first class, her navy-blue uniform the exact ratio of professional and seductively tight prescribed by the airline. Still, despite her porcelain skin's gamine appeal, the Rice history professor failed to notice her. Luther fidgeted in his seat, thoughts pummeling him. He was returning from DC, where for the last several days he and Lackland listened, cataloged, and transcribed tape after tape exposing the sick underbelly of politics. Agents delivered the tapes to 935 Pennsylvania Ave, from Loyola and Tigre's homes, their business, the boat, and the hotel room they occupied in Austin.

The fact only he and Lackland listened to the tapes surprised Luther at first. While Luther mentally ingested the tapes, his surprise transformed from concern to fear, then outright terror.

Luther heard Lackland overview the tapes to Moss, telling his boss about the oncoming political melee. Still, Luther studied history. History repeats itself. Luther understood two facts. Facts Lackland, Moss, and Tucker missed. Truisms that Liu, despite her brilliance failed to identify:

➢ First: The professor knew he rocketed to the top spot in someone's dead pool. He calculated his chances of surviving the year, not appreciating the odds. Luther knew Lackland, Tucker, Liu, and even Moss occupied top spots on some reaper's wish list.

➢ Second, the most important fact, something Moss and his cadre of FBI agents missed: *Power doesn't share secrets.*

• • •

Austin, Texas
The agent who protected Tucker opened the door and looked into the room. "Liu, I got Moss, he'll arrive in a half hour."

She looked to Tucker. "Good, that'll give us time to catch up." Liu started with the downfall of the governors. She shared every detail, including Foxx Kauffman's over-the-top reaction. He peppered her with questions, engaged, focused, despite or because of the pain, which added edge to his awareness.

"The men you killed, Leon Loyola and Arturo Tigre, were Puerto Rican. Childhood friends, tight. They joined the Marines to escape poverty. Tough guys."

"Good shots," said Tucker.

"Yes, not too good, thankfully."

"In the Marines, they did everything together. Loyola showed a propensity for old-fashioned soldiering, expert marksman, top-notch at hand-to-hand combat. Loyola outweighed Tigre by 40 pounds but was shy, quiet, firm. Tigre proved to be an electronics and surveillance wiz. Outgoing, brash, and talked a good game. Not the soldier Loyola was. Still, due to his skill, the Marines valued Tigre more. In *the video*, Tigre talked, Loyola executed Greene and Thompson."

"I'm lucky, then," said Tucker.

"What do you mean?"

"The little one, Tigre, shot at me, not Loyola. Luck."

"Save that for Moss."

"Ahh…sure. So, what happened to the governors?"

"They lawyered up. They're out of jail for now, still they'll do prison time. Their political careers are kaput. The recording played in a room jammed with reporters. The story turned into a news feeding frenzy. Still, this is just beginning."

"What do you mean?"

"I'll be able to tell you more soon. I mentioned Tigre and Loyola were Marines. When they retired, they started a freelance protection company. They specialized in surveillance but did high-end bodyguard work too. They protected senators, the Secretary of Commerce, the Secretary of Energy, and several well-connected PAC leaders. The working theory is Loyola and Tigre fought for the American Dream, built a profitable business, then got disenchanted with the crooks they protected. Something set them off. They started killing, but more interestingly, they started recording."

"Excuse me?"

"Swindell, Steel, and Howe aren't the last politicians Tigre and Loyola will take down. Four years ago, before they started killing, they wore wires and recorded their clients. Erasmus left with a team, headed by Lackland. Our guys scoured through Loyola and Tigre's homes and office. Lackland located dozens of tapes hidden in Tigre's basement. Moss told me more politicians, PACs, business leaders, and influencers show up on those tapes. Dozens, probably more."

"Crap."

"Oh, did I mention, you're a national hero of sorts? You're all over the news. 'The FBI agent who stopped Loyola and Tigre.'"

Tucker watched Moss silently enter the room. "I'm just a guy with a gun." He looked at Moss. "Liu, you're the reason the FBI covered Austin. You're why we caught those guys, not me."

Liu spun around when she heard a steady clap behind her. "Tucker, I knew little about you a few days ago. Liu told me you were solid. Still, you've become a bit of a legend. Don't let it go to your head. Liu's correct, you're getting a ton of press, but back on Pennsylvania Avenue, Liu's getting her due. We understand who got us there, but I appreciate you ensuring I knew."

"So, these guys..." continued Tucker.

"Loyola and Tigre," Liu said.

"Were they responsible for the earlier killings, before Greene and Thompson?" asked Tucker.

Moss answered. "That's the pickle, probably not. No record of them visiting California. No record exists of them visiting Texas before last week, but Liu's reviewing Texas again. I asked the California team to scour the West Coast. To date, zero indication Loyola or Tigre visited California, Alaska, or the West Coast. Honestly, we'd write them off as coincidences..."

"But," continued Tucker, "you can't because someone snuffed a Pennsylvania mayor and California congressman with the same weapon."

"Yes," answered Moss. "Luther, Lackland, and the DC boys uncovered a treasure trove of info, and we're hoping for some link to Loyola and Tigre's associates, or a network. But we'll let the press operate under the assumption this is over..."

"But it's not," finished Liu.

Moss smiled at Tucker. "I promoted Liu to lead agent for the investigation; the California and DC teams report to her. She reports to me. Liu wants to stay here; she feels it all starts here. So, you'll be her right hand in Houston, Senior Special Agent Tanner Tucker."

"Wait…" started Tucker.

"Liu filed for your promotion months ago, recent events allowed your promotion to get rubber-stamped expediently. You're a national hero. Eyewitness accounts absolve you of wrongdoing, still we need you to recount what happened."

Tucker smiled his crooked smile and thanked Moss and Liu. She watched thoughts traverse his face, mapping emotions, documenting a path through pain. Liu worried about Tucker's bodily health, but had not considered the internal, mental, and spiritual challenges a man like Tucker faced.

Something about the promotion turned him inward. Like her, Tucker spent his career training to make the shot. He executed his technique to precision. Hurdling the barrier between training rounds and bringer of death, no matter the lawfulness of the action, remained a leap most agents never took. Tucker now stood on the other side of the barrier, without her, alone.

• • •

Tanner Tucker sat darkly absorbed. He felt blessed Moss and Liu allowed him time to collect himself. The new Senior Special Agent experienced gratitude for his promotion. Hearing Moss's words returned Tucker's thoughts to the men who died. Tucker knew nothing about them during the gun battle. He now glimpsed Loyola and Tigre through Liu's words. The two men bought the American Dream. They, like him, served their countries, them as Marines, he in the FBI. Loyola and Tigre held higher aspirations for our government than the politicians they policed.

Tucker had not mourned the two men or analyzed his actions. He wished the situation differed, not demanding mortal consequences. His first moments of consciousness were intoxicatingly bedazzled by the phantom kiss. Next, the excitement of the case offered a buttress of distraction. The time to sort his feelings arrived, unwelcomed, without the privacy sought for such moments.

He processed his emotions in front of two experienced FBI agents, who despite their rank and success, possessed no experience as counselors or priests. No one here granted absolution or offered condolences. Moss, Liu, Luther, the reporters, had days to process and glean from the events in Austin. Tucker's circumstances forced him to catch up in minutes. The girth of information overwhelmed him; the sheer magnitude of pressure proved crippling to most.

Still, Tucker grew up at his father's feet, a man who operated businesses with integrity. When his father served as a two-term congressman, he emphasized his desire to fulfill a duty, not gain status. Tucker worked with his mother in supporting roles in dozens of charities. She never sought the limelight. She served out of passion, not the senseless search for accolades. Tucker learned the true meaning of servant leadership. His parents' integrity, his carefully crafted character buoyed him now, helping him rise from the darkness. This moment, when Tanner Tucker desired nothing more than private hours to cry, he rallied instead. He donned his crooked smile. His team and Liu needed him now, not hours from now.

At first, Tucker heard himself speak. He remained unattached to the words, reciting from memory, not allowing himself to experience the moment. Reliving the memory, knowing the background, would be too painful. More so, the facts he now possessed allowed him to postulate the horrifying truth.

"Bates, Harmon, and I searched for sound trucks, or anything that could be a recording base. We knew nearby hotel rooms offered the best chance for a base camp for the senators' killers. Honestly, we didn't have the manpower to cover hotel rooms. So, we searched for vehicles.

"Harmon went north, Bates west, and I covered the area toward the river. I remember repeating, *think like Liu*. These killers always seem steps ahead of us. Why use a sound van? Too obvious. Then it hit me. When I was younger, my dad and I canoed Lady Bird Lake…a damned section of the Colorado River. I thought maybe the killers set up shop there, tried to look like tourists. If the killers were near the lake, who'd look there?

"So, I jogged to the river; kayakers were everywhere. I saw a boat with a small Evinrude motor tied to the dock. Seemed weird because I never saw a motorized boat on Lady Bird. It's not allowed. Then I spotted it."

"What?" asked Moss.

Tucker continued, his voice sans emotion. "A huge antenna, too big for a small boat. Even if local authorities popped them for a motorized boat, the boaters claim ignorance, get off with a warning. I tried to observe the boat without looking like I was observing the boat. A large man—probably Loyola—sat, casually reading, and appeared relaxed. I decided not to address him, not without backup. I debated my next move. Then the little one, Tigre I guess, returned."

Tucker paused, trapped in thoughts. He remembered the colorful Hawaiian shirt Tigre wore, the casual shorts, and soft canvas shoes. A broad smile highlighted his face.

"Tucker, I can tell this is tough, but please continue."

"Tigre carried two snow cones, he brought Loyola a snow cone. Sorry, something about the snow cones bothers me. From what you told me, these guys were buddies their entire lives..."

"And Tucker, they murdered three men."

"Yeah..." said Tucker.

Liu and Moss waited on Tucker. He understood they needed the information in his head. Liu wanted to press him but allowed him to pace his response. As always, Tucker comprehended his duty.

"Tigre steps on the boat and hands Loyola a snow cone. I hoped they'd eat the snow cones there. Stay put. They stood side by side, backs to me. I knew. It's the guys from *the video*. There's zero doubt. Zero. Tigre stood like the host on the video. I watched the damn tape a hundred times. I considered calling for backup, but Loyola decided for me. He brought the engine to life.

"They needed to hear me over the engine, and I wanted to establish authority; I wanted no doubt it was over. So, I called out 'FBI, hands in the air.' I fired two shots into the sky. Then it went to hell.

"The boat revved. I looked to Loyola who captained the boat. My mistake. The little one, Tigre, spun and popped four rounds. The first shot, spot on, hit me in the chest. Knocked me on my ass. I'd be dead if not for the vest. The next three shots were erratic. Trying to shoot from a moving boat threw him off. His last shot clipped me in the left arm, near my shoulder. I remember rising, sprinting toward the end of the pier for a clean shot.

"Tigre lost his balance, trying to maintain a shooter's stance on a moving boat. Loyola spun drawing his weapon. I had no choice. I had the advantage; they were only 10 or 15 yards away, but I stood on solid ground. So, I unloaded three quick shots into Loyola, the last few into Tigre. My head started spinning; my body surrendered. I stumbled backward. My last thought: what happened to the snow cones? When you're bleeding out, randomness dominates your brain. When I woke, people surrounded me."

"A lot of bikini-clad women surrounded you, you mean," said Liu.

"I got shot, and that's your memory," said Tucker, for the first time remembering her words from the beach, then allowing himself to relive the kiss.

"Anything else?" asked Moss.

"That's all I remember. But yeah, something else."

"Okay."

"Gonna sound stupid."

"Spill it."

"When Tigre shot me, he knew I wore a vest. He didn't want to kill me. Just put me down."

"That's ridiculous, Tucker, we're trained to aim for the trunk of the body. He fired at your core because that's how the Marines trained him."

"I understand, but I don't believe it. That's why I'm struggling. He wanted me on the ground, incapacitated, but he wanted me alive."

"Even if you're correct, there's no way prove it," said Moss.

"Yeah…if you guys don't mind, I need time to sort this. I'd like to see my family, talk to the docs, the normal stuff you do when you wake up in a hospital."

Liu smiled at him. She denied her feelings to herself, but she felt something for him, and he needed to process that as well.

Moss spoke first, "Look, you need time, you'll get it, but you mentioned the word *normal*. Understand, normal left the building for you. You're the press's hero du jour. Washington exploded when Thompson, Greene, and Heater got offed. You think you know crazy, but you don't. From what I got from Lackland, Washington's due for a much-needed rectal exam…and your lives are about to get complicated."

● ● ●

"Balls in Your Court"
Foxx Kauffman / Columnist / *The Times*
March 9, 1993
Austin, Texas

The Politikill is over.

Accepting bribes returns as politicians' favorite unpenalized indulgence. Crossing the blurry line between palm-greasing and payola again becomes PAC's most popular sport. Illegally influencing policy via extravagant gifts retakes its traditional place in corrupt businessmen's plans.

Yes, I understand the illegality of the above activities. Do you understand anti-corruption laws have proven universally ineffective? Odds dictate, politicians return to corruption as usual. Sorry, I meant business as usual. Here both statements are correct, interchangeable.

I'm a columnist, not a reporter. Still, overviewing the basic facts seems important. FBI Agent Tanner Tucker engaged in a gun battle with two assailants. While details remain sparse, reports claim Tucker, while taking fire, shot and killed 40-year-old Leon Loyola and 39-year-old Arturo Tigre. Loyola and Tigre, formerly of Puerto Rico, resided in Washington, DC.

Authorities confirmed both men were in DC on the day of US Senators Eagle Thompson's and Alan Greene's executions. Loyola's and Tigre's height and size matched images from *the video*. Inside sources confirmed both men were in DC the day of John "The Heater" Hall's murder.

Loyola and Tigre served in the US Military in the latter part of the Vietnam War. The two headed an independent security agency for a decade. Their agency protected politicians, Broadway stars, and East Coast financial elite. They specialized in high-end video and audio surveillance. The two served as jacks-of-all-trade in the security business, protection, prevention, and training. Neither man married, possessed a criminal record, or had living family in DC or Puerto Rico. Their personal circumstances allowed the twosome to remain invisible.

As security contractors to the elite, imagine the corruption Loyola and Tigre witnessed. They protected the right hand of the political graft-masters. They stood beside politicians selling the American Dream publicly and selling out Americans privately. Soon articles, books, news programs devoted to these men's lives will clog the zeitgeist. Still assessing their path, even today, with little information, proves simple.

Both men rose from abject poverty. Both selected the US Marines as their ticket to the American Dream. No greater believer exists than the impoverished who earn their ticket to success. No soul burns hotter than someone who captured the American Dream, then watches their beliefs sullied.

So, witnessing the corruption of this country, up close, created white-hot anger. Being paid to protect politicos selling out America piecemeal fractured the core of Loyola's and Tigre's beliefs. What the men witnessed turned them from protectors of the elite to predators of the corrupt.

The FBI confirms the two executed Greene, Thompson, and Hall. Using technological savvy, Loyola and Tigre ended the political careers of Governors Swindell, Steel, and Howe. We don't know what scouring the murderers' offices and homes will reveal.

How will history remember these men? As assassins? Or as dark heralds highlighting the need for change?

Unfortunately, the chance for change rests in the unsteady hands of the US political elite. The very people Loyola and Tigre sought to scare straight. I can predict your rebuttal. Voters hold the power to correct this problem. Are you sure? Political ads sway voters. Political action committees fund political advertising...well, you get the point.

A lifelong DC resident, I possess immeasurable hope but scant faith of our politicians spearheading real, meaningful political change. Despite the hard lessons these two former Marines tried to imbue, DC may be too dense, too corrupt, too money-thirsty to learn a damn thing.

I witnessed Thompson's and Greene's deaths on *the video*. I held a front-row seat to witness the fall of three governors in Austin. So, not surprisingly, I vacillate between relief Loyola and Tigre's vendetta ended, sadness that one of the greatest stories in history crashed to conclusion, and curiosity to watch what comes next.

Loyola and Tigre's quest ended.

Still, an uneasy feeling, a voice from afar, a rattling in my head, an unrelenting internal scream tells me I missed something. I don't know what I missed, but I can't wait to find out. Stay tuned, because often the ending is when things begin...begin to get interesting.

•   •   •

May 1993

Then...nothing happened.

No politicians faced indictment, no PACs disbanded for illegal practices, no business leaders expelled from ivory towers. Radio silence ensued. Papers and news programs painted Loyola and Tigre as extremists.

Erasmus Luther understood that power shapes public perception. Most people naively accept the lone gunman fantasy because the alternatives present far deeper terror. Erasmus, unencumbered by the populace's blissful ignorance, detected the miller's lathe shaping history in front of him. He grasped the gremlins of impropriety ran amok.

Liu and Tucker asked him what he heard in Washington. Luther declined, blaming his consulting status with the FBI. By not telling Tucker and Liu the tape's contents, he rationalized they had a chance at life. Not a big chance, but a chance, nonetheless. A chance he no longer possessed.

Positive power brokers deemed his death a necessity, Luther awoke surprised each day. He slept little, worried incessantly, looked over his shoulder constantly, and harbored no appetite. He lived in crowds, spending time with coworkers, his housemates, and when possible, Tucker and Liu. His lean muscled body morphed to just lean, sickly lean almost. To further his despair, Allie wrote, delaying their date. She referenced a family illness. She promised to apologize for the delay in a manner he would wholly approve. He did not have her phone number; hence, he could only return post his disappointment. He enjoyed her words' intrigue but doubted his chances of living another month.

When his date with Allie arrived, he broke down and told Liu and Tucker. He kept enough secrets from them. His friends deserved to share his excitement. He allowed Liu to gloat and take credit for his progress with Allie Arrington. Tonight stood as the high point of the rest of his short life. Someone should know.

• • •

Liu watched as Tucker rotated his left arm. The action had become a tic of sorts; he repeated the action often since the shooting. Once Tucker regained consciousness, he bulldozed through recovery and physical therapy. He returned to duty in less than four weeks. The

Bureau mandated Tanner attend physical therapy every week and meet with an FBI-appointed psychiatrist twice a month, for another four months.

Still, Liu observed his greatest healing, his strongest balm, was standing by her side. The FBI agent in her made note of the fact. The woman hungered for Tucker more. In her career, the FBI agent overruled the woman in her, choosing career over all else.

They wished Luther luck on his date when they saw him earlier. The two agents relaxed in the lobby of Liu's complex where they met often, sharing a Fuzzy's pizza and a bottle of cheap wine. Cheese hung from Tucker's chin, and he caught her looking at him. He shrugged and smiled his crooked smile. Liu felt the FBI agent in her lose ground to the woman.

"Luther looks like shit," Tucker started.

"I don't think he's sleeping."

"Since his trip to DC?"

"Yes."

"I took him out for beers, got him drunk, I can't get anything out of him. Has he told you anything?" said Tucker.

"Nothing."

"When's the shit hitting the fan? It's been months. What's Moss saying?"

"Nothing, and I don't think he believes Loyola and Tigre's tapes will see daylight. He's different now, not himself. Something's off."

"Look, I don't share this a lot, out of respect for my father. He's a great man, but he's got demons."

Liu remained quiet, knowing Tucker searched for something with his words.

"Dad's an alcoholic. He stayed sober since I was a teenager, but during my childhood it ate him up. Despite the booze, he worked at being a good father. Each evening he sat red-faced at the dinner table, barely keeping his wits. He went to bed soused every night. The next morning, he woke up and left for work, a functional alcoholic. His alcoholism was Houston's worst-kept secret. Everyone knew, but no one addressed it. Then, someone did—my mother.

"She challenged him to tell everyone about his addiction. He needed to own it. She compared secrets to black mold, destroying homes, rotting them from the inside. Mom explained to Dad that his secrets threatened our home's foundation, destroying our family from the inside.

"He got to meetings, let go of his secrets, worked with Mother to support centers for people with addiction. He became a champion for others with addiction. He used his brokenness. Dad's one of the more influential Houstonians, so his openness helped others get sober.

"Luther and Moss can't tell us about Loyola and Tigre. Moss lived the FBI life for years; he's used to secrets, so if something unsettles him, it's a monster. The bags under Luther's eyes could carry luggage. He keeps losing weight too. They're scared. The secret's killing 'em."

Liu said nothing. She long ago recognized her fear. She wrestled her feelings by doing her job.

"Look, as intriguing as the information found at Loyola's and Tigre's homes is, it's not our case or our job. Our job is to find Joseph, Little, Lane, Cole, and Freel's killer."

"Don't forget Whiteman," Tucker said.

"A woman killed Whiteman, not the same."

"You sure a woman didn't off the others?"

"Lane and Joseph were killed while hunting…"

"You're a Yankee, so you don't understand. This is Texas. Country girls mount two bucks by their fourteenth birthday. Maybe we're looking at this wrong. When men kill women, the crimes lean toward sexual motivation or control issues. There's no sign of that with Freel and Cole, the only female victims. Women are more inclined to kill women if you remove sex and control as motivations. What if we need to analyze Whiteman closer, because the killer's female? What if our killer has always been a woman?"

• • •

Allie Arrington may be a lot of things, but Erasmus Luther decided she did not exaggerate. She promised to dress to dazzle, and she did not disappoint. He watched her for years at the Arrington Gala. She dressed to impress, wearing full-length gowns radiating elegance and grace.

When they met at the farm, she looked fetching in tight fawn pants and a pressed white shirt. Even though he could not unpeel his eyes from her backside, she dressed functionally. Today, Allie dressed for an audience of one, the luckiest bastard in the world. She wore a slinky dress that stopped tantalizing just below her rear, showing off her impossibly long legs. The sheer fabric invited examination of every facet of her fit form. The neckline plunged tantalizingly low. Allie's breasts appeared ordained to escape with a sneeze or cough.

He prayed she battled allergies. Life's worries flew away, like birds at a gunshot. The polite history teacher ached to throw his date over his desk and let his pent-up frustration rule the day, but decorum prevailed.

Erasmus watched her smile. She understood her dress's effect, planned his painful pleasure to the nth degree. He imagined her walk across campus, male students half her age dumbfounded. Many smarting from torqued necks. The thought aroused him more.

"God…" he caught himself saying, unsure of how to survive the evening without acting like a hormone-enraged 19-year-old.

"I'm afraid not. Just a girl in a dress trying to look nice for you."

"Admitting you succeeded seems a blithering understatement."

He understood his appearance shocked her, but for different reasons. Luther wore his best suit, but it hung on him because he lost so much weight in the last few weeks. His usually vibrant eyes sported dark patches underneath. He spent most of his 30s and early 40s looking 25. Tonight, he appeared his age, or older.

"You look tired, Erasmus Luther."

"I was, before you entered the room. I'm okay now. You're a knockout."

"Thank you. I planned to save this for later, but you obviously need stress relief. Dessert usually arrives after dinner…but if you wanted…"

He wanted; working out years of attraction took time and multiple attempts. They arrived late for dinner.

●　　●　　●

The Brenner's maître d' seemed perturbed upon their arrival, but after admiring Erasmus' comely companion and the professor's stupid, broad, relaxed smile, their server quietly divined the reason for tardiness. After they sat, Luther said, "You know, I'm not starving. My roommates left town, we could just…"

"Dr. Luther, you enjoyed dessert early, and like you, I enjoyed it. Still, if you desire to enjoy dessert later, you promised this girl a meal. And I deserve a chance to get to know you better."

An inappropriate comment about knowing every inch of her almost tumbled from his lips. He conquered the urge. In their previous meetings, Allie seemed impressed when he appreciated the qualities others missed. Her beauty left most men unable to discover her other attributes.

Reviews rated the Brenner's Steakhouse service, food, and décor exquisite. Luther failed to notice. He reveled in not just the appearance but the entire aura of Allie. Like always, with her conversation flowed. Stress and anxiety, which coated him like a Houston sweat in August, evaporated. His soul lightened and his body strengthened concurrently. Allie gifted him an evening without fear.

He could not talk about his trip to Washington. So, he told anecdotes from his years teaching the world's best, brightest, and occasionally exasperating students. She told stories of her time at Rice, glossed over her time in New York, then somehow ended up talking about her brother, Bo.

"I left my job when I went to work for Wyeth in New York. After Wyeth and I parted ways, I headed home with no prospects. Apparently, Wyeth told Bo how much I helped him. So, when I hit the Houston airport, Bo waited for me."

"Look, your mother said you don't talk about your brothers."

"I don't, but it seems like we are getting…"

"Yes, it seems that way," confirmed Luther.

"If you want to learn about me…"

"I do."

"Then like I overheard my mother say, I have no choice but to tell you about them. Okay."

Luther nodded.

"Like I said, Bo waited for me at the airport in Houston. He drove me straight to Odessa, where he had an apartment set up for me. Bo married, but his wife despised my mother, me, Wyeth, Pete, especially Kyle, or anyone who had any influence over Bo. She wanted him to herself.

"A former Miss Odessa, with daddy issues, she struggled with insecurity. Bo served the role she needed—protector and father figure. Also, she recognized a rising star. She got her claws into Bo and pulled him as far away from us as she could.

"With Bo's newfound influence, she became a bigwig in a small town. She ran charity events and women's groups. Bo just wanted to work. We saw him at holidays if we were lucky. So, him waiting at the airport stunned me.

"Briana, his wife, showed no interest in his business, never came into the office. Her passions revolved around spending Bo's money. Bo probably thought she'd never know I worked for him. She didn't for a while.

"Bo drove things forward and led with technology but struggled with details. I stepped in and ran his office. I hired sharp women who oversaw compliance, billing, etc. Bo's revenues soared. Once the office ran smoothly, I became Bo's lead land man—or woman—securing mineral rights all over Texas. We hit a home run outside of Fairfield, Texas, a big life-changing oil lease. Everyone got rich, the landowners and Bo. I made life-changing money with the percentage bonus; we were riding high.

"Then Wyeth died, and Mom came into town. She needed us, and Briana, forced by Bo, hosted dinner. At dinner, Mom asked how I enjoyed working for my brother. With Wyeth's death hanging over me, I forgot to warn her to avoid the subject. Briana blew a fuse. She threw Mom and me out of her home. She forced Bo to leave with us. He slept at my apartment for weeks before he dared venture home.

"A month after Wyeth's death, Bo wrote me a huge severance check. He apologized but said he needed to protect his marriage. A year later, an Austin bureaucrat broke a commitment to lease state lands to Bo.

"Bo purchased millions of dollars of job-specific materials. In my absence, no one counseled him to spread his risk. He put most of his eggs in one basket and lost millions. Not only did Bo's chief competitor land the job, but Bo found no place else to get rid of specialized drilling equipment. He sold the equipment to that asshole for pennies on the dollar. That's what broke him. Months later, Briana sued for divorce, but before the divorce finalized, he committed suicide."

Luther struggled to put the pieces together. "I've attended the Arrington AIDS Art Galas; I've heard Bo left you and your mom millions. Why didn't his wife get everything?"

"When Bo lost the deal, he took a big hit. He became the butt of jokes in Midland and Odessa. Wildcat oilmen are tough by nature. But the business can make them cruel. Briana traveled in the same circles as the oil baron's wives. She heard the cruel jokes, and she believed the mistake finished my brother. She was wrong. Before I left, Bo and I set up two additional companies to purchase land that had some oil potential and long-term commercial value.

"Some of that land borders I-10, but most of the acreage abuts a future development called the Grand Parkway, on Houston's west side, near Katy. Bo predicted explosive growth there. Since his death, Mom and I sold off pieces for ten times what Bo paid. Still, the land we kept will be worth hundreds of millions in the next twenty years. We pay the taxes by leasing the land to livestock owners, scattered oil leases, and selling timber rights.

"If Briana's attorney conducted discovery, he'd have found all of Bo's assets, if it had gone to trial, but it didn't. Briana died of alcohol poisoning after a night of partying with her Midland/Odessa girlfriends. Apparently, she was the life of the party, celebrating her windfall. She died at home later that night."

"Wow," Luther mustered.

"Between land leases, the proceeds from selling Bo's company, and selling some of the land...we can help others."

"Like the Arrington Arts Gala."

"Yes."

Allie then peppered him with questions. She admitted her passion for history. Allie knew about Luther's father. She asked about his childhood and listened intently.

He recounted a junior high adventure when everything turned. "My best friend Foxx and I ran a game he created. We called it the Kiss Ass Committee. Everyone made fun of brownnosers for kissing the teacher's ass, but Foxx became convinced of a quantifiable grade increase if teachers liked you. He joked he had a brownnose, since he was half Jewish and half African American..."

Luther watched as Allie's demeanor transformed. "You're friends with Foxx Kauffman?"

"Yes," Luther answered.

"Hmm..."

The tenor of the evening changed. After he finished his story, she excused herself and left for the bathroom. He felt as if an earthquake left a chasm between them. Upon returning, she feigned politeness, but the familiarity they enjoyed evaporated.

Allie declined dessert. "Dr. Luther, while I powdered my nose, I called home. Mom needs me to return tonight. My driver's outside."

Then Allie departed. She promised no opportunity for another date; she simply left. He sat at his table in shock. Luther looked to the maître d'. The elegant man shook his head, imparting his thoughts. "You idiot, how'd you mess that up?"

He drove home asking the same question.

Luther jerked his vehicle hard to the left, avoiding a speeding Mercedes. The caw of the horn rung in his ears. To exacerbate matters, this was the second near collision on the short drive home. The terror he experienced since Washington settled upon him again, wrapping him as unwelcomingly as a comforter in a Southeast Texas summer.

Sweat gathered on his sallow forehead. Allie's sudden departure troubled him. He understood why the knowledge in his brain endangered his life. But Luther could not fathom why Allie turned so cold, so fast. Maybe she slept with Foxx Kauffman. Luther's association with Foxx might disgust her. Still, the theory made little sense. Foxx, never a discreet man, shared his most prolific stories with Erasmus. Since the professor got no calls about Foxx's rendezvous with an unbelievably gorgeous Texas blond with an elfish haircut, he assumed that must not be the case.

Erasmus almost missed the turn into his neighborhood, a turn he navigated thousands of times. Why did a woman who tantalized him earlier, suddenly treat him like he reeked of eau de pig shit? Despite the dark fate he considered inevitable, his thoughts rolled back to her dress, her eyes, her rich voice, and the sight of her walking away.

He stepped out of his car, forgetting to lock it, and turned to his front door. He stared at his feet until he heard it—the gurgling rumble of old American metal, a gray '68 Chevelle pulled slowly toward him, window rolled down. The car slowed, and the driver stuck his head out the window.

"Hey man, I gotta package for Doctor Luther. You him?"

Luther's internal antenna tripped. He left the question unanswered and sprinted toward his car. The distinct sound of a pistol fire and the clink of bullets bouncing off his International Harvester rang in his ears. Luther fell short of cover. A brawny hand jerked Luther behind the vehicle. Luther turned to face the second attacker before recognizing Tanner Tucker.

Tucker forced Luther down, then stood firing into the Chevelle. As Tucker's fire provided cover, Luther watched Natalie Liu rise from behind a pony wall, bordering the front of Luther's home. She peppered the Chevelle, unloading her service weapon. Luther heard glass shatter, unclear if it was the Chevelle's windshield, his home's windows, or likely both. The squeal of tires marked the Chevelle's departure.

Tucker sprinted for his car and chased the Chevelle. Liu stood over Luther. She held out a hand to help him up.

"You okay?"

Ordering his body not to shake, he looked into Liu's eyes. Luther aspired to reflect the confidence she projected. He took inventory before speaking.

"Yea."

"Get inside, let me call this in."

Luther wanted to follow her direction, but stood, unmoving in shock. He overheard Liu breaking down the events of the last few minutes. She called in the Chevelle and the partial license plate, then requested backup.

When she hung up, she jumped straight to business. "Did you recognize the shooter?"

"No."

"I got a partial on the plate, did you get the number?"

"Sorry, no one's shot at me before, so I didn't have a plan," he said. "Will Tucker be okay?"

"Tucker has a knack for being okay."

"How did you guys know to check on me?"

"We wanted to cover you leaving the restaurant, but you didn't tell us where you made reservations. So, we staked-out here."

"You didn't answer my question, how'd you know to be here?"

"Lackland and Moss run together three nights a week. Someone gunned them down tonight. Both dead. Leaving you the only person alive who knows what's on Loyola and Tigre's tapes."

Erasmus analyzed his situation. Bullet holes decorated his car, gunshots shattered the two front windows of his home, nothing money could not fix. Explaining the firefight to his professorial roommates presented an unwanted challenge.

Not as troublesome as his mother arranging his funeral, he thought. Score one for the home team. While Liu stood outside, he opened his front door. Glass shards intermingled with his designer rugs. Luther took a deep breath, traveled to his fridge, and removed two beers. The professor popped the top of the first Budweiser longneck and finished it in a gulp, before sitting the survivor on the table. He dropped the empty bottle in the garbage and flopped into his spot at the breakfast room table. He picked up the second beer and held it to his head, neck, and wrist, allowing the bottle's frigidness to cool him. Trying to imagine a day with more diverse highs, watching his dream girl enter his office, her pistoning off him moments after; to the lows, being shot at in front of his home, watching Allie depart without explanation. Comically, as he considered his day, the shooting failed to register as the nadir.

Luther popped the top of the second beer and swallowed half of the elixir before letting it rest on the table. He started laughing, then could not stop. Liu entered his kitchen sporting a funny look. She seemed concerned, so Luther spoke up. "I'm not going into shock and I'm not crazy."

Liu nodded unconvincingly.

"Someone tried to kill me, and it wasn't the low point of my day."

"Your date was that bad?"

"No, it went incredibly well, then it didn't."

"Sorry." Now seemed an inappropriate time to explore Luther's love life. Liu patted him on the shoulder and sat beside him.

Luther took another swallow, finishing the bottle. "Drinking's not the best idea right now," Liu scolded.

"I'll take that in consideration for next time." Erasmus Luther rallied to regain composure. He decided to participate in the solution versus letting the situation control him. "What do we know?"

"Tucker's headed back. The shooter's long gone. He got nothing. We called it in, shouldn't be hard to find. The car was collector quality."

"I'm sorry about Moss and Lackland."

Liu's reassuring smile vanished. Time for him to comfort her.

"Lackland and Moss became friends as rookies. Moss was my only boss in the FBI; he raised me professionally. I considered him my mentor, and I'm honored he considered me his protégé. He and

Lackland became my FBI dad and uncle. They took turns trying to set me up with their sons and nephews. I ate dinner at one of their homes six to eight times a year. I know their wives, kids, and grandkids."

"So, what now?"

"We have a conundrum."

"You think?" Luther jabbed. "Which one are you referring to?"

"I don't know what's on those tapes, but if you tell me, Tucker or anyone not in authority, especially the press, you're breaking the law. You swore secrecy when you accepted the assignment."

"Yes…"

"And if you don't tell anyone, you're trapped in someone's crosshairs."

"That sums it up. Who do you think took a shot at me tonight?"

"The public doesn't know about your involvement with the case. So, nobody's trying to exact revenge for Loyola and Tigre. Clear that option from our queue. Probably a politician, or several of them, implicated in the tapes you listened to in DC."

"Do you think they'll come back?"

"Sure, but not soon, they'll need to regroup. They tried to hit you, Moss, and Lackland tonight. Coordinated surprise attack. They lost that advantage."

"So, what happens now?"

"No idea. Someone squelched the Loyola and Tigre tapes. I can't guess what happens next. I got nothing about the investigation into Moss's and Lackland's deaths or tonight's attempt on your life. I'm positive the assignment won't land in my lap, I'm too close to the victims."

"So, I'll ask again, what'a we do next?"

"We do our jobs. Uncover who killed politicians back in the mid '80s. Discover why and work from there. That's our assignment: locate the genesis of these murders and stop this.

"Then I jump every bureaucrat hurdle, I crash through every political wall. Finding answers may take decades, but I'll hunt down the assholes who killed Lackland and Moss. I'll find out who's behind tonight's attempt on your life, even if it kills me. But for now, our assignment remains unchanged."

The two awaited Tucker's return. The local police arrived, called by a neighbor, and took a report. Liu handled the details, but Luther answered several standard questions. After the cops departed,

Luther moved to his sofa, just to relax for a minute. Something about a guardian present released the demons haunting him. He woke twice, pulled from sleep by the trumpeting sound of his snores, each time looking for Liu before nodding off. His stiff sofa, adjacent to her, more welcoming than his bed's goose down pillows. Sweet dreams and nightmares intermingled moments later.

• • •

Luther woke to the smell of coffee brewing. He groggily looked over spotting Tucker passed out on his recliner; a turn of his head revealed Liu sitting at the table, coffee mug in hand. She wore her clothes from the night before but looked refreshed. He stumbled to the table; Liu met his glance guiltily.

"I made myself at home, I took a shower when Tucker stood watch, hope you don't mind."

"No problem," Luther said.

"Also, your bed was unused...so..."

Luther poured a cup of coffee and sat next to Liu.

"What did I miss?" asked Luther.

"A lot, actually."

"Sounds foreboding."

"Yes."

They sipped their coffee, Luther waiting for Liu to talk; she did not. Luther pushed, "Are you going to tell me? Not telling me will freak me out more."

"You sure?" Liu said, stating fact more than being clever.

Luther nodded.

"Tucker didn't return because he overheard a dispatch from a black-and-white. They spotted a car meeting the description I called in, parked near some warehouses off Clinton and Fidelity. They called for backup. By the time Tucker arrived, the cops taped off the crime scene. The car sat idling, that's how the locals found it. Your shooter sat in the passenger seat, bullet through his head."

"Self-inflicted?" asked Luther.

"No," said Tucker from the couch, not opening his eyes. "Do I smell coffee?"

"Yes," said Liu.

Tucker stretched as the tablemates watched.

"Aren't you supposed to say you're not sure, the crime lab will tell you tomorrow?"

This time Liu answered, "I'll say that if it makes you feel better. But we're sure it wasn't."

"And how are you so sure?"

Tucker stretched while walking to Luther's coffee table. He put his hand on Luther's shoulder, bracing him. "Because DC cops found the guys that gunned down Moss and Lackland."

"Dead?" asked Luther.

"Dead."

Act 3: The Plot Twist

The radical change of direction that twists the book's outcome

Four Miles from Harrogate, North Yorkshire, England, 1937

"Steady, Philippa, steady," whispered Lord Harrington.

Philippa and her father stalked the stunning stag for hours. The massive red deer invoked excitement, even for someone of her father's experience. Philippa's earliest memories, colored with horse rides and hunts with her father, returned to her now. She wanted her last memory with him to be as special.

She considered the appropriateness of her father's words. She needed steadying, steeling. Not for this shot, but for tonight. Her last night. She planned this night years earlier, saved for her departure. Every detail re-examined and perfected.

Since today marked her 18th birthday, and tomorrow her wedding, she requested a hunt with her father as her birthday gift. Cyril, the head gamekeeper, accompanied them, of course, but per Cyril's practice, he trailed yards behind. Philippa paused, lingering in the moment.

Philippa surveyed the land one last time, taking in the Kelly-green dales and stunning countryside. Her heart hurt, missing her home already. Philippa forced a deep breath, refocusing on her target. The gunshot rang through the countryside. The large red staggered, then bolted. Philippa knew the deer would not run far.

She turned, winking at Cyril, allowing him to feel her appreciation for all the hunts, the years of devotion, and to communicate the shot's purity. Cyril lowered his field glasses and returned her wink. His smile confirmed shared respect. The gamekeeper waved and three younger men, his game staff, joined him.

The group followed the stag's trail, finding the beautiful fallen creature a few hundred yards ahead. "Nice shot, Lady Philippa," said Cyril beaming, as proud as her father. He witnessed every shot Philippa took in her eighteen years. "Roger's a few miles back with the horses. Your mum waits impatiently for your arrival. Big plans today and of course, tomorrow."

"Thank you, Cyril," Philippa said kissing him on his cheek. The old man blushed, wringing his hat in his hands.

"Ah, my Lady, I'll miss you. Nothing but blessings for your wedding. Mr. Hysler better bring ya' home often."

Philippa handed Cyril her rifle, nodded, but said nothing. As the gamekeeper's crew remained to dress and transport the stag, Philippa and her father started the walk through the dales, along a hand-stacked wall of weathered stones.

"Father, when we arrive home, I want to visit the stables, to groom Minerva...one last time."

"Of course, dear."

"Thank you."

"Philippa, I know the family asked much of you."

"Yes," she said, continuing her walk.

"You do not love Jonas yet, but he is your brother's best friend, the best man at your brother's wedding."

"Yes." Philippa no longer desired to fight her situation. Her parents arranged this wedding years ago, and despite her disagreement, plans remained unchanged.

Jonas Hysler and Philippa's older brother Thomas met at boarding school. That summer the Hyslers visited from Germany and vacationed with the Harringtons at Ridley Castle. In her formative years, Thomas alone proved challenging for Philippa. Jonas and Thomas together stressed the limits of intolerability.

Alone, Philippa defended herself against the two teenage terrors. To avoid confrontation, she and the cook's son Ronald awoke early departing the castle to explore the lake and stalk wildlife. The two often spotted fallow or roe deer. On the grandest of days, they followed a red stag.

She perfected avoiding her brother and Jonas through the day. The lazy twosome slept through breakfast. However, the boys proved unavoidable in the evening. Dinners remained safe thanks to the formal setting; however, after dinner, Jonas and Thomas targeted Philippa for their misadventures.

Unfortunately, after the Hyslers departed that first summer, genuine horror rooted for Philippa.

"What a pleasant visit, don't you think, dear?" said Philippa's mother, Lady Antonia Maria Harrington.

"Quite nice," responded Lord Harrington, swirling a burgundy in his glass.

"Are you excited they committed to return next year?" asked Lady Antonia.

"What?" said Philippa as Thomas laughed.

"The Hyslers will return each summer," answered Philippa's mother.

"Why?" said Philippa, making no effort to mask disdain.

"Well, several reasons, first, Jonas and Thomas are quite close."

"Let Thomas go to their house," begged Philippa.

"Philippa, that is not how we speak at the table."

Philippa put her head down and huffed.

"Also, your father and Mr. Hysler completed an exclusive importing agreement. The Harrington Partnerships will be the British importer of Hysler Spirits. The economy is terrible, especially in Yorkshire. Half the men remain unemployed. Please understand how lucky we are, Philippa."

Lord Harrington looked up from his dinner and nodded.

"Your father flourished, thanks to his partnerships; still, adding Hysler Spirits ensures growth of our products in Germany and adds an important trade partner in the UK. Since you and Jonas will marry one day, our families should spend time together."

"What?" said Philippa in horror.

"The merger makes perfect sense; Jonas is enamored with you. Thomas will become Earl when your father dies, which we hope is not too soon."

"Here, here," replied Lord Harrington.

"You, my dear, need a suitable husband. Who could be more suitable than Jonas Hysler?"

"Anyone, Mother, anyone."

"Philippa Harrington, the Hyslers remain Germany's most prosperous family, tracing their heritage to Charlemagne. You will marry him. They visit us, as a courtesy each summer, so you can spend more time with Jonas."

"I will not."

"Philippa, you will. Over time you will learn to love Jonas."

That evening, Philippa's plan formed. The pre-teen saved every pound, pence, and shilling to propel her escape from Ridley Castle. The Hyslers' visit each summer served as Philippa's personal hell. She prayed often that she could learn to love or even tolerate Jonas.

Her prayers remained unanswered. Jonas proved brash, incorrigible, reckless, and arrogant. Each year after the Hysler visit, Philippa's resolve to abandon her family sharpened.

With Lord Harrington's example, Philippas's brother, Thomas, blossomed into a fine man. The future of the Harrington estate ensured by his business acumen and the selection of a fine wife, Lilian, the Earl of Coventry's daughter. Lilian became Philippa's dearest friend.

So today, Philippa's 18th birthday, her final day at Ridley, stood as the last opportunity to inspect the stables and groom her horses. Her birthday also served as the last night to hug her mother, who Philippa adored despite their differences.

Philippa studied her father as she traversed the path.

"I will miss you the most," said Philippa.

"Why, I will miss you too. You are getting married tomorrow, not severed from the family. I venture to Germany occasionally on business, and Jonas travels to London often."

Philippa smiled sorrowfully.

That evening, Lady Antonia aspired to outshine Aurora herself. The castle, decorated for following day's wedding, looked breathtaking, even by Ridley's lofty standards. Philippa thanked the butler, footmen, cooks, and entire staff for a perfect evening. She requested the night just be family and staff. She wanted one more night to enjoy her childhood, which ended tomorrow.

Despite Lady Antonia's disapproval, Thomas did not attend Philippa's birthday, choosing Jonas' stag party. Thomas explained to his disapproving mother that Philippa would celebrate more birthdays. Jonas' stag party represented a once-in-a-lifetime opportunity. Lilian attended Philippa's birthday, offering regrets for her husband's decision. Recently, Lilian allied with Philippa in her loathing of Jonas.

Philippa received extravagant gifts from her father, the staff, her absent brother, and Lilian. Still the most special gift, and the timeliest, passed from mother to daughter. Lady Antonia's accent denoted Genoese upbringing. "My father was once the Italian trade minister in Japan. Our family lived in Tokyo for 18 months. I was 16 and promised to your father, but not yet married. Weeks before our departure, my family dined at an embassy event. A young man, about my age, sat beside me. I did not know until later that he was the third son of the Emperor. Polite, very formal. I thought little about our interaction. Still, I think the young man found me interesting."

"He found you intoxicatingly beautiful, more likely," added Lord Harrington.

Lady Harrington ignored her husband. "Two weeks later, a day before we departed for Genoa, a beautiful packet arrived from the young man. I cherished this gift and now pass it to my only daughter."

The lacquered antique Japanese box previously adorned her mother's dressing table. "Stunning, Mother, thank you."

"Philippa the box is only part of the gift."

Philippa's eyes widened as she opened the intricately detailed box. Inside rested a stunning six-inch Japanese hairpin, elegant and beautiful in every way. A tear streamed down Philippa's cheek. Her mother stood and walked behind Philippa, patiently braiding her daughter's hair. Lilian rose and moved to Philippa's side, holding Philippa's hand as Lady Antonia worked. "Happy birthday, Philippa!" With her work completed, Lady Antonia kissed her daughter then pushed the long, elegant pin through her daughter's hair.

Turning her daughter's head toward a mirror, she whispered, "Perfect."

"Indeed," concurred Lord Harrington.

"Breathtaking," added Lilian.

"Thank you, Mother."

"You are welcome, dear. Now, I must check on the wedding cake."

Philippa Harrington never heard her mother's voice again.

• • •

Philippa lingered, cherishing each good-bye. She hugged Lilian, then sat on her father's knee, which she had not done in years. After collecting each gift, Philippa sullenly walked to her room. Once behind her closed door, she retrieved her bag, hidden for months, and carefully packed the beautiful box from her mother and gifts from Lilian and Lord Harrington. Philippa sat, crying, coming to grips with losing her family, this place, her home.

She walked to the mirror. How could she leave? Was marrying Jonas Hysler so terrible? Philippa looked at herself in the mirror, her hair elegantly styled with the gorgeous Japanese hairpin. Why desert her father, her dear mother, her home? Ridley was part of her. She breathed deeply and looked to her bag, doubting her chosen path.

Crashing pulled Philippa from her thoughts. Apparently, Thomas arrived home. Her brother and Lilian's quarters occupied a separate hall of the castle, but Philippa overheard Thomas's slur, "Lilian, Lilian, where are you?"

"Dear God, Thomas, you are inebriated, don't for a moment..."

Philippa debated checking on Lilian before deciding her sister-in-law had proven capable of taking care of herself. When Philippa again heard crashing in the hall, the sound did not alarm her. Philippa assumed Lilian sent Thomas packing.

Philippa's door swung open; Jonas Hysler stood on the threshold pissing drunk. "Thomas told me he was coming home to tangle with lovely Lady Lilian. If Thomas can call on Lilian this evening, I can call on you."

A thousand thoughts assaulted Philippa's brain. How did Jonas get past the staff? Did Thomas help him? Was Jonas, the man she hated more than any other, intent on raping her? Thoughts she entertained of staying here, in her home, emptied from her. Jonas's drunken intrusion confirmed what 12-year-old Philippa ascertained. She could not marry this indulged, arrogant, self-important bully.

Philippa Harrington long ago chose to leave her family, country, and even her name behind, instead of marrying Jonas Hysler. For now, Philippa endured the only available option: playing along. "Jonas, I am your wife tomorrow, not tonight. I want our wedding night to be special..."

Philippa paused in terror as Jonas advanced. "Jonas, our first night together cannot be a drunken foray. A foray you will not remember." Philippa prayed tonight's memory would not torment her forever.

The 18-year-old's words failed to slow Jonas. Still, if she heard Lilian earlier, maybe Lilian could hear her. Philippa started to scream.

Jonas expected this and leapt, muting her with his hand. He wrestled her to the bed, holding one hand over her mouth, the other switching between holding her arm and gropingly removing her dress. With her free arm, Philippa scraped Jonas' eye. He recoiled but quickly returned to the attack. One hand was still over her mouth, a knee held her right arm down. Jonas' other hand tugged down her dress.

Philippa kicked, tried to scream, and managed to topple a vase which shattered on the floor. No rescuer appeared. Philippa understood who her rescuer must be and embraced the depths of fury required for emancipation.

Philippa found being left-handed a tremendous advantage. Especially if an adversary ignores that fact. Philippa reached back and pulled the Japanese hairpin from the tight bun fashioned earlier by her mother. Shocked by how easily the fury rose to greet her need, Philippa bathed in the emotion, coddled it, called upon its power. With one quick motion, Philippa jammed the pin into her attacker's eye.

Jonas Hysler screamed. Philippa violently kicked Jonas to the floor then grabbed her bag. Philippa's last view of her room featured splattered blood and Jonas kicking and cursing. Philippa turned and hurried down the back staircase while straightening her bloodstained dress. Bag in hand, Lady Philippa finished her descent, thankful she packed appropriate travel clothes.

She took her last view of Ridley's Grand Hall, decorated for a wedding she never wanted, that would now never occur. Philippa Harrington, the future Gertrude Arrington, stepped for the first time, but not the last, into an uncharted future.

•　　•　　•

July 4, 1993
"Hey, Ima" said Foxx, stepping through her door, still bleary-eyed from last night's carousing.

"Hello, Foxx," said Ms. Kauffman, stirring her homemade chocolate pudding. "Kiss your Ima, I can't step away, I'm in the middle of it."

Foxx, excited about eating his mother's cooking, obeyed, bending to kiss her weathered cheek. Now 80, Ima only rallied to cook during holidays and his birthday. Foxx never missed a chance to eat her cooking. He once flew from Los Angeles to DC for his birthday, returning to his West Coast assignment the next day. None of the world's epicurean palaces held more pull for Foxx than a meal prepared by his mother. He knew she spoiled him as a boy. Foxx's friends, including Erasmus, never declined a sleepover at the Kauffman house. Ima's meals featured an eclectic blend of Caribbean, Jewish, and Soul.

Amita Kauffman came to motherhood late in life. To complicate matters, Foxx's Jamaican father died in the Korean War before Foxx's birth. So, Foxx looked dissimilar to his classmates. The unmarried Amita Kauffman bravely raised her child in the 50s and 60s. She battled prejudice by winning overs teachers, principals, neighbors, and shopkeepers with kindness, boundless goodwill, and chocolate babka, apricot rugelach, macaroons, and signature Caribbean chocolate rum pudding cake made from her Jamaican grandmother-in-law's recipe. Foxx swore the pudding cake ensured his Georgetown scholarship.

Foxx spent weeks covering the deaths of Deputy Assistant Director Moss and Special Agent in Charge Lackland. Foxx assumed the execution of the FBI agents connected to Loyola and Tigre; however, no proof emerged. Moss' and Lackland's deaths failed to register as the most terrifying development. The indifferent but uniform responses from the FBI, DC police, and law enforcement agencies reeked of high-level cover-up.

Each agency released eerily similar statements. Basically, *"Moss and Lackland were in the wrong place at the wrong time. Sources pointed to a gang initiation."* Many newspapers did not run an article on the deaths. Foxx's own paper disallowed the Moss and Lackland story in Foxx's usual column. Instead, his publishers jammed the story deep in a Wednesday paper. Foxx's high-ranking sources, reliable insiders, and low-ranking snitches repeated the gang initiation story. The reporter heard the story so often from so many usually reliable sources, he questioned his intuition.

Foxx survived enough brushes with death not to court another, still something stuck in his mental craw. He pushed his troubled thoughts away, deciding not to obsess about stories, non-stories, and gangland slayings on his birthday. Tonight, he welcomed the opportunity to stuff himself to the point of loosened belts, food sweats, and epic burps.

Each dish proved amazing; Foxx savored each bite and relished his mother's presence. Sadness gripped him. He understood Father Time stamped these special meals, this time with her, with an approaching expiration date. He enjoyed every moment. In his early career, Foxx's assignments took him overseas often. As his status grew, he pushed his editor for a chance to work DC. Over time, Foxx became the paper's DC-based columnist. With Loyola's and Tigre's deaths, the dead end in the Moss and Lackland slayings, Foxx decided someone granted him a chance to slow down, enjoy life, and get fat inhaling his mother's cooking.

• • •

While cleaning, mid-conversation, Amita Kauffman shook her head, removed her apron, and said, "Foxx, I am so sorry, a package came for you days ago."

"Delivered here?" he asked to the backside of her retreating head. "Ima, don't worry, it's just junk mail." His voice echoed back to her as she reached her office.

"Oh, I don't think so. Someone handwrote my address, had a funny cartoon written on it. Looked personal," her voice echoed.

Amita Kauffman felt a chill embrace the room as she handed Foxx the envelope. Her son took the envelope and collapsed in his chair. He looked at her as if he saw a dybbuk's hand upon her shoulder. His reaction seemed out of place. After all, the envelope only said:

HEY FOXX

• • •

Amita Kauffman's perception, though incorrect, stuck within a razor's edge of truth. Foxx did not see a dybbuk or a good old-fashioned Anglo-Protestant ghost. He just received a letter from one, though. Foxx looked at her as raw emotions cascaded through him.

"Foxx, what's wrong?"

"It's just work, Ima, I...a...I have to go."

"Do you want my letter opener?"

"No, no, no," he repeated, nervously scanning her apartment, wondering who watched. Foxx grasped involving his mother in whatever this was...correction, *is*...might get her killed. The reporter carefully selected his words. "I love you so much."

"I love you too, Foxx."

"I know I usually help you clean up. I'll make it up to you, but I have to leave right now."

"Foxx, you look scared." He did not hear her. Amita Kauffman talked to a slamming door and the sound of Foxx's footsteps banging down the stairs.

• • •

Houston, Texas

Thick, knotty emotions like concern, discomfort, and even fear surrounded Natalie Liu. Still, her most disconcerting emotion, one she never experienced, entered her vocabulary: paranoia. Liu, as many before her, considered Joseph Heller's quote from Catch-22: *"Just because you're paranoid doesn't mean they aren't after you."*

Liu and Tucker sat in Erasmus Luther's office, pouring through newspapers. She examined current national papers while Tucker attacked Texas-based papers from the '80s. The newspapers served as her distraction, not the reason for her concern.

Liu's eyes furrowed as she debated. No newspaper connected Luther's shooting to Moss' and Lackland's deaths because no one knew Rice University's history professor worked with the FBI. Also, the attempt on Luther's life basically went unreported. One generalized blurb with no follow-up stories appeared days later. No paper mentioned Luther's attacker's fate.

The only reporter or columnist that might put it together lived in DC—Foxx Kauffman. Liu's new boss forbade Luther, Liu, and Tucker to inform Foxx. Kauffman knew nothing of the attempt on his best friend's life.

Liu tried to follow the investigation of Luther's shooter, but authorities shut her out. Her new boss, Carmen Angelo, informed Liu another team spearheaded the investigation of the attempt on Luther. Moss' and Lackland's murder investigation, also not hers.

Her assignment remained to find the root of the political killings, period. Angelo told her, "Stay in Texas, harvest your field, get it solved, stay out of other people's crops." Over the last month she felt abandoned on a deserted island.

Angelo trimmed her Texas team to Tucker and Luther, then reassigned the California team. Her DC group now comprised one administrator.

Liu would happily accept the evisceration of her team if the FBI devoted the resources to ferreting out the powers behind Lackland's and Moss' murders and the attempt on Luther. Instead, the FBI assigned Special Agent in Charge Mitchell Doherty, a man considered a connected political crony and a blustering idiot. Doherty only kept his mouth shut about one thing—his inability to solve cases.

Despite the lack of answers about Moss' and Lackland's deaths, the dearth of resources devoted to investigating the attempt on Luther's life, and the execution of Lackland and Moss, and Luther's shooters, none of those issues proved primary on her lengthy list of concerns. Her team's reduced resources, although problematic, failed to reach the number one spot. Liu's most troubling concern, the one she suffered to her core, was her severe lack of sleep.

Liu repeatedly asked Angelo for a security detail to cover Luther around the clock. Someone wanted Luther, an FBI asset after all, dead. Angelo repeatedly denied her request. She directed the same request to local authorities—denied. Liu received the same pushback. The person who tried to kill Luther died; no threat existed. So, she and Tucker assumed the mantle of the professor's bodyguards, on top of their investigation. One of them shadowed him when possible. Luther liked her and Tucker. Still, she identified with his anguish. He sickened of the babysitting but needed their presence as a mental salve. Despite his grumpiness, Luther showed appreciation.

She looked to Tucker, her mental salve, and accepted that fact. Liu understood the responsibility for stopping this crazy carousel now rested solely in hers and Tucker's hands. She also grasped they needed help from the man who lived as their ward, Erasmus Luther. She returned to her assigned papers, making notes, not knowing how or when the next clue may present itself.

When with Tucker, Liu hid her disappointment in the agency. She clearly saw the strings, the strings some puppeteer several pay grades above her now manipulated. Natalie Liu was far from naïve. She perceived the puppeteer's presence before, but never quite as close, never so intimately concerned with her work. The Special Agent in Charge admitted defeat, accepted utter failure, resigned herself to one fact. The puppeteer's proximity ensured Loyola and Tigre's tapes would never surface. Natalie Liu was wrong.

• • •

July 7, 1993

Gertrude considered the gloom surrounding her daughter. Months ago, Allie bordered on happiness...or the facsimile of happiness allowed by Allie through her hardened veneer. Allie's veneer, like her every emotion, was colored by her brothers' deaths. The young professor intrigued her daughter. Gertrude read Luther's books, well before Gertrude met Erasmus or knew of Allie's interest in him.

How could Allie resist? Erasmus Luther was smart, handsome, interesting, and literally the last suitor in the world Allie should consider. Danger and attraction often traveled as a pair. Most women desired the unavailable suitor. Gertrude's heart ached for Allie.

As a girl, Gertrude, or Philippa more accurately, showed no interest in the cultured young men of her class. The cook's son, the dirty, chiseled young man who worked with the gamekeeper and the townsman who delivered coal to Ridley Castle, intrigued Philippa. Dirty hands, thick shoulders, and an accent that sounded nothing like her brother's refined diction caught her attention. She spent decades examining the impulses of her attraction. Simply stated, she wanted the opposite of everything Jonas Hysler represented. Polite and polished in the bright light of society, but showing his true nature—haughty, demeaning, even cruel, when unsupervised.

Few women, or men for that manner, endure cruelty happily. The men who liberally dispensed cruelty, no matter their social status, appearance, or wealth, proved unattractive to her. Her attraction template cemented at an early age, the antithesis of refinement and cruelty. She found herself drawn to burly, kind, creative, and adventurous men, without a hint of polish or viciousness. So, she chose here, this place, Silsbee, Texas. Polish seldom cracked the entree menu here, and Gertrude gratefully called this place home. Unavoidably, like any town, large or small, politics existed, as did the haves and have nots. Still, minimum snootiness prevailed, except in the upper levels of the small-town society, which she avoided.

Gertrude enjoyed four passions:

1) First, her children, of course. She lost two tragically. Now preserving her boys' memory and protecting Allie endured as Gertrude's spiritual cornerstone.

2) Second, her horses, and not just because of their beauty or her background. She embraced their pure intuition. Horses read your confidence, felt your doubts, but mostly horses do not care about bank balances or the cars in your garage; if you could ride, you could ride.

3) Third, the world's greatest equalizer: education. The poorest person in America might surpass the wealthiest through education and work ethic. Everyone possessed an opportunity for an education, perfectly equal in quality, no, but opportunity, nonetheless. To Gertrude, America stood as the greatest country in the world, despite the imperfections.

4) Finally, The United States of America. She watched America develop from world power to a superpower to the superpower in her residency. Gertrude learned, then taught the country's laws, systems, and intricacies. She understood America grew because of the opportunity for fairness, the perception of equality, and the absence of a caste system. America, like most countries, struggled with racism and inequality. Still, she enjoyed helping hundreds of students break the bondage of racism and poverty through education. She loved her adopted country, and in her own way protected it.

Gertrude wrestled with the fault of her boys' deaths. Yes, contributing factors abounded in both cases. But what if, as she feared in her darkest thoughts, the fault rested with her? In her youth, the peony, her mother's favorite flower, charmed her. The delicate, extravagantly bloomed, and subtlety scented flower often decorated Ridley's Grand Hall. Like Gertrude's boys, peonies bloomed briefly. The flower grew perfectly in the greenhouse behind her Yorkshire home. Still, peonies flail in the withering Texas heat and clay-based soil. What if she planted her children in the wrong place, the wrong environment?

She savored tea as she watched the news. The DC columnist at the center of the Thompson and Greene story years earlier talked on screen. Most of her life, she perused the few newspapers sent to her home and the dozens at the school library. At first, she read to stay informed for class, then because she loved newspapers, and finally with specific purpose. Since retirement, her eyesight worsened. She now only read the Beaumont and Houston papers. Begrudgingly, she relied on TV. The proliferation of news programs benefitted few more than her.

She looked across at her beautiful daughter, her best friend, her biggest challenge, and her most ardent supporter. "Allie, please turn up the news, Foxx is on TV again."

Allie shook her head. Her daughter shared no interest in her mother's fascination, yet she stood, smiled sardonically, and adjusted the volume. Sadness again gripped Gertrude. She loved Allie dearly and would be lost without her. However, she wished her daughter left her side years earlier when the opportunity to escape…whatever this is…was still available. Or frighteningly, as Bo's and Wyeth's deaths hinted…no chance for escape ever existed. Maybe the foursome, or now twosome, were doomed all along.

• • • •

Houston

Erasmus Luther and his acting bodyguards, Tucker and Liu, crowded around the TV in Tucker's small but luxurious bachelor's loft. Each read Foxx's articles, but the promise of more information left the threesome, and the country, wanting more. Foxx appeared comfortable on television. He reclined, seated with the gorgeous anchor, formerly from Texas herself. Tucker turned up the volume catching her mid-sentence, "…the nation's most watched nightly news show, I'm in Washington, DC, covering for Nick Stone." She smiled into the camera, smoothly welcoming viewers. "In history, few stories exist of humans rising from the dead. If you're Christian, Jesus, of course, tops the list. If you're a George Romero fan, the progenitor of the zombie genre, you're familiar with the premise," the anchor continued. "But zombies remain fictional, and Jesus performed miracles far from the bright lights of modern cameras, so today we'll examine the greatest resurrection in recent history.

"Leon Loyola and Arturo Tigre remain dead but enjoy resurrection through what DC columnist Foxx Kauffman jokingly labeled, the *Tapes of Wrath*. Foxx, for those few who failed to read your story, please overview how the tapes came into your hands and what you shared so far in your columns."

"Thanks," Foxx said. "The tapes landed on my doorstep last week. I needed time to process them before I felt capable of broadcasting Loyola's and Tigre's life work."

Luther glanced from the screen to the enthralled agents. "I've known Foxx my whole life. He's lying about something, I don't know what, but he is."

"Shh," the only response he received. The professor's attention returned to the TV.

"Foxx, explain Loyola's and Tigre's life work."

"Exposing corruption, Kayla."

"Okay, fair, they exposed corruption, and even in death expose additional malfeasance. They also killed men in cold blood."

"I noticed you did not say innocent men," Foxx rebuffed.

"Thompson, Greene, and Hall paid an exorbitant price for their crimes."

"Did they? Greene and Thompson sold out our country. Hall purchased changes in policy to benefit himself. Prosecutors might label Greene's, Thompson's, and Hall's actions treasonous. This country executed traitors in the past."

"Treason, Foxx? You're stretching the definition."

"That's fair. But the definition of treason: the act of betraying one's country. We can debate treason's definition, but that's not why you asked me here."

"Agreed."

"I'm here to share Loyola's and Tigre's words."

"Okay, start from the beginning."

"I spent months studying them. I mentioned in an earlier column, Loyola and Tigre were Puerto Rican natives, best friends, and Marines. Once they became private citizens, they started a security company based on Loyola's protection skills and Tigre's technological savvy. From what I know, they believed in the American Dream. Loyola and Tigre became, if not wealthy, successful beyond their dreams. They felt they owed something back."

"That's how this began?"

"The retired Marines started their company to make a profit, yes, but also to guard the American Dream. Protecting politicians served as their way of giving back. They were not naïve. Sure, they understood there were cracks in the system. However, when they worked for the politicians, patriarchs, and protectors of America, they witnessed the country's underbelly.

"The corruption troubled them. I'd bet they had drunken discussions dissing their crooked clients. Then, something pushed them from alcohol-induced conversation to deadly action. Loyola killed for our country before. A man of Loyola's background might make the leap in logic needed to justify the murders of Hall, Thomson, and Greene. Then Tigre took the helm.

"Tigre possessed a flair for the dramatic. I think he handpicked the venue for the deadly opening act. The Watergate Hotel, long ago the setting for the fall of Richard Nixon. Watergate introduced many Americans to political scandal. I'm positive Tigre wanted to show us things haven't changed. He jerked us back to the origins of our political discomfort."

"Why select Thompson and Greene?"

"Ongoing investigations state Thompson abused the system for decades. A good man when he arrived in Washington, a hero. He used his GI Bill to become an attorney, worked as a prosecutor, ran for Congress, then the Senate. Decades in Washington corrupted him. Thompson went to Washington with a thousand bucks in his pocket. He owned no businesses; his family possessed no trackable source of wealth. He served our country, worked briefly as a lawyer, then became a career politician. On a government salary, how did Thompson become a multimillionaire?" He waited for a response from the anchor. She remained silent.

"Explain to me how a man with zero business holdings, no investment portfolio when elected, and no family wealth, owned a palatial River Oaks home, held membership to three country clubs, and divorced a collection of extravagant wives. Tigre and Loyola selected Thompson because he represented the tintype of the Capitol's populace, a cesspool of career politicians whose votes follow their investor's direction."

The anchor added, "Your choice of words…intentional? You just said politicians have investors."

"Very intentional. I understand politicians have honest grassroot supporters, working the phones, putting out signs, and door knocking. These volunteers represent the best part of America.

"Still, successful political campaigns feature strong financial engines. I'm labeling the PACs and large individual donors what they really are—investors. These investors, or backers if my word makes you uncomfortable, invest in the politician's ability to change policy. Investing in Wall Street stocks can make millions of dollars for a trader. I'll argue, investing in politicians who change policy is a sounder investment. Policy changes divert the flow of millions, billions, and yes, sometimes *trillions* of dollars."

"That's cynical, Foxx."

"Cynical and true."

"We covered Thompson. Why did Loyola and Tigre choose Greene? Thompson's opposite, new to politics, liberal leanings, ran on environmental causes..."

"You answered your own question. Loyola and Tigre wanted us to witness how easily and early the system corrupted him. Also, they put every politician on notice."

"With that, we'll go to break. Stay with us for excerpts from the *Tapes of Wrath*. Additionally, Mr. Kauffman promised to unveil explosive new information next segment."

As commercials started, Tucker said, "Can we talk to Kauffman?"

Liu fought to hide frustration. "I tried, not our case. Angelo restated our job is to find the perpetrators of the deaths before Greene and Thompson. He narrowed our focus, resources, and personnel significantly."

"But what if these tapes address the early murders?"

"They don't," said Luther. "Or not the tapes I heard."

Liu wanted to interrogate Luther. He refused to answer her questions. "We have a simple task. Technically, we"—she made air parentheses—"*solved* the Thompson, Greene, and Hall murders. The Moss and Lackland murders, not our case; the execution of Moss' and Lackland's murderers, not our case. The attempt on Luther, not our case. The execution of Luther's shooter, not our case. Spot the pattern?"

"But can we...?" Tucker started.

"No, stay focused. We missed something. Loyola and Tigre are not the first chapter. I don't understand how or why the murders started. We'll find out. Us three, in this room, *we* will."

• • • •

Washington, DC

Foxx Kauffman smiled at his comely host. Her abilities proved equal to the industry buzz. Unfortunately, before the interview, she adeptly redirected his advances. Foxx laughed to himself. Maybe he lost his touch. More likely, the station's seasoned female reporters forewarned her.

He sipped the water delivered during the break. His host spoke first, "Great job so far. Remember, you promised a bombshell tonight."

Foxx thought *bombshell* an interesting word selection. The young anchor measured as a bombshell on any scale.

"I'm sure your coworkers discussed my ability to deliver."

The anchor glared at him. Foxx imagined her repeated and unwelcomed opportunities to thwart awkward and even practiced flirtations. "Foxx, I'm sure you're a nice man, check that, I'm not sure at all. You're a commitment-phobe and serial flirt. I'm engaged…"

"I don't see a ring."

"I don't wear it on air…"

"The network feels a ring reduces the number of male viewers."

"I didn't say that."

"Still, it's true." Foxx watched the producer start the countdown. He took another drink before he and his perfectly polished host turned to the camera.

"Foxx, you supplied an edited tape to us, overviewing what you covered so far. I think this is an appropriate time to play it. A note to our listeners: investigators confirmed this is Arturo Tigre's voice."

Foxx thought to himself. Few people realize how often they hear the voice of the dead—Janis Joplin or Buddy Holly for instance. The ruminations of dead haunt our radios daily, each with something powerful to share. Do listeners consider the ramifications?

Whether the words to a song or JFK's inauguration speech, each day, listeners experience the echoes of dead men. Each singer, politician, poet, or newswoman, whose voice or likeness someone recorded, obtained immortality, spited death.

Foxx wondered if Tigre and Loyola grasped their immortality. The slow churning of the tape preceded the vibrant voice of Arturo Tigre, his Latin lilt adding rhythm to his words:

"Hello, Foxx. I'm Arturo Tigre, here with my friend Leon Loyola."

"Hola," mumbled Loyola.

Tigre continued, *"We haven't met. Still, we know each other. You follow our work, and we enjoyed the humor you laced through your columns. We **were** fans. Sorry for the slip, the past tense, but if you received this tape, we're quite dead."*

Loyola's chuckle resonated in the background. *"More importantly, our government failed us again."*

An extended pause followed, the only sound, the chugging a recorder turning in rhythm. *"When we died, the investigator's first order of business would be to search our homes and business. They found dozens of tapes containing congressmen, judges, bureaucrats, executives, and PAC leaders breaking our laws. I witnessed the people charged with improving our country have no goals other than lining their pockets. They accepted bribes and dispensed favors."*

Again, the sound of the tape grinding in the recorder.

"We gave the government months to release the tapes or announce their existence. They buried the information, or you would not be hearing my voice now. Leaders had a chance to do the right thing; they failed. Possibly, someone destroyed the tapes. More likely, one agency possesses the tapes and uses them to leverage others. Imagine the blackmail potential, immeasurable. Have you considered that? I have."

Again, Arturo invoked drama, his pause as intentional as his dialogue.

"Our government at the highest level reviewed these tapes and did...nothing. I'll bet some people who knew about these tapes died already. Since we don't want people to die in the coverup, and because Leon and I have no desire for our tapes to be leveraged for political chicanery, Leon developed a little plan."

Pause.

"Foxx, this tape serves as our opening act."

Again, a long silence.

"This is the voice of Nebraska Senator Dick Crooks speaking to Agro-businessman Hoagie Black."

Foxx and the host listened as Hoagie Black committed to wire $50,000 into a Grand Cayman holding account for the senator's commitment to support a bill endorsing legislation to further cripple family farms. Yes, the senator and the businessman dance around wording. Still, there was no doubt Black offered Crooks dollars in exchange for a vote.

Tigre's voice returned, *"Don't worry, there's more to come, next week a federal Judge agrees to...oh, so sorry, you'll just have to wait. But before I go..."* The tape stopped.

The anchor took a deep breath. Foxx forced the network to play the tape for the first time on air, so the anchor's emotions mirrored her listeners. Every station wanted this footage. Other stations did not agree to his conditions, so Foxx waited until one did. The anchor addressed the camera. "More to come. When we return, Foxx promised one more revelation from Loyola and Tigre."

As the cameras cut away, the young anchor's eyes shot to Foxx. She said nothing, in shock from Arturo Tigre's words. Foxx watched a thousand questions form in her head. The entire break passed in silence. The young anchor rallied as the countdown ended.

"Foxx, for the last two days you've published portions of the tape's transcript, instead of reviewing the entire tape. Why?"

"Old-fashioned marketing. We give readers enough to whet their appetite, then hit them again, more readership, more content, more advertisers. You understand the game. As a reporter in Houston, you did the same."

"Yes, I did," she said. "You're here to promote tomorrow's edition, I presume, the big reveal?"

"Ex...actly. You get something, the only station playing the tape, I get increased readership, the American public gets the truth. Everyone wins..."

"Well, not quite everyone," the anchor steered the conversation. "When we announced your appearance today, attorneys for Senator Crooks and Mr. Black contacted us."

"Yes, we got the same calls," said Foxx.

"Their attorneys threatened us with lawsuit upon lawsuit."

"But our job remains reporting the news. I received the tape; I reported the news. Before I released the tape, I confirmed the voice on the tape belonged to Senator Crooks. He'll have no luck denying that fact. He has an awfully specific speech pattern. Also, he and Mr. Black call each other's name several times on the tape."

"Foxx, these tapes will never be admissible in a court of law."

"Correct. The recording's covert, the conversation's participants unknowing. The tape won't hold up in court; probably a judge rules it inadmissible. But the tape matters in the court of public opinion. Nebraska remains a family farm state; Crook will get voted out.

"The tape, while not admissible, paints a picture of corruption. A young DA targets Crooks' prosecution as a steppingstone to advance her career. Likely, someone turns on someone for a lighter sentence. Howe turned on Swindell and Steel. He leaves the minimum security country club prison he occupies in six months. Swindell and Steel will spend considerable time incarcerated."

Like a comedian that does not step on their laugh, the young anchor waited for Foxx to drive the point home.

The reporter pushed, "Now the moment we've waited for, your big reveal."

"It's not mine, it's Mr. Tigre's, so we'll let him speak for himself."

The grind of the recorder began again.

"Foxx, we've never met, but I liked you. I don't want your life endangered, or the lives anyone who listened to our tapes. Therefore, this is the only tape you'll receive. No need for the government to silence you, Foxx. Enjoy your star turn. From now on, you'll report the news, but you won't be the news."

Grinding tape served as background noise for the tension.

"Soon, more tapes drop into the hands of reporters. If that reporter stays silent, or someone silences them, the exact tape ships to another reporter. There are thousands of reporters; every tape gets out."

The tape played the powerful sound of silence…then.

"I know what you're thinking, there's a way to stop the tapes. There's not. Too many copies, too many systems, too many contingencies, too many reporters to stop us.

"Reporters, watch your mail. Uncles Arturo and Leon may send you a present. America, sit back, order a Coca-Cola, popcorn, and Twizzlers. Enjoy the show."

•　　•　　•

Arturo Tigre's words lingered. Samantha Book nudged closer to her husband in the darkened living room. She tucked her children into bed earlier. A seductive purple teddy, Pete's favorite, adorned her body. She knew the tenor of tonight's newscast. So, she dressed to take his mind off DC drama. Experience told her, despite her husband's concerns, he would hunger for her tonight, as he had from the moment he spotted her.

When first-term Congressman Pete Book arrived in DC, the Texan and former Marine effused confident appeal. He sat beside her today, more handsome and muscled than the day they met. Most men let themselves deteriorate with age. Pete remained militaristic about diet and workouts. He understood his appearance wrapped the package the voters bought. He implied without saying that her figure and their children's appearance reigned equally important. When she requested a personal trainer, Kyle Kenner hired one without question. When she asked for a chef to provide health-conscious family meals, Kyle Kenner interviewed several within days.

Before she met Pete, Samantha coordinated the gala to welcome new congressional representatives to the Capitol. Stunning women inhabited the room, many looking to become congressmen's wives or dalliances. Samantha remembered spotting Pete for the first time. He cut a swathe across the room, bumping representatives, PAC leaders, and Washington elite out of his way. She did not comprehend why but watched Pete clear a path toward her.

She remembered their conversation clearly.

"Let's dance," the young congressman said.

"I can't dance, I'm working the event."

"Let's go dancing after."

"Look…"

"Pete."

Then she recognized him. Incoming Congressman Pete Book. Samantha knew every sitting congressional representative; knowledge equaled power in her profession. To prepare for tonight, she studied pictures of the incoming representatives. She smiled, impressed he used his first name and not his new appellation.

"Congressman Book," she said, hoping he did not realize her failure to identify him at first glance.

"Pete's fine."

"Pete, like I said, I coordinate DC events, so I'm surrounded by senators, representatives, judges, executives. I watch them all, been hit on by most, sometimes within steps of their wives. So, maybe I'm tarnished, but I'm simply not interested in…"

"Married?"

"No."

"So, I have a chance?"

"I'm **explaining** why you don't," she answered exasperatingly.

"Boyfriend?"

"Not your business. Now, Pete, you passed dozens of beautiful women to get to me…"

"Did I?" he said, never breaking eye contact.

Two words, two words that weakened her knees, and foretold her impending marriage. She heard hundreds of lines from the country's foremost purveyors of bullshit. This was no line. Her heart softened like butter left on a kitchen counter.

She smiled. "You did…"

She did not agree to go dancing with him that night or the next several times he manufactured opportunities to see her. Still, she grasped the inevitable. In time, inevitable won.

When they made love, she knew no man ever desired her more. He ravaged her as if he craved her for years, releasing a lifetime of pent-up passion. How could she not fall for him?

After she admitted she loved him, and not before, he confessed, almost guiltily, his family swam in old-oil money. His father paid for the wedding, honeymoon, the whole shebang. She married Pete one year to the day after their meeting. They married in her small hometown, Pete's idea. They married weeks after his proposal, leaving little time for formal announcements. Everything happened so fast.

Pete told her she would meet his parents at the wedding. He kept everything close to the vest. She also did not meet his best man and chief of staff, Kyle Kenner, before her nuptials. When she questioned why she had not met his best friend or family, he quelled her concerns.

Despite short notice, her entire family attended the wedding, dozens traveled in from all over the country. Pete Book, the young congressman, had guests from DC, new congressional representatives like himself and DC veterans. Pete's political crew from Texas arrived in force. Only Pete's mother and father showed up from his family. Both departed the moment the ceremony ended. Her husband's only old friend in attendance was his best man, Kyle. His other groomsmen were DC's newest young elite.

She met Kyle and her future in-laws for the first time at the wedding rehearsal. Samantha readied in the backroom with her bridesmaids. The priest and wedding coordinator went over instructions with her, her bridesmaids, and her father moments before. The wedding coordinator remained as the priest took leave to counsel groomsmen, ushers, and family.

Samantha remembered being extremely nervous as her bridesmaids each left the room, taking position. Then Samantha and her father assumed their place. In moments, for some bizarre reason, she would see her fiancé's best friend and future in-laws for the first time.

As she walked down the aisle, Samantha spotted Pete's best man. Kyle Kenner looked like he recognized a ghost from a past life, his stare transfixed on her. His glance ripped to Pete, then volleyed to her.

As she walked down the aisle, she glanced to where Pete's parents sat. Pete's mother made no attempt to hide a confused look. His father looked on angrily. To this day, Samantha never received an explanation for their reactions.

Samantha seldom spent time with her in-laws. Pete's parents visited DC infrequently. When they did, Pete never invited them to stay over. Pete's parents showed no favor for Samantha and Pete's children. Her parents stepped up to fill the void, showering her children—their grandchildren—with gifts.

Born and raised a Virginia girl, she appreciated staying near home. Her husband owned a townhome in his old congressional district. Pete returned to Texas to manage his office and for political rallies. Yet, Pete seldom took her to Texas. He took the kids once a year to visit his parents. He encouraged her to take a girlfriend's trip or a Mommy vacation.

She wondered if he kept a Texas-based girlfriend, but his passion for her upon his return dashed her concerns. Years ago, she leaned about an art event he attended at Houston's Rice University. She begged to attend. She loved Wyeth Arrington and could not believe he was Pete's childhood friend. Each year, Pete offered another reason he needed to attend alone, with only Kyle in tow.

He returned for her passionately each time he traveled. However, when he returned from that event specifically, she learned she needed to prepare for repeated romps.

The specificity of his manic machismo disquieted her. Samantha banished her fears with comments other wives shared with her.

"I wish my husband looked at me the way Pete looks at you," said a senator's wife.

"He looks like he wants to take you into a closet and pole you right now," said a judge's much younger girlfriend. She considered the woman's suggestion and led Pete to a closet moments later.

"He always looks like he's searching for a place to hump you," said her sister at their family's Christmas party, not knowing Pete had just mounted her in their parent's bathroom moments earlier.

Pete Book proved to be a good husband and father. Yes, he harbored secrets, so did she. She chose not to begrudge him his.

She rubbed her husband's knee, softening him for the question she must ask, the question every congressperson's spouse must ask after what they just witnessed.

"I remember meeting Crooks at an event."

"Yes," he said.

"How well did you know him?"

"Not well."

"So, a lot of your friends…they're in trouble?"

"Probably."

Then the question circulating DC living rooms: "Do we have anything to worry about? Is there a tape with your name on it?"

"No."

She understood that answer circulated most DC homes, and like others, she hoped the answer true. Heartened by his lack of justification, Samantha considered the power of his singular word. She believed her husband, but even if he was lying, she remained all in, one way or another. She rubbed his knee again and stood.

"Then you deserve a reward."

Her teddy hit the ground and Pete Book redeemed his reward, there in the living room, in front of the political talking heads on TV. Later, when Pete slept and she kissed her children again, Samantha Book considered the oncoming storm. She tried to remember the last time a hurricane hit DC wondering if her family occupied safe harbor or if anyone did.

• • •

September 4, 1994

About 18 months passed since Loyola and Tigre rocketed into America's conscience. This morning, Foxx reread the *Atlanta Journal Constitution* story about Georgia's stalwart Senator, I.M. "Rob" Robbin. The latest subject of the *Tapes of Wrath* resigned. A New Jersey casino owner forgave the senator's gambling debt for a commitment to filibuster a new gaming tax. Engrossed in the article, Foxx found himself pulled back into reality by a timid knock on his door. "Someone left this package with the night watchman for you." Belle, from the mailroom, offered a box. Foxx signed for it, recognizing the contents immediately. He shook the small rectangular box to confirm.

He waited for Belle to leave, then ripped open the box. A dozen tapes fell onto his desk. Then he spotted the greeting he prayed to see again one day:

HEY FOXX

"

———

ENJOY THE BOXX

The contents assuredly were the motherlode. Of course, Tigre, in death, boldly delivered the box here, to Foxx's newspaper's front door, executing the mother of misdirection.

Someone mailed the previous *Tapes of Wrath* indirectly to reporters. Tapes showed up at a reporter's brother's home, neighbor's mailboxes, secretaries' apartments, and, once, a reporter's kids' dormitory. All marked to the reporter. Unlike Foxx's delivery, each of the mailed envelopes looked normal on the exterior, but once opened contained a second envelope with the greeting:

HEY THERE (various reporters' names)

"
___

And of course, a tape.

Loyola and Tigre, in death, stayed truer to their word than the plethora of politicians they dethroned. Every two to three weeks a new tape appeared. The timing, delivery method, and geography of the tape's delivery proved inconsistent, thwarting the chances government intervention.

The two former Marines served as the security team to the elite for years and enjoyed unusual access to Washington's ruling class. Foxx bet they collected a slew of material. Unlike Foxx's first tape, most arrived regular mail, postmarked from various locations. Foxx destroyed the envelope containing his tape to protect his mother.

Law enforcement confiscated each inner and outer envelope sent to reporters. The smarter reporters took photos of the envelopes before confiscation. Yesterday, a young reporter, who wanted a piece of the action, assembled photos of the surviving envelopes and posted them for comparison.

No two outer envelopes looked the same. Some addresses were typed, others hand-addressed. No two letters appeared to originate from the same typewriter. Of the hand-addressed envelopes, no two bore similar handwriting. Someone addressed one in extravagant cursive. Other handwriting varied from chicken scratch to block print. One envelope mimicked the handwriting of a 90-year-old with Parkinson's, another a child's work. The envelopes changed in size and color. Because the tapes' delivery funneled through family members, the timing proved wonky. Foxx assumed damning tapes sat in some reporter's Aunt Mabel's infrequently checked PO Box. Never once, before today, did a reporter receive a second tape.

Tapes filtered to newspaper columnists, television reporters, and even anchors. One tape landed in the hands of a Seattle rock DJ, another shipped to a New York shock jock. Recent tapes arrived in the hands of a British tabloid reporter and a glossy East Coast fashion magazine editor.

Tapes arrived in Washington State, California, New York, London, Tallahassee, El Paso, New Orleans, Michigan, and the list rolled on. The unknown mailer or mailers seemed determined each tape got through. Foxx assumed authorities stopped a few.

On each tape, Tigre made an introduction of the tape's participants. Then, a politician, judge, businessperson, or executive, sold out America in an assortment of sordid ways. Tapes arrived in inconsistent intervals but far enough apart, so the misdeeds received the focus of America's media. Corrupt political elite members got their unwelcome star turn.

Tapes arrived postmarked from towns and cities around the country. The funniest postmark originated from Post, Texas, a small town outside of Lubbock. Foxx assumed Tigre, a purveyor of the dramatic, found himself unable to ignore the irony.

After the fourth tape, Tigre said, regrettably, that the tape was their last. As a DC resident, Foxx felt the entire city enjoy a gigantic sigh of relief. Weeks later another tape appeared featuring a laughing Arturo Tigre. The dead man claimed he perpetrated a false promise, like the promises our politicians broke to the American people daily.

Three tapes later, Tigre again bemoaned the shipment of the last tape. Another recording arrived a week later. Tigre asked the politicians if they enjoyed another broken promise. The political soap opera continued. Loyola and Tigre were reborn with each tape, energized by the dying career of another politician.

Judges ruled the tapes inadmissible in court. Foxx laughed; of course, corrupt judges protected crooked politicians. To be fair, Foxx understood in most legal settings, even an honest judge rules the tapes inadmissible. The tapes' inadmissibility failed to alter their veracity.

Upon each tape's release, public pressure dictated investigations. Ambitious DAs stepped forward, happily prosecuting the case. The press, in each politician's district, attacked, running lead stories with legs. After the first tape, reporters prayed for a recording to fall into their hands.

Tapes featured a minimum of two speakers breaking the law. Many recordings featured three participants. One tape featured seven congressional representatives and two PAC leaders.

The new tape's on-air release became appointment-viewing for the nation. Updates on the soiled politicians set daytime rating records for the networks. A noted poet described the situation. "I awake discovering an interminable battle with disease ending, not terminally, with the oft-predicted death of our country, but with the promise of a cure and an enlivened republic."

To date, 16 business executives resigned; indictments ensued. Four federal judges faced investigations: two resigned. One Supreme Court Justice compromised himself but avoided indictment. Seventeen PACs fired board members. To date, tapes featured 21 House of Representatives members. One killed himself, three resigned, several faced indictments. Law enforcement promised more to come.

Five additional senators stepped into the darkness, with two resignations to date. Tapes implicated another governor. Tigre and Loyola recorded the mayors of Boston, Chicago, Philadelphia, and Baltimore at a convention. All four still occupied their positions, but investigations loomed.

If politicians survived the investigations, most would not win reelection. Some may survive, crippled politically, yet, like cockroaches, enduring. Already, many corrupt public servants faced replacement. Shiny new public servants stepped forward, men and women whose moral fortitude remained unknown and untested, unlike the long-dimmed lights of their predecessors.

The military trained Loyola well; high-profile clients paid for his protection. Tigre, the master of high-tech recording equipment, served by Loyola's side. The two often wore wires. Tigre showed creativity, placing miniature microphones under dining tables, inside kitchen equipment, and laced through wicker patio furniture. He recorded the very people who paid for his protection. Foxx assumed that before Thompson's, Greene's, and Hall's assassinations exposed Tigre's audio skill, the former Marine placed equipment in the restaurants and hotel boardrooms of political power brokers.

People asked why Loyola and Tigre selected Thompson and Greene. Foxx validated his guess via research. Neither Thompson nor Greene used Loyola and Tigre's company for security.

Therefore, the senators failed to recognize their assassins. Foxx supposed Loyola and Tigre found out via their recordings about Greene's rocky financial position and Thompson's rampant corruption.

John "The Heater" Hall probably mentioned his meeting at Le Donphant with Congressman Cash. Tigre likely taped The Heater bragging about his upcoming meeting.

A revelation overtook Foxx. Loyola and Tigre sat on these tapes, some over a decade. They knew the rampant nature of the corruption. Yet they could do nothing. Many conversations captured on the tapes led back to Loyola's and Tigre's client base.

If caught, prosecution awaited the retired Marines. Foxx assumed DC power brokers would ensure the two friends died in their cells. Ironically, while living, the release of a tape crippled Loyola's and Tigre's ability to record the next corrupt oligarch.

Foxx grasped the conundrum. By killing Loyola and Tigre, Tucker liberated them. The two old friends freed in death, as they had not been in life, to affect change. Foxx wondered if one, or either, laughed while dying.

When they killed The Heater, they must have known they disclosed the modality of collection, as authorities found no other recording devices in restaurants, hotels, or politicians' homes. Tigre probably decided the risk increased dramatically.

So, if they could not collect information from restaurants and hotels, if they could never release their client tapes, and if Washington remained on high alert, the two would be pushed to take bolder risks to expose politicians. The Southern Governors Conference, for instance. Tigre's need to top his last act proved fatally intoxicating.

How long must the two have planned their deaths, knowing the inevitability? Why did they move from Loyola's world of violence, executing the guilty, to Tigre's world of technology, exposing the guilty?

Foxx prayed the answers lay in the tapes in front of him.

• • •

September 6, 1994
Erasmus Luther bolted up in bed, covered in light sweat, wide awake now from his brief but troubled sleep. He first thought, a

nightmare ripped him from his slumber. Then the rapping repeated, loud, familiar. He looked to the bedside clock: 1:07 a.m.

Why did Liu or Tucker not quell the disturbance? Since the shooting, the two acted as constant companions, guardians. His human *crutches*, he admitted. A strange addiction formed, he felt comforted with them present and struggled with anxiety when responsibilities pulled them away.

Weeks ago, the three agreed the danger dissipated. Months passed since the attempt upon his life, and no further attempts followed. Despite Tucker's and Liu's efforts, Luther remained unprotected at times, usually when on campus. He sat trapped in his thoughts. The rhythm of the knock assaulted his ears again, nonstandard, haunting, with the nonsensical rhythm of a child.

Still, his thoughts prevailed. Someone dispersed the tapes, or better stated, the political atom bomb throughout the public consciousness. Maybe Luther presented less of a threat to whoever dictated his execution. Likely, the person who ordered Luther's death now faced more daunting threats. Luther's roommates would not answer the door, of course, because they moved out. Despite universal admiration for Harrison Ford's whip-toting, adventure-seeking, history professor, *Indiana Jones*, Luther's history-teaching roommates proved averse to gunshots or FBI agents sleeping on their couch. Luther's former roommates moved out within days of returning from their conference to gunshot holes and glass repair.

Now, Luther found himself alone, isolated. He wrote unanswered letters to Allie. He still struggled with her sudden turn. Luther knew Allie's newfound aversion to him revolved around his oldest friend, Foxx Kauffman. She dominated his thoughts. Liu forbade his attendance at the 1993 Arrington AIDS Art Gala. In retrospect, Luther admitted he acted like a three-year-old brat when told he could not attend, stressing he was an adult.

Liu joked adults do not pontificate about adulthood; they do the right thing. To pacify Luther, Tucker attended in the professor's stead with a note from Luther for Allie. Unfortunately, only Gertrude attended, apologizing to gentlemen who attended just for a chance to dance with Allie. Gertrude offered no explanation for her daughter's absence. Tucker secured a dance with Gertrude and placed the note in her hand.

"Is this from the awkwardly handsome history professor?" asked Gertrude.

Tucker confirmed.

After the gala, Tucker consoled Luther. "I don't know Allie well. I danced with her once and then her mother tonight. I get your fascination. There's something regal about those women, the way they stand, dress, talk. They're intoxicating."

Luther, in a rare moment of jocularity since the shootings, ribbed. "You have your crush, stay away from mine." Luther noted when anyone referred to Tucker's obvious infatuation with Liu, Tucker joked, diverted, or ignored the subject. Tucker chose the latter.

Despite the lack of news coverage, and despite Liu and Tucker ordering the professor's former roommates to stay silent about the shooting, news spread. The campus proved incongruent with secret-keeping.

News of an attempt on a teacher's life circulated within twenty-four hours, confirmation the attempt targeted Luther outed hours later. Soon intellectually curious students deducted FBI agents followed Luther, and the buzz grew tenfold. Next, someone divined that the agents who followed Luther also "solved" the Thomson and Greene murders, and a gossip hissy fit took launch. The next leap in logic occurred:

1) Luther wrote about assassinations;
2) the FBI agents who stopped the assassination protected Luther;
3) therefore, Luther aided in stopping the assassination.

On campus, excitement grew from overwhelming to crushing. The release of each Tigre-narrated tape led to rabid questioning from Luther's associates, acquaintances, and students.

Students and teachers discussed Luther, Tucker, and Liu sightings. The school faced a conundrum. Administrators wished to support Luther's mental health and encouraged time away. However, school leadership failed to resist the story's pull.

Luther declined time off, pushing himself into his work and the responsibilities of the Politikill case. The attempt on his life rocketed his demand. Luther's classes filled within moments of availability; the university pushed him to teach extra classes. He refused. Luther became the most requested guest at university donor events. He attended occasional functions when Liu and Tucker could cover him, welcoming any distraction. His lack of availability increased demand.

At events, organizers and large donors pushed him to a corner pressing him to recount his last few years. His consistent refusal to do so increased the onslaught.

A groundswell of sales of Luther's books occurred around campus, then spread to a lesser degree around the city. Alumni who shared the university's fascination with Luther fueled sales. Luther enjoyed the increased royalties, if not the notoriety.

The strangest but oddly predictable trend ensued. Despite Luther's haggard appearance, his demand with the fairer, smarter gender increased. Women who never noticed him now battled for moments of his time. This proved convenient, as Luther craved companionship.

No one cared to talk to him about history anymore, except very recent history, which he remained duty bound not to discuss. He crafted systems to avoid questions. He discovered the less he discussed himself, the more the gravitational appeal he possessed.

Ironically, Luther, without intention, upped his flirting game, never his strong suit. He now asked detailed questions about his companions, adding to his popularity. He enjoyed any distraction from the gnawing fear that served as his constant consort.

He ached for Allie but abandoned hope of reconciliation. Occasionally, he surrendered to newfound temptations. Luther allowed long associated but never interested female colleagues to take advantage of him. Fetching junior professors, gorgeous doctoral candidates, a campus administrator, and one comely cafeteria worker fulfilled his prurient needs, sometimes while Liu or Tucker slept on his couch.

Liu watched disapprovingly as he hurried out the latest assuager. She voiced her concern but admitted there were less healthy ways to deal with his recent grasp of mortality. Everyone handled near-death differently, and she chose not to bemoan Luther his methods. Tucker never commented.

The knock again. Now awake, Luther, riddled with fear, internally begged the intruder to leave. Then he recognized the knocks' rhythm, the reason he associated the rapping with childhood. The knock belonged to him, his childhood knock, when he visited Ima Kauffman's house, his and Foxx Kauffman's secret knock.

He leapt from bed and scurried to his door. Luther peeked through the peephole to confirm Foxx, alive and well, occupied his front stoop. As the door opened, Foxx jabbed, "You look like the Devil took a dump down your throat."

"Thanks." Luther paused. "Good to see you, old friend."

"Raz, looks like you need a friend."

Luther hugged him, feeling stress melt from his body, as he had not since his night with Allie. The professor decided not to take that comparison any further. Still, seeing Foxx was a godsend...or was it?

"Wait...why are you here?" asked Luther, bracing for the answer.

"To repay a favor, from when you knocked on my door late one night." Foxx smiled. "Now I'm making a late-night delivery."

"How 'bout if I don't want the favor repaid, not at all?"

"Little late for that, I'm afraid."

"Look, I'm not working for the FBI anymore," blurted Luther, before realizing he spoke to not only his best friend and but also a famous reporter.

Foxx dramatically mimicked shock. Then chuckled. "Raz, I know the FBI pays you. I didn't have to be a reporter to catch that. You never said so, but being friends with Tucker and Liu showed your FBI baby bump, don't ya think?"

Luther pondered, then relented. "Tucker and Liu solved the Thompson and Greene case. I'm off the case. The FBI doesn't need my support for the old stuff."

"Old stuff?"

Luther continued. "Remember, we talked in Austin, the pre-Watergate stuff?"

"Sure, that's why I'm here."

An icy shiver whiplashed through Erasmus, knowing any security he felt was about to dissipate. "Look, let's walk."

"Walk?"

Luther nodded toward his door. "Walk," he confirmed.

Houston weather features unforgiving days, sweltering heat, and sauna-esque humidity. Evenings feature softly breezed warmth, a welcome intoxicant for Houston residents. Luther hurried Foxx out the front door into the tree-lined beauty of Rice University's campus. Once distanced from his home, he began. "Tucker checks my home every week to ensure it's bug free."

"Bugs...?"

"Long story."

"You trust Tucker?"

"I trust him and Liu; they saved my life."

"What?"

"Am I talking to a reporter or my best friend?"

"We both keep secrets or I wouldn't enjoy much of a career. You keep someone's secrets to get someone else's secrets, that's how it works."

"I can't give you much."

"Okay," Foxx said. He spotted fear in Erasmus' haggard eyes.

"When Loyola and Tigre died, two people listened to a collection of their tapes. Someone selected me as one of the two. The other guy, Lackland, was best friends with Deputy Director Moss. FBI brass, including Moss, assumed Loyola and Tigre didn't leave much to glean, a coupl'a tapes possibly. Moss was wrong; he paid a heavy cost, he and Lackland are dead now."

"I know," Foxx stated, "I tried to cover that case."

"Tried?"

"I didn't know about the tapes yet. I assumed a connection to Loyola and Tigre but got nowhere. Lots of dead ends."

"I bet." Luther deliberated going further, before choosing the WTF protocol. "So, I'm a history professor."

"I've heard."

"Moss, despite being a hardened FBI veteran, naively assumed the government would release the evidence. Zero-point-zero chance of that happening. Before Moss' and Lackland's executions, I bet the tapes would get squelched."

"By the government, at least," added Foxx.

"Exactly. The government couldn't predict Arturo Tigre's counterattack from the grave. So, before the tapes matriculated into America's psyche, the information in my brain labeled me a dead man."

Foxx asked, "You know what's on the tapes? Guess I didn't need to fly to Houston."

"I only listened to about a third. Lackland transcribed better, he got through more tapes."

"Oh, so anyhow, back to Liu and Tucker saving your life."

"Okay, I was on a date with...wait."

"Yes?"

"Have you slept with a beautiful tall blond?"

"You bet," said Foxx, sporting a wry smile.

"I'll be more specific."

"Smart."

"Have you slept with a gorgeous blond from Texas, elf-like haircut, from a tiny town called Silsbee? Girl loves horses?"

"Don't think so. I don't get here often, and Texas doesn't travel to me," he said. "What's her name?"

"Allie."

Foxx answered with raised eyebrows.

A perturbed Luther added, "Allie Arrington."

"No, I haven't."

"Anyway, I was on a date with Allie. It started well…"

"Mmm…huh," said Foxx.

"Stop it, that part of the story will not be included."

"Don't skip over my favorite parts."

"Sorry, the date started well, then I mentioned your name and her attitude changed. The date ended in seconds, *seconds*."

"That sucks, maybe she hates the news. I don't know. If you're this caught up on her, I'd remember her."

"In vivid detail."

"Not over her, huh?"

"Not the girl you get over. She's the girl you write poems about, the reason artists learn to paint, why sculptors perfect the human form, the reason playwrights exist."

"Okay, delightful distraction, but back to Tucker and Liu saving your life."

Erasmus recounted the night of the shooting as Foxx listened intently. "Why didn't I know about this?" asked Foxx.

"Not a lot of coverage; the story got buried."

"Why didn't you call me?"

"Liu, Tucker, and I discussed it, but we were not allowed to tell anyone."

"Why now?"

Luther shrugged.

"I'm sorry you went through that without me, Raz." Foxx paused, stuck in thought. "So, the guy who tried to kill you ended up dead later that night? Same night Lackland, Moss, and their shooters died?"

"If you were playing a board game, It'd be *BINGO*."

"Wow, you're connected to this mess?"

"Yes. But releasing the tapes saved my life, for now. Each time a dirty politician's exposed, one less person trying to kill me."

"Have the networks aired the tapes you've heard?" asked Foxx.

"Most, not all."

"They're about to, I got a box of all the tapes. Someone shipped them to me in case a few didn't get through."

"Those tapes paint a target on your back."

"They don't. I put copies in my editor's hands. The paper has 'em. Copies sit at the TV station I freelance for sometimes. Several news radio buddies hold copies. No way to stop the tapes' release. My editor organized a release schedule."

"You've listened to them?"

"Every one," replied Foxx.

"So, you know everything?"

"I've waited a lifetime for you to admit that."

"Not what I meant. The tapes, they're in the press' hands now?"

"Well, not all." Foxx reached into his jacket and pulled out a cassette. "Not yet."

• • •

Across Town

Tucker stood at the front door, exposed, endangered. This bust belonged to another agency, not remotely an FBI case. Natalie Liu squatted under the open window, as Tucker motioned for her to stay put. Dime-store curtains flapped in rhythm to a box fan. In her time here, Liu learned box fans were a Texas staple. She and Tucker arrived first. They did not show up with sirens blaring, like most Thursday night cop dramas. The two parked down the street, muffling every move on their path to the perp's house.

The sound of bullfrogs and crickets interlaced with their perp's incoherent screams. A crying, begging woman joined the disturbing domestic refrain. Liu tried to fathom how she landed here, squatting beneath a window, once again in harm's way.

"Why are we here?" Tucker asked on approach.

"You know why."

Someone above Liu's pay grade intentionally dismantled her team. Her DC-based administrator, Nancy, resigned. Liu's attempts to contact her proved fruitless. Nancy returned to her childhood home in the Tennessee mountains and disappeared. Liu hated that

Nancy seemed unreachable but comprehended her cranky but wise former assistant's motivations. Nancy came from the orneriest of mountain clans. Liu, who at this moment, wished for a mountain hideaway, hoped Nancy found safety under her clan's protection.

Liu's new boss disassembled her California team. Now, only she and Tucker remained from the Houston team, their local aide shipped to an oversees assignment. Her new boss, Carmen Angelo, informed her that the funding used to pay Erasmus Luther dried up. Additionally, Luther's FBI contractor status was under review. Her boss ordered her to share no further information with the professor.

She assumed the only reason she and Tucker remained together was to be paraded in harm's way together, even targeted together. Liu comprehended her and Tucker's best chance for survival existed by each other's side. Tucker never complained, never questioned, remained vigilant about staying in proximity.

Natalie Liu, last year's fastest rising FBI agent, found herself free-falling from favor and marooned in Houston. She just became a Houston resident, transferred here against her wishes. Liu still reported to Carmen Angelo, so he could monitor her. She and Tucker found themselves lent out to other agencies, mostly Angelo's running buddy in the ATF, Lyle Fiddler. Tucker and Liu supported the Bureau of Alcohol, Tobacco, Firearms, and Explosives, when needed for backup or added force, which is why they arrived here today.

She and Tucker found themselves lent to operations where someone mopped up blood afterward. The FBI recruited Liu for her IQ and problem solving. Now she served as a storm trooper, hired gun, deep in the meat grinder of other agencies' agendas. The sound of bullets clinking off Tucker's government-issue sedan became a too-familiar sound.

Tonight, Liu and Tucker arrived first because Fiddler called them first, even though they were not the closest team. If Fiddler's pattern remained consistent, support was not imminent. Help usually pulled up after she and Tucker settled the situation.

Tonight, from what Liu gathered, they needed to collar a minor league ATF target. Hick O'Connell, a small-time gun trader, junkie, and drug dealer, lived here for months with his girlfriend and her kids. ATF knew about Hick and had him under round-the-clock surveillance. They used Hick as feeder bait to find trophy fish.

On the drive over, Tucker called in favors with the locals. Apparently, ATF softened their surveillance, now following Hick in intervals. ATF agents suspected O'Connell made them. He seemed twitchier than normal, like a water balloon stretched to its limits, ready to burst. Tonight, when a neighbor reported gunshots, the locals called Fiddler. Fiddler phoned Liu.

Liu considered herself a below average Bible student. However, lately, she identified with Uriah the Hittite, ordered by King David into the mouth of battle. Then David demanded all allies abandon Uriah.

Like Uriah, Liu felt deserted.

If she died today, her death would not hide a king's sins. Blundering bureaucrats or political despot plotted against her to unfetter themselves from collected misdeeds. She considered resigning but running from this problem presented poor survival planning. Tucker of course remained.

Liu and Tucker never shared their concerns with Luther. The professor remained shaken enough. Somehow protecting Luther distracted her and Tucker from their internal concerns. Luther assisted Liu, when possible, but he faced increased pressure from Rice as well. To complicate matters, Angelo dropped four additional Houston area cases on them.

Thankfully, the dark power behind the attempt on Luther's life took a body blow with each *Tape of Wrath* release. Every politician exposed weakened the collective evil host.

When Tucker killed Loyola and Tigre, the aftermath blew up in authorities' faces. The *Tapes of Wrath* were birthed. The tapes' appearance caused drastic change in some unnamed authority's priorities.

Now, some evil arbiter seemed afraid the public capture of the pre-Watergate murderers may lead to more tapes, secrets, and uncontrolled exposure. Liu convinced herself an off-the-book hit team hunted for the perpetrators of the earlier murderers.

The Special Agent in Charge found herself delayed at every turn. Liu's new boss buried her under inconsequential cases, non-agency priorities, and oft-requested paperwork. Internally, Liu's only goal remained finding the Adam, the author of this graphic novel. If she survived another night, she just might succeed. Liu forced her thoughts back to this deadly moment.

She nodded, then Tucker stepped to the door's side before knocking. "I am sorry to disturb you friendly folks tonight. No big deal. Someone reported a disturbance. I'm just checking to make sure everyone is okay."

The familiar and terrifying sound of a readying shotgun provided the resident's only response. The cheap front door's center exploded into sawdust and shards.

"Get back, get back 'fore I kill another one."

Another one, thought Liu in horror.

Tucker motioned, demanding she remain in place. Then he zigzagged across the yard. Liu remained in the best position to end whatever nightmare unfolded behind the shotgun shell-shattered door. By exposing himself, her partner accepted his role—bait. Tucker dove behind an abandoned truck as another shotgun blast peppered the vehicle.

Liu spent tense seconds praying for her partner's life.

Then, glass shards showered Liu. Hick threw a small lifeless body into the yard. The window above her had been open, but the small dead body Hick used as a projectile shattered the rotting frame. Liu sat frozen, staring at the child's lifeless eyes, nothing more than black marbles now. Liu felt the roots of horror set, embracing the fertile ground of dreams, promising the dead girl's repeated nocturnal appearance.

This beautiful little girl would never ride ponies, enjoy a first date, share a kiss. Liu fought every emotion as the stain expanded on the girl's blood-soaked unicorn pajamas. She struggled to stay professional. Emotion gets you killed.

Screaming from inside the hellish home taunted her. Liu wanted the shot, but first glanced at the truck serving as her partner's cover. Emotions hurdled through her body when Tucker's voice addressed the author of their circumstance. "Hey, Hick, we're only here because a neighbor called us," Tucker lied.

Another brush with bullets, another chance to lose him. Even in the middle of mayhem, Liu found herself forced to picture life without him...again. And again, she forced her emotions in check, and beseeched Special Agent in Charge Liu, to snatch the baton from the smitten Natalie Liu who had no place in this melee.

Liu watched as her partner repositioned himself to communicate with her and view the lifeless body in the yard. Liu needed no translator to interpret Tucker's emotions as he studied the small, beautiful, dead child laying between them.

Tucker motioned for her to stay down, then again engaged the freshly minted murderer. "Hick, I'm sure the child's death was an accident."

Liu again appreciated her partner's calm under fire. Their recent mop-up assignments provided abundant chances for practice.

Liu listened intently by the window. The man's voice sounded close, but so did sniffles, mumbles, and cries. Liu disseminated one adult female occupied the home, probably two children, maybe more. She needed Hick's voice as her compass, so she wanted the killer to keep talking. Liu's greatest asset: Hick did not know she existed.

She motioned for Tucker to continue the conversation. Hick flew without a plane tonight, agitated and tripping hard.

Tucker nodded. "Hick, buddy. Can I help you in there? Ya' need food?"

"If I needed food, I'd call Dominoes, dipshit," shouted Hick.

Liu assessed Hick stood too close to the others. She received no indication of help's imminent arrival. Once again, the solution fell to her ... and Tucker.

"What can I do then? I heard kids inside. Need something for the kids."

"You a babysitter? You didn't look like one when your scared ass dove behind the truck."

"I have an allergic reaction to buckshot up my butt," said Tucker. "Anyway, what can I get you? Need a car?"

Nothing.

Tucker continued. "I'll get a car if you release these nice people. A fast one. Mustang maybe?"

"Sure...yeah ... a car. I'll take a hostage with me, so you don't get ideas."

"Sounds great; not the hostage part, but the car."

"You don't make the rules. I do. Unless you want another dead body on the lawn. Get me a car."

"I got a better idea. I'm the only one here, so take my car, no one can follow you. Here's the plan: I toss you my keys, you leave the hostages, even-Steven."

Liu waited. Hick considered Tucker's solution, as much as a laced junkie considers anything. "So, you'll just toss me your keys?"

"Yep, do we have a deal?"

"Yea, I think…"

Just then, the wail of sirens shattered Tucker's plan. Two police cruisers squealed onto the street. Liu glared at Tucker, cursing under her breath.

"You lied, you said you're the only one here," blurted Hick.

"I wasn't lying…" But no one, even Liu, understood Tucker over the sirens. Tucker took control of the situation, waving down the officers bounding out of their cruisers.

Liu's inner antenna pinged. Hick was in no condition for this pressure, he would blow. Liu's senses keyed on a screaming woman. "No, Hick, no, no…" A vicious slap followed by the distinct sound of the woman's body hitting the floor.

Liu did the math: only kids left standing…and Hick. The kids sounded young, only four or five, and the only adult now upright in the house held a shotgun. *Aim high, aim high, aim high.*

"I'm sending out another dead body, asshole."

In one fluid motion, Liu stood, swept back the curtains from the shattered window, spotted Hick, based on his voice's last location, and pumped three quick chest-high rounds.

Tucker bull-rushed. Her partner crashed through the door, finishing the job the shotgun started. Tucker rolled, then flipped to his feet, gun drawn. He stood over Hick's dead body. Officers entered behind him. Relief washed over Liu as Tucker bent over and collected the two little girls. An officer checked the battered mother.

Tucker walked outside and handed the two girls to another officer, a recent arrival on scene. He walked to Liu. "Great, plenty of backup now."

Liu let her back slide against the house. Gravity propelled her butt groundward. Tucker collapsed, joining her. "How much longer?" asked Tucker.

"Until we run out of luck. Or until whoever busted our asses down to shit detail runs out of luck. Hopefully, they end up on a tape soon or dead."

"That'd be great."

"Tucker, you can resign. Start your life in politics, there're openings popping up every week…"

Despite the adrenaline pulsing through him, Tucker laughed. They sat together, ignored by the ATF team and HPD officers now onsite.

"Tucker, what do you want?"

"Natalie," he said, dropping formality. "I know what I want, I have from the moment I saw you." He looked at her hungrily, as he always had. Liu admitted, she hoped he always would.

"If I'm going to die soon, I'm going out with a bang."

"I've waited a long time."

"You've been patient."

"Natalie."

"What?"

"It's gonna be more than one bang."

•   •   •

The Next Day

Foxx departed; dumpster fire delivered into Erasmus' hands. Luther refused to let Foxx overview the tape. He lied to Foxx, "Best for me to hear it myself." Luther dialed Tucker and Liu a dozen times.

His calls remained unanswered. Their duties no longer dictated they return his calls. They stayed friends; he drank with them often. Luther hoped they would always be friends. Tucker and Liu now seemed pulled in dozens of directions. Luther's status remained under review as an FBI and CIA contractor.

The press deemed the Politikill case solved. No reporter explained how Loyola and Tigre committed the crimes previous to the Watergate executions. The press failed to let facts interfere with a well-packaged story. Luther theorized someone needed an expedient ending to the drama. Laying all blame at the feet of Loyola and Tigre fit the bill.

Luther traversed campus again, waiting for the return call. He started calling Liu last night. Luther checked his watch, almost 3 p.m. A nagging concern for his friend's safety winnowed into his troubled soul.

No chance he listened to Foxx's tape alone. Luther refused to occupy the role of lone carrier of national secrets again. He barely survived last time. The professor maintained his sanity, admitting to his psyche's tattered edges.

Luther reveled in the university's tree-lined streets. He enjoyed everything more now. His failed assassin showed Luther's life's fragile nature. Until recently, he pictured himself dying fat, long tenured, liver-spotted with age, coffee at his side, studying ancient history text in a Chesterfield chair. Now his life mirrored James Dean. Live hard, leave a good-looking corpse. Luther thought, in his case a haggard, moderately attractive corpse.

He turned toward home, hoping for a message from Liu. She seldom left him waiting long. Luther fumed. *Whatever occupied them better be damn important.*

Luther meandered home, relieved to spot Tucker's car in his driveway. Luther long ago entrusted Tucker and Liu with keys to his home. He opened the front door but did not see them. A ragged rhythmic bumping originated from the guest bathroom.

"Tucker, Liu," Luther called. The banging stopped.

"Be right there…needed Liu's help…looking at a bruise on…my shoulder," Tucker said unconvincingly.

Luther examined his home. The decor remained neat and clean, but misplaced items caught the professor's attention. An apple lay on the wood floor, the convicting fruit rolled several feet from the table and fruit bowl. Someone shoved his recliner against the south wall. The crocheted throw that laid across the couch occupied the floor.

"Hey, I'm a doctor. I'll look at the bruise," said Luther.

"You're a doctor of history," replied Liu.

"You're an FBI agent, I feel equally qualified," answered Luther, happy for his friends. He wondered when the duo's chemistry would explode. Luther just did not predict the eruption would redecorate his home. Luther leaned toward professorial decorum.

Liu and Tucker emerged from the bathroom. Both appeared more relaxed than Luther remembered.

"I've tried to get in touch with you for hours."

"Sorry," said Tucker.

"Tough day yesterday," Liu muttered. Luther watched as the weight of the world seemed to crush her. "A girl, beautiful girl, was murdered. We were there…"

"Liu took out the killer. We needed to…decompress," added Tucker. "That's why we haven't been in touch." Tucker inspected his shoes.

Liu disengaged from the conversation and started brewing coffee.

"You called a dozen times. Why d'you need us so badly?" asked Liu, back turned to her companions.

The professor inspected Tucker. The agent's face communicated no emotion. Luther knew Tucker ached for Liu. Still, the agent would never sell out his partner, even when evidence pointed to multiple indiscretions in Luther's home. Luther looked to the couch, Tucker followed his gaze, then to the kitchen. Luther raised an eyebrow. Tucker should play poker for a living. His face admitted nothing.

For the first time since he arrived home, Luther's thoughts returned to the tape. He enjoyed the mental break Tucker and Liu's indiscretion offered. But the time arrived to reintroduce worry to its regularly scheduled program in his brain.

"Let's go for a walk," said Luther, motioning with his head.

"You just got back."

Luther nodded to the door. Liu turned off the coffeepot. Exasperated, Liu and Tucker followed Luther outside.

Once they exited, Tucker said, "No one bugged your place, I check weekly."

Luther did not answer. Instead, he kept walking. "Foxx came by."

"Foxx Kauffman?" questioned Tucker.

"Do you know another fox? Besides your partner."

Liu blushed slightly, but replied, "Aww...thank you." Tucker remained nonresponsive.

"Foxx flew in from DC."

"Hmm," said Tucker and Liu in unison.

"To return a favor," said Luther sullenly.

All thoughts of folly evaporated.

"Favor?" asked Liu.

"In kind," returned Luther.

"He left a tape?" asked Tucker.

"What's on it?" followed Liu.

"Don't know."

Tucker looked ticked. "You've had it for fifteen hours and you didn't listen?"

"I'll never again be the keeper of our nation's secrets."

"So..." said Tucker.

"We listen together," said Liu.

"That's the entirety of my plan," said Luther.

Liu asked, "What did Foxx say?"

"Not much. Tigre mailed Foxx the tapes, all of them. Tapes already circulated, plus some that didn't get through. Plus…this one," Luther said, removing the tape from his shirt pocket, surrendering it to Liu.

"Foxx will release the others first. He'll give us a few weeks before that one hits. You guys in?"

"In," replied Tucker.

Liu nodded.

"Where do we listen to it?" asked Tucker.

"I have a key to my dean's office."

The three strolled through campus. Luther considered two of his favorite people. They possessed the same potent chemistry and camaraderie. Both seemed blissful, relaxed, chatting back and forth. Even without catching the agents in the act, he would spot the change. Hell, anyone would.

"So, you two…"

Tucker looked down and jogged forward, gentlemanly, avoiding the topic.

"Yes," answered Liu.

"'Bout time," said Luther, "He loves you, you know?"

"Yeah, I got that."

"So, what now?"

"Unsure. It's complicated."

"Complicated?"

"I saw a child murdered, then I watched Tucker almost die…again. Yesterday was the worst day of my life, then it wasn't…for a while." She paused, taking in the campus, breathing the air, as if for the first time. "Tucker and I, all of us, we've been through a lot together. So, yeah, complicated." She took Luther's arm and walked on.

Minutes later, Luther removed a key from his pocket as the threesome approached the dean's office. "I don't use Dean's office much."

"Wait, the dean of your department is named Dean?" Liu asked.

"I guess his mother preordained him," answered Luther.

The three funneled into the large, stately office, and Luther searched for a tape player. He plopped the tape into the player thinking, *screw it, screw it all*.

•   •   •

The rhythmic sound of turning tape greeted them. For a full minute, the clicking served as the tape's only output. Tucker, Liu, and Luther exchanged confused looks. Luther prayed for continued silence. Hopefully, he dodged being an insider again. Then Arturo Tigre started.

> *"So, this is good-bye, I'll miss this. Sure, I'm dead. I'll miss this, nonetheless. If you're listening to this tape, my final recording, the other tapes got out. Which is why you hear joy in my voice. Puerto Rico and America blessed us. Leon and I were compelled to give back. A little addition by subtraction.*
>
> *"You probably wonder how we got here. We started recording our clients years ago. We had no idea what to do. With the recordings, I mean. I felt like a coward. Leon too. We possessed absolute proof that crooked politicians sold out America. Belittling our taxpayers, voters, and our servicemen and women. Our circumstances trapped us. Releasing the tapes painted targets on our backs.*
>
> *"Then a drop of magic entered our lives. Leon worked for a senator out of Pennsylvania. The senator hired us because something scared him shitless. Leon worked as his bodyguard. I did the senator's advance work. One night, the senator got shitfaced. He babbled to Leon that two friends died recently—a judge from Jersey and the mayor of some Pennsylvania town."*

Tucker stopped the tape. "Holy shit."
Liu nodded. Luther sighed.
Tucker pressed the tape again.

> *"Leon shared the senator's drunken ramblings. I got curious and looked up the senator's friends; both died weeks apart. Authorities treated neither death as a homicide. No one connected the death, besides our client. Turns out both dirty, both investigated, both got off.*

"*Only Leon and I knew about our scared senator. So, Leon got him drunk again, played on his fear. Leon told him we could only protect him if he told us everything. Even drunk, the senator balked, but admitted the Jersey judge had connections throughout Atlantic City.*

"*Leon and I assumed mob hits. We set the information aside, didn't think about it. One day Leon asked, 'what if it wasn't the mob?' Both deaths lacked the professionalism and vindictiveness of a mob hit. No missing fingers, peeled toenails, or signs of torture.*

"*What if the killer just hated corruption? The executions seemed emotional. A fake hunting accident means you get someone in your sites, you see them, you choose to pull the trigger. Forcing someone to commit suicide, you don't get more emotional than that. The deaths seemed personal. What if some common citizen without our training, or expertise, did something about crooked politicians? What if someone else showed courage when we did not?*

"*We felt like cowards. We couldn't release the tapes in our possession while we lived. Still, what if Leon and I used our talents…to act?*

"*We placed recording equipment in places frequented by politicians. We mostly got gossip, but occasionally we got gold. We accumulated clues to understand who was already bought or who could be bought easily.*

"*We killed the senators at Watergate, and we killed the scumbag at Le Donphant, who bragged about his upcoming meeting in the same booth the day before. But, death offered a certain cleansing these politicians did not deserve. Thompson did not deserve martyrdom. After Le Donphant, we grasped our stupidity. We telegraphed our operation. Law enforcement would look for simple recording devices.*

"*We needed new ways to record and distribute information. If you're listening, the plan went to shit. That simple.*

"Luckily, our death freed us to distribute the recordings we feared to release in life.

"I can tell you we didn't get everything we heard on tape; it'd have been impossible. The filth only begins with the tapes we sent.

"Something else really important: there's no great evil empire, no puppet master behind the corruption. We witnessed a flawed system and tiny unethical men and women lacing their pockets and protecting their asses. No wizards, just spoiled, entitled assholes. But hopefully, we created space for the public to elect people of honor. Maybe there's hope yet. We love our country. Remember, there're honest politicians out there. We've seen them, we've prayed for them. Maybe we made their jobs easier."

• • •

The clicking tape marked time. Tucker, Liu, and Luther sat without a shared word.

Tucker spoke first. "Luther, Foxx said nothing else?"

"Nothing."

Liu started, "Loyola and Tigre confirmed they weren't connected with the earlier killing."

Luther pondered before speaking. "Someone...inspired them. Any chance the judge's and mayor's deaths were coincidental?"

"No," answered Liu. "Remember the ballistics report. The deaths were intentional, orchestrated, not as professional as Loyola and Tigre's attacks."

"Clumsy, amateurs, civilians maybe," added Tucker.

"What now?" asked Luther.

"You do nothing. You no longer consult for the FBI. Understand?" Liu stared him down.

"Okay," Luther said, attempting to hide relief. Being an old-fashioned history teacher sounded wonderful.

"What do we do?" asked Tucker.

Erasmus Luther, the man named for conflict, looked at Liu as she wrestled internally. Liu and Tucker did not tell him, but Luther extrapolated someone sidetracked, even shit-canned Tucker's and

Liu's careers. The agents tried but failed to hide the fear they experienced daily.

He could not comprehend their daily challenges. However, he understood from experience these two people did not scare easily. Courage meant doing your job when afraid, making Natalie Liu and Tanner Tucker the most courageous people Luther encountered.

Time passed before Liu answered, "We go to the beginning. Every fiber of my being screams that no one, *no one*, wants us there."

"We've been to the sticks of Texas a dozen times. We got nothing."

"We go again."

• • •

Silsbee

Gertrude stepped out of her cottage and ambled toward the old barn. She did not knock, instead Gertrude waved into the camera her daughter installed.

"Hi, Mother," Allie's voice echoed mechanically through the speaker. "We'll be right down." Mechanical grinding signaled the lock's release.

Gertrude entered the chic living room and modern kitchen. The boys remodeled the loft decades before. Allie updated the boys' area upstairs, creating an office and reconfiguring bedrooms. Allie also overhauled the barn's lower level. The interior echoing a posh downtown apartment more than a rural home.

Gertrude studied the stairs leading to her boys' former area, or the Romp. She refused to climb the stairs after Bo and Wyeth died. The thought of the climb tortured her. Allie never forced or even asked her mother upstairs. Allie respected the difficulty of the physical climb for the aging matriarch. The emotional climb proved more daunting to Gertrude. She longed for Wyeth's laugh and the comfort of Bo's presence.

Gertrude stuffed those memories in the past where they belonged. The distinct sound of Allie descending the steps and the gurgling sounds of a baby played like a comforting melody in Gertrude's ears. Today promised to be her favorite day in years, a special occasion. The grandmother vibrated with excitement.

"Mom, I brought down Beth's bag, so you won't have to go upstairs."

"Thanks, dear." Gertrude took Beth from Allie and launched into baby talk.

Today represented Allie's first Mother's Day out. For weeks, Gertrude prepared to babysit Bobbie Wyeth Arrington Luther, or just Beth, Gertrude's granddaughter.

• • •

Houston

Liu remained glued to Tucker's sofa, unafraid of sexual tension between them or what might happen because it happened. She no longer calculated the odds of a tryst with Tanner Tucker damaging her career. Without Henry Moss as her mentor, no career path existed. She pictured herself exposed, naked, to face the world's dangers, no one to trust, no protection.

Almost no one. Tanner Tucker, her guardian angel, watched over her. The most logical, the safest place remained on his couch. Liu, despite her challenges, found herself far from a distressed damsel. She served as Tucker's protector as well. He proved man enough to admit to the fact.

Liu stewed on the sofa, stripped of her support team, her resources, and mentor. They, whoever "they" were, wanted her under thumb or dead. "They" could take Tucker away from her. The thought of standing at Tucker's gravesite, smelling fresh dirt, hearing his eulogy, watching Tucker's father console his mother haunted Liu, kept her eyelids pinned open, staring at ceiling fans in the night's heat.

Liu listed her assets: 1) Luther; 2) Tucker; 3) her health.

"They" tried to eliminate Luther. "They" repeatedly placed Tucker in the line of fire. "They" put her in harm's way. "They" possessed power over all Liu's assets.

But did "they?"

"They" could not take her experiences with Tucker. "They" owned no deed to the knowledge percolating in her brain. "They" possessed no influence over her biggest assets, the reason the FBI hired her, the unique way she processed, her talent for deconstruction, her dogged determination; her ability to stay on task.

"They," like all movie villains, possessed weaknesses. "They" needed to protect their image and career. She now found herself free of those concerns.

Arturo Tigre's words gut-punched her. In retrospect, he presented the biggest gift—knowing "they" did not exist as an entity. *"No puppet masters, no wizards, just spoiled, entitled, selfish assholes."*

Yes, she needed to survive the threats "they" presented. Daily, she must prove capable of that task. Still, "they" were someone else's problem.

Her job did not revolve around solving "they."

With renewed focus, she pushed "they" aside, returning to her task, coldly analyzing her assignment.

Tucker brought her cereal in the morning, soup for lunch, and a salad for dinner. She reviewed and re-reviewed her notes. She quizzed Tucker incessantly for his memories. In the organized filing cabinet of her brain, something remained amiss.

Before Angelo completely deconstructed her team, before he dropped multiple nonrelated cases on her, before she became a storm trooper for other law enforcement agencies, she considered a question. The question seemed important. Tigre's words returned. He talked about the emotions of the killings. Liu repeatedly eliminated one of the original killings, the Ollie Whiteman stabbing, because the killer was a woman.

Then logic flowed like a waterfall. Due to her training, she possessed superior marksman scores. She remembered Tucker, stressing Texas women's hunting acumen. Maybe a woman cross-haired the California State Congressman. Maybe a woman executed former Mayor Steph Joseph, in a similar hunting accident. The best ballistics lab in the world verified the same weapon killed both men. Could a woman force Judge Urey Little to type his suicide note, then overdose? A woman with a gun to his temple, sure.

The two female school board members murdered in Beaumont. Cole and Freel were common school board members. Their deaths felt close, personal. Men kill to show power, women kill to preserve safety, for revenge, or sometimes out of rage. Cole's and Freel's deaths signaled rage.

Liu looked to Tucker. He reread the files too, but stayed quiet, distant, giving her the space, she needed.

"You just reviewed the Ollie Whiteman murder," Liu said. "You went to Port Arthur; you know people there."

"Yeah, Mom and Dad met in high school there. They'll be in Port Arthur this weekend."

"What do you remember about the case?"

"The murderer was petite, pretty, about Whiteman's age, or slightly older. Elegant, according to the bartender. He doesn't remember her saying a word, she just whispered in Whiteman's ear. The bartender never heard her."

"Did she order a drink?"

"Yes, but he doesn't remember her speaking, she pointed or signaled."

"Anything else?"

"You know all of this."

"Anything else?"

"The woman wore gloves. The bartender considered the gloves a fashion statement. In retrospect, no prints, I guess. The woman seemed high-class for Whiteman. Out of his league. The bartender, young guy, noted the woman looked twice his age, and he knows she killed Whiteman, but he joked he'd have taken his chances."

"Men," grumbled Liu.

"You asked."

"And?"

"They got little from the crime scene. Lots of blood. No weapon left behind; lab guys guessed an ice pick."

"What else?"

"The killer's left-handed, stabbed Whiteman three dozen times, most of the stab wounds happened after he croaked. No prints, a few hair samples, strands of gray and black hair. All the blood belonged to Whiteman. Minor signs of struggle; he died quicky. Based on the lack of Whiteman's struggle and the fact the woman stole his wallet and car, there's little chance this was self-defense. The perp came to the bar to murder Whiteman."

"This wasn't a straight-up kill-and-cash grab. You don't stab someone thirty-plus times if there's no emotion. Shit, Whiteman's...the beginning."

"Possibly."

"You said your mom and dad are in Port Arthur this weekend."

"Attending a wedding."

"When?"

"Tomorrow around noon."

"A lot of your dad's political cronies will be there?"

"Sure."

"Can we crash the wedding?"

"I'll grab my tux but the truth is, if you wear that lavender dress, we can crash any damn party you want."

"You keep trying to get me back in that dress again."

"I've tried to get you in that dress to watch you get out of it."

"In your dreams, Tucker."

"Every damn night, Natalie, every one."

• • •

March 4, 1986

"Thank you for the ride, Allie."

"You're welcome. You don't need me to wait?"

"No, dear, I arranged a ride home," answered Gertrude.

"Okay." Allie looked at Gertrude quizzically. "So, I'm leaving you, dressed to the hilt, in Audrey Hepburn sunglasses and designer gloves, outside a crappy hotel in Port Arthur, Texas." Allie raised her eyebrows.

"Dear, it is not like that."

"Mom, for what's it's worth, you look stunning."

"Thank you."

"I haven't seen you wear the Oriental hairpin. I remember the first night I saw it."

"I try to forget that night, I hope it has not haunted you."

"Not too much, no."

"I only wore it once before, long ago, on my birthday. It proved…useful. Allie, dear?"

"Yes."

"I love you as much as I loved the boys, more, I think. You know that, right?"

"Sure…thanks. I love you too. Strange conversation to have outside of a rundown hotel."

"Allie, the best conversations occur in the most unusual places and in the most unusual times."

"Guessing this is both."

"Yes. Till tomorrow, dear."

Gertrude watched her daughter drive away. The older woman's elegance was shocking to the eyes in counterpoint to her grimy surroundings. She stood; a perfect red rose in a bouquet of fading dandelions. The former mother of three, current mother of one, braced herself for the task at hand.

She crossed the hotel's parking lot to an equally rundown bar. Gertrude checked before Allie left. He parked in the exact spot as every Tuesday when he arrived from DC.

Allie taught Gertrude to drive after Bo's death. The two joked Gertrude learned to drive at the age most adults stopped driving. She told Allie she needed independence. Her words held a symbol of truth. When Gertrude's faithful neighbor, Milly Rae, died, Gertrude lost her most reliable ride. Over time, she embraced driving and loved the freedom.

Still, the reason for her newfound auto passions revolved around tonight. This night planned with down-to-minute detail. Gertrude opened the door of the bar. The rank smell of stale beer and cigarettes gobsmacked her senses. She coughed, taking a moment to adjust to her surroundings. Still, nostalgia comforted her. She remembered sweetly her long-ago New York days with Claire at O'Connor's. She stood reminiscing, wondering about her long-lost friends.

As Gertrude hoped, the bar featured downlighting. Once her eyes adjusted, she could navigate without removing her sunglasses. She spotted him sitting across the bar, bullshitting with the bartender. She studied him for months.

He remained mildly attractive. A 59-year-old, 6'4", twice divorced, hard drinking, scratch-golfing good old boy who knew everyone. Most nights, he networked or attended political events, but not Tuesdays.

Tuesday, he kept to himself. He drove to this local bar, away from reporters' prying eyes and the political elite. Whiteman got blitzed, often stumbling to his car, before driving home or taking a taxi. His Tuesday routine seldom wavered. She braced herself before approaching him.

Walking over, she paused. What if Whiteman failed to find her attractive? She carefully selected men in her youth, each drawn effortlessly to her. She aged since her time as the moth's flame, gracefully, yes. Still, age proved an unforgiving bitch, even to Gertrude. Maybe her beauty faded more than she considered.

An appraising look from the young bartender gave Gertrude confidence. The toothy smile on Ollie Whiteman's reddened face as she took the stool beside him, relieved her fears. When the bartender approached, she did not speak, simply pointing to what the congressman drank. A Whiskey neat.

When the bartender delivered her drink, Whiteman nodded approval and added, "Put that one on my tab."

Gertrude smiled, communicating her gratitude.

"Have you been here before?" asked Whiteman.

Gertrude could tell he disappointed himself with his tired opening. She herself expected more from a lifelong politician. He recovered, "'Course you haven't, I'd remember."

Gertrude waited for the bartender to drift away before speaking. "Quite kind, thank you," she said in a hushed voice. "It just occurred to me," she lied, "I have seen you in the papers. How is that?"

She watched as Whiteman's chest puffed. "I'm the congressman from this district."

"Oh, how nice," she whispered.

He looked over and asked her name. She used her long-discarded birth name, what did it matter. "Philippa," she whispered.

"Philippa, I like that. It's beautiful."

"My mother selected my name; it means lover of horses." She used all of her might to cover her accent.

"And do you, love horses, I mean?"

Gertrude/Philippa battled revulsion for this man. Her next words remained central for the trap she set. Her script required perfect delivery. "I especially love stallions, the big ones." She looked at him and smiled, letting her words bounce like a red rubber ball through Whiteman's lurid thoughts. Like her old dog, Loper, Whiteman chased the bouncing ball.

"I like fillies myself, especially the small, elegant ones, like yourself."

In her youth, Gertrude's father taught her to fish for trout, his favorite. Lord Harrington stressed the importance of presenting the lure, then setting the hook. Ollie Whiteman sat primed to suffer the fate of the trout from her long-ago memories. Like the trout, Ollie Whiteman failed to comprehend danger.

Gertrude presented the lure.

"How sweet. I am recently divorced. It has been too long since a stallion rode this filly; there is something about building up a sweat from a hard ride," she whispered, hoping he could not feel her skin squirm when her gloved hand rubbed above his knee.

She mustered every fiber of her soul to hold the act just a little longer, a little more, to hide her revulsion. The powerful, crooked politician unwittingly rushed toward his fate. Gertrude prayed her masquerade held.

Ollie Whiteman, noted orator, career politician, backroom dealmaker, and backslapper remained speechless. His eyes volleyed from the bartender then back to her, then repeated the process. Her smile offered Whiteman the perfect blend of innocence and carnal suggestion.

Hook set.

"Corky, put this on my tab, I'll settle up next time," said Whiteman.

Ollie Whiteman paid for his sins that night, he just never paid his bar tab.

•   •   •

The Following Morning
Almost home.
Almost home.

Whiteman's Lincoln Town Car drove smoothly, despite the unsteadiness and shock of the still inexperienced driver. No longer Philippa, never Philippa again. Only Gertrude, blood-soaked Gertrude, shaking Gertrude, muttering Gertrude.

Almost home.
Almost home.

Gertrude planned Whiteman's execution, convinced this task belonged to her. How naïve, juvenile, unacceptable for a woman of her experience. She proceeded through her initial steps, pre-murder, girded by intricate planning. In retrospect, she needed more time to prepare for the actions after she killed Whiteman.

He enthusiastically agreed to pay for a room at the grimy hotel. She tried to push the memories away but failed. The congressman so easily led to his slaughter, currently recoloring his hotel room in dripping, sticky crimson.

The former college football star, opened the hotel door, waving her in with flair. She smiled, removed her sunglasses, and winked, placing her eyewear on the dresser. He jumped her at once, in full arousal, clumsily pawing. She pushed him away. She could ill-afford to leave much of herself behind.

"Charming…if you don't object, I have a better plan," said Philippa/Gertrude.

Ollie stopped. She continued, "I must shower, to a…remove the bar's less appetizing odors. There's a perfume in my clutch. Please undress and get in bed. The wait will be worth it." She smiled; the wait would be worth it for her.

She watched him undress. "May I borrow your shirt?"

He smiled and handed the button-down to her. She walked to the bathroom and turned on the shower. Gertrude enjoyed the water's warmth with her hand but did not enter the shower. She let the shower run, biding time to collect resolve.

Gertrude removed her clothes, except her panties, and put on his shirt. She let the starched cotton shirt hang over her body. Gertrude left it unbuttoned enough to distract him from the fact that she still wore leather gloves. She shook her head and removed the long silver antique pin from her hair, now holding it in her left hand.

Gertrude looked down and unbuttoned her shirt one more button. She turned off the shower. "Are you ready?" she projected from the bathroom.

"More than you can imagine," he answered.

"Please tell me you have undressed completely, I want to see all of you," she lied.

"I am, I promise."

Gertrude wanted him exposed to the world that found him. She could not reveal what he did to Bo, without leading authorities back to her family. Leaving his old naked body bleeding and exposed for all to see offered a just punishment. She needed the world to know Whiteman died pathetically, in a rundown hotel, without dignity.

She waited a moment more, allowing her hatred to galvanize, to shield her. Rage gurgled below her calm demeanor. Hate built, not slow, as she expected, but microwave fast. She worked to keep her emotions under control, fighting for sanity. Gertrude hoped that despite this act, parts of her could remain untainted.

She emerged, seductively, from the bathroom. Whiteman lay naked; erect.

"I like your hair down," Whiteman offered.

"Thank you. Let me climb on top of you. Hands behind your head please," she said faking another smile.

He complied.

"Close your eyes; it's more fun with your eyes closed," she coaxed. She took in Whiteman. Once a stallion, he held much of his form, still alive and well. Her son was dead. Gertrude's rage took the reins.

Even the greatest of stallions age, and when they become useless, end up at the glue factory.

The silver Oriental hairpin that long ago served as her protector, now served as her ticket to purgatory. The first stab took everything...her hate, anger, bitterness, loss. His eyes popped open, but he reacted slowly. She went for the meat of his neck, and he bled profusely. The second stab proved easier, then third easier still, then the fourth, fifth, sixth, seventh, eighth, ninth, and 10th followed. After she passed a dozen strikes, stabbing the corpse of Ollie Whiteman was no longer hard. Stopping proved difficult.

Gertrude ended her attack when she ran out of breath, arms spent from exertion. She climbed off the bleeding meat clump, former Congressman Ollie Whiteman. She worried little about leaving evidence. Investigators would not select a small-town Texas teacher, with no criminal record, no filed fingerprints, rarely photographed, with no association to the victim as their lead suspect. She took Whiteman's car keys—her ride home—and his wallet, to simulate a deadly mugging.

Gertrude took off his bloody shirt and stuffed it in the hotel's trash can. She stuffed the rest of his clothes, the hotel towels, and the sheet in the trash can next. She wanted nothing for the hotel workers to cover him in before they called the authorities. Gertrude redressed in the outfit of her arrival.

The femme fatale wiped up as she could, rinsing her hairpin before returning it to her hair. She looked in the mirror. Blood speckled her hair and face. The shaking started as she took in the reflection of Whiteman's body bleeding out. The reflection triggered near madness. She fought to swallow it back, knowing the image resided as an imprint for nightmares to come.

She considered showering but decided against it. The congressman parked his car steps away. The shaking progressed, and chills overtook her. Gertrude doubted her ability to navigate home.

She grabbed the garbage receptacle and the evidence it contained before stepping into the humidity. She started the car and began her expedition home.

Now she found herself:

Almost home.

Almost home.

She stabbed Jonas Hysler in her youth…in self-defense. Later, Gertrude witnessed Bo and Wyeth kill Jonas and another man. Still, nothing prepared her for this haunting drive.

She saw the lights of her home in the distance, calling her as sirens once called sailors, promising safe harbor. She pulled in the driveway, shaking. Gertrude tried and failed four times to type in the gate code. Then Allie buzzed her in.

Allie walked out to greet her, a quizzical look on her face. The darkness hid the evidence of Gertrude's deadly endeavors, while she sat in the car. When she emerged, Allie started a sentence Gertrude knew in advance would remain incomplete.

"Mom, where did you get the Lincoln…?"

She watched as Allie inspected her mother's bloodstained face. She knew her Allie, always observant, reconstructed the evening in her head. Allie looked from her mother's face to the tussled hair to the garbage can stuffed with Whiteman's bloody clothes. A bloody shirtsleeve hung from the side.

"Is he dead?"

"Yes."

"How long did you plan this?"

"Since Bo died."

"Why didn't you ask for help?"

"I didn't want to involve you."

"A little late now, I guess. Well, tonight won't be the first time I ditch a car."

"Yes," Gertrude said, still battling shock but happy to have her ally, her Allie.

"Let's get you in the shower. Mom, I love you."

"I love you too, Allie."

"Once you warm up, I'll dump the car...Wyeth showed me where." Allie guided her mother inside and started the shower. She assumed the role of protector, undressing her mother, as Gertrude undressed her as a child. Allie tested the water, then helped her mother step inside. "Mom, stay here, I'll be back."

"Okay, dear," Gertrude said, looking forward, not turning to her daughter, shaking despite the steam now rising from her skin.

Before Allie left, she turned back. "Mom, is this over?"

"No."

"Okay, Mom, okay."

●　　●　　●

Saturday, September 17, 1994

Erasmus Luther, officially back in professor mode, labored over his least favorite task—grading essays. He admitted, however, that reviewing students' written words, the boldness and creativity of their thoughts, proved the easiest way to spot talent. Yes, he aspired to catch syntax errors, still not his strength. Thank God his publisher assigned their best editor. Syntax was important, he understood, but birthing an original thought remained the kernel of genius.

He tried, unsuccessfully, to lose himself in the papers, the semester's first. The chance to see her loomed painfully close. Luther lately learned the entrails of fear. Still, now he experienced a more soul-slicing emotion—consternation. He looked at the wall calendar again, twelve days to the Arrington Aids Art Gala.

Twelve days.

Questions riddled him. Should he go? Does she want to see him? Can he handle her rejection? What if she welcomes him? Why is he drawn to a woman who prided herself on remaining distant?

Allie lived in a remote town. He did not have her phone number, unsure even if she owned a phone. When she spoke, she offered little of herself. She appeared to like him but seemed unaffected if she spent months without communicating. She saw Luther at September's gala, or at times and places of her choosing.

Female colleagues asked him to attend the gala, implying, hinting, cajoling even, to be his date. He dodged every subtle suggestion. The last year, many women had him, his body at least. Unfortunately for him, one woman owned his heart.

Twelve more days. Luther no longer feared for his life or even his sanity. He processed his emotions finally, unhealthily, but finally. He only feared her rejection. More so, he questioned his courage to face it.

• • •

On the drive from Houston to Port Arthur, Liu instructed Tucker to dance with every woman present. His mission, ask each woman—politicians' wives and female politicos—about their memories of Ollie Whiteman. Not as an investigator, conversationally. Per Liu's direction, Tucker danced with woman after woman.

Most dance partners remembered Whiteman, all remembered how he died, found naked in a seedy hotel. The women shared funny stories about Whiteman, tales of his flirting, golfing, and drinking prowess, but little else. Tucker found his task annoying and pointless. To be fair, Tucker experienced agitation beyond levels he thought possible.

Liu wore the lavender dress. She graced him with the first two dances. The soft, elegant dress struggling to cover her taut, fit body enthralled him. Looking into her eyes, and taking in her form, left him rigid, painfully so. She smiled pretending not to notice…for a moment.

"We're here on business, remember?"

Censure did little to correct his animal arousal. She tried to pull away after their first dance, but he held her for one more. A second dance, less than five minutes, a welcome mental vacation from the stress enveloping them both, seemed so little to ask. She smiled and remained in his arms. She playfully used her smile, body positioning, and proximity to taunt him beyond endurance.

Or did she just taunt him without trying?

Before their arrival at the wedding, Liu proposed a simple plan. Tucker knew many of these people. Tucker asked a politician's wife to dance. The women accepted each time. Then Liu swooped in for the husband. Tucker's dance partners varied, some quite old, others like his mother remained breathtaking. Most women stayed in appropriate wedding mode; all complimented his dancing. Some second and third wives challenged propriety, a few proved flirtatious, and one woman outright propositioned him. Tucker understood if he faced this level of wedding shenanigans, Liu danced under full attack.

Why did he ask her to wear that dress? If the lavender-cream gown rendered him helpless, constantly seeking opportunities to view every exposed inch of her flesh, what did it do to these men witnessing her exotic beauty for the first time? Suffering these men, any men really, but especially these professional glad-handers, with their paws on her, their eyes searching for the opportunity to hunt her bare skin, enraged him. He glared as Liu raised a dance partner's hands from her backside to the small of her back. Tucker fumed, envisioning each man's lurid thoughts. He begrudgingly admitted their thoughts mirrored his own. Tucker never considered himself a jealous man, but now raged with the greenest emotion.

Now, he stood without a dance partner, enraged. Earlier, the two agents arrived with a grandly wrapped present. Tucker's father and mother waved them in upon arrival. Tucker told the bride's parents he and Liu ate earlier, would be of little bother, and were in the area on non-related business. He wanted to visit his parents, congratulate the bride, and say hello to old friends. The bride's parents, the former governor and her husband, old family friends, welcomed him and fawned over Liu.

Seeing his dismay, his mother approached, a beauty in her day, and still today, and asked him to dance. Tucker accepted, celebrating any reason to stop watching men paw at Liu. He took a deep breath and smiled.

Escorting his mother to the dance floor, he banished his thoughts and presented the polish he learned from her. She smiled sadly for the first few moments of their dance. Tucker knew his mother's every move. She examined, analyzed, and, as always, waited to present her findings. She already processed the data, or she would not have requested this dance. She now engaged in the final polish of her arguments, ordering them to present her findings politely, ensuring their usefulness to the listener. A former electrical engineer, a rare trade for a female in her time, his mother chose life as a politician's wife. Few processed information better.

Tucker started the conversation, choosing not to wait for his mother's analysis. "Mother, I danced with a lot of women tonight, few look as beautiful as you." Tanner Tucker was not playing favorites. His mother reigned as one of the most intriguing women present.

"Very sweet."

Not ready to engage, he thought. *Classic Mom.*

A second song started, and his father tried to cut in. Tucker's mother gave her husband *the look*. The multimillionaire retreated without argument.

When his mother's lessons became inevitable, which always seemed the case, Tucker learned to embrace the moment. This woman, his dance instructor, role model, homework tutor, taught him everything. "You are the best dancer here," she said, engaging the conversation. "My girlfriends fawn over you, complimenting your every turn."

"You taught me. By complimenting me you're patting yourself on the back."

She laughed, dismissing the validity of his comment.

"She watches you. Almost as much as you watch her."

"I'm sorry?"

"You watch her. At first, I thought it was because she's your FBI partner. Then your true intentions became obvious. You're smitten."

"More than that."

"Yes, appears that way. The playing field might not be as uneven as you assume. Your partner came unglued when Eileen Haus danced with you. That flirt had her hands all over you. Ms. Liu steamed. As an interested observer, I found her predicament entertaining."

"We're here for your viewing pleasure," ribbed Tucker.

"Lucky me," she said perfectly executing another turn. His mother proved herself incorrect. Tanner was the second-best dancer here. To this day, his mother remained the best social dancer he knew, using her skills to charm her husband's contemporaries.

"She's every bit as jealous of you as you are of her. I thought the observation may comfort you."

"I doubt that's the case but thank you."

"And keep you from killing her dance partners. Remember you're at a wedding. Although I understand you can decapitate most men present with little thought, it would be poor form."

There it was, as always, message delivered. Tucker comprehended the underlying nugget. Protect our family's reputation. She expected, check that—*required*—her son protect his family.

He smiled to confirm, lesson noted.

"Your partner is dancing with your father, how nice. I'm sure he considers it a terrible imposition. She is so awful to look at. Ahh, the trials your father endures," she said, shaking her head.

Tucker spotted Liu laughing while being led around the floor by his father. She seemed more comfortable than with her previous dance partners. Tucker exhaled gratefully.

"Well, this might do the beautiful Ms. Liu in," said Tucker's mother.

"What do you mean?"

Just then, a tap on his shoulder pulled his concentration from his mother. A gorgeous young strawberry-blond asked to cut in. His mother departed before his declination. So, left no choice, Tucker danced with the bride's sister, maid of honor, and the former governor's youngest daughter.

"Good to see you Tanner," she said.

"Hello, Katherine." He remembered her as Texas's most annoying, flirtatious, and spoiled debutant. Still, he admitted she grew up...well.

"Mom didn't tell me you were coming," she led.

"I decided last minute."

"You just showed up at the biggest Texas wedding in years with no invitation. Nothing has changed, I see."

"I heard you graduated college."

"Yes, you look dapper tonight."

"Thank you, young lady," Tucker said, accentuating their age difference.

"You're defying the aging process. You get more handsome with age," she said, pulling closer, brushing against him as intimately as Liu earlier.

"Ahh...thanks..." he said.

"You interest me."

"Okay."

Tucker replayed memories of Katherine as an annoying child in his head, fighting other thoughts. He did not remember maid of honor dresses being so revealing, so accentuating. Katherine looked inviting.

He tried to pull back, creating space between them. Her grip held him in place, too close for comfort.

"I feel…" She paused, glancing belt-ward. "Sorry, I meant…I see…you like the dress."

She toyed with him. He searched for reasons. His family spent vacations with the governor's family, he watched this girl grow up, she always had an angle. He prayed for the song's conclusion.

"Aren't you going to ask me?" Her face, form, posture, and voice loaded with innuendo.

"Sorry?"

Then everything changed. "Aren't you going to ask me about Ollie Whiteman?"

Tucker failed to offer an answer.

"You're an FBI agent, I know that. You asked every woman here about Ollie. Is the FBI reopening the case?"

Tucker flipped through his mental Rolodex, bringing everything he knew about Katherine forward: teenage beauty queen, runner-up in the tennis state championship, full ride athletic scholarship to University of Texas and a *journalism* major…shit.

Her hand that formerly rested on his shoulder, ran down his chest. She peered into his eyes, "You can't stay silent forever."

Yes, I can, yes, I can, he repeated to himself. When the hell will this dance end? He remained silent and spun her to buy time. She bit her bottom lip, then smiled.

"Nicely done," she remarked.

"Thanks."

"What's your answer?" The song mercifully ended. He attempted retreat.

"One more dance for old times' sake," she continued, not losing her grip.

The dance continued. Katherine bided her time.

"I won't quote you. I won't mention you by name. I need something from you…"

Just then he felt a tap on his shoulder, thank God…Liu. Unlike his mother predicted, Liu seem unconcerned about Tucker's gorgeous dance partner; Liu appeared agitated.

She did not cut in. She seemed lost in another world. Tucker stood confused before Liu unceremoniously jerked Tucker from his inquisitor.

"Say good-bye to your mom and dad, we're leaving," Liu said, speaking as his boss, not the beauty he lusted after all evening.

"Okay…"

"Now," she said and marched out of the banquet hall. He enjoyed every step, finding himself powerless to pry his eyes away. Tucker glanced to his right and left. Other males of the species joined him.

He doubted she experienced an inkling of the jealousy he endured. Only after she passed from his line of sight did he turn to say his good-byes.

He forgot Katherine's presence, an unfamiliar sensation for her. He nodded good-bye before walking to his parents.

"Thanks for the story, Tanner."

That story could prove dangerously inconvenient.

• • •

Liu walked to the car. She processed Tucker's father's words and the evening in totality. Liu dismissed the collection of men who ogled, groped, and propositioned her. She endured hands sliding to her backside and eyes directly connected to her decolletage. Those men's contributions to the evening proved inadequate, as she assumed their performance would demonstrate if she accepted their advances.

She processed the night's highlight—her dance with Tucker. His attempt to remain gentlemanly, while aching to ravage her, remained sexy beyond measure. Other dance partners showed less refinement. She would reward him, unfortunately much later, based on her newfound knowledge.

Before Tucker's return from his good-byes, she needed to assess how she felt watching him dance with other women. In deep self-exploration, she admitted seeing Tucker in the arms of other women, even women she did not consider rivals, challenging. Women relished their time in his arms. She did not anticipate feeling so possessive. Liu suggested he dance and mingle. She hated her plan.

His dance partners treated him as tantalizing fare, expertly prepared filet, and each woman looked starved for protein. The polite, polished women found him irresistible. Liu needed to conquer her jealousy before addressing Tucker. Liu hoped his departure tour took time.

She prayed for time to process the range of her…desire.

Because their first break in months, the biggest break in the genesis murders, the executions leading to Loyola and Tigre's deadly campaign, was there all along, with Tucker's father.

Since their initial coupling, driven by raw emotions and trauma, Liu understood the need to return to a strictly professional relationship. But the draw proved too strong. Liu breathed deeply, remembering the word she shared with Luther—complicated.

Earlier, Natalie enjoyed a much-needed break from dancing and pawing, when she noticed Tucker dancing with his mother. She witnessed Tucker's obvious respect. Suitors coerced Liu to dance. She rebuffed each. Observing Tucker with his mother, taught Liu much about his origins. She examined each dance step, each laugh, learning about him by the second. Watching Tucker with one of the people who molded him proved enthralling. Liu ascertained the origins of Tucker's dance competency.

Mr. Tucker tried to cut in, rebuffed by his wife. Liu wanted to continue monitoring Tucker's interaction with his mother but must not miss this opportunity. She strolled to Tucker's father and requested a dance. He accepted.

"Nice to see you again, Ms. Liu."

"Thank you, Mr. Tucker."

Unlike previous dance partners, Tucker's father maintained polite spacing. She smiled, noting the son's gallantry in his father. Far from equal to his son or wife on the dance floor, he led competently.

"I enjoy watching my son and wife dance. She's a beauty, isn't she?"

Complimenting his wife at conversation's start—a classic move of a man behaving properly. Mr. Tucker's hands remained positioned on her back, far from her rear.

"Yes, she's exquisite. You're a lucky man."

"Luck had little to do with it. I pursued her, fighting off rivals. Studying her likes and dislikes became my hobby. I questioned her friends. Even tracked down an old boyfriend, got him drunk and plied him for intel."

He chuckled. "I paid an admissions clerk for her class schedule. Ended up in one of her classes. I asked her out several times, she said no. Thankfully, I owned a pickup and made myself available when she and her roommate moved. I humped boxes all day. Got nowhere."

"What happened?"

"Her roommate asked me out, in front of her."

Liu giggled. "What'd you say?"

"I told her roommate the truth. She was beautiful, but my heart belonged to someone else. I looked deeply into Clancy's eyes with my best puppy-dog impersonation, and I walked out."

"And that worked?"

"My wife followed me out. She asked if I could drive her to their old apartment, to collect the final few boxes. She kissed me on the cheek to say thanks. It was over for me."

"How much did you pay her roommate to ask you out?"

"Tanner said you're bright. I didn't pay her." Liu gave him a knowing look. "...I did offer. She turned me down. The roommate agreed, because my feelings were sincere, if not my plan."

"How long did it take your wife to find out?" Liu laughed.

"Not long, but long enough. Agent Liu?"

"Natalie."

"Natalie, why are you here?"

"Tanner wanted to see you."

"Bullshit. Tanner's a wonderful but unwilling dancer. I've watched him dance with every woman here. Betting you asked him to perform that function."

"You didn't capture your beautiful wife's heart because you're stupid."

"No..." He smiled. "Or lack of persistence, so again, Natalie, why are you here?"

"I need your promise of confidentiality."

"Young lady, unlike most politicians and businessmen, I have found success keeping my mouth shut. I'm sure Tanner told you that, but yes, you have my promise."

"Remember when Tanner got the press, for stopping Loyola and Tigre?"

"Of course."

"Our careers were fast-tracked, then I lost my boss," Liu selected her words. "Then the tapes hit, ruined lots of careers."

"Yes, a few of my friends among them," said Mr. Tucker matter-of-factly.

Unsure of how to respond, she continued carefully, "Lots of backlash. Since then, your son and I have experienced some…challenges."

Her dance partner nodded, keeping his mouth shut, as advertised.

Liu understood she said too much, but her career circled in the toilet. She tired of being shot at in raids outside her jurisdiction. So, she continued. "Anyway, Loyola and Tigre's campaign began with Greene and Thompson. But politicians died before them."

"I read something about that. The story died quickly."

"Loyola and Tigre knew about the earlier murders, but someone else committed them."

"You're trying to find out who," said Mr. Tucker.

Liu nodded.

"And you're here to ask questions. So…ask."

"Your son said you knew Ollie Whiteman. What can you tell me?"

"On the surface, a backslapping good old boy."

"And?"

"Absolutely for sale."

"I have to ask; did you ever take advantage of that fact?"

"No. To be fair, I understand the question. I'll understand if you choose not to believe me."

"I work with your son. He's your greatest testament, so I believe you."

"Thank you for that."

"Did the fact he was for sale get him killed?"

"I recall some chatter, but judging by the ugly way he died, I didn't think so…I mean before this dance."

"Is there anything else you can tell me about Whiteman?"

"He shamelessly flirted with my wife, was an outstanding golfer, decent politician, and a terrible poker player."

"Did any other political friends die around that time?"

"No, it was a tough patch, though."

"Why?"

"Tanner's only sister died, he probably told you, in November 1985, on my birthday."

"No, he didn't tell me. I'm so sorry. How did you lose her?"

"Thank you for asking…cancer. Don't understand how she got it; there's no family history. She was my baby, resembled her mom in every way, but acted like me." He smiled. Liu did not want to disturb his reminiscing. So, she just kept dancing.

"She died at 11:52 p.m. on my birthday."

"I'm sorry."

"People think it's terrible. That she died on my birthday. But she held on for me. For that day. Her last thing was being there for me on my birthday. Hell of a gift to give. Your last day, for someone else." Liu pretended to ignore tears streaming down his cheek.

After a few moments, Tucker's father left the warmth of the past and mentally returned to their dance. "On top of that, my best friend from college died months later. We weren't close anymore—I married. He didn't. He wasn't much on hanging out with a married guy's family. Still, we stayed in touch. I saw him a coupl'a times of year."

"How'd he die?" she asked offhandedly.

"He was injured around Christmas, hunting accident, stray bullet…"

Liu lost step, only her dance partner's firm hands kept her from tumbling.

"You okay?"

"Yes. Sorry, did you say…hunting accident?"

"Yes."

Cannons, fireworks; hell, atomic bombs exploded in her head. This could not be coincidence. *How the hell did they miss this guy?*

"He died from the gunshot?" she asked, shell-shocked.

"Not exactly, he recovered from the gunshot but picked up a bug in the hospital. Some superbug, Mirshad?"

"You mean, MRSA? They listed his cause of death as MRSA?"

"I think."

"What's his name?"

"Cat Conroe, short for Wildcat Conroe, used a nickname because his parents named him Eugene. Also, his family's been wildcatting since the thirties."

"Did Tanner know about Cat?"

"Tanner met Cat a few times. He went with me on a business trip to Midland, and we met Cat for dinner. But he was young. Tanner traveled to Ireland, to get away after his sister died. Her death did a number on him, on all of us. I attended Cat's funeral when Tanner was overseas. I don't think I ever told him about Cat's death. Just never came up. This related to Whiteman?"

"Were Whiteman and Cat friends?"

"Not sure. But both were scratch golfers. Ran in similar circles, although not the same city. I'd bet they ran into each other at golf scrambles."

"Cat, was he like you, I mean, honest?"

"Coming from that family, whew. I don't think he ever had a chance to walk a straight line. The Conroes lived and died by the next oil well. They spent money like it was on the two-fer-one buffet. Straight-up bullshitters."

"He ran the company?" asked Liu.

"Pffff...no, his dad runs the company, no one else'll run the company while the old man's alive."

"Was his family part of a political action committee or fundraising group?"

"Don't think so. They did things old-school. Good old-fashioned glad-handing. Cat officially ran their sales division but was really the chief officer of four-man scrambles and ass kissing. Played golf every week, bought dinners, took clients to strip clubs, hosted high stakes poker games, etc."

Liu's mind sorted, filed, and processed. "Can your son or I call if we need more?" He nodded. "I got your promise earlier, but I want to add something. Staying quiet may help me and your son stay alive, so I'd be grateful."

Her dance partner stopped smoothly, pulled his fingers across his lips in a zipper motion, half bowed, then exited.

Liu started her search for Tucker as soon as she parted ways with his father. She found herself perturbed by his stunning female dance partner. The horror reflected on Tucker's face redeemed him, a wolf caught in a steel trap, ready to chew off his paw to escape.

Now reclining on the hood of Tucker's car she awaited his return. She smiled as he exited the hall and jogged toward her.

"You're in a big hurry to leave. What's up?" Tucker leaned on the car beside her.

"Let's take a walk."

Tucker admired her dress, then looked at his tux. "We're not exactly in hiking gear, let's get in the car. We talk on the drive home?"

"We're not going home." Liu motioned vigorously.

Tucker and Liu took a few steps. Liu said, "I don't want to talk in the car."

"You're getting as bad as Luther."

"Maybe as smart as him."

Once they walked twenty yards from the car, Liu recounted Tucker's father's words. Tucker listened intently, apologizing for not knowing about Cat Conroe's demise.

"Why didn't he come up in our searches?" Tucker asked.

"Not sure, but I will find out. My guess, he wasn't the chief executive of the company, his family wasn't directly involved in any PACs. Also, in family businesses, they move around money. Cat may not have been a payrolled employee."

She continued, "There's 1,000 to 1,500 hunting accidents per year. Even with the FBI's resources, we couldn't track everyone. Again, the doctor didn't code the cause of death as a gunshot wound or hunting accident. Hell, I'm not sure a police report exists. Where's the Conroe Oil headquarters?"

"Midland. If I remember correctly."

"How soon can we get there?"

"Liu, it's Saturday. We didn't bring a change of clothes. Honestly, I won't be able to think about anything else if you're in that dress. Let's stop in Houston, long enough to grab a set of clothes and power nap. We can be in Midland Sunday. Let's not storm the doors yet. Let's spend a day in town, at Midland's library, researching the Conroe clan."

"Fine, fine."

"There's something else," Tucker said.

"Yes..."

"The last woman I danced with," started Tucker.

"Old girlfriend?"

"I wish."

"Excuse me?" said Liu feeling jealousy bubble beneath her calm demeanor.

"No, that's not what I meant, I mean it'd be easier if she was my ex-girlfriend. It's worse."

Liu crossed her arms, imparting a look he witnessed often, the cut-to-the-facts stare.

"She knows I'm an FBI agent."

"And?"

"A few people told her we asked about Whiteman's death."

"Inconvenient, not the end of the world."

"She's a reporter."

• • •

Sunday, September 18, 1994

Pete Book lay in bed, looking at his bedroom ceiling. He enjoyed his new DC home, elegant to-the-minute detail. The senator announced his 1996 Presidential run. Pete planned to use the home's dinner table as the setting to leverage support from his immense network. Still, Pete, Samantha, and the smartest supporters understood that Pete Book could not capture the Presidency in 1996.

The current President possessed a strong DC base and incredible grassroots support. Voters would re-elect him. Whoever Book's party put forth against the president in 1996 served as political fodder. The party historically put forth an old loyal warhorse as a service award, allowing the aging politician one last lap in the sun before putting him out to pasture. Everyone understood #42's imminent return for a second term.

Book's goal with the presidential run: gain national attention to present him as a force for 2000's election. DC players believed Book moved to 2000 front-runner status with a decent showing this cycle. Next cycle, the field appeared wide open, and no incumbent stood in his way.

The campaign demanded Book's energy, but his senate seat was not due up. There was no risk of him losing the seat. So, when he failed to win his party's nomination, as anticipated, his senate seat guaranteed a safe landing spot.

To Pete Book, Sundays were sacred. His life spun out of control Monday through Saturday. True, as a political animal he enjoyed the push. However, a day with his wife and kids renewed him. Also, any day he slept past 7:00 proved pure luxury. When his private phone rang at 4:59 a.m., anger flashed through him. Only Kyle Kenner dared call him at this hour, but Kenner knew better.

Zero chance of the phone waking Samantha. So, Pete groggily rolled out of bed and trudged to the office. Halfway there, the phone stopped. Book turned to return to bed. Then the phone started again.

He picked up the phone as the clock clunked behind him, 5 a.m. "Hello," he said in his best polite but annoyed voice.

A nasally female uttered four words, "Hold for the President." Pete Book found himself fully awake.

• • •

Gertrude sat on her front porch enjoying one of the best days of her life. As a horse person, she rose early. Allie updated her. The campus staff completed final arrangements for the Arrington AIDS Arts Gala. She instructed Allie to select two of Wyeth's paintings this year. Allie fought her. They donated just one in years past.

She did not tell her daughter this was the last Arrington AIDS Arts Gala, or at least Gertrude's last. As Allie prepared breakfast, Gertrude watched Beth scoot around the porch, babbling in the incoherent way uniquely beautiful to grandmothers.

Gertrude finished reading Foxx Kauffman's article and laughed. Of course, how could she not see it coming? How did she not foresee this toxic ending to the four-part play she haphazardly set into motion before it got away from her? She remembered from her time studying the classics how a play broke down:

Act 1: *Introduction or Exposition.* In this case, a heartbroken woman revenges her son's death and takes it upon herself to correct a broken system. Still, her actions corrected nothing; the system proved too corrupt. So, abandoning hope, she stops.

Act 2: *Plot Arch or Rising Action.* Someone more talented and equipped, two men she never met, unexpectedly took up the mantle and continued her quest. Enter Loyola and Tigre.

Act 3: *Plot Twist or Climax.* Authorities kill Loyola and Tigre. Everyone assumes the story ended. Enter the *Tapes of Wrath.*

Act 4: *The Final Catastrophe or the Reckoning.* The Reckoning. She liked that; she remembered the rough definition by memory from her days as a political science teacher. The payment of accounts due or a judgment to be paid.

Foxx Kauffman smartly used the word as the title of his latest article. She smiled. Gertrude consumed with passion the great

Russian authors, Dostoevksy, Tolstoy, Turgenev, and Pushkin. She enjoyed the Brontë sisters, Jane Austen, Dickens, Twain, Hemmingway. She most loved Virginia Woolf, whom she met briefly as a young girl.

Still, no written word in her lifetime granted the joy of Foxx Kauffman's article, "The Reckoning."

Gertrude beamed at her granddaughter, understanding her closing chapter awaited. Gertrude's reckoning. The cancer returned. No doctor told her. Allie, despite her razor-sharp intuition, failed to guess. But Gertrude felt her body's deadly copilots return to the helm. No need to confirm the fact.

A woman who twice fought off an attacker recognizes the enemy's tactics. She beat cancer twice, and though not a doctor, she understood the bleak chances of a third conquest. More importantly, she found herself bereft of the will or inclination to battle her foe again.

She looked to the crystal blue sky, the horses grazing to her left, and at the beauty of little Beth Arrington scooching from toy to toy. Not a bad way to go, with her horses, in the home she built from nothing, beside her beautiful and determined daughter and her blessing of a granddaughter. Reckoning be damned.

• • •

"The Reckoning"
Foxx Kauffman / Columnist / *The Times*
Sunday Edition
Re-printed in *The Houston Chronicle*
Washington, DC / September 18, 1994

How did you guess this would end?

Seriously, I am asking the question.

Did you think the politicians, bureaucrats, judges, and business executives soiled by the *Tapes of Wrath* might accept their punishment with grace?

Did you expect apologies?

Did you hope these men would donate their ill-gotten gains to the Sisters of Mercy?

I like Disneyland, I do, but our situation bears no resemblance to a fairy tale. No glass slippers on the horizon.

In a predictable DC twist, the *Tapes of Wrath* now seem less interesting than The Reckoning. You heard me. The release of new tapes reached appointment-viewing status. Now new tape broadcasts seem passé. How can that be, Foxx, you ask?

Well, kids, it's because our elected officials turned on themselves. One of the first politicians implicated in the scandal, Sonny Howe, the Governor of South Carolina, started the ball rolling. Sources close to Governor Howe confirm, in return for a reduced sentence, Howe provided proof that he and both South Carolina senators received large, under-the-table donations to gain permit approval for a new resort hotel. South Carolina legislators shot down the resort's construction once before. Environmentalists argued the construction would endanger the Hawksbill, Kemp's ridley, and leatherback sea turtles. Howe worked through sycophants to ensure the resort's approval the second time around.

Did South Carolina's Governor sell out his colleagues? And Howe?

When Sonny Howe brokered his deal, the "Sell Out Your Friends and Finger Pointing" Tour began. So far seventeen politicians highlighted, or low-lighted, on the *Tapes of Wrath* testified against their brethren, for the promise of reduced sentences. Politicians and business leaders *not* on the original tapes face indictment because of the testimony of sullied colleagues.

You can predict the sequel, right?

The second generation of soiled souls sells out a third generation of dastardly DC residents.

The third movie in the trilogy: an epic finger-pointing session.

Gosh, what fun.

Still, the biggest news: the FBI announced a deep internal investigation. California Congresswoman Libby Lyinstein who headed an FBI Oversight Committee, found herself outed on the *Tapes of Wrath*. She admitted she and others applied pressure to the FBI and the Director of National Intelligence to keep the tapes underground. She confirmed the FBI confiscated the tapes from Loyola's and Tigre's office and homes. Under pressure, the FBI buried the tapes.

Months ago, a street gang allegedly killed FBI Deputy Director Henry Moss and Special Agent in Charge Lyle Lackland. Someone executed Moss and Lackland's murderers later that night. That story got suppressed.

Are these murders related to the tapes? Probably. FBI agents took down Loyola and Tigre in Austin. So, let the conspiracy theories begin.

Wait, there's more. Lyinstein has two young children and would crucify her own mother for a reduced sentence. She spoke candidly about federal law enforcement officers openly for sale. Lyinstein hinted corrupt officials used lower-ranking agents as unwitting hit teams.

When these corrupt agents named by Lyinstein enjoy their date with prosecutors, one can only imagine who will be sold out. Their agencies task these men and women to keep our country's secrets, not the secrets of the sins against our country.

The press will attack these stories like politicians on a plate of payola, a buffet of bribes, a gorg'arama of graft. Okay, you get the point. So, pick up any paper, open any magazine, turn on any television, because you, dear readers, own a front-row seat to The Reckoning.

●　　●　　●

Samantha waited by the door for her husband's return. He woke her hours earlier, telling her #42 summoned him. She, like her husband, found herself wide awake.

Why did the southern charmer, POTUS, the world's most powerful man, and the leader of the rival party, call her husband?

Samantha donned her Sunday best because she did not know the day's agenda. Also, overdressed proved a smaller sin than underdressed in her world. She called their nanny, Lita. Yes, Lita agreed to watch the girls on Sunday for time-and-a-half. So, the girls now occupied the playroom learning Spanish. Samantha surveyed her beautiful home, not knowing her future.

Then she heard the distinctive sound of their security lock turning. Samantha stood, ready. Despite his early wake-up call, her husband appeared energized. Samantha chose to mirror his mood.

"You're excited," she led.

"Oh God, yes," he said.

"I'm a politician's wife; I understand there're things you can't say, but tell me what you can."

"I'll tell you everything, everything."

She took a deep breath to prepare.

"So, when I answered the phone, the President asked me to get ready fast and come meet him. So, I showered quickly…"

"And put on your best suit, you look handsome."

"Thanks. You look gorgeous. Ready to be First Lady on a Jacqueline Kennedy scale."

"Wow, thank you." Samantha allowed herself to briefly enjoy his words, but her need to hear the story overwhelmed the compliment. "But, back to the President."

"So, I'm out the front door, thinking I'd grab a cab, but a limo and four Secret Service agents are waiting. I thought they'd drive me to the White House. They didn't. They dropped me at the Smithsonian, shepherded me in, and escorted me to the John F. Kennedy display. Remember where that is?"

"Of course, you took me there on one of our first dates."

"The President stood in front of a collection of JFK photos, admiring the display. He did not turn. He made me wait. Then said, without turning, 'I met him, you know? I shook his hand.'"

"Yes, Mr. President, I love that story."

He turned, smiling, and said, "Me too."

Except for the Secret Service, the place was deserted. But the Secret Service made themselves scarce. Forty-two walked; I followed.

"I come here before big decisions. I think about what he'd do."

I stayed quiet. "Many people sainted him now, but he was imperfect, you know. He made mistakes…"

The President seemed to drift in thought. "Still, Americans remember Kennedy as one of the greats. He understood the American people don't tolerate indecision. Set big goals, stick to them."

"Kennedy spoke the words: 'We choose to go to the moon.' He had no idea how our nation would achieve the goal. But believed in American's ability to find a way. I'm not sure if that was Kennedy's greatest speech, but it forever changed our nation."

"Tomorrow, my speech will change this nation forever, Pete."

Time passed as we walked. I heard radio chatter, I knew the Secret Service surrounded us, but I no longer saw them. I started to speak. He held his hand up, silencing me.

We kept walking.

"Pete, I've made mistakes, most of us have. Now's not the time to consider my mistakes. We're presented with the opportunity to find long-term solutions."

"Today, you remove yourself from the Presidential Race."

"Sir?"

"We both know you won't win this election. Save your supporters' money and withdraw."

I started to speak, and he held up his hand again.

"My people tell me you are clean, squeaky clean."

"I made mistakes too, sir, but I planned to be President since I was 19 years old, and…"

"Tomorrow, I'm selecting you, from my rival party to lead a team to investigate DC-based corruption. You pick your team with no influence from me. You report to no one except the American people."

"But sir…"

"As the leader of this, let's call it task force for now, you'll receive more free press than your supporters could buy. You'll be a presidential front-runner in 2000, along with my VP and the Governor of Colorado…"

"Chad Cash," I murmured.

"You'll be in charge of DC-based corruption. Cash's team will investigate non-DC-related corruption, the governors, local politicians, judges, etc. The Vice President will serve as ambassador between the groups and your hammer if you need one."

"Then, at the height of the trials, you and your team propose real changes, term limits, campaign funding limits. I'll highlight these in tomorrow's speech, help pave the way."

"What if I withdraw from the race and someone implicates you before the next election? I'd miss a hell of an opportunity."

He nodded.

"You think so? You'll be the great knight battling to cleanse DC. Your day will come soon enough, Pete. Still, stay in the race. Your choice, but this opportunity goes to someone else."

I stood there for a long time.

Then he spoke. "You want to be President. You'll get there. But don't you want America to remember you as the man who cleaned up Washington? If you don't take this opportunity, someone else will. Picture how history will remember the man who gets this job. Pete, picture it..."

"Even if historians question my presidency, I'll be the President that gave *you* the power to get this done. My greatest act, my moon shot."

•   •   •

Samantha's voice jerks him back to the present. "He's smooth."

"Yes, with your permission, I'm asking if I can withdraw..."

"Of course, Pete."

"Can you imagine what I'll find?"

"No, dear, I don't want to."

•   •   •

Monday Morning, September 19, 1994
Gertrude put down her Monday copy of the *Beaumont Enterprise*. Newspapers delivered markedly different news to her in consecutive days. From the heights of yesterday's Foxx Kauffman article to today's lows.

Someone dug up old bones.

To be specific, somebody's re-examining Ollie Whiteman's death. Gertrude checked the *Houston Chronicle*; no mention there, thank God. Still, the fact that the article showed up in the Beaumont paper, printed thirty minutes from her home, seemed more disturbing.

She stood deliberately. Much to do, little time. All her advanced work proved essential. Fake passports ready, forged birth certificates on file, "hightailing-it" backpacks ready to go.

Just a simple phone conversation to get started—the toughest call she would ever make. Technically simple in today's world, emotionally a hurricane. She needed her ally.

She made her way to the barn and knocked. Allie greeted her, sporting Beth on her hip.

"Allie, dear, please saddle up Voltaire for me, I am riding into town."

"Mom, I'll drive you."

"Dear, if I wanted a car ride, I promise you would be the person I would ask. I do not. Please saddle Voltaire."

"You understand I'll follow you and keep tabs, right?"

"Allie, another day, any other day, your company would be welcome. Today, I ask a favor. I will saddle Voltaire myself if you choose not to oblige."

"Okay, Mom. Watch Beth for me."

"My pleasure."

"If you're not back soon, I'm coming for you."

"I would expect nothing less."

Gertrude assumed Philippa died with Ollie Whiteman, years earlier. Time to dust off the old gal. She calculated, then whispered to herself, *6:30 a.m. here, about 12:30 p.m. there.*

•   •   •

Tuesday, September 20, 1994

Liu bull-rushed forward, not waiting to research the Conroe family. She and Tucker arrived in Midland on Sunday morning and tried to intercept Conroe family members. The family estate and both daughters' homes stood empty. They checked the homes again yesterday, same result. They staked-out Conroe Oil Monday as well. No family member showed for work.

Yesterday, Tucker checked Sunday papers and found nothing from Katherine about reopening the Ollie Whiteman case. This morning, he tore through the Houston, San Antonio, Austin, and Dallas papers. Nothing about Whiteman. He did not find copies of Katherine's paper, the *Beaumont Enterprise*, in Midland. Not surprising, most towns only carried papers from the major metro areas.

Liu researched Katherine. The young reporter wrote the *Beaumont Enterprise's* society page, puff pieces about weddings, cattlemen's balls, and local celebrities. Liu acted unconcerned but worry stalked Tucker.

Following procedure, Liu tried to report to her boss, Deputy Director Carmen Angelo, to no avail. Calls remained unanswered. She preferred to go into Conroe Oil soft, asking for help, not full-blown FBI bravado. Tucker called his father once they reached Midland. Mr. Tucker recommended avoiding the old man, and Dee

Dee and Norene, who he called the "surly sisters." Dee Dee handled accounting and Norene oversaw operations, both carbon copies of their father. Mr. Tucker counseled his son to start with Mother. The matriarch arrived first each morning.

So, here she and Tucker sat, Tuesday, 6:45 a.m., coffee in hand, ready for anything, when a newish, champagne-colored Cadillac Coupe De Ville rolled into the company's lot. Liu sipped coffee, watching the white-haired woman emerge from the car, taking time to retrieve her cane and Thermos from the Cadillac. Thermos in hand, the woman started her walk inside.

Liu watched as the old woman glanced to her left and spotted the agents resting against Tucker's sedan. Mrs. Conroe paused, gauging them, taking an extra second to analyze Tucker. Instead of continuing her path to the door, the woman hobbled boldly, if slowly, toward Tucker.

The old woman's eyes bounced between the two agents. Each time the octogenarian studied Tucker; Liu caught hints of recognition wash across the woman's face. The woman's face, ripe with cunning, finished her approach and spoke before Liu identified the pair.

"I know you," the woman said, pointing her cane at Tucker.

"No, ma'am, but you met my father."

"You look like 'im."

"Thank you, ma'am. I'll consider that a compliment."

"Do as you must," the woman said. A wry smile cracked her withered face. "What's the FBI need with an 85-year-old grandmother on this spry Tuesday morning?"

They both looked confused. They had not identified themselves.

"Ahhh." She let the agents marinate on her assessment. Then she solved the riddle for them. "I remember Cat mentioning a few months 'fore he died, Tuck's son joined the FBI. Not a thing you forget." The woman pointed to her noggin for emphasis. "Come in. You probably wanna ask questions, and I want my favorite cushion under my ancient butt."

She turned without their affirmation and walked to the door with surprising vigor. "Just back from family vacation late last night, so give me time to get our office running."

Tucker stepped forward to open the door for the matriarch but found it locked. The old woman dangled keys, shaking her head. Tucker laughed, took her keys, and opened the door. Once inside,

Mrs. Conroe appeared undeterred by the FBI's presence. She turned on the office lights, started the five-gallon coffee urn, and adjusted the thermostat. She poured herself coffee, not offering a cup to Liu or Tucker, and motioned for them to follow.

They settled in her office and waited while Mrs. Conroe cleared voice mail. After she finished, she asked, "So young...and not quite as handsome as your father...Mr. Tucker, why are you bothering me?"

Liu started, "Mrs. Conroe..."

"Betty."

"Betty, I'm Special Agent in Charge Natalie Liu, and you guessed, this is Senior Special Agent Tanner Tucker."

"Fancy titles."

"...Ahh, thanks. We're here today..."

"What'd my idiot husband do?"

"I'm sorry?"

"My husband, what'd he do this time?"

"Nothing, or nothing as far as we're concerned. We're here about your son."

"Whew, he didn't do nothin' this time, he's dead," Mrs. Conroe said without remorse or humor.

Liu tried not to smile. She began questioning Mr. Tucker's advice. This old woman, not her husband, was the brains behind Conroe Oil. Liu examined Betty's wall and noted the degrees hanging behind her, an undergraduate degree from Texas Woman's University, a law degree from Oberlin College.

The old woman followed Liu's eyes. "Everyone assumes I got a law degree to keep my old man out of trouble."

Liu asked, "Is it true?"

"You said you weren't here to talk about him, so not today."

Based on Tanner's father's commentary, and Betty's colorful statements, Liu wondered what might happen if the IRS turned attention to Conroe Oil. Still, Conroe Oil's finances, no matter how inventive, remained outside today's purview.

"Mrs. Conroe, I hate to ask, but we need your help. I need the details of your son's death."

"So, you don't believe 'the hunting accident' bullshit?" Mrs. Conroe cackled. "Been waiting for you to stop by for years. Figured just a matter of time."

The room stood silent for a thirty-count as Tucker and Liu considered Betty's words. Tucker's expression mirrored Liu's, relief, an acknowledgment that answers may finally be revealed.

After gauging the moment's ramifications, Liu asked, "You knew your son didn't die because of a hunting accident?"

"Not for sure, 'til today. But now I do." A dark expression colored the woman's worn, wrinkled face. "Honestly, I'm surprised he didn't die sooner."

Liu raised her eyebrows, encouraging Betty to continue.

"Our business grew gangbusters when Cat operated in good-old-boy-land. Everything went our way, every time. You gotta call in hefty favors or apply powerful leverage to keep that rolling."

"Can we review your books from Cat's time? To look for large cash outlays?" Tucker asked.

"Oh, you're so sweet, naïve, and proper. Like your dad."

"We'd find nothing in the books?" Liu questioned.

"No," Betty answered.

"Mrs. Conroe, sorry, Betty, each of us have something the other wants. We have zero interest in tearing through your financials, and you don't want us to."

Betty nodded.

"Also, we both want to know who killed Cat?"

"Oh, you may want to, but I already know."

"Excuse me?"

"I know who killed him, or at least who shot 'em."

"You do?"

"Took me a bit to figure it out, but sure."

"Mind telling us?"

"After we come to an agreement."

"Ma'am, I'm an FBI agent, I'm not here to make deals," said Liu.

This time Betty cackled. She stopped and looked at them, slapped her knee then cackled more. They waited for her to stop. "Did you just say a government agency won't make a deal?" More cackling. "Ohh, girl, to be so young, beautiful, and dewy-eyed."

"Ma'am, we can get a warrant..." Tucker started.

"My friends say I'm starting to show signs of Alzheimer's. I forget all kinds of stuff, all kinds. What if the Alzheimer's...?"

"What type of agreement, Betty?"

"You leave before my husband arrives."

"Done," Tucker and Liu confirmed in unison.

"You have no memory of where you found this information."

"Done. If your information's correct."

"It's correct."

"Anything else?" Liu questioned.

"You forget about Conroe Oil. No mention to any government entities."

"How can you guarantee we'll keep our promise?"

"Cuz'a Dudley Do-Right's father," Betty said, nodding to Tucker. "His word's rock solid."

"Okay, you have our word," Liu confirmed, nodding to Tucker. "Who killed Cat?"

"Well, Cat was good for business. Too good, 'cuz he was crooked. I raised him. I loved him, but he was almost, *almost*, as twisted as the politicians he ran with. The answer's obvious when two people from Cat's poker game ended up dead. My son and the no-good, ass-kissing congressman, Ollie Whiteman."

"Poker game?" asked Liu.

"My husband funded a poker game for Cat, politicians and movers and shakers. High stakes, people lost thousands of dollars, cars, in one case a home. My son showed no inclination for work, but he golfed like a PGA veteran, fished like a pro, and majored in extracting money from politicians at the poker table."

"And?" nudged Liu.

"And Ollie Whiteman was into Cat for $250,000. One of my daughters dated Whiteman. After she heard how much money Ollie owed Cat, she said the idiot played poker as badly as he performed in the sack." The old woman cackled again.

"No one from the poker game told the cops about the deaths?" asked Tucker.

"Sure, they'd call the cops and report 'Two members of our illegal, high-stakes poker game died.' That's not gonna happen, son."

Liu and Tucker waited. Betty Conroe wanted to continue. "Anyway, when Cat got shot, the family thought the wayward bullet was an accident. I assumed Whiteman pulled the trigger."

"Then Whiteman ended up dead," led Liu.

"Now you're thinking my family killed Whiteman. Honestly, my husband would'a killed him. If he thought like me. But my husband had nothing to do with Whiteman's death. I know for sure."

"How?"

"The man can't keep a secret from me."

Liu tried to hide her smile, failing. "Can anyone?"

"No," Betty stated. "Possibly as a young woman, not anymore. Besides, a woman killed Whiteman. It was messy, crime of passion."

Tucker and Liu sat, too enthralled to interrupt. "A year before Whiteman died, my husband picked up a boatload of drilling equipment dirt cheap from a young, cocky rival. Kid got overextended, had lots of equipment for some new project, then something changed. We won the drilling contract the kid thought he won. We printed money on the deal. My husband bought Cat a deep-sea fishing boat and a Mercedes. I don't have details, but I can guess. You can too."

"So, the young oilman, he killed your son?"

"Not a patient young woman, are ya?"

"Sorry," said Liu.

"No, wasn't the young oilman. He committed suicide. The kid lost millions. Plus, the kid's wife snuck around with a no-good, philandering, scratch-golfing, poker-playing scoundrel."

Liu could not help herself. "Your son?"

Betty touched her nose while pointing at Liu. "That's how Cat got the inside info."

Liu continued, "After that, you guessed who it was?"

"Who do you think I am, Agatha Christie? No, still not enough clues."

Liu felt a step behind. "How did you know?"

"The married woman, Briana I think, died weeks after my son, before Whiteman."

Liu pushed. "How?"

"Papers claimed alcohol poisoning, but if you put pieces together, it's cockamamie."

"You put it together and told no one, even though you knew who killed your son?"

"Let's do the math. If I told my husband, he takes revenge and is too damn stupid to cover his tracks. I lose my husband. God bless him. If I told my daughters, they're smart enough to do something. Maybe get away with it. But there's a chance I lose 'em too. That's a no go. If I told the cops, they ask how I figured it out. Cops start snooping around. I look ridiculous in stripes."

"You could make an anonymous tip," suggested Tucker.

"But, if the boys in blue put the pieces together, law enforcement's up my backside. So, I told no one. Not 'til today. 'Cuz today we have a deal."

"Okay, so, who did it?"

"My son bought his ticket to an early grave, fair and square. Still, it eats at a mother. I don't know who exactly, but I know who approximately. I'd have done the same damn thing if I were them."

"Who then?"

"The family of the upstart oilman, of course."

"What's the family's name?" Tucker asked.

In Liu's childhood, she loved nothing more than jumping off things. As a toddler, she leapt from her bed or the sofa. Teenage Natalie Liu jumped from trees or her parents' home. When she returned from college for the summer, she and her friends jumped from bridges or cliffs into the lakes.

Liu experienced moments of fear staring down before the jump. The jump's height appeared more daunting from the launch point than the ground. She loved the instant courage invoked to leap. Ahhh, then the thrill of the fall. Finally, the ultimate rush, plunging into the water, surrounded by a new ecosystem, a moment of pure ecstasy.

Natalie Liu felt that now answering in rhythm with Betty Conroe.

"Arrington," they both said, but only Natalie continued. "Bo Arrington, that's the guy's name."

•   •   •

Gertrude's well-maintained farm truck pulled slowly into the parking lot of Beaumont's Parkdale Mall, the only mall within forty minutes of Silsbee, and the perfect place to begin their subterfuge.

As promised, the limousine awaited them, near the mall's movie theater. The limousine driver transferred Allie's and Beth's hurriedly packed luggage into the limousine's trunk. Allie moved Beth's child safety seat, while the driver opened the door for Gertrude.

Once Allie secured Beth, she climbed in herself. The well-maintained limousine smelled of leather and jasmine car spray. As the black limousine pulled from the parking lot to begin their journey, Allie took a deep breath and said, "Mom, this happened so fast."

"Yes," Gertrude confirmed. "Exciting."

"Not the word I'd use."

"Ahh, Allie, you will understand soon enough."

•   •   •

On the limousine ride from Beaumont to Dallas, Philippa Harrington told Allie everything.

The five-hour ride proved the most rewarding of Philippa's and Allie's lives. Philippa's daughter now comprehended Gertrude Arrington existed for Allie, not a myth or a made-up entity, but an actual person created for Allie and her brothers' benefit, to ensure their safety, to protect them.

Philippa never before felt contentment. Today she embraced the word. Someone listened to her entire story—her mistakes, her past, her deceptions. Her daughter knew her, every flaw, mistake, misdirection, and still loved her.

Of course, the children's mysterious British father, as Allie suspected, complete bollocks.

Allie's mother shared everything—grief, adventures... lies... murders. Gertrude laughed to herself. Allie naively—a strange word for her—thought her life could not prove more interesting. Wrong, incorrect, an immeasurable miscalculation. The next strange chapter of Allie's life began today.

Allie's daughter, Philippa's granddaughter, now possessed unimaginable opportunities. Still, Gertrude experienced regret. Her granddaughter would never remember the place that she, Allie, Bo, and Wyeth built, molded, and improved from the ground up.

Allie's words pulled Philippa from her thoughts. "Mom, come with us."

"No, dear. I want to die in my home, and Silsbee, Texas, is my home."

"It's back, isn't it, the cancer?"

"Yes, dear."

"Why didn't you tell me?"

"Giving you extra time not knowing seemed a simple gift within my power. Dear, no one, not the boys, not my father or mother, proved more loyal than you. My Allie, my ally, my best friend. I will miss you."

Philippa sat in her seat, studying Beth, hoping her granddaughter would never experience the horrors Allie experienced. Philippa/Gertrude, all of her, both of her, prayed Beth enjoyed a bond with Allie as strong as Gertrude shared with her daughter.

"How much do they know?"

"What a loaded question. Who exactly do you mean?"

"I guess law enforcement...to start."

"I feel them closer. Or why dig up Whiteman again? They will put together the pieces pretty fast. If they asked the right questions. I will pay for what *I did*."

"Mom..."

"What *I did*, Allie, do you understand? What...*I...did*."

"Yes, Mother. When I arrive, late tonight, how much will they know?"

"Exactly enough, only enough. You understand the life you must live now, correct?"

Allie nodded.

"Some beautiful flowers, like the moonflower, bloom best in the shadows. A life in shadows can still prove exceptional."

"I understand."

"That's your life, but not your daughter's, as long as you accept your role."

"I accept."

"Why fly out of Dallas instead of Houston?"

"A few more hours with you, simple as that," Philippa said and smiled. "You cannot contact him, you understand?"

"Beth's father?"

"A difficult request, I understand. Mr. Luther is a charming man, much more attractive than he recognizes, a rare quality in our world."

"Yes, rare."

"Allie...please understand the inherent dangers of contacting..."

"Mother, I understand the dangers perfectly."

Act 4: The Final Catastrophe or the Reckoning

The payment of accounts due or a judgment to be paid.

The Drive to Silsbee, Texas

Erasmus Luther sped from Houston to Silsbee, Texas. Liu called Luther from the road to update him on Ollie Whiteman and the connection to the Arringtons. Luther understood by making the call, the FBI agent ignored a directive from her leadership. Luther checked his watch. He would arrive hours before Liu and Tucker.

He ignored specific instructions himself. Liu told him to get to Silsbee, check into a motel, and wait. Still, he needed to talk to Allie. She owed him that.

He remembered their dinner conversation. Allie discussed Bo's death. Luther possessed a piece of knowledge Tucker and Liu did not—the certainty of Allie's involvement.

So, despite Liu's orders, Luther planned to arrive early. His heart, brain, hell, every fiber of his being demanded answers. Instincts told him neither Allie nor her mother wished him harm. He prayed his instincts proved correct.

Luther arrived at the Arrington's home and pulled to the gate. He waited, but the gate did not open, and he spotted no activity in the home. Luther admired several horses grazing in the field. Someone left one old stallion saddled. Luther opened his car door, nothing happened. The remnants of a bonfire smoldered a hundred yards from the barn.

He walked to the fence and climbed over. He went to the house first and rang the doorbell. No answer. Zero movement. He pulled the door, finding it open. Luther stepped inside. Nothing changed since his time here. Except the occupants hurriedly rearranged the pictures. A quick review of the photographs proved the picture of Gertrude when she was young and all photos of Allie missing. The lovely, lacquered box and hairpin remained in place.

He explored the home, knowing Tucker and Liu's arrival, best-case scenario, remained hours away. Driving from Midland to

Silsbee meant nine hours of windshield time. They called him at 10 a.m. after two hours on the road. They would not arrive before 5 p.m.

When he got to the kitchen, a note posted on the fridge with a bumblebee refrigerator magnet caught his attention:

Make yourself comfortable, tea and ice water are in the fridge if you get thirsty. I will return soon. Gertrude Arrington.

The note, not addressed to anyone specifically, seemed unusual. More interesting, the date of the note—today.

Of course, he never told Gertrude or Allie the FBI recruited him to investigate the Thompson and Greene executions. Erasmus considered his date with Allie and her response to the news that he and Foxx grew up together, best friends.

If Allie followed the story, which surely she did, she witnessed Foxx break the story of the first tape, the Watergate murders of Thompson and Greene. She proved her intelligence to Luther repeatedly. Allie considered the facts and assessed the connection using information only she possessed. Luther wrote about famous assassinations, a noted expert. Foxx Kauffman received the tape from an unnamed source. Allie ascertained Luther's involvement in the investigation. The next assumption for her was that Luther delivered the tape to Foxx.

Luther completed his tour of the home, seeing nothing else out of order. He stepped outside and walked the premises, noting a few horses remained stabled. Luther ventured to the barn. The entry door remained ajar, propped open by a doorstop. Luther stepped into a space as elegantly furnished as a modern New York penthouse. Signs of quick departure grabbed his attention. Still, he allowed himself to examine this space, *her* space.

Rich gray furniture and stainless steel highlighted the living room. The modern kitchen appeared as well equipped as a midtown restaurant. The walls featured several Wyeth Arrington paintings and other modern works. Luther looked to the piece over the fireplace, recognizing the Salvador Dali print. Surprised, knowing Allie, that she placed a Dali print in the middle of her brother's original masterpieces. Luther moved closer to the print then softly touched the surface. He reexamined the room. Allie displayed the Dali painting in a place of honor. Holy shit, an original Dali.

Luther stood in place, taking in everything. Like the pictures in the main house, someone left the barn apartment slightly off-kilter.

He poked around the rest of the downstairs, finding nothing. His gaze carried him to a rustic staircase leading upstairs. Once he climbed the stairs, an open area acted as an office of sorts. The office recently contained a computer and printer; unplugged cords littered the room, but no computers or printers.

He walked to a bedroom. Someone shoved an enormous bed in the corner. The other side of the room stood empty, containing no furniture or clues of the area's previous use.

He took a deep breath and rummaged through each drawer of Allie's desk, hoping to locate a note or clues from Allie. Luther found nothing.

He turned and noticed one unexplored door. Once opened, his eyes ravaged the images inside. Despite his circumstances, despite the certainty the woman he loved was a killer, he stood in the doorway of Allie's barn/apartment with his erection pushing, pressing, painfully against his corduroys, in utter shock.

• • •

With Allie's plane safely away, and tearful good-byes behind her, Gertrude slept a majority of the limousine ride home. The physical activity needed to prepare the house for...guests, added to her exhaustion. Between waking and sleeping, in her moments of cognition, she cataloged today among her favorites. Despite her estimation of impending doom, Gertrude vowed to hold that sentiment most dear. Someone now knew all of her secrets, all of them. "Liberation" seemed the most accurate word to describe her state of being.

She returned to Silsbee, her adopted home, with much to consider. Gertrude and Allie found themselves forced to act hastily. Somehow, as a team, she and Allie conquered the vital tasks— everything, even the most fatal of details.

She would arrive before 6:30 p.m., her favorite time of the day, when satsuma sunsets decorate the Texas sky. Her neighbor's son arrived to round up the horses around 7:15, a task the boy performed in exchange for saddle time. A wonderful arrangement for everyone. Yesterday she asked him to saddle up Voltaire around noon, hating that Voltaire would be saddle-bound so long.

Even if she returned to an empty house, not her estimation, the Lord provided exit strategies. Gertrude's third date with toxic Mr.

C hung over her decisions. She dreaded most the emptiness of her home. A home haunted by the spirts of her dead sons and now departed daughter and granddaughter.

She considered burning the place down, freeing apparitions she must face around each corner. Gertrude held the thought captive, recognizing the dark fantasy remained outside her genuine desires. Her home, the beautiful pastures, and grazing horses represented the palette to paint her last memories. Even if a higher power provided only minutes in her home, those minutes provided incalculable value to her.

Those minutes, possibly all she had to treasure, besides the knowledge of her daughter and granddaughter's safety. Beyond the reach of the most ambitious lawman, wrapped in layers of deception, wit, and guile. Hidden deep in the bosom of political and financial resources impossible to unravel.

Safe.

• • •

Liu's calls to her boss remained unreturned. She considered, but decided against, calling local law enforcement. Cat Conroe, Ollie Whiteman, and Briana Swanson Arrington's killer remained free for nine years. The Arrington family hosted fundraising bashes and shown no inclination toward flight from the law. The Arringtons demonstrated the opposite modus operandi, complete lack of fear.

Liu and Tucker took turns behind the wheel to speed up their 550-mile trek. Shorter routes existed between Midland to Silsbee, full of back road twists and turns. Instead, Tucker coaxed Liu to pass through San Antonio to pick up Interstate 10, predicting, a faster arrival. Now, thanks to an empty gas tank, Liu begrudgingly stopped at Stuckey's.

Despite their mission, Tucker brimmed boyishly with excitement. He spotted the Stuckey's billboard an hour earlier and prodded Liu to stop there. "We need gas anyway, gotta be Stuckey's."

Liu had not seen Tucker so excited in her time with him. Check that, she had, but in a completely different arena. After they stopped, Tucker practically begged her to go inside, she declined. Tucker started the gas pumping, then hurried into Stuckey's.

Liu topped off the gas. Upon his return Tucker held up a Stuckey's bag. "My turn to drive," he said to her.

"I'm good. I concentrate better when I drive."

Tucker drove a majority of their time together, due to his familiarity with Houston. Today provided a straight shot on Interstate 10, few turns, clear direction, so Liu jumped at the chance to sit behind the steering wheel. Tucker struggled in his role as a passenger. Still, Liu refused to surrender the driver's seat. After they pulled out, Tucker opened the bag.

"Can you eat while you drive?"

"Why?"

"Gotta try this." Tucker pulled out a large tube-shaped object covered in pecans.

"What's that?"

"A Stuckey's pecan roll," answered Tucker.

"That thing must weigh a pound."

"Close. Stuckey's is a southern tradition. Started in Georgia as a roadside pecan stand. They grew into this massive chain of roadside stores based on the founder's wife's pecan candies. Still, the mother of them all, is the pecan roll. Try it. You can't be a real Southerner without trying a Stuckey's pecan roll."

Tucker took a huge bite from one side. "Okay, I marked my territory, that's my side, the other side is yours."

"Sure," Liu said. A bite into the bar validated Tucker's excitement. "That's good."

"Since you're driving, slow down before you get to Beaumont. The highway patrol uses the area near the refineries as a speed trap. Notorious."

"Okay."

"Not exaggerating. As a teenager, they wrote me a ticket for going fifty-six miles an hour in a fifty-five zone. Assholes. Especially if they need to hit their quota, so slow down."

"We're federal agents in pursuit of an interstate murderer. We'll be okay."

"That and a buck will buy you a cup of coffee. These guys are ruthless."

Liu took another bite of the pecan roll and returned the indulgence to Tucker. She steered the conversation back to their task. "Okay, what do we know?"

"From the gala, I remember Pete Book grew up with the Arrington boys."

Liu prodded, "Is he in on it?"

"Not sure. He benefitted from Ollie Whiteman's death, which, according to Mrs. Conroe, the Arrington family orchestrated. However, Book also benefitted from Eagle Thompson's murder. If you believe Loyola and Tigre's tapes, the Arrington family didn't participate in Thompson's murder."

"Tigre could have lied."

"Sure, but why?"

They both sat silently, then Liu continued, "Okay, what else?"

"Kyle Kenner, Book's right hand, grew up with the Arringtons too."

"Kenner...in on it?"

"Too early to tell. The police report said a woman who matched the Arrington matriarch's general appearance killed Whiteman."

"Gertrude...I remember the name because it's old-fashioned. Did Gertrude Arrington kill Whiteman?" asked Liu.

"I'll know better when we arrive. Whiteman's killer was left-handed, not cinch-sure proof, but probably a dead giveaway if Gertrude Arrington leads with her left hand."

"How about the daughter?"

"No proof or appearance of her anywhere. Still, means nothing."

"Not what I mean. You danced with her; Luther is crazy about her; your thoughts?"

"She guessed we arranged everything, so Luther got a dance with her. She seemed smart, decisive, bright."

"Not too terrible to look at."

"No," Tucker said, not elaborating.

Smart man, Liu thought. "Gertrude's involved. So far, that's all we got."

"They're loaded, but the mother lost both sons. I'm not an art buff, but even I saw Arrington's Aphrodite on my trip to New York. I remember when Wyeth died from AIDS. Betty caught us up on Bo."

"The mother, Gertrude, speaks with an accent. Does the daughter?"

"No. I don't remember an accent. But she doesn't sound small-town Texas. She possessed a lot of her mother's grace."

"Do you remember the mother's accent?"

"Vaguely, didn't mark her as a murder suspect at the time. So, I didn't pay attention. Australian or British, maybe, I can't tell the difference."

"What do you think we're walking into?"

"No idea, and that disturbs me. Probably unwise to underestimate these women."

•   •   •

Erasmus Luther dropped to his knees, staring at the two nude portraits of Allie Arrington. He replayed his conversation with Gertrude before his first date with Allie. Wyeth Arrington, by habit, nervous tic, or process, painted four renditions of each model.

Always four.

Only two known copies of Wyeth's most famous model, *Arrington's Aphrodite*, existed, well outside this room. Cassandra Hinds, Wyeth's benefactor, held a copy in her personal collection. The most famous copy sold for a record amount at auction years ago. The remaining paintings, until a moment ago, remained unviewed by anyone, except painter and model.

Erasmus, like most Americans, viewed photos of *Arrington's Aphrodite*, currently on display at The Met. The painting rivaled the most famous works of any modern American painter. After attending the first gala, he located magazine photos of the second *Arrington's Aphrodite*, the one in the Hinds collection.

Both versions, stunning in their beauty, left few clues to the model's identity. Critics assumed, with Wyeth's death, the model's name would remain lost to history. The professor studied the painting hung to the left. The painting showed the model's petite peach-shaped bottom. Artful, but offering no clue of the model's identity. Unless, as in his case, from one exuberant engagement, you recognized the distinctive birthmark on the lower part of her back. A birthmark, vaguely resembling a rapier. A birthmark identifying the model. Erasmus assumed few held the key to solve the mystery, as he did, from the painting.

Luther understood a fact only three people on the planet comprehended. The four paintings presented a progression.

Four brief moments forever captured in time of Allie turning from the creek toward the painter.

The first painting in the sequence, the painting to Luther's left, presents the model's rear. Allie turned from Wyeth, unaware of his presence. The first painting communicated the model's bliss and tranquility.

Conversely, the second painting, *Cassandra Hinds' Aphrodite*, represented the model noting another's presence. Allie begins the turn. No chance to identify the model.

The third painting, the most famous *Aphrodite*, the version at The Met, Allie's face turned almost into view, taunting observers. Another millimeter turned toward the painter promises her identity.

The final painting in the sequence, the picture mounted to Luther's right, extinguished any doubt of the model's identity. No mystery to solve. Allie completed the turn.

Luther remembered the conversation with Allie. Wyeth stalked out his sister's creek swims. He painted his sister. Allie attempted to hide her resemblance to the painting subject. Aphrodite's flowing hair, gone. Allie's sported a short, elfish haircut.

The other giveaway; the overall feel of the painting. Wyeth Arrington's other paintings featured sharp, crisp strokes, very current, seeming of the present day. The *Arrington's Aphrodite*, now *Arrington's Aphrodites*, presented a softer, timeless quality as if painted from a dream, or at the very least from memory. Art experts placed the value of Wyeth Arrington's paintings in the hundreds of thousands of dollars. Still, The Met version of the Aphrodite's soared well beyond those estimates.

Erasmus, a historian, never considered himself an art critic. Still, he grasped why this painting, or now a series of paintings, forever represented Wyeth's master work. The Aphrodite series captured Wyeth's youth, painted from memories of his home, as an homage to a woman he loved more than any other—his sister. A sister, by her admission, he spoiled with every effort. One of the first two women he loved.

Still, as enticing, arousing, and mind-bending as these paintings were, more riddles awaited Erasmus Luther. Before her hasty departure, Allie addressed an envelope to him. She placed the envelope in a location easy to spot at the base of the paintings. He took a deep breath before opening the envelope.

He read the handwritten postcard featuring four words: *"You remember the spot."*

Luther hurried down the stairs, out of the barn, through the field, then followed his memory. He walked for twenty minutes before reaching the entrance into the woods, the path to their picnic. A pink kerchief marked the trailhead. Luther did not remember the kerchief from his last outing. He chose to believe Allie left the kerchief for him. The professor followed the meandering path down to the creek. Allie left the same wicker picnic basket atop a checkered tablecloth. He gasped when he opened the lid. No pimento cheese, sourdough bread, or chicken salad awaited. The basket contained one life-changing object. Moments earlier, as Luther sat dumbstruck in front of Wyeth's lost Aphrodites, the professor assumed he experienced the most earth-shattering moment of his life.

Allie's parting gift proved Erasmus Luther wrong.

•　　•　　•

After shock, Luther's emotions tilted toward surprise. Allie boldly left the envelope for anyone to see. Then Luther realized only he possessed the knowledge to follow the cryptic clue to the wicker basket's location and then translate the basket's contents. His head raced with possibilities. Luther understood Allie Arrington recruited him, in the most basic way possible. The FBI no longer paid him as a consultant, not for months, although he tried to help Tucker and Liu when possible. With Allie's hidden message, Erasmus switched sides, now a traitor to Liu and Tucker. He analyzed the situation; the facts validated his actions; he assumed many traitors felt the same about their motives. Not only would he no longer aid the FBI, but now he planned to subvert their investigation.

Carrying the picnic basket and tablecloth, Luther left the picnic site and returned to the Arringtons' pasture where he walked among the horses. A beautiful chestnut noted his presence with soft neighs and a nervous departure trot. Luther walked to the smoldering fire. He found a knotty branch nearby and poked the fire. Nothing discernable remained in the still smoldering ash. He found himself strangely happy. If he could not translate the fire's mysteries, maybe the FBI crime lab would struggle. Still, he stirred the ashes, encouraging the embers to burn hotter, then added the picnic basket and tablecloth for good measure. The flames kicked up, enlivened by the addition. He watched the flame's hungry talons embrace the wicker basket and gingham tablecloth.

Erasmus Luther now sat on the weathered but well-maintained front porch rocker, waiting. The small soft rubber contents of the basket, stuffed in his pocket to be shared with no one. He waited for the Arrington's return, or Tucker and Liu's arrival, in whatever order they occurred.

He returned to the fire to ensure the flames reduced all evidence to ash. In time, he saw the distinctive headlights of a government-issue sedan stop by the gate. Like him, they pulled to the side to allow the Arrington family an unimpeded path to their home.

Like him, they climbed the fence, admittedly more gracefully. He waited as they approached.

Liu and Tucker debated as they walked toward him.

Tucker asked, "When'd you arrive?"

"Fifteen minutes ago," Luther lied smoothly.

"We'd have arrived earlier, but someone got pulled over for a speeding ticket outside of Beaumont."

Luther laughed. "Everyone knows that's a speed trap."

Tucker looked to Luther. "We were talking...should we hide the cars so they don't know we're here?"

"I don't think that's necessary. They expected us, Gertrude left a note on the fridge."

"Of course, she did," said Liu shaking her head. "Of course, she did."

•　　•　　•　　•

Luther watched Liu and Tucker explore the property, offering no assistance or guidance. The threesome walked to the bonfire together. Luckily, the wicker basket and tablecloth burned before the agents arrived. When the agents split up, Liu explored the house and Tucker walked to the barn. The professor followed Tucker.

Luther's inner prankster demanded to see Tucker's reactions when he witnessed the Aphrodites. He reminded himself to act shocked when Tucker found the paintings. Luther retraced his steps, touching everything he touched the first time through the barn. He vowed to retrace his steps inside the home later.

Tucker, appreciating the elegance of the modern apartment built into the barn, looked to Luther. "Nice place."

Luther nodded.

"I know you're not an art expert, I assume the Wyeth Arrington paintings are original."

"I think so."

"Holy crap. That's a…"

"Original Salvador Dali, yes."

Tucker examined each art piece, then inspected the kitchen and the rest of the downstairs. Luther remained by his side. Tucker, like Luther before, explored the bottom floor before climbing upstairs.

After ascending the stairs, Tucker inspected the master bedroom and former office area.

"Appears furniture from this bedroom, the computer, and printer ended up on the bonfire."

"I'd guess that."

Tucker continued, "I understand about the computer. But why burn furniture?"

"Can't imagine," Luther lied.

Luther hung back in the office when Tucker opened the door to Allie's art gallery. A room reserved for two masterpieces.

Luther showed nothing when Tucker entered the room, stopped cold and uttered, "Ohh…wow."

• • •

Tucker spent a moment overcoming shock, then another moment appreciating the beauty in front of him. Luther watched as Tucker's mind raced. The professor watched Tucker's inward gentlemanliness finally pull him from the painting. His eyes seemed broader, larger, almost cartoonish when he addressed Luther.

"I'll...a...get Liu," Tucker mumbled. Luther understood Tucker's word economy, remembering his own inability to articulate on his first dance with Allie. Yes, her beauty proved distracting. Yet, the timeless conveyance of wit and intelligence Wyeth communicated in Allie's face stood as the painting's ultimate treasure.

Luther reveled in the painting, understanding this may be his last moment alone with her or her rendering. In later life, when Luther traveled back to this moment, with his Allie, the memory often lasted for hours, other times mere seconds.

Liu arrived. Luther heard her marvel over the downstairs decor, the Dali, and original artwork like Tucker moments before. Then he heard her march up the stairs.

Tucker led her directly to the paintings. Her first reaction, not as visceral as Tucker's or Luther's, proved equally shocking. She stood facing the pictures for four or five minutes before venturing words.

Tucker said, "Liu..."

She shut him down by raising her hand. So, Luther and Tucker waited as Liu's mind processed the information in front of her.

When she spoke, she appeared serene, relaxed. "I'm one of the first people to witness these paintings...."

"Yes," said Luther.

"Incredible. Erasmus, your girlfriend is breathtaking," stated Liu as fact, more than observation.

"She's not my girlfriend anymore," Luther stated.

"There's the fact that she may be a cold-blooded killer," reflected Tucker.

"There's that," said Liu. "If I was a guy, I might try to power past that."

• • •

Gertrude's small farm pickup pulled in front of her home. Earlier, she thanked the limousine driver, who over their marathon drive back from a Dallas-area private airport shared the details of his escape from his African homeland. He told stories of his childhood, his tribe, and the slaughter of his people. His family escaped to the US decades before.

She told him the United States served as her safe harbor as well, while withholding the details of her long-ago departure from Great

Britain. The driver dropped her back at Beaumont's Parkdale Mall parking lot, near the movie theatre. The driver helped Gertrude to her truck. She paid cash and tipped well, in return collecting a promise that he would forget every detail of their journey, no matter the circumstances.

"Madame, my family would reside in unmarked grave, if others lacked discretion." Gertrude assured her driver and new friend of similar circumstances. The old woman enjoyed the thirty-minute drive from Beaumont to her Silsbee home.

She did not know what to expect on her return home but assumed her greeting's inclusion of flashing red and blue police lights. Upon arrival, the former British heiress, retired schoolteacher, and executioner looked to her right at the two cars parked outside her gate. She smiled. The greeting lacked flashing lights, more dignified than she anticipated.

Her nosy neighbors would appreciate the consideration. She remembered the International Harvester parked in front. The vehicle belonged to Allie's beau, Erasmus Luther. The other car she did not recognize, obviously government-issue. After Allie's date with Luther, she informed Gertrude of her suspicion of the professor's involvement in the search for the perpetrators of the deaths of corrupt politicians. Gertrude's chest puffed a little with pride. Her daughter's diagnostic abilities still dazzled Gertrude.

She hit the remote control, opening the gate to her home, and drove slowly to the front of the house. Erasmus Luther and a handsome man and woman awaited. Gertrude collected her purse, then opened her truck's door.

When she looked up, she recognized the handsome man who offered his hand. "Hello, ma'am, I'm Tanner Tucker, we met once before. We've been waiting for you."

"Not too long, I hope, I hate to be an inconvenience. I remember you from one of the galas."

"Yes ma'am."

"I left you some tea, lemonade, and ice water; I hope you indulged."

Once he helped her out of the car, Tanner extended his arm to Gertrude. She enjoyed seeing manners, even in these circumstances. Gertrude walked to the porch, taking each step slower than she needed. She understood the importance of appearing helpless, even crippled. Once on her porch, Gertrude sat, deliberately exaggerating the effort.

She looked to the face she knew best. "Mr. Luther, please be a dear and retrieve the tray I left on the kitchen table. Collect four chilled glasses from the freezer and the pitchers of cold water and tea in the fridge. There is homemade lemonade as well. Bring that too."

"Yes, ma'am," he said departing.

"So, it's just you three today?"

"Yes," Tucker answered too quickly, before he noted Liu's shaking head. "I'm Senior Special Agent Tanner Tucker; this is my boss, Special Agent in Charge Natalie Liu."

"So nice to meet you both," said Gertrude. "Yes, ahh, now I recognize you from the news, you are the young man who killed Loyola and Tigre."

"Yes, ma'am." Tucker looked to his shoes.

"I cannot believe I did not put that together when we danced. Still, sometimes when you see someone out of context… Well, a shame really about Mr. Loyola and Mr. Tigre. I guess they got the last laugh, though. With the tapes, Mr. Tigre made for a haunting ghost, more terrifying than anything Dickens or Mary Shelly created. Well, to the intended audience at least. Young lady, I remember you too. You oversaw the investigation."

"Yes, ma'am."

"You did not help yourself to something to drink earlier?"

Neither Tucker nor Liu answered. Gertrude considered their reaction. "Ah, I see, you thought I might have poisoned the lemonade. How clever." She waited for Luther to return with the tray, glasses, and three small pitchers.

With her left hand, Gertrude poured a sampling of each pitcher into her glass. She smiled to them then drank the muddled concoction. She waited to prove her point then poured herself a glass of lemonade, also with her left hand.

"I do not like iced tea, I make it for guests. I prefer my tea hot, I always will."

Tucker looked to Liu, acknowledging that Gertrude Arrington was likely Ollie Whiteman's killer.

They waited. Liu nodded, and he poured himself a glass of tea. Luther pointed to the lemonade and Tucker obliged. Liu waved Tucker off.

Gertrude sipped her lemonade and looked over her glass at Liu. "Young lady, you are fetching."

"Thank you," said Liu, flustered. The agent chastised herself, *don't get caught in this woman's web of charm*. Liu assumed men, and maybe women, had fallen victim to this woman's easy likeability before. "I met your daughter in person at the gala. She's gorgeous."

"Yes, she is, thank you. I assume you have been here long enough to solve one of modern art's mysteries."

"Yes, we found the missing paintings from your son's Aphrodite collection in the barn. Breathtaking."

"Indeed."

Liu wondered aloud. "Did your daughter ever take the acclaim of *Arrington's Aphrodite* to heart?"

"Allie seldom accepted compliments about her beauty. The paintings were an anathema to her. She valued anonymity. She changed her hair, traveled little, avoided cameras, but now it does not matter."

Gertrude continued, "Interesting fact, I am the former owner of those two paintings, after my son's death. Per my daughter, my beneficiary, the paintings have a new owner."

"And who is that?" Liu asked.

"Per my daughter's request, those two paintings now belong to Mr. Luther. An extravagant gift. The rest of our art is to be auctioned off to support Rice University, AIDS charities, and cancer research at Hermann Hospital. Once the FBI completes their examination, I'm sure. I mailed letters to those charities. They will be expecting the proceeds. So, they will pester your agency until the artwork is released."

Liu looked at Luther, who stood flabbergasted. Gertrude seemed to understand his lost look.

"Mr. Luther, I see your struggle. In truth, I cannot estimate what either painting is worth. With the new back story, fascinating really, the model for *Arrington's Aphrodite* has been identified and is missing, her mother a suspect in multiple murders. If you parted with either painting, you would never need to teach again. Still, you and I understand you will never sell." She smiled sweetly at him.

"No, ma'am, never, you have my promise."

"Ms. Arrington, did you just say your daughter was missing?"

"Yes, dear, vanished. I came home to find the bonfire and her place a mess. I went looking for her, of course, that's where I've been."

"Ms. Arrington, I don't believe you," said Liu.

"I am so sorry for your distress, dear," answered Gertrude sweetly, neither confirming nor denying Liu's statement.

"Ms. Arrington, we're here because we consider you a suspect in the death of former US Congressman Ollie Whiteman."

"I stopped counting at two dozen," recounted Gertrude.

"Excuse me?" blurted Tucker.

"I lost count after I stabbed him twenty-four times. I only stopped when I became too tired to continue. Very cathartic. You can find the murder weapon in the beautiful, lacquered box, just inside." Gertrude heard Luther gasp.

Liu, Tucker, and Luther sat quietly, surprised by her easy admission. Gertrude admired her property, taking it all in. "It's easier than you think to kill someone, if hate protects you."

Liu continued, "And you killed others?"

"Yes, many others."

Gertrude named the victims the threesome identified in Luther's office years earlier, slowly explaining how she targeted each crooked politician and committed each murder. "Each politician broke their vow to the American people. I provided a public service…of sorts, but none gave me the gratification of Whiteman."

"And your daughter-in-law, Bo's wife, Briana Swanson Arrington, and Cat Conroe; you killed them too?"

Gertrude paused, looked momentarily confused, then her smile returned broader than before. "Yes, of course, I killed them as well."

"And how did you kill them?" asked Liu.

"You already possess the facts to put me away. Let a woman keep some of her secrets," Gertrude said.

"And your daughter knew nothing of this?"

"Not until a few days ago, when I told her. She threatened to turn me into the authorities but left instead, I guess." The old woman gazed sadly at the bonfire.

Liu pushed, "How did she not know sooner?"

"Oh, I am quite proficient at keeping secrets. Keeping secrets is a skill to some, to others a necessity. To me, probably both."

"Pete Book and his chief of staff, Kyle Kenner, you knew them since they were children."

"They played in the barn, ran these fields, and shared lemonade on the porch, much like you now. Of course, they did not wonder if I poisoned their beverages." Liu noted Gertrude possessed a near constant twinkle in her eye.

Liu checked on Tucker and Luther, to confirm this woman had not lulled them into a false sense of security. Luther appeared captivated by her charm; Tucker appeared resolute, professional, on guard. This woman proved more deadly than she appeared. The agent again reminded herself to not fall for the charming hostess routine. Gertrude murdered over a half-dozen men and women.

As if reading her thoughts, Gertrude spoke, "Ms. Liu, stop worrying. I have shown no propensity to kill officers of the law. Well, the honest ones. You three are free from danger, especially Mr. Luther, with whom I have a certain affinity."

Gertrude locked eyes with Luther. She smiled warmly at him. "I feel he is part of the family."

For his part, Luther only nodded.

Liu made note but continued, "As I said, you've known Pete Book and Kyle Kenner their entire lives and they have benefitted from a few of the murders."

"What a happy accident," said Gertrude.

"Did Pete Book have any idea of your activities?"

"No."

"You did not kill Ollie Whiteman to help Pete Book?"

"No, I killed Ollie Whiteman because he accepted payment to circumvent my son's success. The scoundrel's intervention contributed to my son's depression; my son's depression led to his suicide. I will admit to encouraging Pete to fight for the vacant seat, which he did successfully."

"Pete Book is clean."

"Natalie, may I call you Natalie?"

"Yes," answered Liu before catching herself.

"Natalie, I raised Pete Book. He spent more time here than his home. He was and is an arrogant prig, probably a narcissist too. Pete, like all men, possesses blind spots. However, as a politician, Pete is spotless, too motivated to be involved in anything dirty. Not because of a strong moral compass. Pete is just too ambitious to allow corruption near him."

Liu found herself sidetracked. The next statement flowed from her mouth before her brain corrected the action. "His wife, she looks a lot like your daughter."

"Spookily so," added Tucker.

"Yes," Gertrude continued. "Pete had a bit of a crush on me in his youth. Many students become fascinated with their teachers. The crush passed to my daughter when she matured."

"Was the feeling mutual?" asked Luther.

"No, my daughter detests Pete. She never liked him, even when they were kids. Dislike grew into disdain when Allie reached about 15 or 16."

"Any idea why?" asked Luther.

"Allie never told me. She possesses her mother's talent—or curse—for keeping things locked inside."

Liu took control of the interview again. "Did you or your daughter ever communicate with Leon Loyola or Arturo Tigre?"

"No, but I would have loved to meet either."

"You have no idea how they picked up your lead and ran with it—killing politicians, I mean?"

"Oh, I never knew." Gertrude sat quietly, relishing Liu's question. After a moment, she observed. "They did much more than follow my lead."

After Gertrude answered the question, she made a distinctive clicking sound, obviously a call for a pet.

Liu asked, "Do you have a dog?"

"No, I hope you don't mind. I called my old horse, Voltaire, to the porch. I give him an apple each day. More of a pet than a horse. With my daughter's departure, he is all I have left."

Before Liu approved and dissented, a horse trotted toward the porch. "Mr. Luther, please retrieve an apple from the table," said Gertrude. Luther left to retrieve the fruit.

Gertrude started to rise from her chair but appeared to struggle. Tucker held out his arm to help her rise, and she took it, letting him guide her up. Liu watched as the two stepped past the small table where the pitchers rested. Liu turned her attention to the approaching horse.

Why's the horse saddled?

Liu knew immediately, but too late. In one smooth motion, Gertrude Arrington threw her body into Tucker, just enough to cause him to lose balance. As Tucker tumbled, Liu, by instinct, attempted to stop his fall.

Liu looked up as Gertrude Arrington mounted her horse, in the manner of a woman who performed the action thousands of times. The horse raced away at full gallop within seconds.

Once Liu caught Tucker and corrected herself, she drew her pistol, considered firing, before holstering her pistol.

"Do we chase her down or explain to my boss, if he ever returns my phone calls, that an old woman gave us the slip?"

●　　●　　●

Erasmus Luther found himself running through a field, chasing a horse, which struck him as ridiculous. He possessed neither the ability nor inclination to keep pace with FBI agents. Still, he attempted to stay close.

The horse proved easy to follow, parted tallgrass, translating Gertrude Arrington's escape route. Earlier, Gertrude Arrington's glance toward him, and offhanded comments confirmed what Allie's hint implied. Allie's gift staggered him as well. Not the financial value, which meant nothing if you never planned to sell the paintings, but the emotional value.

She wanted him to possess a memory of her, something to remind him of her. Maybe she yearned for him the way he ached for her. Her bequest hinted to that fact.

The path lead into the nearby woods, a horse trail he and Allie explored the day of their first date. Then Luther remembered, and understood the discovery waiting for them, and he slowed, then stopped in the field. He put his hands on his knees and heaved, fighting tears.

No need to rush, Gertrude Arrington awaited them. Erasmus Luther understood he no longer pursued a suspect. He, like Liu and Tucker, followed a path to an impromptu funeral. Luther watched as Tucker and Liu continued their sprint. The professor stood, then trudged slowly, delaying the inevitable, in no rush to witness awaiting horror.

●　　●　　●

Luther walked into the woods, a full five minutes behind his compatriots, following the path he remembered. He rounded the corner and found Liu and Tucker watching the swinging husk of a body. The empty vessel that minutes ago possessed the spirit of Gertrude Arrington.

The matriarch hung from the noose Allie discounted as Halloween decor during the couple's long ago horse ride. Gertrude's horse nudged her dead body with his muzzle, calling to her in a strange mix of grunts, whinnies, and whines, unsuccessfully beckoning his owner to return from the dead.

"I can't imagine the secrets that woman just took with her," said Liu.

No, Luther thought, *no, you cannot.*

• • •

Luther watched from afar as months passed in a blur. Courts enforced Gertrude's behest. The FBI released a majority of the artwork to Christie's for auction, the proceeds funneled to the charities Gertrude specified.

Eventually, authorities released Allie's *Arrington's Aphrodite* paintings to Luther, an extravagant gift even by Texas standards.

The fact the paintings' subject was the missing daughter of a murderess and potential accessory flamed the value. National news organizations often featured the Aphrodites in exposés to grab ratings. Christie's placed the value of each painting over $25,000,000. The auction house projected the paintings would sell for substantially more based on the press. Cassandra Hinds offered him $40,000,000 for the pair.

The Houston Museum of Fine Arts contacted him months before the paintings found their way into his possession. He never discovered how they knew he was the owner of two Wyeth Arringtons. Luther signed an agreement to allow the museum to display the Aphrodites for the next ten years while he decided upon a long-term plan.

Luther's lawyer drew up a complex contract assuring their safety, demanding the museum take out a $60,000,000 insurance policy. In time, he grew to love the arrangement. He walked to enjoy the paintings every few days, and to be fair, the museum offered the paintings protection well beyond his means.

Luther sold the reproduction rights to a national printer for $1,500,000 and a substantial percentage of the gross sales price. Luther donated the proceeds to Gertrude's chosen charities. His dean called Luther into the office and offered the professor a substantial raise. In return, Luther agreed not to leave the university for the next five years.

His classes, full before, now boasted a substantial waiting list—a luxury allowing Luther to cherry-pick students. He ensured only budding historians, and not fans of his celebrity, took his courses.

Luther negotiated two semesters on and one semester off, using the off semester to travel, guest professor at a college of his choosing, or work on his next book. He presold the rights to his upcoming book, *The Politikill Investigation,* for seven figures.

On the surface, Erasmus Luther's life mirrored perfection. Sometimes, the ocean's surface appears calm, while untold drama unfolds beneath.

Luther still lived without roommates. The attempt on his life gained legendary status, and few academics wanted to risk their lives for an easy commute.

Liu said good-bye earlier today, before returning to Washington. Days earlier, she rejected Tucker's proposal.

Luther found himself constantly surrounded but lonely. Few people understood him. Like Tucker, hurting from a spurned proposal, Luther lost the love of his life. Still, Tucker possessed the upper hand. His heartbreak occupied a known location. Also, federal law enforcement did not hunt Tucker's love interest.

Luther inspected the artifact Allie left behind, holding it in his hand as he did often when he felt alone, the small rubber pink pacifier he kept in his pocket always. The artifact announcing his daughter, communicating his fatherhood. Four handwritten letters adorned the pacifier, four letters she knew he could translate: BWAL

Of course, the first two letters were a female version of her brother's names. "A" stood for Arrington and "L" stood for Luther. No misery drove him like…knowing. Luther fathered a daughter he may never meet. That thought troubled him beyond craziness.

He once again, without consent, became a keeper of secrets. He woke and fell asleep waiting for someone to put together the facts: 1) Allie Arrington birthed a daughter; and 2) the daughter's father, a history professor, participated in a murder investigation, which led to Allie Arrington's mother.

He feared the natural assumption. The history professor retarded the progress of the investigation. Admittedly, true…near the end.

As time passed, his fears lessened.

Erasmus, a researcher by nature and profession, searched hospital records for proof of Allie's pregnancy. No birth record, no day care record, no social security number existed. His daughter, BWAL, like her grandmother and to a degree her mother, proved a mystery.

He remembered an offhanded comment to Liu the day they met. The Luther men are attracted to darkness. The love of his life proved that fact. Allie Arrington, at the very least, went missing with his daughter, at most a murderess herself.

On the surface, Luther's life looked incredible. Rock star history professor, best-selling author. But when he looked in his mirror, a heartbroken father with a daughter he never met, in love with a woman he could never hold, stared back at him.

• • •

Newly appointed Deputy Assistant Director Natalie Liu stood facing Tanner Tucker, feet from where they first met at the airport. Tucker's crooked smile, the smile she already missed, taunted her. She reached up and kissed him.

Days before, Tucker dashingly executed his proposal, beautiful and touching, making it harder when she said no. He handled her rejection with the grace and class she expected. She examined him now, waiting for him to crack or beg her to stay, knowing he proved, in their time together, constitutionally unable to do either.

He only offered exactly what she needed right now: support…closure. Tucker, perfect, the man she wanted, and the man she could never possess. He worked well as her number two the last few years. Still, despite his efforts, she recognized he was not born to play a supporting role to her career.

Liu also understood she possessed none of the tools to function as a politician's wife.

"Please reconsider your resignation?" she asked Tucker.

"I can't. Time for me to pursue the family business. They waited long enough. Also, my district's congressional seat is wide open, thanks to our friends Loyola and Tigre."

"Will you win?"

"With my father's reputation and the news coverage we received, yes, I'll win."

"So, you'll be in Washington soon?"

Tucker nodded.

"You can visit my apartment. I might finally let you rip the lavender dress off me."

Tucker's crooked smile and sad eyes served as Liu's answer.

"If it means anything, I hope you take me up on the offer." Liu felt a tear run down her cheek. He reached and wiped the tear away. She remembered he wiped off her face at their first meeting. "I'd rather get shot at with you than eat crème brûlée with anyone else."

"Okay," was his last utterance.

He kissed her on the forehead before walking away. Two flight attendants tried to gain his attention as he passed. The women giggled, then turned to see his tight-fitting jeans. He walked away, oblivious of the attention. She waited for him to look back; he did not.

She understood Tanner Tucker. He did not turn back out of any sense of pride or to protect himself. He did not look back because he would see her crying, and he understood, despite her tough exterior, she may run to him. She never forgot the kindness he granted her, being strong enough to walk away.

• • •

February 1996

Within weeks of working for Pete Book, Anna translated Kyle Kenner's cryptic warning. Disappointed she did not put pieces together sooner, the tainted answers evident to anyone who paid attention to the clues. Still, Book and Kenner seemed to master the art of distraction. No proof existed of Book's wrongs. Her word against his.

Anna understood Book completely. However, she struggled with how Kenner allowed himself to be pulled into the abyss. She now sat across the table from Kyle, not nervous like years earlier for her interview, but terrified. Anna asked for this meeting to turn in her resignation. She only hoped she possessed the courage to blow this whole thing up, to end Book politically.

Kenner, for his part, seemed disheartened, beaten by the world. Before she uttered a word, he slid a stuffed envelope across his desk to Anna.

"So, this is how it works?"

Kenner nodded.

"You've done this before?"

No answer. She imagined from her time with Book's team, Kyle completed this horrific process many times. He did not seem calloused and cold; instead, he seemed raw, greatly pained by the process.

"You tried to warn me before I started."

No answer again.

"But you made sure, years ago, the contents of this envelope would ensure my silence."

Kenner seemed content to let her process, adding nothing. Anna opened the envelope, which contained stacks of hundred-dollar bills and a folded piece of letterhead.

"No amount of money will keep me from going public," Anna said. She mustered all her courage to keep from shaking. "You can keep Pete's money; I don't want it."

Kyle looked at her, then to the letterhead.

Anna opened the folded stationary and read the typed contents. She recognized the signature; the offer was real.

"You knew I couldn't turn this down."

Silence.

"So, I'll be Congressman Tanner Tucker's Chief of Staff. I have not interviewed with him."

"Not necessary, I called him myself. I helped when he arrived, got his team set up, made introductions. My word goes a long way with him. He needs someone...like you. He'll rise quickly through the ranks. You'll be in charge of that rise; you'll ascend with him."

"Is he like Book? Before you answer, you know what I mean."

"No."

"Does Tanner Tucker know any of the crap that goes on here?"

"What do you think?"

"He doesn't. Your help to obtain this position...is contingent upon my silence?"

Again, nothing from Kyle.

"You knew this is everything I've wanted. You're a bastard for giving me this."

•   •   •

Over Three Years Later

"New Year, New Hope, New DC"
Foxx Kauffman / Columnist / *The Times*
Washington, DC / December 31, 1999

Almost fifteen years ago a retired political science teacher from small-town Texas acted. Her actions, driven by personal loss and a corrupt political system, changed this country forever. She killed a politician who accepted financial gain to ruin her son, Bo Arrington. Then she killed other equally corrupt political figures.

Were her actions misguided, heavy-handed, and illegal? Yes.

When that woman, Gertrude Arrington, endeavored to correct our system, she did not comprehend the suffocating weight of the burden. After a short time, Gertrude surrendered her self-imposed yoke. Correcting a system so corrupt, so dangerously astray from our Founding Fathers' vision, proved too much for her.

Her actions inspired two former US servicemen, Leon Loyola and Arturo Tigre, to take up her odyssey. Their initial attempts to correct the system also failed. Killing corrupt politicians proved a poor solution, as these two men, like their unknown spirit guide, discovered. For each mosquito they killed, dozens of bloodsuckers survived to drain the American people.

Loyola and Tigre's greatest progeny, the now famous *Tapes of Wrath*, led to real change. Politicians exposed on the tapes exposed others for lighter sentences. These tapes, now studied worldwide, have been translated into dozens of languages.

The tapes led to our President asking Chad Cash from his party to investigate non-Washington-based corruption. Then #42 selected a senator from his rival party, Pete Book, to investigate DC-based corruption. Despite an obvious dislike for each other, Book and Cash worked together to facilitate change.

Encouraged by the American public, Chad Cash and Pete Book focused on one platform: the elimination of career politicians. Our forefathers, believed the best political servants stepped away from their occupation to serve in the government for a brief period then return to the free market. Our country's founders failed to predict the toxic infection to the system known as career politicians.

According to a wise reader and contributor to this column, an elected official or Washington bureaucrat should view their time in Washington as jury duty. A duty they owe the country. A task so challenging, so onerous, they cannot wait to return home. Another oft-contributor added, "I want my politicians working so hard, giving so much, they can't wait for their time in DC to end."

A DC assignment, either elected or appointed, must be viewed as a mission trip or charitable outreach. Many people remember their time helping others as the best time of their lives. In the future, I hope our public servants feel similar pride.

Returning home, sharing what you learned, and applying the lessons in your neighborhoods represents the truest calling.

Another key point: people do not do charitable work for financial gain. Helping others remains the gift offered for your service.

Cash and Book oversaw significant policy changes. New laws allow senators to serve two elected terms, effectively twelve years maximum. Congressional representatives' maximum stay in Washington now stands at four terms or eight years. Politicians can extend their Washington residency by occupying different bureaucratic or political posts. This practice offers opportunity for political cross politization.

Governors' terms are still decided by each state, but most states have adopted two-term maximums.

New laws no longer offer senators and congressional representatives a retirement program. The lack of a retirement program further discourages political lifers. A call to politics is a service call, not an invitation to financial gain. Additionally, the lack of a retirement program encourages public servants to reengage in the private sector.

Politicians must return to the real world, facing the consequences of laws they passed.

New policies reduce campaign contribution maximums. As much as Senator Book and Governor Cash tried, they could not eliminate the political action committee. Still, Book and Cash crippled the organizations, reducing PAC's maximum contributions.

More importantly, no longer can a business or a PAC run an advertisement supporting or denouncing a candidate. PAC members, like all Americans, can contribute to campaigns and the candidates. Candidates must run their own advertisements.

Each candidate must take ownership of their position. If a candidate slanders or attacks a rival, now the message must come directly from the candidate. A PAC, company, or unnamed organization can no longer slander one candidate to further the career of another. Politicians must be solely responsible for calling out their competition, at best, or backstabbing, at worst.

New policies chopped advertising and travel budgets, with a maximum spend defined by office, to be reviewed by a nonpartisan group of retired academics and business executives every four years.

Penalties for accepting or making a bribe ballooned. In the past, people caught accepting or taking a bribe escaped with a fine and minimum imprisonment. Now the starting sentence for accepting or making a bribe is ten years for first offenses and twenty years for additional offenses. No parole is offered. Any business caught in the act of bribery faces minimum fines of $1,000,000. Any employee involved in the incident faces the sentences outlined above. In extreme cases, politicians accepting bribes can be indicted for treason.

Yes, correct, someone accepting a bribe endangering our country can be tried for treason and face capital punishment.

The goal of these policy changes: make the voter the most powerful person in a candidate's life.

Now you ask, "But Foxx, what about career bureaucrats?"

Spectacular question.

If politicians no longer stay in Washington, won't the bureaucracy step up and fill the corruption void? Bingo. Most likely, yes.

Bureaucrats grasp system manipulation better than most. To correct this conundrum, Book's and Cash's teams crafted a bill, recently passed into law.

Bureaucratic leaders can serve in any post for a maximum of eight years. Mid-level bureaucrats must circulate through different bureaus, each eight years, like a doctor going through specialty training, to learn the best and worst of each agency's practices. Also, after four years, bureaucrats receive a bonus to leave government employment and return to the business world.

After four years in the private sector, the former bureaucrat can return as a government employee, bringing with them real-world knowledge, again receiving a bonus. The policies reward bureaucrats for circulating through the private sector and bringing best practices back to Washington.

There has been more change, but I am not a political science teacher, and I don't recall getting your tuition check. So, let's attack the provocative question. What do we know about Gertrude Arrington, the murderess, the progenitor of political change?

Volumes of information exist about Leon Loyola and Arturo Tigre. Books overviewing their history litter bookshelves, including one by yours truly cowritten with my best friend, historian Erasmus Luther. Hollywood already produced two movies about the pair. Multiple documentaries exist outlining everything from their upbringing to the technology they used to crash the beast, our warped political system.

Conversely, research into Gertrude Arrington proved unfruitful. To date, we know little about her. Which makes her staggeringly interesting.

Gertrude Arrington is a myth; she never existed. No record exists of her before she arrived in New York just before WWII. Long-term associates recognized she was British but knew nothing of her upbringing. Someone forged her documentation, including a birth certificate. When she rode to her death, she left a bonfire, reducing to ash any photos or proof from her past.

Only a driver's license photo exists. In the driver's license photo, she wore no makeup, left her hair down, covering most of her face. Mrs. Arrington proved notoriously camera shy, and no one understands why. She served as a teacher at a Texas high school, and her photo never once appeared in the yearbook, not once.

She served as the yearbook committee faculty advisor her entire career. According to a former student, she was always sick or traveling the week of teacher photos. He remembered Gertrude searching the final prints of the yearbook, deleting any snapshots that included her, even in backgrounds. The student found her aversion to the camera strange, but he remembered her stating the yearbook's purpose—highlight her students, not her.

She hosted an annual fundraiser at Rice University, raising millions for Rice and AIDS research. The university president remembered her unusual "no cameras" requirements for the event. Many philanthropists live for the camera, not Gertrude Arrington.

We know she raised three accomplished children. Two remarkably successful sons now deceased. Noted American Painter Wyeth Arrington and millionaire oil baron Bo Arrington. Gertrude Arrington's daughter, Allison Arrington, attended Rice University on full scholarship. Over time she worked for both brothers. According to a former employee of Arrington Oil, Bo's business grew substantially during Allie's tenure. Art collector Cassandra Hinds credits Allie for taking Wyeth's painting career to the next level.

Allie also served as the unwilling subject of Wyeth Arrington's most famous painting, *Arrington's Aphrodite*. Allie may also be murderess Gertrude Arrington's only living relative. No one knows if Allie Arrington is alive or dead. The extensive manhunt, or I guess woman-hunt, has yielded zero results to date.

Gertrude ended her own life years ago. A reporter, like myself, can argue, for better or for worse, criminal or patriot, Gertrude Arrington changed American government. At minimum, she remains the architect for redefining the way American government works. At maximum, arguments can be made she stands as one this country's most important contributors.

Our citizens currently enjoy a honeymoon period, an American political rebirth this woman died to accomplish. I finish this column, excited to enjoy this political renaissance. Sadly, I understand, somewhere in a room, a crooked politico searches for the cracks in our new system, trying to find a method of personal gain, planning to screw it up again, without Gertrude Arrington, Leon Loyola, or Arturo Tigre to correct them.

• • •

Kyle Kenner walked through his perfectly decorated apartment. Everything, in place, even after his outrageous and successful dinner party. A night at home, rare in the heat of coordinating a front-running bid for Presidency, proved a pleasant respite. Kenner's boss and longtime "friend," Pete Book, reigned as political darling du jour. Pete "By the" Book, the man who cleaned up Washington, selected by a president from the rival party to lead the Senate task force in charge of investigating political corruption.

The candidate predicted to win his party's Presidential nomination and compete against the rival party's fast-rising star, Colorado Governor Chad Cash.

Kyle reveled in the afterglow of last night's dinner party. The gathering proved a boffo success, with gourmet food, dinner, and dancing afterward, behind closed doors. Privacy remained mandatory for a man who made Kyle's choices.

One friend always protected his secret, his oldest friend. He missed Allie dearly since her disappearance five years ago. Another person knew his secret—his employer. Book used Kyle's past to control and manipulate him.

To assuage Kyle's needs, he sought brief companionship but never long-term relationships. For two reasons, he still worshipped a man who died fifteen years earlier. Then of course there was the fact his boss would never allow it.

So, Kyle shuffled around his perfect apartment, currently on top of the political hill, connected to the powers that be, but completely miserable...when his phone rang.

Strange, no one called him on his home line. Pete and Samantha dialed his new cell phone. Even his mother switched to his new number. Probably a solicitor.

When he picked up the phone, he heard a beloved voice say seven simple words, "Kyle, you've paid your dues. It's time."

He stood listening to a blaring dial tone, wanting to talk to her for hours, needing to tell Allie he missed her. Kyle missed talking to her, laughing with her, being open with her. He wanted to tell her he still loved Bo, and always would.

Still, no time to reminisce.

• • •

January 1, 2000

Foxx Kauffman wondered how often his profession ruined his holidays. He enjoyed a perfectly acceptable evening. New Year's Eve, as a single man of note, proved entertaining. Foxx enjoyed the fruits of his D-list celebrity. A recent article in *Time Magazine* about Foxx's friendship with Erasmus Luther added to his carte blanche.

Still, he awoke this morning, pulled from his bed and comfortable companion by a phone call. Not from a politician seeking press coverage or an event coordinator beseeching him to cover her party. This call originated from Kyle Kenner, a man known for thoughtful silence. His boss, Pete Book, stood on the precipice of power, in line to be the next President of the United States.

Their meeting location proved ironic. The origin of Loyola and Tigre's deadly campaign, the site of Nixon's falls—the Watergate Hotel. Foxx arrived and was greeted by the quiet and graceful man. Without his boss present, Kyle Kenner appeared happier, relaxed.

"To what do I owe the pleasure?" Foxx asked.

Kenner motioned for Foxx to sit on a nearby sofa. Kyle said nothing for moments. The reporter studied Kyle. The man noted every sound, enjoyed each movement, welcomed all smells. Kyle Kenner's mannerisms resembled a newborn child witnessing the world for the first time.

Foxx chose not to disturb him, letting Kenner enjoy his reverie.

Kyle considered Foxx, as if he forgot the reporter's presence, then said the strangest thing, "I've been released from my debt."

"I'm sorry?"

"I made a terrible mistake once, a mistake that changed everything. My mistake led to death, rape, and maybe worst of all, a false life. That mistake left me indebted. I did terrible things, terrible things to repay my debt. But my debts have been paid. I'm free."

"Care to expound?"

"No."

"Then why am I here?" Foxx questioned.

Kenner patted a file sitting beside him.

"What's that?"

"Find out yourself."

"Is your boss corrupt, like the politicians he prosecuted?"

"Pete Book's the most honest politician in DC; the worst man, but the best politician."

"Why did you work for him?"

"Like I said, I owed a debt. Today I repay it. Then, I'm free."

"Something in this file will ruin Pete Book?"

"I hope so, yes."

"But you were friends."

Kyle reclined, sat forward, and reclined again. Wistfulness overtook his face. "*No.* I have one friend. *One.* You can guess her name. I miss her. Once, I thought Pete was my friend. I was young, naïve. Poor judge of character, I guess."

"This information…if I release this, people will guess the source. Giving this envelope to me will ruin your career."

"God, I hope so."

"What will you do?"

Kenner smiled. Never in Foxx's life did he witness such unadulterated joy. Kyle rose and walked away. No, thought Foxx, Kenner did not walk away; he strolled, glided even.

"Where can I find you to verify this?" Foxx said, flapping the file. Kenner never turned. Foxx rose and chased Kenner out the door. Foxx looked back and forth; Kyle Kenner disappeared.

"What the hell just happened?" Foxx Kauffman asked the pigeons, now his only companion.

• • •

London

Today not only began a new year, but a new millennium. Allie Arrington, now Nanny Smith, of course, decided the new millennium could do without Pete Book. She called Kyle from a single-use cell phone she purchased earlier. Even if Kyle sold her out, which she doubted, finding her in London from a ten-second call made from a burner phone seemed unlikely.

Awash with relief, she took in her surroundings. Her uncle/boss secretly paid her a large bonus and granted her a week off. So, she enjoyed New Year festivities in London, while Lilian and the staff joyfully took on Lady Antonia.

Now, with her last connection to her old life behind her, Allie Arrington wandered the streets of Notting Hill, bundled tightly, but warmed knowing Pete Book's voyage to the Presidency just hit an iceberg.

Unlike Allie, who lived life anchored to her Silsbee home, Nanny Alice Smith proved quiet the adventurer. On vacations, with the help of a false passport arranged by her uncle, she traveled to Europe's great cities. On days off, Nanny Smith hiked the Yorkshire countryside or just explored the castle grounds, still her favorite pastime. As often as she could without being obvious, she observed the paintings of her ancestors. She resembled a few of the portraits, but not like her uncle, Lord Thomas Harrington, the mirror image of his grandfather.

Thomas, like his father before, became a politician of note. Still, Thomas's business acumen proved beyond compare in the United Kingdom. While many English estates languished in disrepair and debt, Ridley Castle's influence spread through the British Empire and worldwide. Over time, Thomas Harrington proved more than a businessman. He became a shaper of markets and a master of macroeconomics. He advised the Queen and quietly counseled the Prime Minister.

• • •

Allie's last day in the US, the day she said good-bye to her mother, remained the most painful and interesting of her life. When Allie arrived at a small airport outside of Dallas, a private plane awaited, accompanied by the aged butler of Ridley Castle, Bernard.

Bernard greeted her, and the flight from Dallas to Great Britain proved as fascinating as the limousine ride with her mother. The enchanting Bernard oversaw Allie's every need, but he proved especially attentive to Allie's daughter. The butler remembered her mother as a girl when he served as Ridley Castle's second footman. Bernard inundated Allie with stories of her mother's childhood adventures.

"The staff cherished your mother, all the young male staff, well...we were quite in love with her." Bernard continued, "Young Thomas, now a fine man, was a stinker, but not your mother, she was cherished.

"The old gamekeeper, who passed years ago, bless his soul, said your mother was a marvelous shooter, better than her father, brother, and even her grandfather, a noted huntsman. Do you hunt?"

"I have, with my brothers. Once on my own. Missed my shot, clipped the target."

Bernard looked at her awaiting explanation; none came.

"Lord Thomas molded into an exceptional man. I enjoyed my life in his service. His wife, Lilian, a saint. She softened his rougher edges, made him a better man. Lord Thomas adores her; however, it complicated matters that Lilian failed to bear children."

"That's terrible," said Allie.

"Yes, but prayers have been answered."

"I'm sorry," she said.

"I assumed you put it together or your dear mother informed you. Your daughter may be the heir of Ridley Castle and Thomas Harrington's estate."

"Excuse me?"

"It's simple these days, a simple DNA test will do and prove that your daughter is the heir. Oh, how his evil cousins will tither. The arrogant Blythes eyed your uncle's estate for decades, world class fools they are."

She sat quietly. Allie prided herself and her ability to analyze situations, see around corners, see through deception, but now found herself off-kilter.

"So, my daughter, Beth, is Lord Harrington's heir?"

"Yes and no."

"What do you mean?"

"A child will be found at the doorstep of Ridley Castle with a note. The note will explain the child's relation to the long-lost Lady Philippa Harrington. Lady Antonia Harrington, named for Lord Thomas's beloved mother is born. DNA results will prove this true, and your uncle, who loved his sister dearly, will make legal arrangements over time for his heir, your daughter. Your Beth will be no more."

"Do I disappear, never see Beth again?"

"Far from it, you become Nanny Smith, Lady Antonia Harrington's nanny, a member of my staff. Your responsibility will be to take care of your daughter. If you choose."

"I choose."

"When she graduates, you can leave service or remain with us. Your choice."

"Sounds like there's more."

"You can be her confidant, friend, role model. You can be the wind that carries her to grand adventure. Unfortunately, she can never know your true identity. Are these terms acceptable to you?"

"Yes," said Allie, or Nanny Smith forevermore.

"Our ruse must be complete; you will be treated as a servant, paid as a servant, and will receive no special treatment, despite your lineage."

"I understand. Can I work the horses too? When I'm not with my daughter."

"Of course, the stableman will appreciate the assistance."

She nodded. "I accept these terms in full."

"And your daughter will be the beneficiary of your sacrifice."

Their verbal contract complete, he smiled. "Let's talk of more pleasant things. You will enjoy the castle and grounds, quite exceptional."

"I would expect nothing less with such a grand man in charge," Allie said.

"Your flattery warms these old bones." Bernard spoke for hours about the family history, her new quarters, the arrangements in progress for Antonia's education. He recalled grand stories from recent and ancient castle lore.

In time, he asked to be dismissed, then stepped away. Allie considered her incredible life, how regal her mother made their home, and how blessed her upbringing. She imagined how different her life would be if her mother stayed in Yorkshire. Of course, Allie understood, she would never have been born if her mother stayed at Ridley Castle. She prayed for her mother, asking for safety. When Bernard returned, she asked the question that vexed her. "Why did my mother leave?"

"She never told you?"

"Actually, today for the first time. But please tell me what you know?"

"I was 20 when your mother disappeared." Violent emotions ripped across his face. "I don't know everything, of course. Your mother was promised to marry a man she did not love and in fact detested. She tried to do as her family asked. But the night before their wedding, the wanker tried to rape her. Philippa fought back, taking his eye in battle. Your grandfather needed someone with tight lips to clean up the mess. I felt honored by his selection. I and your grandfather alone witnessed the evidence of the attack."

"Good for you, Mother," Allie said before she could stop herself.

"Indeed. After your mother's blow to the young thug—she disappeared, never to be seen or heard from again." Allie remembered her deadly meeting with her mother's former fiancé and his henchman, a memory successfully packed away before today.

"The son was from a prominent family, the Hyslers. Papa Hysler made every attempt to keep his son's dastardly deeds hidden.

Thomas, your grandfather, and grandmother, fought to have this thug, who had been Thomas's best friend, arrested.

"At the time, the Hysler family's wealth squashed the investigation and the story. Your grandfather ended all businesses dealings with the Hyslers. The Harringtons suffered consequential financial losses by severing the relationship."

"You said the Hysler family used their wealth to squash the story. From what you said, my grandfather was wealthy."

"Ah, Allie, there are levels of wealth. The Hyslers at the time were one of Europe's wealthiest families. Lord Harrington's attempt for justice was thwarted at every corner. Over time the Harrington family used their influence to chip away at Hysler's empire. Several years ago, Jonas Hysler disappeared in Texas."

"He more than disappeared," said Allie.

Bernard chuckled. "Bravo, quite exceptional news, Nanny Smith."

Allie smiled at her new name, being used for the first time.

"Over the last few decades, your uncle's fortune rose at a similar pace to the Hysler family decline. After your mother disappeared, your grandfather spent exorbitant amounts of money to find her as did her brother decades later. To no avail. I was present when Lord Thomas got the phone call from your mother. She reversed the charges and could talk only moments. The Lord brimmed with excitement. He would have talked forever if she allowed. He is beside himself to meet you. Be prepared, he desires to know everything about your mother."

"Is he a man who can keep secrets?" she asked.

"He is your mother's brother," answered Bernard, a twinkle reflecting in his eye.

Allie and Beth napped on and off the rest of the transatlantic flight. Allie dreamed of castles, knights, and courtiers before Bernard shook her awake. She looked out the window, and Bernard pointed to her new home, Ridley Castle, as the plane circled for landing. They touched down moments later at a private airstrip, the plane's passengers greeted by a Rolls Royce Silver Cloud.

A few moments later, the limousine pulled in front of a small inn. Bernard opened her door and held out his hand. "Young lady, your future awaits inside. You can be completely candid. Your uncle, or new employer as it were, emptied the entire inn. The employees received the day off. I alone will oversee your, Lord Thomas, and Lady Lilian's stay tonight."

She walked inside; Beth cradled in her arms. An elegant man and stunning woman about her mother's age greeted her. "Young lady, you are as beautiful as your mother," said the woman.

"Thank you, you are breathtaking. What do I call you?"

"I am Lady Lilian; this is your uncle, Lord Thomas Harrington."

"Pleasure," said the man, who never broke eye contact. Allie saw questions dancing behind his hard hazel eyes. "Please sit."

Allie sat as Lady Lilian stepped over to her, looking excitedly at Beth. "May I take her? Only if you are comfortable, of course."

"Yes. From my conversation with Bernard, I gather we need to get used to one another." She handed Beth—or now Antonia—to Lady Lilian. Lord Arrington's wife sat gracefully and began rocking Allie's daughter while singing a lullaby.

"Bernard, he reviewed the conditions of the arrangements?"

"Yes."

"You may contest. You are in fact my heir, before your daughter."

"Not possible. I cannot be a public figure."

"Yes, so your mother said."

"What do you know?" asked Allie.

"Very little, I'm afraid."

"What would you like to know?"

"I did not appreciate your mother in my youth. My wife loved her, but I was young and foolish. Philippa proved wise beyond her years...and brave. Please tell me everything."

"Everything?"

"Indeed."

"I'm not sure, so much happened, so..."

"Allie, tonight is the last time I will allow myself to use your given name. I counsel the Queen and the Prime Minister. I served in various capacities for the British government for over 50 years. Do you really believe there is anything you can add to shock me?"

"I do," Allie said without pause.

Bernard ventured in and out of the room, but Allie hardly noticed. First, her Uncle Thomas recalled everything about Lady Philippa Harrington and her departure. Then Allie spent hours telling her uncle and aunt about her mother.

"What name did she use in the United States?" asked Lilian.

"Gertrude Arrington."

"Your mother just did not look like a Gertrude."

Allie smiled returning to her story. She told them about their home, about Bo and Wyeth.

Lady Harrington had seen Wyeth's paintings and stressed her love of his work.

Allie told them about Hysler's late-night attack in Silsbee and discovering that her mother was much more than she appeared. Still, her mother was a mystery to her until today. Bernard brought them a shepherd's pie, and the three continued talking. Beth remained content in Lilian's arms.

After she completed her story, every sordid detail, exhaustion took its toll, and she excused herself. Lilian begged to take Beth/Antonia for the night, and after much consternation, Allie agreed, deciding she needed to embrace her new family. Bernard took Allie to a room that he arranged for her. A warm bath was drawn, and a tea cart parked beside her bed. She thanked him. After her bath, Allie collapsed into bed and dreamed of her mother. The next morning, when she awoke, she felt her world collapse. She dressed quickly and sprinted downstairs to check on Beth.

Thomas waited for her. He sat in a high-backed chair, tea in hand, reviewing a black leather binder.

"Is Beth...?"

"Beth, or Lady Antonia, is fine. Lilian and Bernard spoil her as we speak."

Allie first felt relief, then Thomas' face told her everything she needed to know. "She's dead, isn't she; my mother's dead?"

"Yes," he said, anguish colored his face.

Allie Arrington, Nanny Smith, a woman in a new country, who fled her only home, cried, then she cried some more. Days later, Bernard introduced her to the Ridley Castle staff, and within a week, Nanny Smith functioned within her new duties. She accepted her new role and stepped forever into shadows.

• • •

A candle-wielding vendor stepped into her path, causing Allie to come back to the present. She smiled at the vendor while waving him off, then pulled her coat tightly around her, and returned to her walk. Despite the weather, carts littered the street with vendors selling everything from fruit to jewelry to garments. The carts were sandwiched between boutiques, gift shops, and bookstores.

With Pete Book behind her, there remained one American to consider—Erasmus Luther. Each day, she considered reaching out, and each day, for her daughter's safety, she chose not to contact him. One day, maybe she would call, but not today. A few shops away, she spotted an adorable travel bookstore. Time to plan her next trip, time to forget about Pete Book and her past. Time to embrace her future.

• • •

January 2, 2000
Natalie Liu knocked again, then returned to waiting for the congressman to answer. She had never visited his apartment before, despite the temptation. Twice she spotted him at DC restaurants with fellow political types. Each time, she avoided being seen. Liu admitted she loved watching him from afar, always would. Twice she snuck into the back of a room to watch him speak, embracing the darkness' anonymity. Washington, DC, remained a town of collision and the two collided. She worked events he attended. When she approached him, after she spoke, he greeted her with more warmth than she felt her departure deserved.

Each event, a different date accompanied him, always gorgeous, never the same woman twice. She never talked about him to her friends; she found herself incapable of enunciating his name. Texas changed Natalie, and she accepted her metamorphosis. Now the highest-ranking female official in the FBI, Natalie Liu had everything she wanted; well, almost everything.

She dated since Texas, one fizzled fiancé and another close call. Suitors proved deficient by comparison...to him.

He never took advantage of her offer to rip the lavender dress off. They lived in the same city, but he never pursued, called, or even sent a note. Natalie tried to imagine the scar tissue carved into his heart, a wound she inflicted personally, gash by gash.

One day, she hoped he could forgive her, allow her to show her scar tissue cut as deep. Her explanation may fail to affect him, as he believed, rightly so, her wounds were self-inflicted. Liu spurned his proposal, left him days after, and chose her career over him. Liu relished her position within the FBI, and understood she could not have him and it, but why did the choice sit on her heart every day? Liu welcomed the pain, knowing she truly lived and loved to enjoy the level of turmoil she chose for herself, willing to pay the toll for her decisions.

In recent years, Liu's career soared. The FBI and other law enforcement agencies morphed into drastically different places. The ripple effects of the *Tapes of Wrath* turned into a tidal wave of change. Besmirched politicians tuned into informants, selling out dozens of crooked law enforcement officers, including Lyle Fiddler of the ATF, the incompetent Mitchell Doherty, and Liu's former FBI boss Carmen Angelo. Several former law enforcement leaders faced jail time, indictment, or public evisceration during the aftershock.

Liu knew she made the right decision.

Now she enjoyed Tucker from a distance, or ran into him, usually circumstantially, until today. Given no choice, today she stood in front of his door, with her walls up, ready for anything.

He opened the door. With her defenses instantly breached, she stood, jaw ajar. She recalled him picking her up before the gala, the first time he witnessed her in the lavender dress. She wondered if his internal thermostat popped like hers now. Damn, he aged well.

He wore boxers, that was it, and he sported serious bed head. A line of drool drifted down his mouth. Still, most women would fail to complain. She remembered his narrow hips topped with abs and firm chest.

"Wow," she said.

Tanner Tucker raised his eyebrows, saying nothing.

"You have a huge line of sleep drool running down your chin." She reached and wiped it off. She watched him battle before selecting a smile.

Liu enjoyed her view, before he turned, door open, and walked inside. She listened as he shuffled around the kitchen. He did not slam the door in her face, but she received no invitation to enter. Just an open door.

She said out loud, "Come in, Natalie. Why thank you, Congressman Tanner Tucker, I will." Liu walked to the kitchen as Tanner put on a pot of coffee. He placed a mug in front of her, with one packet of sugar, Sweet and Low, and creamer. *He remembered her coffee order.*

Tucker looked comfortable in his kitchen, piddling around, washing a plate, and placing it in the dishwasher. She savored every move, knowing this was a treat, a dessert after a month-long diet, a thunderstorm while sitting on the back porch, appreciating his beauty.

He made no attempt to put on a T-shirt or robe, at ease in his boxers. Natalie admitted, his comfort pissed her off some, not understanding why. She tortured herself, wondering how many women witnessed this marvel of God's masculine engineering. Natalie burned with jealousy, while accepting she forfeited her right to that emotion.

Tucker still had not uttered a word. She recounted events they attended together. Each time she addressed him first, and every time he remained pleasant but used an economy of words, a rare feat for a politician.

"Tanner."

He looked up.

"Please put on a shirt, a robe, something really baggy."

He looked disinterested and walked to his bedroom. Tucker returned still in boxers, but he added a tight white T-shirt, offering her little relief. *That's how it's going to be*, she thought to herself.

"Tucker, I'm here as a courtesy."

Nothing.

"In about an hour, my team will arrest Pete Book."

He remained quiet.

"His Chief of Staff, Kyle Kenner, provided all the documents. The evidence is overwhelming. Kyle turned papers over to Foxx Kauffman. You'll read all about it. Pete's going to jail. He's over. Doesn't seem related to our case back in Texas. Book seems clean politically, no bribes, he is not owned by PACs, no campaign fund issues. It doesn't line up."

He stayed silent; she continued.

"But, he and Gertrude Arrington, or whatever her actual name was, were friends."

"Did he get busted for paying off women to keep their mouths shut?"

She looked at him, stunned.

"You knew?"

"No, I assumed, based on limited information."

"You did nothing about it?"

"Look, I hate Pete Book. He's an ass. But I had no proof. I guessed. My Chief of Staff, Anna, worked for Alan Greene, loved the guy, never shuts up about him, compares me to him constantly. I always lose those comparisons, by the way. Pretty girl, that shouldn't matter but it does here.

"Anyhow, after Greene died, before joining my staff, she worked for Book. Kyle Kenner helped me out when I hit DC. Treated me like a little brother, helped me pick a staff. Great man. Anyway, Kyle called and endorsed Anna. I hired her immediately. Anna never said why she left Book's office. She's a great leader, takes charge. But when I'm around, feels like she's waiting for me to hit on her. Or say something grossly inappropriate. She glares at me like I'm the enemy sometimes. Seems Kyle was protecting her somehow, getting her the job as my Chief of Staff.

"Also, I've met with Pete, away from his wife. Seems like that kinda guy. You understand."

"I do."

"Why are you telling me?" asked Tucker.

"First, as a courtesy to the best friend I ever had." She paused. "Wished I still had."

"I can't only be your friend, Liu. Too late."

She focused on the word *only*, letting it carousel through her soul, allowing the pain to ravage her before she spoke. "And you were my right hand in Texas. Do you think it's related?"

"Yeah."

"Why?"

"Because I danced with Allie Arrington once, you remember. She liked Kyle. Luther told me later she and Kyle were best friends. Even though Kyle worked for Pete, Allie hated Pete Book."

"Just a feeling?"

"More than that."

Liu continued, "I talked to Foxx, he got the impression Allie Arrington called Kyle. Maybe asked Kenner to trash Pete's career. I don't know why or why now."

"Interesting, we heard nothing from or about Allie Arrington in years. Weird she stuck her head up. Must be a big motivation for her to risk that."

"Yes."

"She bristled with hate when I mentioned Pete. My guess, she waited until he got so close to his goal, he could taste it. I didn't know her like Luther. Call him. I got five minutes of data, but Allie Arrington made an impression."

"Gorgeous," said Liu.

"Look, you're gorgeous." Liu realized the words escaped his mouth before he corrected himself. He paused. His next words would be calculated, unlike the earlier three. "It was more than that. Her appearance was a distraction. Probably, she enjoyed the convenience. Most beautiful women do—free drinks, better service, etc. However, her looks aren't what you remember. Beautiful women pass in and out of a man's line of sight. We don't remember most. Allie was spooky smart, brimming with intelligence; she couldn't hide it; it spilled over."

"You got all that in one dance?"

"Instantly. Like when we met, the minute you stepped off the plane in Houston. That's why I remember her, why I can't forget you." He stopped, appearing lost in introspection. Liu chose not to disturb him.

Then something clicked, like Tucker packed his vulnerability away, placing it in a hidden corner of his soul. "Hey, when you finish, put your coffee cup in the sink. Let yourself out. I need to shower, and you got an arrest to make."

He removed his T-shirt, smiled, and dropped his boxers. He paused, knowing his effect on her. She tried to refrain but enjoyed every second of his exhibition. *Now he's just being cruel,* Liu thought to herself. She battled the implied invitation to join him in the shower.

As he strolled away naked, he said, "Next time you come to one of my speeches, sit in the front row. I know you're there, might as well enjoy the view." His last words echoed as he left the room. "You're not the only one with an FBI pedigree."

She laughed, simultaneously enjoying and analyzing his departure, reveling in one fact. Tanner Tucker was not over her. She looked toward his apartment's exit and considered her task. Pete Book's arrest could wait for an hour. She stared at the bedroom threshold he stepped through a second ago. His T-shirt and boxers remained on the floor, glittering bait on a hook, tempting in every way. The soft patter of a water spraying across tile, the creak of the shower door beckoned her.

• • •

July 2000, Paris, The Sorbonne
Erasmus Luther packed his notes, while watching attendees depart. His publisher booked a European lecture series. Luther decided a free trip to Paris, London, Athens, and Rome offered a wonderful break. He spent a moment appreciating his grand surroundings. Luther wrestled with nerves before his engagement, so this moment presented the first opportunity to appreciate the stunning architecture, rich colors, timeless beauty of his surroundings.

His elegant host approached. "Doctor Luther, how may I be of service?"

"Well, actually…" His unfinished sentence lay dormant in his mouth. A woman walked away holding the hand of a beautiful young girl. The *petite fille* looked back and waved happily. The woman did not turn but continued toward the exit.

Luther shoved the remaining documents into his briefcase, muttered something unrecognizable, then raced toward the same exit Allie Arrington departed moments before. He crashed the door, anticipating the need to chase her, but she stood, waiting. She held a finger to her pursed lips and motioned for him to follow.

They strolled together. After a few moments, Luther guessed their destination. The three walked toward a small, fenced park littered with statues. Seconds later, the girl reached for Allie's hand, then reached for his. She considered him, inspected him, measured him. She smiled, signaling he passed some internal test.

Then she said one word or one sound: "Weeeeeeeeeee." He looked confused. The girl's eye encouraged him, begged him to understand. She pulled on his finger again, uttering the same sound, "Weeeeeeeeee." Understanding washed over him. Allie smiled, and the two swung the beautiful girl back and forth, high into the air. At the apex of each swing, the girl yelled, "Weeeeeeeeeee!"

The girl, five or six, resembled her mother, but evidence of his parentage presented in her darker features and eyes. Allie smiled, not saying a word. Caught in his thoughts, he stopped swinging his daughter. She tugged on his finger again and repeated, "Weeeeeeeeeee." The sound previously offered as a request now bordered on a command. The professor smiled and Allie and he started swinging their daughter again.

When they reached the park, Allie returned her fingers to her lips, beseeching him to remain silent. Then she looked to the little girl. "Antonia, take your pad and go to each statue, sketch each one so you remember them, then translate the plaques from French to English for me."

"But Nanny Smith..." Erasmus noted the girl's diction, distinctly upper-crust British.

"Antonia, I'm offering you a simple assignment. Execute the task or I'll demand you translate them to German as well."

"Yes, Nanny Smith." The girl took her pad and pen before skipping off.

"Nanny Smith?"

"She doesn't, will never know, I'm her mother."

"I'm sorry."

"It's okay, I'm paid to play with my daughter every day, it's a dream job."

"So, she doesn't..."

"She'll never know you're her father."

Silence dominated. Moments later she continued. "I can't offer much, but I'm giving you this, today."

"I'll take it." The little girl bunny-hopped from the first statue to a second. "Is she that fast with language?"

"Yes."

"Smart?"

"Extremely." She followed their daughter's progress, then reengaged the conversation. "I follow you, from afar. I saw you were speaking at the Sorbonne, so I took Antonia for an outing." Allie's eyes seldom left Antonia.

"I'm sure she was bored beyond measure."

"No. She's an unusual child."

"Wait, if she doesn't think I'm her father, why'd she wave at me as you left?"

"Don't flatter yourself, she waves at everyone."

"I've never gotten over you." He surprised himself with the rawness of his words.

"Thank you, quite a compliment."

"Are you married or dating anyone?" he asked, terrified of the answer.

"No, Antonia is my life. How about you? Do you date?"

"I don't exactly date."

"So, you're a male slut," Allie toyed, but in her expression' Luther witnessed pain.

He laughed, hoping to diffuse her response but did not answer, instead steering the conversation away from his inadequacies. "Thank you for this. Can I take you two to a café?"

"Yes, there's time," Allie answered, looking at her watch.

"Can I ask a question?"

"You better hurry. There's only two more statues."

"Did you help your mother kill all those people?"

"A complicated question, but sometimes yes. She killed Whiteman and most of the politicians. After Whiteman, I became her point woman, did the research, etc. She's the better shot, so the hunting accidents after Whiteman were her."

"You said after Whiteman. Cat Conroe and Bo's wife died *before* Whiteman."

"I killed them," she said plainly. "They screwed over Bo. I lost Wyeth and could do nothing about it. But I could do something about Bo."

"Did your mother find out?"

"She assumed my sister-in-law drank herself to death. I don't think Mom knew about Cat. Funny, Mom got so distracted by the politics, she never considered the personal side."

"But you did."

"Cat had as much to do with Bo's death as Whiteman. I guess at some point Bo told Mom about Whiteman but not about Cat. I worked for Bo, he told me everything."

"And why did you kill your sister-in-law?"

Allie's temperament transformed from her normal cool demeanor to white-hot rage. "That bitch sold out my brother. She wasn't only letting Cat slip it to her, she was slipping him company secrets. And she threatened to expose Bo."

"I'm sorry. I don't understand. Expose?"

"Do you remember the picnic?"

"Sure."

"You asked what it's like to have a gay brother. I was surprised. You guessed the wrong brother. You assumed Wyeth was gay; he wasn't. Bo was."

"Oh."

"He played football, succeeded in the oil business, hunted. Girls went crazy over him in high school and college. No one guessed, but I did. I'm sure Wyeth and Mom did too, but we never talked about it."

"Wow."

"Anyway, Bo left that bitch nothing in his will. Briana threatened to expose Bo, but Bo took that off the table by killing himself. Nothing more she could do to him. Her family came from money, so before they married, her family attorneys forced Bo to sign a prenup.

"That pissed Bo off. Out of spite toward his in-laws, he had her sign one as well. Of course, he became wealthier than her parents. She called after his death and threatened to expose Bo if my mother and I didn't let her have everything. She demanded I meet at her home. I...obliged."

"You shot Cat before, correct?"

Just then Antonia skipped toward them. "All done, Nanny Smith."

"Great job, Antonia." The translations were completed, rudimentary drawings covered half the page. Even from several feet away, Erasmus deciphered each image. "My friend offered to take us to a café."

"I never met one of your friends before, Nanny Smith," Antonia said.

Erasmus hurt for Allie, glimpsing how lonely her life must be. She caught his stare and as usual translated his thoughts.

"Antonia, he is special to me, and he doesn't believe you can translate the inscriptions into German. I bet you could. If he loses our bet, he offered to buy chocolate croissants."

Antonia looked back and forth. "Be honest, Nanny Smith. You just want more time with your friend."

Exactly like her mother. Luther grinned. "True, but either way, if you sit on that bench and translate the inscriptions into German, chocolate croissants await."

She held out her hand to seal their deal. After they shook, she skipped to a nearby bench.

"Just like you," Erasmus said.

"Yes."

"Your mom murdered so many people; you were close to it."

"Yes."

"In retrospect, your mom, do you think she was crazy?"

"I understand a lot more now. Mother's family unknowingly forced her into an extremely dangerous situation. A powerful man tried to rape her. She escaped using her wits and guile. No one protected her. She and only she became her protector for decades, she distrusted men. When Bo, Wyeth, and I came along, the Momma Bear hormone added to the cocktail. Once Bo died, she was lost. She loved her students, part of her adopted a little of each of them. She became Momma Bear to the world, deciding she needed to protect us all from people like her attacker and Ollie Whiteman. My only choice became to protect her."

"Why tell me this now?"

"Despite what you think, I did and do care about you. Also, I know you'll tell no one."

"Because of our daughter?"

"And I hope part of you loves me."

"Still, probably always."

"But also, the guilt over hiding your daughter's birth from you, then taking her away. I need you to understand those choices proved unavoidable."

"Is Antonia safe now?"

"More than you can imagine."

"Is she well cared for?"

"Yes, the best of everything, except maybe her father in her life."

"Can I see her occasionally?"

"I'm afraid not. I can give you this day."

He looked over as his daughter focused on her task. A sliver of tongue peeked through her lips. She got that from him.

"Can I see her again?"

"Honest answer, probably not. Seeing you is a risk."

"Can you tell me her full name, where she is, so I can follow her from afar?"

"No."

Luther watched as she shifted. He did not want Allie to consider today a mistake. He understood, to see his daughter again, he must offer no doubt of his commitment to her plan. So, he mimicked most men. When backed into a predicament, he changed the subject.

"I gotta ask, Pete Book got taken down recently...not killed or anything. Kyle Kenner exposed Book's habit of sexually abusing staff members, then paying them to stay silent."

"You're asking if I had anything to do with it?"

"Did you?"

"You bet."

"How?"

"Kyle and I were best friends. He was my date to every high school event. Kyle even returned from Rice my senior year to take me to Homecoming and Prom. Kyle and Pete were friends too, but I never held that against Kyle. My junior year, I noticed Kyle and Bo going for walks together, near our home. Over time, I surmised Kyle and Bo were...close."

"Oh."

"It worked for me. What girl doesn't want a gay best friend, handsome, sweet and completely devoted to her?"

Luther remembered his jealousy flaring when he watched Kenner and Allie together at the Arrington AIDS Gala and now understood their closeness. "But?"

"But he made a big mistake. He told Pete everything, but Pete wasn't the man Kyle thought. Pete was honest in school, dedicated to his studies. And Pete's parents gave him everything but their attention. He felt entitled to anything he wanted, and he wanted me."

Luther nodded, not knowing what to add.

"Mostly because, unlike other girls in school, who fell for his good looks, his family money, and his bullshit, I detested him."

"So..."

"One night he cornered me and tried to..."

"What happened?"

"I kicked him square in the balls."

"Bet that slowed him down."

"No..." She remained unmoving, held in place by pain's dark grip. "As I was leaving, he said, if I didn't let him...he would tell everyone my mom was a slut; he overheard some things, things *I* said, which made it worse."

"What did you say?"

"I told him my mom would not want her daughter raped to keep her secrets."

"Good for you, Allie, good for you."

"That's not the end."

"I'm so sorry, Allie. You don't have to tell me this."

"I do, I want someone to understand. Next, he said…if I didn't sleep with him, he'd tell everyone Bo and Kyle were gay."

"So, you…"

"Yes."

Erasmus watched as distaste, no, more than that—disdain, hate, fury—passed through Allie.

"You didn't tell anyone?"

"I couldn't. First Pete knew…about Bo, and if I told my brothers Pete raped me, they'd kill him. I'm positive about that."

"Once your brothers died?"

"Mother never found out; she loved Pete. She lost her sons. I couldn't take Pete away from her. The bastard became her replacement son; he was good to her at least."

"Did you tell Kyle?"

"After the boys died, yes."

"What did Kyle say?"

"After I told Kyle that Pete raped me, Kyle said he should have known. He felt betrayed. But confessed Pete blackmailed him too. Kyle admitted he was the one that told Pete about Bo.

"Kyle understood he inadvertently gave Pete ammunition to blackmail me. Then Kyle told me about the women Pete paid off, the number of times he covered for Pete. Kyle wanted to resign. He hated Pete and the way he treated women. But I told him he couldn't quit. I begged him to stay with Pete. Kyle pledged his loyalty to me that day, he owed me a debt."

"You collected?"

"Working for Pete, despite Pete's sins, became Kyle's penance. Kyle kept me informed, acted as my mole. I released him from his debt when he handed Foxx Kauffman every illicit detail."

"Why'd you wait so long?"

"I needed Pete to get close, so close he tasted his goal. I needed him to know it was me who finished him."

Antonia said, "Nanny Smith, I am finished. Someone owes me a chocolate croissant."

Erasmus replied, "I do." Allie and Erasmus stood.

Antonia walked between them, handing the pad to her mother (or Nanny). Once Allie put the pad in her purse, Allie took Antonia's finger. Then the child latched onto Erasmus's digit and giggled, "Weeeeeeeeeee!"

With Allie's help, he swung his daughter as she laughed contagiously.

Luther enjoyed the greatest day of his life or so he thought.

• • •

August 2017, Rice University
Erasmus Luther walked to his dean's office. The 66-year-old professor had not fretted over his job in decades. Being a tenured professor, a published author, and a mild history celebrity offered stability. Still, his new dean sacked two tenured professors and a few staff members, claiming they were stodgy and failed to change with the times. Luther's last book sold well, but not like his seminal works in the '90s. His celebrity faded over the years and honestly may no longer exist.

The dean's last-minute request troubled him. The last decade trudged by slowly. Luther seldom saw Foxx, now busy at his new CBS gig. He saw Liu once last year while attending a DC conference.

The man who became his best friend in Foxx's stead was now a little busy. Texas Governor Tanner Tucker visited Luther's class once a semester as a favor to his old friend. They occasionally dined together, and those meetings remained highlights for the professor. Luther became reticent to seek new friends, not recovered from his wild ride through the '90s.

To protect Allie and his daughter, he did not search for them. He never received a note or communiqué of any kind from Allie.

When he reached the dean's office, Fran, the longtime administrator, greeted him. She survived three deans and appeared unthreatened by her new boss's propensity for cutting the old guard.

"Fran, can you tell me what this is about?" he asked.

"No."

"No, you don't know, or no, you can't?"

Fran's traditional rolling of the eyes confirmed the second.

"So, I wait."

She nodded, pointing with her pen for him to sit his "ass" down. She did not say *ass*, but her pen implied it.

Luther sat for thirty minutes; he never waited this long for his last dean. He started to leave when three well-dressed, fit men departed the office. Luther stood and watched them leave.

The young dean said, "Erasmus, you waiting for me to roll out the red carpet? Come in, damnit."

Luther entered and said, "Hello, Dean Keyes," attempting to add decorum to their meeting.

"Ya, ya, sit down. We don't have time to polish your old awards and dust off long-ago best sellers."

Now Luther felt pissed but sat. *Respect the office even if you don't respect the man*, he told himself. "What's this about, sir?"

"Those men were from Scotland Yard, a contingent of the Royal Guard who protect traveling dignitaries."

Luther remained silent, not comprehending how this applied to him.

"Sir Thomas Harrington was an Earl or Marquess or something. Hell, I don't know. He's about a hundred years old. Anyhow, he still advises the Queen and the Prime Minister. The Queen made him a duke."

Luther shrugged, not knowing the association.

"The duke's a financial savant, expert on global markets and macroeconomics. Ba-ba-billionaire. Even if he weren't a duke, he'd be one of the most powerful men in Europe. Shaped financial policy, created markets, the Queen doesn't make a move without him."

"Okay."

"His grandniece is brilliant, degree in economics, master's in language. She's his heir, next in line. She'll be a duchess, grew up mingling at Windsor and Buckingham. Now, she plans to attend Rice University to study history for a semester or two. She requested you as her mentor during her time here. She'll attend each of your classes."

"My classes are full."

"Exceptions are made, the girl's world-class bright."

"Got it."

"So, you'll do it?"

"Do I have a choice?"

"No. She'll arrive the week after classes start. Her protection detail wants to understand how things work when classes are in session."

A long-ago conversation rang through his head. Clues fell into place.

"Her name is…"

"Lady Antonia Harrington…"

"I don't recall mentioning her name before."

"You didn't."

Allie Arrington, Nanny Smith, or whatever name she used now, granted him a huge favor. Luther lived 66 years, which equaled over 24,000 days or 578,160 hours. He enjoyed only two hours with his daughter, less than .000003% of his life. Allie somehow helped his daughter find her way to him.

Luther left the dean's office and stared into his future. A future including his daughter. Maybe, just maybe, a future with Allie.

•   •   •

The time from his summons to the Dean's office through the start of classes passed with the speed of a snail on depressants, pulling a dumpster into the wind, uphill. Now in each of his classes, a trio of well-appointed men attended, selecting different seats daily. The threesome did not take notes, listen to the lecture, or acknowledge his existence. Each scanned the room.

Antonia Harrington's team informed no one of her arrival date. So, he quelled excitement when she entered fifteen minutes after class started. The campus and local papers announced her impending arrival weeks earlier. Her appearance surprised him; she looked nothing like he remembered. The cherubic child of memory transformed into a coltish beauty. Like her mother, her limbs seemed impossibly long. Even from this distance, he noted her long, slender finger. She gazed at him, smiling, offering no hint of recognition.

After his meeting with the Dean, Luther felt liberated to search for details about his daughter and Allie. His research for Allie proved fruitless. Few traces of her existed. He located no online documents referencing Nanny Smith, no photographs either. When he visited Ridley Castle's website, her name appeared nowhere.

He enjoyed the online photos of the castle and pictured Antonia playing hide-and seek. Luther hurt for time lost with her but found solace that she lived in a uniquely magical place. He could not have hoped for more. When her granduncle passed, Antonia would become Great Britain's wealthiest woman. Still, that fact failed to counterbalance the pain of not being able to see her, hold her, or watch her ride her first horse.

Finding information on his daughter proved shockingly easy. She served as a member of Great Britain's Equestrian Team and an alternate for the 2016 Olympics. She spoke five languages fluently and became passable in two more.

Unfortunately, he found British tabloids a wealth of information about Antonia. She rejected two marriage proposals and possibly another. He found pictures of her laughing while on an African mission trip and sunbathing at Cannes. Still, the pictures proved incapable of diminishing the shock and awe of seeing her in person.

She grew up playing with Britain's upper crust and dining with royalty. He found her origin story. Someone left her on Ridley Castle's doorstep, note attached, claiming her lineage. A DNA test proved she was the granddaughter of Sir Thomas's long-lost sister, Lady Philippa Harrington.

Luther let that roll around in his head. Gertrude Arrington, the kind, sweet murderess who poured him tea years ago, the sister of a duke.

Sir Thomas kept the story of Antonia's origin suppressed for a decade, but as Antonia stepped into the spotlight, so young, so smart, and so beautiful, the story leaked and became a press feeding frenzy. Luther scolded himself for not researching, then reminded himself why he decided not to search for them years earlier. He could not be forced to spill information he did not possess. Dangerous people survived the Politikill era. He and Allie may still be on their list.

Luther refocused on his students, struggling to stay on point. Ironically, today's lecture focused on Liu and Tucker's pursuit of Loyola and Tigre. He watched his daughter settle into the back of the room.

When the class ended, her detail escorted her out.

Saddened he had no chance to greet her, he packed his leather satchel, left the building, and started his walk home. When he stepped into the Texas morning, he spotted Antonia seated alone on a bench. A few students approached her, recognizing her. She greeted each. He observed her from afar, relishing each movement before turning for home.

A firm hand anchored him in place. Luther turned, greeted by a member of Lady Antonia's protection detail. "Professor, she awaits you."

"Okay," Luther said. He delayed, allowing the students to depart, then walked toward the bench.

He paused a few steps away, not knowing the proper protocol. Was he supposed to bow or something? Why did he not study that? He looked to one of her security detail members for direction. The behemoth shook his head. Luther imagined a speech bubble above the guard's head with one word in capitals: IDIOT.

Her voice jerked him from his thought spiral. "Doctor Luther, please sit," Antonia said pleasantly.

He obliged.

"I remember you, we met once."

"Yes, I remember. I'm surprised you do."

"You bought me a chocolate croissant."

"You earned it."

"Mother had few friends, so I made note...of you."

Luther's heart hurt for Allie, her loneliness. Then he grasped the power of the first word of Antonia's statement. "Wait, you know she's your mother?"

"Of course."

"Did she tell you?"

"That question disappoints." She smiled impishly, intending no ill will. She waited for Luther to catch up. *Wow, she's giving me crap.* "Of course, she didn't tell me. You were a friend; you understood her capacity for secrets. Also, you should assume I would gain a small part of her cognitive ability."

"Of course. Have you told her you know?"

"I told her months before she died. She never told me but seemed proud I arrived at the conclusion myself."

Luther sat quietly, experiencing the pain of Allie's death. Loneliness engulfed him, even though he had not held her for over a decade.

"I am so obtuse. It did not occur to me you were uninformed. I am so sorry, Dr. Luther."

"Thank you."

"I assumed you corresponded, but in retrospect, I see how that might prove problematic."

He realized he was crying. He did his best to recover. "Not to bust your bubble, you're not Sherlock Holmes or anything. Not difficult to make that jump. You look exactly like her."

His daughter laughed, lifting his soul from the dark place it lived seconds before.

"Touché, Doctor Luther, touché. But...not exactly like her." Her words hung in the air, an open invitation.

"Did you enjoy class?"

"Of course, for review, I have read all of your books."

"Wow, thank you."

"Mother kept copies on her bookshelf and occasionally left your books in my room. She kept one with her always."

"Thank you for that. You can't grasp what it means to me. To follow protocol, what do I call you?"

"People call me different things, depending on their station and familiarity. I would like very much if you called me Antonia. No need for titles between us. We are in the US, your home court, your rules."

"Where are you staying?"

"For now, my uncle secured the top floor of the Sam Houston Hotel. Still, I am working with my team to make other arrangements."

"Really?"

"Yes, I researched a home, steps from campus. Just one professor lives there. The home would be perfect. My team can share one bedroom, leaving one bedroom for me and another for the professor."

"I know the place," Luther smiled. "Might be small, compared to your usual accommodations."

"Looks cozy from the photos my team provided. Castles can be drafty." She smiled. "Not by happenstance, the arrangement provides extra time to get to know my father."

The End

Acknowledgements

After my first novel, *Payback Jack*, several readers stated the offbeat acknowledgments were their favorite part of the book. I am unsure if their comments stand as a compliment to the acknowledgments or insult to the book. I can only say ... your call, bro.

My first thanks go to Linda Migura, the first and last reader of every manuscript I produce. Your dedication to attempting and occasionally failing to put me on the right path is my favorite part of the literary journey. To Denise Kingham, my test reader extraordinaire.

To my wife, the beautiful, intelligent, and driven Lori Sojka, the only woman I have and will ever love. Thank you to my daughter Abigail Sojka, the coolest and most adult person I know, which is a testament to you and your incredible mother. To my brother, Jeff Sojka, our adventures started me on this path.

To Myrtis and Thomas Gilmore for the love and plethora of well-deserved spankings. To Donna Bloodsworth Scruggs, who taught me how to read. Depending on your opinion of my writing, you can thank her or accept my humble apologies.

Thank you to the teachers at Silsbee Elementary, Jr. High and High School for helping a child with rampant ADHD navigate twelve years. A special thank you to Mrs. Johnson, Mr. and Mrs. Edwards, Mr. Atmar, Mr. Meldrum, Mr. Leigh, Mrs. Seabrook, Mrs. La Toof, Mrs. Voigtman, and all the teachers who took extra time with me. You should each be nominated for sainthood.

Thanks to Michelle Scrimger and Nick Massad of "The Sam" (or the Sam Houston Hotel) for befriending a first-time author. My family felt so honored to work with you. I hope Texans forever revel in your hotel's elegant confines. Additional thanks to Erin Woolsey and Kelsey Creech of *Public Content*, the best darn PR Firm in Texas. A shout out to Ruben Dominguez, the coolest reporter in H-town.

Much gratitude to *The Silsbee Bee* and *Beaumont Enterprise* for feeding my fledgling brain in the 70s and 80s (when music was actually good, not like this crap today – oh wow, sorry, tangent... have I really gotten that old?)

To the incredible staff of the Silsbee Library, Pam Hartt, Naconna Armfield, and Joni Sheppard (and her incredible son Bryson). Your team was amazing to work with during the book signing.

Thanks to Wal-Mart for my first real job and to the Walton Family for the scholarship that allowed me to pay for my first two years of college. Many thanks to the Ella C. McFadden Trust for helping to pay the rest of my way through Texas Tech. Mr. Walton and Ms. McFadden, I know you are long gone, but you helped so many of us.

Thanks to the Silsbee Class of 1985, for your support, which is surprising, because let's admit it, I could be a royal pain at times, sincere apologies.

A special thanks Sherry Jacks Davis. You helped promote my book better than an advertising agency. Your organizational skills are a blessing to the entire class of 1985. To my friend Carl Wright, who did not get a shout-out last time, when we all know you deserved one.

To my other friends in high school, college, and ATO fraternity brothers at Texas Tech: I made a lot of terrible decisions, and you were right there by my side...*you're welcome.*

Thanks to Keller Williams for providing an escape for me when I ran kicking and screaming from the corporate world. To Esmeralda Martin who helped promote *Payback Jack*—you rock!

A special thanks to Lori Sojka, Paul Crandall, Denise Kingham, Annette Webber, Fred Bauscus, Esmeralda Martin,

Laura Hughes, Steve Irish, Michele LaPoint, Jill Chastain, Heath Hardin, and Shelli Hinkson who helped grow our real estate business. Your competency allowed me time to author this book. A special thanks to our company's, *See TIM Sell's* 2000+ customers: I am so grateful for you.

Blessings to patient and incredible editors Linda Migura, Lisa Petrocelli, and Brandee Miller.

Thanks to the readers of my first novel, *Payback Jack,* for your encouragement, reviews, and calls for a second novel. Your words helped propel me through bouts of writer's malaise.

Thanks to author and mentor AJ McCarthy, Canada's best thriller writer. Thanks to fellow authors John Hazen, Nola Nash, Carolyn Gehduld, and Luke Swanson for your guidance. Imagine how much better the book would be if I listened more. Thanks to *Katy Christian Magazine* for being my first interview. Much gratitude to Karen Leidy, of the *Freestone County Times*, you blessed me with your feedback early on and helped propel me forward.

Thanks to Todd Smith, for pointing out the Henry Kissinger quote preceding these acknowledgments.

Thank you to my unbelievable test and support readers, Denise Kingham, the Smiths (Brett, Mary, Steve, & Patti), the Joyners (Jenni &Troy), Mary Bell, Melanie Aman, Kathy Girgenti, Karen Norwood, Kristen Mann, Beez Beasley, Ed Wiesner, Robert Anthony, Katie Tognietti, the Kilcommins (Joey and Jennifer), Dianna Homolka, Misty Gonzalez, Honey Bumstead, Jim Bob Stuckey, the Bishops (Lori and Alan), Loree Carruth Kaufman, Christy White, Kathy Adams, Charlyne White, Brian Varvel, Heath Hardin, the Bancrofts (Mark & Julia), John Cordes, Greg Graham, Linda Garrett, Tracey Ross-Watmore, Paul Crandall, Shelli Hinkson, Steve Irish, Ed Kamph, Zack Kampf, Bill Holt, Joel Matthews, the Stierwalts (Brian & Kayla), Ariana Montelongo, Cassie Clark Balla, Kem Sandifer, Dee Blake,

Michele Moore Zernial, Charlotte Messer Causey, Karen Chance and Merita Miloti O'Krinsky.

I bet I forgot someone, so if I did, call me! I will set you up with a free book or mention you in the next novel. Unless of course you decide to duck your contributions, which may be smart.

Thank you to *Politikill* publisher, Minna and Reagan Rothe of Black Rose Writing. Your partnership is invaluable. Marty Miller, thanks for the push to stop making excuses, and just finish a book.

To 'Merica. Despite my political commentary, I love you. You're the greatest country in the world, but like any loved one, I hope you can strive for more.

Finally, to Laura Hoffpauir and *The Best Little Bookclub in Texas*, your encouragement meant so much.

Readers, lets be bros. You can follow me or reach out to me at timothygenesojka.com

Book clubs – Let me know if I can hang out with your crew one day.

About the Author

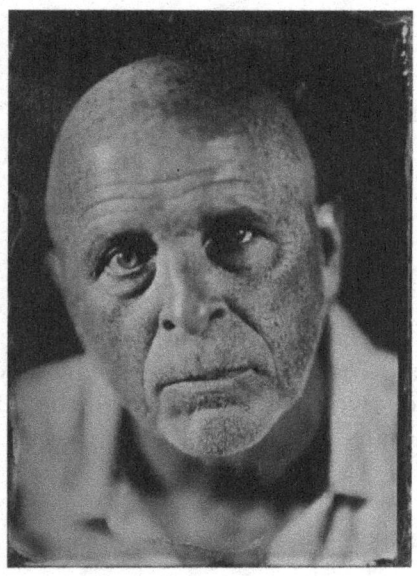

Tim writes for enjoyment, paddle-boards for stress relief, and runs so he can eat Tex-Mex. He has a passion for plot twists and pushing the "philosophically pure" to the point of hypocrisy. Tim enjoys time with his wife Lori, hanging out with his daughter Abigail and playing 42 Dominoes with his mother and grandmother. Sojka's debut novel *Payback Jack* became a #1 Amazon Thriller and received 5-Star Reviews from around the globe.

Note from the Author

Word-of-mouth is crucial for any author to succeed. If you enjoyed *Politikill*, please leave a review online—anywhere you are able. Even if it's just a sentence or two. It would make all the difference and would be very much appreciated.

Thanks!
Timothy Gene Sojka

We hope you enjoyed reading this title from:

www.blackrosewriting.com

Subscribe to our mailing list – *The Rosevine* – and receive **FREE** books, daily deals, and stay current with news about upcoming releases and our hottest authors.
Scan the QR code below to sign up.

Already a subscriber? Please accept a sincere thank you for being a fan of Black Rose Writing authors.

View other Black Rose Writing titles at
www.blackrosewriting.com/books and use promo code
PRINT to receive a **20% discount** when purchasing.

www.ingramcontent.com/pod-product-compliance
Lightning Source LLC
Chambersburg PA
CBHW01072810726
47899CB00009B/2967